MW01201033

# BADL

## A Nora Ke

# DOUGLAS P
# LINCOLN

GC

GRAN
CENTR

NEW YORK   B

# BADLANDS

Copyright © 2025 by Splendide Mendax, Inc. and Lincoln Child

Cover design by Faceout Studio, Tim Green; cover images by Shutterstock. Cover copyright © 2025 by Hachette Book Group, Inc.

Grand Central Publishing
Hachette Book Group
1290 Avenue of the Americas, New York, NY 10104
grandcentralpublishing.com
@grandcentralpub

First Edition: June 2025

Grand Central Publishing is a division of Hachette Book Group, Inc. The Grand Central Publishing name and logo is a trademark of Hachette Book Group, Inc.

The publisher is not responsible for websites (or their content) that are not owned by the publisher.

The Hachette Speakers Bureau provides a wide range of authors for speaking events. To find out more, go to hachettespeakersbureau.com or email HachetteSpeakers@hbgusa.com.

Grand Central Publishing books may be purchased in bulk for business, educational, or promotional use. For information, please contact your local bookseller or the Hachette Book Group Special Markets Department at special.markets@hbgusa.com.

Library of Congress Cataloging-in-Publication Data has been applied for.

ISBNs: 9781538765821 (hardcover), 9781538765852 (ebook), 9781538774526 (large print)

Printed in the United States of America

LSC-H

Printing 1, 2025

# BADLANDS

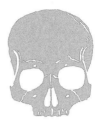

I

*August 2020; precise date uncertain*

THE WOMAN PAUSED and raised her head, looking over the wavering landscape toward the horizon. She blinked, then blinked again, dazzled by the light. As far as she could see lay a land dotted with hoodoo rock formations: spires and domes of rock, giant boulders balancing on slender stems, trembling and ghostly in the heat. This madness of rock and sand rose into a burning sky dominated by the implacable sun. She could see no traces of life: no trees, no grass, nothing beyond a few stunted prickly pear cacti hugging the sand, shriveled up, dead, more spines than flesh.

The woman lowered her head and continued walking, concentrating on placing one foot in front of the other, always northward, where she knew her destination lay. If only she could get there soon, she would be safe.

She finally understood the expression *raging thirst*. She thought she had been thirsty before, sometimes very thirsty; but that had been nothing. Nothing. She thought of the Coleridge poem she'd taught so often in English lit it had become a drone in her head. This was what that Ancient Mariner must have felt watching the very boards of his ship shrink under the sun. The thirst that was upon her now was one that seized her mind, refused to let her think of anything else. She could feel her pulse thundering in her temples; the muscles of her legs were shaky and trembling. Her mouth had dried up many miles back, and now her tongue was cracking and swelling. She could taste the iron of blood.

But to stop now would be the worst possible mistake. She had to keep walking.

To get her mind off the thirst, she tried recalling the last few days, but the memories would come back only in pieces: long, dusty bus rides; furtive traveling by night; the air-conditioned Walmart with its racks of cheap clothes; the shabby gas-station restrooms and McDonald's dumpsters. She recalled burning her money, watching with fascination as the twenty-dollar bills wrinkled in curlicues of flame. The phone had been harder to destroy; in the end, its innards had nevertheless crackled and popped under a burning glaze of lighter fluid.

*One foot in front of the other.*

A sudden surge of dizziness forced her to brace one hand against a rock. She took a deep breath, let it out slowly. The sun stopped wheeling overhead, returning to a fixed position, a hole of omnipotent heat punched through the fabric of the sky. She spat out the blood weeping from her tongue and continued on.

All she had to do was endure. She tried to say it out loud, *endure,* but no sound emerged beyond a breathy hiss. It was hot, brutally hot, but nowhere was it so hot as at ground level. She could feel it through the soles of her running shoes. It was a miracle they weren't actually melting. And, in fact, maybe they were melting: she had once read that in the desert, in full sun, the ground temperature could exceed a hundred and fifty degrees.

Time passed. She walked on. And then came to a tottering stop, feeling a rush of...what?

Of what? She couldn't articulate what she felt. Everything was so different now. Here in this inferno, it was as if she'd already begun her transformation. The way she felt now was different from just a quarter of an hour before—and light years from the beginning, when she first realized she'd lost sight of a road.

*Deliverance.* That was the one word that echoed louder than anything else in her mind: louder than the baking heat, louder than even the dreadful thirst. Even now it rose before her. *Deliverance.*

She could feel the anvil of the sun directly on her head. She counted ten steps forward.

She took off her shirt, peeling it off over her head, and dropped it.

Ten more steps.

She unhooked her bra and shrugged it off. The radiation of the sun now penetrated into her skin.

As she reached for the button of her shorts, she saw movement out of the corner of her eye. She swiftly moved and crouched behind a rock: she'd already seen many things that were merely tricks of her sun-blind vision, but she had to be sure.

This time, it was no phantom or mirage. There was the dot of a person in the distance.

How strange: out in the middle of nowhere, a woman was herding a small flock of sheep. She was maybe a mile away and headed in the opposite direction, and she'd become visible only because she was climbing a low rise with her sheep, taking them over the brow of a ridge.

Had the woman seen her?

She waited, hiding. Nothing. After a while, once she was sure the woman was gone, she eased back up. She unbuttoned her shorts and took them off, dropping them, following with her panties.

The running shoes came off next, and finally the socks. When she placed her bare feet on the hot sand, she felt a sudden, searing pain so excruciating she almost fell to her knees—but she pushed this away as best she could, focusing instead on clenching her last possessions: the objects that, unlike things of this world—money, clothes—she could not, *must* not, give up.

It was like walking on fire. Her body, not her brain, warned her that this could not last long. But there was no reason to be afraid, no reason at all.

One step. Another.

And then, with unexpected abruptness, her legs gave way and she fell to her knees. Her bare skin hit the ground like meat dropping on a searing griddle. She screamed involuntarily, then fell back, writhing in a useless attempt to escape the heat, every fresh contact with the sand scorching anew, as she felt her skin crack and pop. Fluid sprang out from her skin, but it was like no sweat she'd ever experienced. It made a hissing sound. Through a screen of agony she realized she was cooking. *Her body was cooking...*

The screams stopped. There was a brief flurry of echoes before silence fell over the landscape once again. Her body went slack against the sand in a dreadful mockery of ease as the first stage of postmortem change—primary relaxation of the musculature—began.

Only her fists remained clenched.

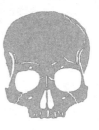

# 2

*Present day*

ALONG THE REMOTE eastern border of the Navajo Nation, dawn broke over the Ah-shi-sle-pah badlands, the sky lightening from midnight blue to pale yellow.

"We're gonna lose the best light," the director told Alex Bondi, who was crouched over a small landing pad, preparing a drone camera for a flight. *"We're gonna lose the light!"*

Bondi ignored him and continued calibrating the drone's compass and IMU. He did not point out that the reason they were late was due to the director's carousing the night before. In order to arrive by the 6 AM sunrise in these remote badlands, they'd had to get up at 2 AM and make a bone-jarring drive over terrible roads. When the director was assisted into his vehicle, he was still drunk. The horrendous drive had shaken the booze out of him—leaving him hung over and pissed off.

Bondi was already beginning to regret accepting the job as cinematographer for the film, an indie Western called *Steele* being financed by a bunch of Houston oilmen. It had sounded like fun—five weeks in Santa Fe, shooting at the Lazy C Movie Ranch, staying in a downtown B and B near the plaza. He'd heard that the director, Luke Desjardin, was "a bit of" a maniac, but he'd worked with maniac directors before and felt he could handle it. But Desjardin had turned out to be not just a lightweight maniac, but a fanatically committed one: a Clase Azul–chugging, Montecristo-smoking, coke-snorting tornado who never seemed to sleep and resented others for doing so.

Two dozen crew were on site—grips, PAs, camera operators, a breakfast caterer, the works. They'd hauled out an RV with AC and a flush toilet. There was no lack of money being spent. A large shade had been erected to keep people out of the July sun, with big coolers of ice water set up on tables. At least the backers weren't parsimonious—or maybe they'd already figured out that filming without basic comforts in a place so brutally remote might cost them a lot more in the end.

Calibration complete, Bondi stepped back. "Ready to fly," he said.

Desjardin's voice was almost as high pitched as a girl's, and so loud that it cut the desert air like a knife. "About time! The sun's going to be up in less than five minutes." He took a deep breath. "Here's the shot I'm looking for—a long, establishing sweep over these badlands just at the crack of dawn, getting in all that golden light and the long shadows."

"No problem."

Bondi's PA stood next to him, ready with a pair of binoculars. He was the spotter, whose job was to keep track of the drone—as much as was possible—in this landscape. But Bondi had plenty of experience flying drones out of sight, using as guidance the video feed on his handheld console.

"I want you to fly past that peak over there," said the director. "You see it?"

Bondi did indeed see it—a creepy fifty-foot spire of black rock that looked like a crooked finger pointing into the sky, cut off flat on top. It was about a mile away, across a maze-like terrain of hoodoos and balancing rocks, riddled with dry washes and miniature ravines. Bondi had to admit it was a perfect location. It was also a hellscape like nothing he'd ever seen before.

"I want you to fly over to it, camera looking straight down, then come around in a circle, raise the camera to center on the spire, and speed past it, panning back as you go by. Can you do that?"

"Of course." This was the shit he got paid for. His only real fear was some mechanical failure that might put the drone down somewhere in that crazy landscape.

"Okay. Roll."

Bondi fired up the drone and raised it to an altitude of ten feet, paused to make sure its GPS made satellite contact and knew where it was, and then bumped it up to sixty feet, high enough to clear the rock formations. He started it off northward at a medium pace, while Desjardin peered closely over his shoulder at the screen, cigar breath washing over Bondi.

"Go lower."

Bondi lowered the drone to fifty feet.

"Lower."

Bondi took it down to forty. This was risky, because many of the hoodoo formations were higher than that. But Bondi had confidence in his ability to navigate through them, and besides, the drone had a radar avoidance system that would stop it from flying into a rock even if he tried it. He normally turned this safety feature off when getting closeups, but in this landscape he decided not to risk it.

"Good...good...that's it...steady on...," Desjardin murmured, peering at the screen, watching the footage from the drone's perspective.

"Lost it," said the spotter with the binocs.

"No worries," said Bondi. "I got it under control."

*Christ, what a landscape!* It was hard to believe it wasn't some surrealist painting, all the little balancing rocks and spires and arches and twisty little dry washes casting long shadows. As crazy as Desjardin was, he knew how to get incredible footage: this should be fabulous, totally worth the effort.

The cut-off spire was coming up now. It was so prominent, he figured it had to have a name. He flew past it, then brought the drone around in a long, sweeping turn while smoothly raising the camera as he did so. The lens caught a brief moment of the fiery gleam of the rising sun before centering again on the spire. Bondi knew immediately that he'd nailed it, feeling the sudden adrenaline rush of a shot perfectly executed.

"Okay…," said Desjardin. "Good…now lower the camera back down to the ground."

He manipulated the controls and the ground loomed up, a pool of fire in the early morning light.

"Lower," said Desjardin.

Bondi brought it lower, keeping the camera focused on the ground.

"Wait," said Desjardin. "What's that?"

Bondi had seen it, too: something on the ground. But the drone had passed by and it was no longer in view.

"Turn back around," Desjardin said.

Bondi brought it around and retraced.

"There!" Desjardin said.

Bondi brought the drone to a halt, hovering over a whitish object partially obscured by sand.

"What the fuck? It's a skull!"

"Yeah," said Bondi.

"And look, there are some bones, too...See them?"

"I do."

"It's a skeleton!" Desjardin said. "Oh my God: someone died out here!"

As Bondi panned back over the scattered remains, he saw nearby a rotten old shirt and a shriveled-up running shoe.

"Take the drone a hundred yards north," said Desjardin, "and then fly it back over, slow, another hundred yards south. Track the skull with the camera."

"Yes, but..."

"Just do it!"

Bondi did as he was told, flying the drone past the remains.

"Again! This time, raise the camera slightly to pick up the horizon, then pan across the skeleton as you go past."

"Um, that's not a prop," said Bondi.

"Who the hell cares? It's perfect!"

Cobb, the AD, spoke up. "Luke, there's nothing in the script about a skeleton."

"There will be! I can promise you that!"

Bondi flew past again, panning over the bones.

"Those are human remains out there," said Cobb. "I mean, are we even going to be able to use this footage?"

"You're damn right we will. They show shit like this on the news every day! Okay, Bondi: do that pan again. That first take was a little rough."

The drone's monitor began beeping and flashing, indicating a low battery. "I should bring it back," Bondi said.

"I can read a meter, too. It's still at fifteen percent. We've got time for another pass."

"It's almost a mile out. We need enough juice to bring it back."

"Do the pass!"

Bondi didn't argue; it wasn't his drone. He did the pass again, but his hand on the camera wheel was trembling slightly and it wasn't a smooth take.

"One more pass!"

The alarm grew more insistent.

"I need to bring it back," Bondi said. "Now."

"One more!"

He sent it back out a hundred yards, then turned it around. Abruptly, the screen went pixelated; the alarm beeped— then blackness. Fifteen seconds later, a stark warning message appeared on the screen. EMERGENCY LANDING EFFECTED.

Bondi lowered the monitor. "We lost it."

"Get the backup drone."

"It crashed—remember? We've got another one in shipment."

"What the hell?" Desjardin roared with frustration. *"Fuck me!"* He stomped around, cursing and yelling, as everyone else stood around looking on in silence. This was not the first time he'd lost it on set.

Finally, he rounded on Bondi. "Well, do you know where it is?"

"I've got the GPS coordinates."

"You saw the message. It didn't crash; it did an emergency landing. It's still good. Let's go get it."

This was met with silence, until finally Cobb said: "You can't be serious."

"What do you mean?" screeched Desjardin, whirling toward the AD.

"In July, hiking a mile into those badlands, with the sun up? It's already close to a hundred degrees. It'll be death out there."

"Who made you the expert?"

But Cobb stood firm. "Don't take my word for it, Luke—that skeleton says it even better. I, for one, have no wish to join it." And then, as the director fumed, the AD added: "I think we'd better call the cops."

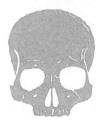

3

How much farther?" Supervisory Agent Sharp asked from behind the wheel. His sleepy eyes, half-lidded, looked steadily forward as if he were watching a golf match instead of driving through sagebrush plains a hundred miles from nowhere.

Corrie Swanson checked her phone. Even though they were out of cell range, she had downloaded the Google Earth satellite images of the area ahead of time.

She located their little blue dot. "Another five miles."

"Five miles," Sharp repeated. "I guess that means the fun part of the drive's about to begin."

Sharp was about as droll as FBI agents came, and she wasn't sure what he meant by this. She looked out the window at the purple sage and bunchgrass; the faraway blue mountains; and, here and there in the middle distance, patches of badlands: clusters of geological bizarreness—boulders balancing on thin flutes of softer material.

Sharp turned a corner and the vehicle dipped into a declivity she hadn't realized lay before them—and suddenly they were driving into a forest of those goblin-like rocks, the vehicle heaving and yawing over a dirt road that abruptly turned from bad to bone shattering.

"Jesus!" Corrie said involuntarily, gripping the armrests.

"Now you know why they're called badlands," Sharp said, his voice a notch higher now to be heard over the racket.

Instead of answering, Corrie merely hung on. It was one thing to view this kind of bizarre sight from miles away—quite another to drive through it on what was more a track than a road. She'd seen pictures, but they didn't do the place justice. Some of the rock formations looked like intestines, bulged and coiled. Others were more like monstrous fungi or the papillae of a giant's tongue, sticking upward in disgusting nodules.

"The locals call these rock formations 'hoodoos,'" said Sharp.

"It's like the dark side of the moon," she said. She glanced into the rear-view mirror, where—far behind—the Evidence Response Team van was creeping along, almost invisible in the dust they were throwing up.

They hit a dry wash that nearly bottomed out the vehicle. Corrie wished he'd slow down, but didn't dare speak out. Dark side of the moon was an understatement. This was more like the place where, during the creation of the world, God had dumped all His leftover rubbish, the bits and pieces of landscape so deformed and grotesque He couldn't find a place for them any-where else.

As they came out of the embankment of yet another dry wash, Corrie was shocked to spy in the distance a small, six-sided wooden hut, made of split logs with a dirt roof.

"That can't be someone's residence," she said. "There's no life on Mars." But as they drove farther, she made out a shabby trailer behind the hut, along with some corrals.

"Oh my God," she said. "Look, someone's there!" And she

pointed toward the figure of a woman who appeared in the doorway of the hut to watch them pass by.

"She's Navajo," said Sharp. "We're in an area called the Checkerboard."

"Sorry?"

"It's a long story about land appropriation. But basically, what we have here are alternating square miles of Navajo Nation land, checkerboarded with square miles of federal land. There are some tough old people living out here, off-grid, carrying on the traditional ways. Some of them don't even speak English."

"But you haven't been in this area before—right?"

"Not in this particular area. I've been elsewhere in the Checkerboard, as well as Chaco Canyon, about ten miles south."

Corrie had heard about the amazing ruins of Chaco Canyon, and intended to go there when she had a break from work—and assuming they made it out of this otherworldly place without being abducted by aliens.

Sharp was wearing his usual impeccable blue suit. Corrie, on the other hand, had dressed for the desert—hiking boots, shorts, a light shirt and broad-brimmed hat—and she carried a CamelBak water pod. The only nod to her federal status was the dangling lanyard holding her badge. Sharp, on the other hand, looked like he was about to appear before a congressional inquiry.

As they drove around a particularly large hoodoo rock, Corrie saw in the distance the white shade tent of the movie crew and their vehicles, including a large RV, parked in a rare flat area among the formations. No one was out and about—she figured they were probably holed up in the RV, staying cool.

"Ready to get your hands dirty again, Special Agent Swanson?" Sharp asked.

"Yes, sir." She mentally tucked away her amazement at the surrounding landscape.

"Since this is the Checkerboard, we're going to be liaising with the Navajo Nation Police. Crownpoint is sending us a detective sergeant named Benally."

"Sort of like a Joe Leaphorn?"

Sharp gave a small smile. "Let's hope he's as good as one of Tony Hillerman's cops. I've worked with the Navajo Nation Police before and they're thoroughly professional. They're also useful in opening doors, if the need arises." He paused. "I'm expecting you to take the lead on this case, Agent Swanson."

She nodded. "Thank you, sir." This was no surprise: she'd expected from the outset that the case would be hers, and she was grateful. She was still in the two-year probationary period of a newly minted FBI agent and was glad to get away from cold case reviews and endless interviews with stupid, unhelpful witnesses.

Sharp eased their SUV into the open area, pulling up alongside the RV. Getting out felt like colliding into a wall of heat. Three people exited the RV on their arrival, and they gathered in the shade under an open tent. It was late in the afternoon and the heat of the day was, thankfully, abating. The three introduced themselves as Luke Desjardin, the director of the film; the cinematographer, Alex Bondi; and another man named Cobb. Desjardin was wearing a big straw hat with a red bandanna draped underneath, a tie-dyed shirt, and baggy pantaloons. Unshaven and ugly. Bondi was young and comparatively normal looking. Cobb was short and radiated intensity.

"So," said Corrie, collecting her thoughts and directing her questions to Bondi, who looked like the most promising interlocutor. "We reviewed the video you sent—they're definitely human remains, and fairly recent. We appreciate your contacting us. Has anyone been to the site yet?"

"No," said Bondi. "We thought we'd wait for you."

"Good decision," said Corrie. "And you say you have a GPS location?"

"Yes." Bondi pointed. "You see that black formation out there? The remains the drone spotted are scattered about fifty yards southeast of it. Our drone ran out of juice and did an emergency landing nearby."

"Right." Corrie scanned the forbidding landscape. The black spire—other similarly evil-looking needles of rock dotted the landscape, but it was by far the closest—looked about a mile away. They'd have to work quickly before it got dark. "Can we drive there?"

"I'm afraid not," Bondi said. "And no trails, either. You're going to have to hike cross-country."

Corrie nodded. Hiking would be a bitch, but at least the air was beginning to cool off. She recited to herself the FBI motto: *Fidelity, Bravery, Integrity.*

The ERT van now arrived in a huge cloud of dust, parking next to their SUV. The doors opened and the team hopped out and began unloading equipment. A few minutes later, they came into the shade of the tent: two ERT technicians and their supervisor, an evidence specialist named Cliff Gradinski. Corrie hadn't worked with Gradinski before, and Sharp had seemed reticent to answer her questions about the man. She looked him over—a thin figure in his forties, with short brown hair, narrow blue eyes, a pencil neck, and a smooth tan face, carrying what she thought was a satisfied, superior expression.

Introductions complete, Corrie prepared to address the group.

Gradinski beat her to it. "All right, everyone, listen up. We've got two hours to sunset, so we'll have to work fast."

His voice was deep and full of self-regard, and Corrie found herself mildly irritated—she was technically his superior, the agent in charge. She glanced at Sharp and saw something glimmer in his eyes—amusement? Or perhaps a challenge? She pushed down hard on her feeling of irritation, telling herself this was an evidence-gathering expedition and it was normal for the agent to take a back seat and let the evidence professionals do their thing.

"Hats, water, and equipment—check," Gradinski went on. "Grab your gear, people, and let's go."

Corrie shouldered her backpack, which contained her notebook, pencil, FBI-issued camera, small first aid kit, headlamp, compass, and water pod. Then she glanced at Sharp. "You're not coming?"

"Dressed like this?" he murmured with a sleepy grin, gesturing at his blue suit, white shirt, and black shoes. "I'm going to wait here in the shade for the detective sergeant. It's your case, Agent Swanson. Good luck."

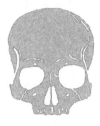

# 4

GRADINSKI LED THE way, heading toward the prominent land-mark, the spire of black rock. The others fell in line behind and started along the hard, dry wash, weaving among the strange hoodoo rocks and sandstone spires of the badlands. The sun cast long shadows. It was still hot, but they made good time—better than Corrie had anticipated. In twenty minutes, they arrived.

"All right, men, let's get to work," said Gradinski.

*Men.* Corrie felt her irritation rise again, but she kept her mouth shut and focused on the site.

The skull and assorted bones lay in a gravelly swale that extended to the base of what people were calling the witch's finger. There was a scattering of prickly pear cacti, shriveled from dryness, and some other desert plants Corrie couldn't identify. Off to one side the drone sat in the sand like a squat spider.

The skull was lying face up, hollow eyes staring into the sky, jaws wide. Bones lay scattered around it on the gravelly ground—a pelvis, long bones, several segments of vertebrae, a partial ribcage. Next to the skull was a mass of blonde hair.

Corrie could see signs of animal disturbance—teeth marks, gnawing—on the bones.

She could hear Gradinski in the background, issuing directions to the two technicians. They spread out and began taking photographs, planting little flags, collecting bones, and placing them in evidence envelopes or containers. They worked fast and, Corrie noted, professionally.

She decided to make a circuit of the site, checking the perimeter. Almost immediately, south of the body, she discovered partially buried and much tattered what looked like a pair of lace panties. Heading along the swale in the same direction, she spied another piece of clothing—khaki shorts. Corrie continued south away from the rock, encountering the remains of a shirt, and then a sock, one withered running shoe, then another.

All in a line.

A strange feeling crept over her. These clothes had not been scattered randomly by animal activity or wind; they had been intentionally discarded. The victim, it seemed, had methodically removed her clothing as she approached the place where she died—or was killed.

She strolled back to where Gradinski was working. He was kneeling over a femur that was partly buried, brushing sand away.

"Mr. Gradinski?"

"Yes?" He didn't look up.

"The victim's clothes appear to have been discarded in a line—"

He raised his head reluctantly from his work. "Excuse me, Agent Swanson? I was distracted."

"I was saying that the victim's clothes appear to have been discarded down that swale, one piece at a time. In a straight line. I want to make sure you and the team map, photograph, and collect them."

"Naturally." He turned back to his work.

Corrie continued circling the site but found nothing more of note. She returned to watch the ER team as they searched the ground for every little bone. Now, scanning the site more closely, she noted how empty it was of evidence. When dead bodies were discovered under suspicious or at least unusual circumstances, there was commonly plenty of evidence to collect: bullet casings, photos of blood spatters, indications of a struggle. But that didn't seem to be the case out here, in the middle of nowhere: there were just bones and discarded clothes.

Corrie believed that every scene had a story to tell—even one like this—a story that went beyond the bones and physical evidence. In the absence of more obviously relevant items, it was better to simply collect almost everything. Of course, most if not all might be unconnected to the victim—but they weren't likely to come back here. This would be their only shot.

"Mr. Gradinski?"

He was still kneeling. "Yes?"

"There are a few things I'd like taken as evidence, in addition to the human remains and clothing."

"Such as?"

"I'd be happy to point them out if you'd care to, uh, stand up for just a moment."

He rose, a pained expression on his face. "All right. What?"

"Those pieces of decayed wood, there, for starters."

"But...they're obviously natural to the environment."

"Just in case."

He rolled his eyes. "What else?"

"There's an old pop-top tab, there. And some of the odd-looking stones closest to the body. Like those two green pebbles near the skull, and that cluster of smooth red and yellow cobbles by the vertebrae, and there are also some flint chips over there—prehistoric, I think—near the pelvis."

"You want us to collect rocks?"

"Uh. Yes, please."

"Really? *Rocks?*"

The supercilious tone set Corrie's nerves on edge. "Maybe it's irrelevant, but I'd rather have more than less. I'm not sure they're all natural to the area." She drew in a breath. "And I'd like a photographic inventory of the plants growing in the immediate vicinity—the cholla, prickly pear, and these other plants, whatever they are. Plus some environmental pictures, including that rock formation. I'm sure you understand—capturing, in essence, a record of the physical environment."

Gradinski stared at her in disbelief. "Agent Swanson, I've been leading ERTs for two decades. I pride myself on a second sense when it comes to evidence—knowing what's relevant and what isn't. May I respectfully ask you to let us exercise our expert judgment? In case you hadn't noticed, we've got very little time."

She looked into that supercilious face and knew exactly what he was thinking: *I'm not going to let some young, green, female agent tell me what to do.*

*Okay,* she thought. Now she understood that little half smile on Sharp's face. There was a reason he'd been evasive about Gradinski—and knowing Sharp, this evidence collection was a test. Well, she was not going to do her usual thing…which would have been to lose her temper.

"I'm aware of your excellent reputation," she lied, trying to make her voice as agreeable as possible. "You probably don't know this, but the young agents talk about your work as being practically legendary. Of course, ordinarily no one would say it to your face, but the fact is, all of us hope you'll be the one leading ERT on their cases." She tried mightily to keep the tone of irony out of her voice. "I hadn't planned on telling you, but I feel fortunate you drew this case."

His eyebrows shot up. "Is that so? I'm glad to know it." She saw that her abject flattery was actually working, as a flush of self-admiration appeared on his cheeks.

"I know what I'm asking for is a bit unconventional," she went on. "All I can say in my defense is, I hope you'll allow a new agent like me to make some of my own decisions about the evidence—even if they're wrong. I just want to make sure nothing is missed."

"Well, of course. We all learn by our mistakes. I'm happy to comply."

She couldn't believe how thoroughly he'd changed his tune.

"We'll be sure to collect those, ah, rocks. And the other things. And anything else you might suggest. Fair enough?"

"Yes, that's much appreciated. And," she added, "please be sure to collect that spearpoint there, next to the pelvis."

Gradinski swung around in surprise, bending down and peering with narrowing eyes. "Will you look at that. What a beauty! Of course we'll collect it. Good eyes, Agent Swanson!" And, with a beaming smile, he gave her a gentle pat-pat on the shoulder.

Corrie didn't know whether to laugh or cry, but she managed to keep her face mild and friendly. She also waited in silence to make sure that Gradinski did indeed collect the evidence she'd indicated. She was pleased to see that he did so, and with the utmost professionalism: photographed, mapped, collected, sealed, tagged, and packed away.

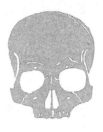

# 5

When they got back to the car, the sun had set and the evening dusk had settled over the badlands, turning the land a dusty pink. The witch's stubby finger was dramatically outlined against a burgundy sky, with a few other equally cruel-looking sentinels forming a backdrop into the far distance.

As the ER team loaded the evidence into the van, Corrie went over to where Sharp was sitting under the tent, drinking ice water. A young Navajo man was there with him, sharply dressed in a police uniform and aviator sunglasses. He had high cheekbones, a crew cut, and an aquiline nose. His short-sleeved blue shirt was tight around his chest, and it looked to Corrie like he spent a lot of time in the gym.

"This is detective sergeant Jack Benally of the Navajo Nation Police, Crownpoint Jurisdiction," Sharp told her. "You'll be liaising with him on the case. I've been telling him all about you—and our last case up in the Manzanos."

Corrie shook his hand. "Pleased to meet you."

"Likewise," Benally said as he stood up. "That was quite a case you had last winter. I hope this one won't be quite so...melodramatic."

"Me too," Corrie said.

"Ice water?" Sharp asked, proffering her a paper cup.

"Heck, yes."

She drank deeply and set down the glass, to find Benally looking at her pensively. "Have you worked on the rez before?"

"No. I'm a new agent. I was assigned to the Albuquerque FO only a year and a half ago—never been to New Mexico before that."

He nodded. "Welcome to the Navajo Nation."

"Thank you. I look forward to working with you." And she did—Benally would have the kind of knowledge of this area she'd never acquire in a lifetime. She recalled what Sharp had said about the Navajo police—how they were useful at opening doors—and an idea occurred to her. "About four miles back we passed a trailer and a hut."

"You mean a hogan."

"Right. Hogan. There was an elderly lady there."

"Oh yes," said Benally. "That's Emma Bluebird."

"Has she been there a long time?"

"Most of her life, I'd guess."

"I was wondering if perhaps we could ask her a few questions. It's possible she saw something, maybe even the victim herself—or might have an idea what happened."

At this, Benally chuckled. "Good thought. The only problem is, she keeps a shotgun by the door and she doesn't like *Bilagáana*—that is, white people—coming around her place. Not that she's prejudiced or anything: it's just that in her experience, having a white person knock on the door is rarely a good thing."

"Maybe you could come with me and explain the situation?"

Benally smiled. "She doesn't like cops, either. But we can try."

"When?"

"Now's as good a time as any."

"We won't get shot?"

He laughed. "Shotgun's not loaded. And she's a peaceable creature at heart. In fact, she's actually a noted weaver. In that hogan she keeps a loom made of juniper branches. Every year she weaves a rug made from wool sheared and spun from her own sheep and dyed with plants and insects collected around here—and sells it. That's what she lives on."

"Really? Amazing."

Benally shrugged. "If we don't make headway with her this evening, I can put you in touch with the trader who buys her rugs. He has a trading post over in Crownpoint."

"Thanks."

They got back in their vehicles and Sharp followed Benally out in his white pickup truck, its doors emblazoned with the green-and-yellow Navajo Nation Police emblem.

The last of the light was disappearing in the sky and the stars were starting to come out when Benally pulled into the dirt track leading to the trailer. He stopped well short of the house, turned off his lights, and waited. Sharp stopped behind him and switched off his engine.

"Aren't we going to go knock?" Corrie asked after a few minutes.

"No," Sharp told her. "It's considered rude in Navajo culture to knock on the door—you've already invaded their personal space getting that close. She knows we're here. We just wait."

Minutes passed. Corrie could see the dull glow of kerosene light inside the trailer, and the old woman's shadow moving against the closed curtains. After another minute, the door finally opened and she stood in it, silhouetted in the yellow light. Sure enough, she had a shotgun crooked in one elbow, muzzle pointing downward.

At this, Benally got out of his police car and, without approaching, waved and greeted her in Navajo. She shouted back in Navajo, and a short conversation ensued. Even though Corrie could not understand it, she could see that it did not go well. Finally, the old woman retreated into the house, slamming the door.

Benally came over to their vehicle and leaned in the window. "Well, I guess that must've been self-evident. She doesn't want to talk to us and wants us off her property."

"I'm sorry to hear that."

Benally shook his head. "You're not going to get anywhere with her. And to be honest, I doubt she has any useful information. But maybe that trader I mentioned can get you an in."

They got back in their vehicles and continued down the hideous road. When they at last reached the highway, Benally turned southwest toward Crownpoint, while Sharp and Corrie headed southeast to Nageezi and Albuquerque.

Sharp turned to her. "So. How did things go with Gradinski?"

"Just fine. We're pals."

"Really?"

"Just ask him. He even gave me a pat on the shoulder." She let a pregnant pause hang briefly in the air. "So—did I pass the test?"

Sharp chuckled. "In more ways than you know."

She looked at him. "I don't understand."

Sharp drove a few miles before responding. "Corrie, after that Dead Mountain case of ours—of yours, to be more accurate—I began to think my mentoring of you was swiftly growing irrelevant. Watching you at work again today, that feeling has only grown stronger."

Corrie sat still, throat going dry.

"In my opinion, you're ready for—lacking a better term—graduation. But there's red tape involved, and we still have to run out the clock for another five months or so. In the eyes of the FBI, I'm still your mentor. But for now, I'm going to remain well in the background—and see how you handle this case on your own."

Sharp was always a hard person to read, but this was the last thing Corrie had expected to hear...especially at the start of a fresh investigation like this. She felt a little like she'd just been thrown into the deep end of the pool. "Sir?"

"You heard me. Oh, I'll have my eyes on you, Swanson. But I'll only step forward if I see you going off the rails...or you ask for my intervention."

As she looked back to the blur of highway, Corrie tried to process this development—and how she felt about it. On the one hand, she'd grown accustomed to having a mentor backing her up, taking ultimate responsibility.

On the other hand: now that she was in the pool, she had to admit the water felt fine.

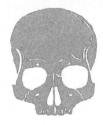

6

THE FORENSIC LAB in the basement of the Albuquerque FO was brand-new—the previous lab having burned—and Corrie loved working in it. No expense had been spared, and it was stocked with the latest in forensic tools, including a scanning electron microscope, radiography, and much more. The previous manager of the lab, a tedious old Englishman who had retired under a cloud, had left her as the only forensic specialist in the entire field office.

As she looked around, she couldn't help but think: *This is all mine.*

Corrie had arranged the bones of the victim on one gurney; and next to it, on an evidence table, she had laid out the evidence gathered at the site. It made quite a contrast—a meager scattering of animal-chewed bones on one side, and on the other a surface chockablock with bagged evidence. Maybe too much evidence. Perhaps Gradinski had been right and she'd gone overboard. Still, she was glad. It made for more work and was a pain to curate, but at least she could feel reasonably sure they hadn't missed anything important.

Making a circuit of the human remains, she looked them over again, wanting to get a feel for the bones. It was hard to explain what exactly she was hoping to see, but having spent several years at John Jay intensively studying human bones, and now after a year with the FBI doing the same thing, she realized that bones could give off a vibe—a mysterious sense of the person they belonged to, who they were and how they died—that she could pick up.

And these bones definitely gave off a vibe. Looking beyond the animal damage, she could see they were the bones of a young, healthy person. Gracile. A woman. The teeth were perfectly aligned and brilliantly white—with no cavities or evidence of dental work. And the hair she had collected at the site was blonde.

She had sent off samples for DNA sequencing, and she knew there would be no problem extracting DNA, since there was plenty still in the bones. But unless that specific DNA was in a database—which was unlikely—the genetic tracking down of her identity from DNA through commercial databases, such as 23andMe, could take months.

Which meant she would need to make a facial reconstruction. Her pulse quickened at the thought of it; this was what she lived for. She had taken a degree in forensic anthropology from the John Jay College of Criminal Justice, but she had also studied sculpture and painting. Normally the reconstruction would be done by a forensic specialist, while the final sculpting of the flesh, hair, lips, ears, and coloring would be done by an artist. Corrie was immensely proud of the fact that she could do both.

A soft knock came at the door and Sharp entered. He masked up, his sleepy eyes taking in the room in silence.

"Welcome, Agent Sharp," said Corrie, feeling a little awkward. He wasn't reconsidering his decision already—was he?

"Thank you, Agent Swanson," he said, walking around the gurney, his eyes on the bones. "I just happened to be in the neighborhood. Mind telling me what you've got—one agent to another?"

"What I've got," Corrie began, in her most professional voice, "is a probable white female, between twenty-five and forty years of age, around five feet eleven, blonde, in apparent good health."

"Tall," said Sharp.

"Yes. The bones have been visually, stereoscopically, and radiographically examined. No sign of injury, no healed fractures, no orthopedic implants, no evidence of trauma. Excellent dental health, good teeth, no dental work. The bones show no signs of unusual labor or repetitive motion."

"Pity about no dental work."

Corrie nodded. "Quite a few of the bones are missing, including one femur, both ulnas, one radius, one humerus, both tibias, and some smaller ones. The missing ones are the larger bones, probably carried off by coyotes or other animals. The remaining bones have also been gnawed on fairly extensively, mostly by rodents."

Sharp nodded. "How long would you say they've been out there?"

"That's a difficult question to answer. Judging from sun damage to the bones, it would be at least two years, probably not more than seven. The condition of the clothing seems to be consistent with that time frame as well."

"Hmmm," he said. "Five years—that's a rather large window to search for missing persons."

"Hopefully we'll learn more once the sequencing comes back."

He strolled over to the table, hands clasped behind his back, peering down. "You have quite a bit of physical evidence."

"Yes," said Corrie, feeling defensive despite herself. "I wanted to make sure we didn't miss anything."

Sharp nodded.

"Starting with the clothes," Corrie said, "they're of the cheapest kind, mass produced in China and Vietnam, in polyester and other cheap materials not suitable to the desert environment. Same goes for the running shoes—they are about the cheapest shoes you can buy. I looked them up online—$8.99. There's almost no wear on the shoes and none on the clothes. My guess is that the victim purchased this clothing not long before her death at a Walmart or similar discount store. These are mass-market brands that are not readily traceable or dateable."

"It's as if she was trying to obscure her identity."

"I had that same thought."

"No canteen or water bottle?"

"None, and no hat, either. And nothing in the pockets. As far as the rest of the evidence goes—" she waved at the miscellany of stones, plant material, and wood— "most of it doesn't appear to be relevant. But that spearpoint was found in the immediate vicinity, and it occurred to me it could have been used as a weapon."

His eyebrows rose. "A murder weapon?"

"Maybe. It's three inches long. It's possible you could stab someone with that as a handheld object. I'm going to do a scanning electron microscope examination, as well as some residue tests for blood and protein."

A nod. He said nothing, but Corrie sensed he was curious about her next steps.

"Now," she said, "I plan to search that missing persons window for a five-foot-eleven-inch blonde woman with perfect teeth. And...I'm going to do a forensic facial reconstruction." She shut her mouth against the ingrained instinct to ask for permission.

Sharp merely nodded again. "I know it's perhaps premature, but do you have any, shall we say...*speculative* thoughts about the victim?"

Corrie hesitated. "Well, I have the sense that she was a poised and intelligent woman."

His eyebrows arched. "Intelligent? Going out in the desert dressed like that, with no water and no hat?"

"It's dumb only if she did it out of ignorance."

"I'm not sure what you mean."

Corrie prepared to reply, then paused just a moment to revise her answer. "Sir, I'm not exactly sure what I mean, either."

His lazy expression morphed into a grin. "Maybe by the next time we bump into each other you will."

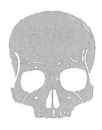

# 7

THE BIRDSONG AND rushing of brook water were interrupted by the sound of a slamming trunk. "Nora, you ready?" came the call.

"Just finishing my coffee," she said back.

For a minute or two, the sounds of nature again filled the air. Then Lucas Tappan mounted the steps and joined her on the back porch, flopping down in an Adirondack chair. She offered him a sip from her cup and they spent a few minutes passing it back and forth in silence, feet up on the railing, enjoying the view over the North Star Nature Preserve.

Tappan had been Nora's boyfriend for almost nine months now. During that time, she had not seen him all that much—he had spent several months back east trying to set up a wind farm business off the coast. When he returned, Nora had begun fearing the moment he might approach her with a black velvet box containing a diamond just slightly smaller than the Great Star of Africa. It wasn't that she was averse to being engaged, and she knew her late husband, Bill, wouldn't object—coming into a vast sum of money was something he'd enthusiastically encourage—but it was too soon for her. Either Lucas sensed her hesitation, or he felt the same way himself, because he hadn't hinted at taking things to the next level...yet.

She finished the coffee, and Lucas took the cup back into the kitchen and rinsed it out. This was one of the things she liked about him: despite being worth more than a billion dollars, he was a demon at dishwashing and an enthusiastic cook. Even more, he hated other people doing things for him that he could do himself. Instead of wallowing in pampered luxury at one of Aspen's numerous resorts, they'd opted for a rustic cabin in the mountains with a fantastic view. Of course, once they reached Aspen/Pitkin County Airport—and Lucas's private jet—everything would change. He was due back on the East Coast in a few days, looking after his corporate interests and putting out fires—for several months, this time—and she'd be back at the Institute. That was why, Nora mused, they'd tried to make every minute of this vacation count.

She'd been dreading leaving their private cabin. And now, as she heard the sound of running water in the kitchen, she flushed like a schoolgirl with a naughty idea. Maybe they could play hooky—stay one more day. And she had an idea how she might bring that about.

"Which did you enjoy more," she asked, raising her voice so she could be heard through the screen door, "Castle or Maroon?"

There was a brief silence while the water turned off before a reply came. "Maroon. A lot more technical, and what an iconic peak."

They had spent the vacation climbing fourteeners—the Colorado peaks over fourteen thousand feet in altitude. Nora had loved hiking and climbing since she was a girl, and during her tenure at New York's Museum of Natural History, she had become a "forty-sixer"—climbing every high peak in the Adirondacks, including the trailless ones. Back here in Colorado, she'd found an even greater challenge—in altitude, at least. It was just one of the many passions she shared with Lucas...and that's what she was counting on.

"I feel the same way," she said. "Long hike, big challenge—but it was worth it." She paused. "Kind of reminded me of Algonquin, second highest in New York. Of course, Maroon and Pyramid are in a different league...And might I point out, Pyramid shares much of the same route?"

She left the sentence hanging. Lucas came back on the porch. "Are you suggesting something?"

"Probably."

Lucas fell silent. Watching him frown in thought, the cleft in his chin coming into prominence and his gray eyes going far away under the curls of black hair, she felt a burst of affection.

"We're all packed up," he said.

"Just one more day?"

He glanced at his watch. "It's already eight thirty."

"It didn't take us long to drive to Maroon. Like I said, Pyramid shares a good portion of the route. It's easier, shorter, less altitude gain—class 3 at most, nothing technical."

When this was greeted with silence, she added: "That would make my tenth fourteener, a milestone. And I think your twentieth?"

Lucas smiled and nodded. "Okay—I know when I'm being gamed. But what the hell? I guess Icarus can get along without me for another day."

She jumped to her feet and kissed him. "Let's head out now—the car's already packed, we'll just pull out our gear when we reach the trailhead."

As she went back into the cabin, her cell phone buzzed. Nora had told her colleagues this five-day vacation was sacrosanct, so she wondered, with some irritation, who was calling. Pulling out her phone, she saw the call was from Corrie Swanson—from her FBI number.

Figures, she thought. Corrie always managed to call at the most inconvenient times.

"Well, well," Tappan said, looking over her shoulder. "An inspector calls."

"I'm not going to take it," Nora said, preparing to bitch button the call.

"Hold on a second," said Tappan. "Corrie doesn't call to just chat—it usually means trouble."

Nora let out a sigh. "That's what I'm afraid of." She took the call. "Hello?"

"Nora? It's Corrie. I hope I didn't get you at a bad time—"

"You always get me at a bad time," she said, with a laugh. "Lucas and I are mountain climbing in Colorado. Got you on speaker."

"Oh, damn. Hi, Lucas! All I need is your opinion on something. Really quick, I swear."

Tappan chuckled at Nora's discomfiture.

"What?"

"I've got some photos I want you to look at. When you have time. On your way home, maybe."

"Photos of what?"

"The remains of a young woman in the desert north of Chaco Canyon. No ID. Been there at least two years, mostly bones. I found a spearpoint under the bones, and I was hoping you might just glance at it."

Nora felt a twinge of interest, then told herself that this was how it always started.

"Just sent them," Corrie went on hurriedly. "Again, sorry to bother you."

On cue, Nora's phone chimed with the sound of incoming images. Corrie was a force of nature when she got going.

"North of Chaco?" Tappan said. "That's terra nullius."

"You're not kidding," said Corrie.

The images popped onto the screen of her phone, showing the bones scattered on the ground, with some closeups of the spearpoint. Nora began flipping through them.

"Nice," Tappan said, still looking over her shoulder.

"A beaut," Nora said. "Paleoindian. It's a Folsom point, fluted—gorgeous." She scrolled more slowly through the next few pictures.

"Could it be a murder weapon?"

"I doubt it," said Nora. "Unless it were attached to a shaft."

Nora kept flipping through the photos and suddenly stopped at one.

"You think it's coincidence, then?"

Nora didn't answer. She stared at the photo. It was another picture of the point, taken at a distance, showing the scattering of bones among the sand and rocks of the desert.

"Nora?" Corrie asked.

Nora continued staring at the photo, enlarging it with her fingers.

"You there, Nora?...Hello?"

"I'm coming in," said Nora. She glanced at her watch. "Should be there by...five."

"Coming in? You mean, here? You want to see the point in person?"

"I'll explain when I get there."

She signed off and looked up to find Tappan staring at her.

"What's this?" he asked. "You just finished convincing me to stay an extra day—and now we're leaving?"

"I know. I'm sorry. There's something in that photo that I've got to see."

"Corrie can wait another day."

"Corrie can," said Nora. "But I can't."

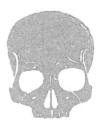

# 8

T HIS WAY," CORRIE said, opening the door into the lab for Nora and then leading her over to a broad table covered with plastic evidence bags.

"That's a lot of evidence," Nora said, staring at the array. It looked like Corrie had taken everything in sight—including half the terrain.

"I may have gone a little overboard," said Corrie, flushing slightly. "I just didn't want to miss anything. Let me get the spearpoint out for you." She rustled around among the bags and pulled one out.

Nora leaned over, faintly curious—but far more interested in something else she'd noted in the photographs.

Corrie unsealed the bag and, using rubber-tipped tweezers, took out a three-inch spearpoint and placed it on an evidence tray. She moved a magnifying glass over it for Nora to use.

Nora bent down and peered at the point. It was very finely flaked from white Pedernal chert: fluted but not stemmed, in perfect condition.

"Just as I thought," she said. "Folsom. Ten thousand years old."

"Folsom?" Corrie asked.

"The Folsom people. They hunted prehistoric bison with it." Nora felt a rising impatience. "Now, there's something else I want to see."

"Hold on," said Corrie. "Any thoughts on how it might be connected to the body? It was lying right where we found the bones."

Nora paused. "Was she carrying it in her pocket?"

"She had no pockets. She'd taken off all her clothes."

"*What?*"

"This is confidential, but she'd hiked out into the desert, taking off her clothes piece by piece, before ultimately dying. I wondered if this point might have had something to do with it. For example, could somebody have stabbed her with it? Or could she have been using it for defense?"

Nora looked more closely. "Can you give me a pair of gloves?"

Corrie offered her a pair of nitrile gloves. Nora picked up the point and examined it closely, turning the point and peering at the edges through the magnifying glass.

"It's been lying out in the open for thousands of years," said Nora. "It's got a lot of desert polish from windblown sand, and the edges are seriously dulled. So, no, I don't think it would have been used as a weapon, unless, as I said, it was attached to a shaft." She glanced around. "And it seems that a shaft was about the only thing you didn't collect out there."

"There *was* no shaft," said Corrie, defensively. "So how did it get there?"

Nora shrugged. It was a beautiful point, but she was itching to move on. "Coincidence."

"Really?"

"Ten thousand years ago, those badlands had some bison. It's not so strange to find something like that out here." She laid the point down and Corrie—with seeming reluctance—put it back in the bag.

"What I really want to see," Nora said, "are those rocks."

"Which rocks?"

"The two greenish pebbles under the bones. They were in a photo. You collected those, I hope?"

Corrie sorted through the bags and finally pulled out two small stones. "Here they are."

She placed the rounded pebbles on the examination tray. Each was about the size of a golf ball and glowed green in the bright light.

As she stared at them, Nora felt her heartbeat accelerate. They were exactly what she'd been hoping they were—what she'd ended her vacation to examine. She positioned the tray under a lens and squinted at them. She could hardly believe her eyes.

"What do you see?" Corrie asked.

"Just a moment." Still wearing the gloves, Nora picked up the stones, one in each hand, and held them up to the light. They glowed a strange, almost ethereal greenish yellow.

"Are they anything special?" Corrie asked.

"Special!" Then Nora hesitated. She needed to make sure. "Can you do me a favor and turn off all the lights? The darker it is in here, the better."

"Why?"

"You'll see."

Corrie switched off the lights. The basement lab had no windows, and the room was immediately plunged into pitch darkness.

"Watch closely," Nora said.

She rubbed the stones together. A cascade of green light

flashed from within the stones, illuminating them for a moment like tiny emerald globes.

"What the *hell*?" Corrie asked.

"You can turn the lights on."

There was the snapping on of lights, and then Nora saw Corrie standing beside the switch plate, frowning. "What was that?"

"These are lightning stones," said Nora. "Very rare. Made from a mineral called prasiolite. I can tell what they are because each stone has hundreds of tiny scratches and divots on their facing sides from being rubbed together—as I just did now."

"What does it mean?"

"Archaeologists believe the ancestral Pueblo Indians used them in shamanistic ceremonies in their kivas. Virtually all lightning stones are white quartz. But green was a sacred color to the prehistoric people of the Americas. It symbolized life, and greenstone items were treasured. You heard me call these rare? Well, they're more than that. The fact is, I know of only one other pair with this coloration in existence."

"How does it work?"

"It's called triboluminescence, and it's still imperfectly understood. These stones were once crystals that, over millions of years, were tumbled and worn into pebble-like shapes. Inside, they're as clear as water. But they have a peculiar electrical quality, generating bright flashes of internal light when you rub them together."

"Any idea what stones so rare were doing there?" Corrie asked. "Another coincidence?"

Nora frowned. "No. Lightning stones were so sacred they were found only inside a kiva—the religious center of ancestral Pueblo Indian life—and never taken out. You never find them anywhere else."

"You think the victim carried them here?"

"It seems pretty likely. I'd like to take these back to the Institute for study."

Corrie shook her head. "I'm sorry, we can't let evidence leave the lab."

Nora had expected this, but nevertheless felt disappointed. "May I take some pictures?"

"Of course."

Nora took out her phone and photographed the stones from various angles. They were extraordinary. The other two prasiolite stones, she recalled vaguely, were in a private collection somewhere. It would be interesting to track them down and learn where they were found, by whom, and in what archaeological context. Maybe these stones came from the same place.

She laid the stones down on the tray. "So the woman stripped off her clothes in the desert and died?" Now that she'd seen the stones, the horror of this was beginning to truly sink in. "Have you figured out who she was?"

"No," said Corrie, "but I know what she looked like."

Corrie led the way to a small alcove, then drew back a curtain, revealing a workspace with a small circular table. On it was a forensic sculptural reconstruction of a woman's head, in full color.

"Wow!" Nora said, staring. "She's stunning!"

The bust showed a woman of about forty years old, with a long mane of blonde hair tied back in a French braid, blue eyes, creamy skin, a thin straight nose, a well-shaped chin, and dimples.

Nora turned to Corrie, who was clearly pleased by this compliment but trying not to show it. "This is incredible. How did you do this?"

"Well, it's part engineering, part art. You start with a cast of the skull. Then you cover it with little indicators that show the depth of flesh at dozens of locations on the face. And then you basically lay down each muscle, one at a time; add the thin layer of fat and skin; smooth it; and paint it—and voilà."

"But the blue eyes?"

"We recovered samples of her hair, so we know she was blonde. Not dyed. Statistically, a person with natural blonde hair of that shade has a seventy percent chance of being blue-eyed."

"And the dimples?"

Corrie smiled. "Artistic license."

"Can you be sure this is accurate?"

"You can't be a hundred percent sure—but this isn't far off. We know she wasn't morbidly obese from the healthy state of her joints. A microscopic examination of the muscle attachments to the bones in her arms and legs indicated she was unusually fit. And her teeth show a lot of attention to appearance and hygiene. Putting all that together adds up to a person of healthy weight, with good skin and hair, and most likely a comfortable economic status."

Nora shook her head, the stones momentarily forgotten. "It's crazy to think someone like this could just drop off the map without people raising hell."

"That's just what I think. A woman this...this regal wouldn't disappear quietly."

Nora peered again into the face. It was so realistic it gave her the creeps—especially the skin, which seemed quasi-translucent, like real skin. "How did you get the skin so realistic?"

"Encaustic. Painting with hot wax. It looks much more lifelike than flat acrylic paint. It was…" She hesitated, and then continued proudly, "My own innovation."

"Well done, Corrie." She had always known Corrie was smart, but this reconstruction showed a truly rare talent. "I think," she said slowly, "that the key to this mystery is going to come down to this face—and those lightning stones."

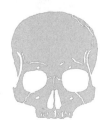

# 9

Corrie sat in her cubicle at the Albuquerque FO, getting her thoughts in order. With the facial reconstruction complete, she was ready to take the next step in her investigation: letting silicon chips, data farms, and search algorithms help her find the blonde, blue-eyed woman who had—it seemed—left behind her normal life one day, started walking into the desert, and kept on walking until she died.

In recent years, the omnipresence of the internet and the proliferation of databases of personal information had revolutionized the search for missing persons. Digital footprints were everywhere. But this case was unusual. For one thing, by missing person standards, it was old—two to seven years old—and that window was large. More than half a million people went missing in the US every year. Those who hadn't gone the route of Jimmy Hoffa were usually found quickly, but that still left many thousands unaccounted for. Corrie *had* a body and a face. What remained was to link them with an open inquiry.

That meant casting a wide net—a very wide net.

She spent another moment doing her best to put herself in the woman's head, trying to understand what her thought processes might have been. She couldn't have simply vanished without others reporting it, searching, raising hell. Maybe she was crazy and had committed suicide or been the victim of a crime. Most likely, she was just lost and delusional from heatstroke. There'd been no obvious signs of violence. Nora had been right: the spearpoint had come back negative for any trace residue of blood or human protein—it seemed not to have been involved.

Thinking of the spearpoint led her once again to ponder the two bizarre rocks—lightning stones, Nora had called them—found with the body. Nora had also said such stones were found only in prehistoric kivas, and that the greenish ones were vanishingly rare. She'd wondered if perhaps the woman had stolen them and run off, but a quick check showed no such stones were missing, and indeed the only known set today was the one Nora had mentioned. The woman obviously hadn't been murdered for them, because they were found by her remains—underneath them, in fact. The woman had discarded all her clothes, which meant she must have been carrying the lightning stones in her hands. Bizarre. Beyond the facial reconstruction, those stones were the only important clue they had.

She roused herself. No matter how or why the woman had disappeared, *someone* must have filed a missing person report. She just had to find it. And this digital detection was work she enjoyed: her experience using and misusing computers went as far back as high school, when she'd hacked into the school's computer system, giving herself straight As and the class bully an assload of Fs.

She preferred doing this kind of hunting at night, when the office was empty and she could slip on her earbuds and listen to Caravan Palace at full volume. She glanced at the clock. Maybe she'd end up doing just that—if the search took long enough.

"So: Do we have our man? Or in this case, woman?"

Corrie looked up to see Agent Sharp in the entrance to her cubicle.

"Sir, the game's afoot."

"Good." He came in and took a seat beside her workstation. "I sent up a second chopper: those badlands cover hundreds of miles, and we want to make sure there isn't another body out there undiscovered."

"Thanks." This was something Corrie couldn't have authorized on her own. "And if possible, I'd like to assign Bellamy and O'Hara to the case. I have some thoughts on how they'd be useful."

"It's your case."

Corrie, hearing how he left this sentence hanging, hesitated a moment. "I was just logging in to NamUs, if…if you'd like to observe."

His eyes lit up uncharacteristically. "I'd like that—as long as I won't be in the way. No doubt you can teach this old dog some new tricks."

The National Missing and Unidentified Persons System, or NamUs, was a vast repository of data maintained by the Department of Justice to help with cases involving unidentified or missing persons. Released initially in 2009, it was upgraded to 2.0 in 2018 and again more recently to incorporate AI, remarkably useful for investigations like this. Corrie had noticed the more senior agents either shied away from it or used it sparingly. Despite the Bureau's cutting-edge image, the J. Edgar Hoover mentality of fingerprint cards and paper files was slow to dissipate, especially among the older agents.

Corrie counted Sharp among those tech-challenged older agents, and casually asking him to watch her at work was, in her mind, a favor for putting her in charge. He had a quick and curious mind, and she felt sure she could in fact show him some new tricks—and that they'd be appreciated.

As Sharp drew up his chair, she brought up her profile on the central NamUs dashboard, showing draft cases currently part of her workflow—less than a dozen, and none of them active. Initiating a new search, she entered the woman's demographic information on a fresh screen—ethnicity, height, gender, last known location. She was forced to leave some of the most vital data—circumstances, date of last contact—empty, but she filled out a succession of other screens with a physical description and clothing. More blank fields meant a larger dataset, but she couldn't help that.

"I'm adding a photo of the facial reconstruction," she explained. "It's not exactly a photo of the person herself, but I can get around that by relaxing the parameters in case I got something wrong in the reconstruction."

"How large a net are you casting?"

"I thought it would be best to start with the state where the body was found. Depending on results, we can widen the search to the Southwest, or the entire country, if necessary."

She had now entered all the data available. Mousing over to the blue search button on the final screen, she clicked it. After a few seconds, a message came back:

1,304 possible results

"Ouch," Sharp said.

Just to get a sense of what she was dealing with, she widened the search to include all states in the Southwest.

14,937 possible results

"Angels and ministers of grace defend us," Sharp murmured.

*Fifteen thousand results.* An image of the past came to Corrie's mind: a vast room smelling of sweat and desiccated paper, library tables arranged in orderly lines, with slanting sunshine and dust motes hanging in the air, a big photo of President Nixon on one wall—and at every table a Caucasian, male FBI agent in a white short-sleeve shirt, poring over fly-specked reports as they all looked for a needle in a haystack. The FBI had come a long way.

She decided not to bother checking the entire country—not yet, at least. She thought she had an ace up her sleeve that might wipe that laconic expression off Sharp's face. Closing the results window, she moved the mouse over to a menu that read ADVANCED TOOLS.

"What's this?" Sharp asked.

"We're going to go see the man behind the curtain," she replied, holding back a smile.

Given her interest in tech, Corrie had been watching the astonishingly rapid rise in artificial intelligence over the last couple of years. The AI developers were eager to bring their technology from their labs and to the market—while at the same time quelling fears that their AI would become "self-aware" and decide mankind was a parasite to be eliminated...the usual end to so many sci-fi movies. To accomplish this, they had gingerly baked AI tools into familiar apps like word processors and spreadsheets, to help with basic tasks like composing letters or creating tables. But Corrie had been experimenting with release candidates of AI subfunctions included in the NamUs 3.0 betas. Now was a chance to see what they could do—on a real case.

A new window had opened in the center of the screen—an empty window, containing only a blinking cursor. On both sides were narrower windows: the search parameters she'd entered on the left, and a hierarchical list of available databases to the right.

"I've activated the NamUs copilot," Corrie said, "and now—since our search is sort of vague—I'm making sure it has all the records and parameters it needs before we unleash it."

"'Copilot.' Oh God—this isn't Microsoft's new Clippy, is it?"

Corrie couldn't help but chuckle at this reference to the software company's awful attempt, years ago, at creating an on-screen "helper." "No. In fact, *copilot* is just a Microsoft marketing term I'm using generically."

"I've heard the proselytizing, but do these AI tools work? How can you be confident they understand what you're asking?"

"Watch and learn," Corrie said. Then—realizing that sounded a little saucy—she quickly added: "If you make sure your search terms are wide enough, and the data pool is large enough, then the AI can do what it does best: encode your request contextually, whittle away the extraneous information and background noise, and build a, um, vector database."

"I was just going to suggest that," said Sharp, bemused.

She realized that, in her haste, she was slinging a lot of terms about. "It's been trained to search these databases like a human would, making educated guesses, ignoring extraneous information, looking for patterns, and, in a weird way, acting on hunches."

"A computer can have hunches?"

"Sort of. A human hunch usually comes from combining past experiences to make a best guess. AI does the same thing. It offers up a string of best guesses—except it's already chewed through more databases than we could in several lifetimes, which gives it 'experience' we could never match."

She began a dialogue with the AI interface:

> ;:: Are the search parameters I entered properly
> formatted?
> ;:: Yes.
> ;:: Can the LLM process the records without further
> context?
> ;:: Yes.
> ;:: I need a missing person process run, using the
> given arguments, least degree of accuracy. Save
> as a flat file in plaintext format.

The cursor returned to its former blinking state. "Are you talking to it?" Sharp said.

"Actually, that's exactly what I'm doing. They call it 'prompt engineering'—using natural-language comments and corrections to lead the AI to a desired result."

A response came back on the screen:

> ;:: Search complete. 712,559 records saved to
> 0001.txt

"Aren't you going in the wrong direction?" Sharp asked.

"I'm just getting it warmed up, so to speak. Now we can start refining the search. The text-to-text model produces increasingly relevant answers each time you instruct it."

Another brief conversation:

> ;:: Perform the same run with greatest degree of
> accuracy
> ;:: Search complete. 13,442 records saved to 0002.txt

"Notice how close that result is to the one I got when I tried the normal NamUs search?"

"It's smaller by 1,500 people—which, I hope, means greater precision."

"If not, we can always blame technology, right?"

"Work it down to a manageable number, and I'll upgrade your pool vehicle to a Lincoln Navigator."

Corrie thought a moment. "We've already given it most of the info we know for sure. That means any of those thirteen thousand, four hundred forty-two records might be our target. There's no way around that. But we can start adding our *own* guesses and hunches. Like containing the search to the Southwest, tossing in the possibility that the target was once a model or actress—that sort of thing. Or people who majored in Southwestern archaeology, or have advanced degrees in the subject. They might have knowledge about those lightning stones from studying ancestral Pueblo archaeology."

"I see where you're going. How about throwing in Indian Affairs personnel, collectors, and antiquities dealers?"

"Good ideas." Corrie typed in the filters, in natural language but longer and more specific, listing all the parameters. She made the AI construct repeat the request in its own words to make sure she'd been understood, then she told it to run the search yet again. It took over a minute before it responded.

> ;:: Search complete. Indexing complete. 1,071 records saved to 0003.txt

"That's still a lot of hits," Corrie said. "But now, in addition to what we *know* about the victim, we've also put in what we *think* might be true. But here's the crucial thing: the software has sorted them by likelihood. So you start with number one and work down, hoping to strike gold long before you reach the bottom of the list. That's the key difference, what AI brings to the search."

"Fascinating," Sharp said. "And new to me."

"So," said Corrie, flushing at the indirect approval, "that's what Bellamy and O'Hara could be doing—looking through that list."

Sharp chuckled. "They'll love it. May I suggest, for your sake, that I be the one to break the news about their new assignment?" He hesitated. "As we discussed—red tape, and all that."

"That would be much appreciated."

Sharp rose. "Exceptional, Agent Swanson."

She hadn't quite managed to wipe the sleepy look from his face—and, since he'd handed this case to her, the compliment carried less weight than if he'd been actively mentoring her. But she could tell he'd been deeply impressed—and that was more than enough.

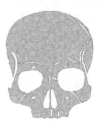

# 10

As the big black SUV bumped along the track with agonizing slowness, Nora gazed out the windows at the landscape through which they were passing. She'd been in New Mexico a long time and had hiked the Bisti Badlands, and so these kinds of formations weren't new to her—but she still experienced a sense of awe and menace when she saw them.

"It's right up ahead," said Corrie as they came around a particularly large hoodoo and entered an open, flat area. "This is where the film crew set up."

Corrie brought the vehicle to a halt and they got out, heat swimming over them in waves.

"The film trailers were parked over there—you can see all the tracks. We've got a mile hike ahead of us."

Nora looked around. "The Navajos have a name for these rock formations. They call them *de-na-zin*. Cranes."

"I can see why."

Nora doused a bandanna in water and tied it around her neck. She noticed Corrie watching. "Do you have a bandanna?" she asked.

"No."

Nora grinned. "I happened to bring an extra...just in case." She pulled a bandanna out of her day pack and handed it to Corrie, who followed Nora's example.

"Thanks," she said. "I'll have to remember that."

Nora hefted her water carrier. The temperature, she figured, was close to a hundred degrees, but the air was dry and thin, and a stiff breeze was blowing. These weren't bad conditions for July.

"Lead the way," she said.

Corrie set off, Nora following behind, threading a path among the balancing rocks toward a black spire in the near distance. A stiff twenty-minute walk brought them to its base.

"The bones," said Corrie, pointing to a forest of little flags stuck in the ground, "were scattered in that area. Those green rocks were right there, about two feet apart. The point was there. And the clothes were spread out in a long line back that way."

Nora looked around, taking it all in. There was something about this place, something ineffable, that spoke to her. It felt instinctively like an unusual spot—and not a nice one.

She nodded at the black finger of rock. "That's known geologically as a volcanic plug. You see a lot of them around here. A small cone once formed and the cinders eroded away, leaving the lava pipe still standing. Sort of like the chimney of a house that burned."

Corrie nodded.

"This formation looks particularly menacing. There's always a chance that, prehistorically, this plug might have been a place of significance."

"As in sacred?" asked Corrie.

"Sacred...or perhaps malign. I'm going to look around a bit."

Nora began walking the site, head down, looking for lithics, artifacts, or anything else of interest. She canvassed the swale, then made a loop around the finger of rock. But she found nothing—just sand and cactus.

She rejoined Corrie in the small puddle of shade at the bottom of the rock, took a long drink of water, then sat down to rest. "Why take off her clothes?"

"That's the rub. I didn't want to speculate too far with Sharp, but...well, part of me wonders if her going out here like this was a form of suicide."

"Anything's possible, of course. But if you want to kill yourself, dying of heatstroke and terminal dehydration is a pretty awful way to go."

"No kidding."

"Perhaps someone else was with her, forcing her to do it?"

"That's a possibility," said Corrie. "Remember that hogan we passed not far back? An old Navajo lady lives there. I really wish I could get her to talk."

"You tried?"

"I did. She wouldn't talk to me or a Navajo policeman. She was more interested in filling my ass with buckshot. I contacted the trader she sells her rugs to, but he couldn't help, either."

"On the way out, let me give it a try," said Nora. "I speak a few words of Navajo."

Corrie nodded dubiously. "Seen enough?"

"Sure have. I can't wait to get back to the AC of that Tahoe."

# 11

About four miles back down the rutted road, Corrie slowed the Tahoe and turned onto a dirt track. Up ahead, Nora could see a hogan and, behind it, a trailer and some sheep corrals.

"That's it," said Corrie.

"Stop here."

Corrie brought the SUV to a stop a good hundred yards from the trailer.

"I'm going to get out. You stay in the car."

"Remember, she's got a shotgun," said Corrie.

"They all do," Nora said. She stepped out into the heat, put on her hat, and, leaning against the car, waited. The sun was so bright it was hard for her to see inside the trailer, and the door to the hogan was closed. It looked like nobody was there—except Nora knew the woman must be around somewhere. The sheep were in the corral, huddled in the shade of a shelter.

Five minutes went by, and finally the door of the hogan opened and a lady with iron-gray hair stepped out, a look of displeasure on her face. A shotgun was tucked in the crook of her arm, broken open and ready for loading. She made a dismissive gesture with her arm, warning them off.

"Yá'át'ééh shimasani"—*Hello, Grandmother*—Nora called out, hoping her pronunciation wasn't too terrible.

The woman frowned and waved her off again.

"Haa'íílá ńt'é?" *How are you doing?*

The woman scowled. Nora could see, in the dim interior behind her, a loom with a half-completed weaving.

"Bilagáana bizaadísh dinits'a'?" *Do you speak English?*

At this, the woman looked puzzled.

"Bilagáana bizaadísh dinits'a'?" Nora repeated. Navajo was such a tongue twister, she thought, she might be ordering moo shu pork without realizing it.

"Haash yinilyé?" *What is your name?*

At this, the woman's face wrinkled up, and for a moment Nora thought she was going to drop two shells into the shotgun barrels—but then she realized the woman was laughing. Her thin, cackling voice came through the air, sounding like a cricket with hiccups.

"Um, is everything all right?" Nora asked in English.

The woman held her sides. "You speak bad Navajo," she said.

"I'm sorry," said Nora, flustered.

"Where did you learn to talk so badly?"

"I took some courses in Santa Fe."

More cackling. "Say something else!"

Nora was taken aback. "You mean, in Navajo?"

The woman nodded.

"Um." She delved into her small bag of memorized phrases. "Háázhó'ógo bee ádíní." *Please speak more slowly.*

This set the woman into fresh cackles of laughter. Nora realized she had no teeth.

At this, Corrie rolled down the passenger window. "What's going on?" she asked in a low voice.

"My Navajo is being made fun of."

"You were speaking Navajo? It sounded like you were choking on food."

Nora suppressed her irritation. The old lady had now leaned her shotgun against the side of the hogan and was waving for them to come over.

Nora called out, "Ahéhee' shimasani." *Thank you, Grandmother.*

At a nod, Corrie got out and followed Nora to the old woman. She went inside and gestured for them to follow.

The interior of the trailer was spotlessly clean and almost empty, save for a large open tub brimful of water, a Coleman camping stove running off a bottle of propane, two wooden benches alongside a crude wooden table, and a wood stove, thankfully not going.

"Welcome," said the old lady in good English. "Do you want coffee?"

"Yes, please," said Nora, and Corrie seconded it. "My name is Nora Kelly, and this is my friend Corrie Swanson."

The old lady bowed her head in acknowledgment but did not offer her own name. She turned the heat on under a tin coffee pot. She pointed to it. "Gohwééh," she said. "Coffee."

"Gohwééh," Nora repeated.

The woman's face wrinkled up in amusement again. She went to a cupboard, took out three enameled tin cups, and placed them on the table, along with a jar of Cremora and another of sugar. She eased herself down while the coffee heated.

A silence fell. Nora had already spent enough time with Navajo people to know that silence was common, and not to be treated as something that needed to be filled with trivial conversation.

Indeed, it was often a token of respect. She took a moment to study the woman. It was hard to tell how old she was. A lifetime in strong sun had produced a face that was deeply wrinkled, almost more than she'd imagined possible. Into this face were set two alert eyes like black marbles, a pronounced chin, broad cheekbones, and a sweep of gray hair tied back in a bun with a blue silk ribbon. She was wearing traditional dress: a purple velveteen blouse with a squash blossom necklace, turquoise earrings, a woven cotton belt, and a long orange calico dress—all very old-style. It amazed Nora that she took the time and effort to dress like that when nobody would see her, and especially in the heat. It said a lot about her sense of self-respect and dignity.

The coffee warmed, and the woman rose and filled their cups. Into her own she heaped several teaspoons of sugar and at least four or five of Cremora. Nora declined both, but Corrie avidly heaped Cremora and sugar into her cup.

Nora took a sip and smiled, even though it was awful—it must have been boiling for days on the stove. She sensed it was finally time to speak. "Did you see all the cars and RVs going past your place last week?" she asked.

"Yes."

"That was a movie crew," said Nora. "They're shooting a movie called *Steele*, a Western, in the badlands."

"Those were some fancy RVs," the woman said, with another toothless smile.

"They found something out there. Human remains."

At this the woman's face froze, the mirth turning to unease. She said nothing. Nora knew that Navajos were extremely uncomfortable talking about the dead.

"It was a woman, and she passed away between two to seven years ago. We're trying to find out who she was."

The old woman shifted uneasily, making no response.

"We want to be able to tell her family."

At this, the woman said, "Where did you find the body?"

"Near the base of that tall black rock mesa a few miles down the road—the one that looks like a stubby finger."

Now the woman's face showed traces of alarm. There was a long shaking of her head. "That is a bad place. A *ch'įįdii* place."

Nora recognized the Navajo word for *ghost*.

"May I?" Corrie asked. She took out a manila envelope, removed an eight-by-ten photo of the victim's facial reconstruction, and held it out to the woman. "Did you ever see someone like this come through here?"

The woman took the photo and looked at it a long time. Then she nodded slowly. "About five years ago, she was here."

Corrie leaned forward, excitement in her face. "Five years? Can you be more specific?"

The woman shook her head. "Time is not that important to me, but it was sometime in the summer. I saw her walk past on the road out there, moving real slow. I was frightened. She looked so strange. I never saw her again."

"You didn't know she'd died out by that black rock?"

"I never go there." She shuddered. "That is a place of *yee naaldlooshii*."

"Skinwalkers, Navajo witches," Nora translated for Corrie in a low voice.

"I never go there," the woman repeated.

"Why is it a place of skinwalkers?" Corrie asked.

The woman looked really frightened now. "I don't know. It's been that way since the beginning of time."

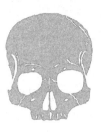

# 12

"MAN, THIS GUY must be loaded!" said Skip, as they eased up the driveway of an adobe house that sprawled along a ridgetop of the exclusive Circle Drive neighborhood in Santa Fe.

Nora didn't answer. She had debated whether to bring Skip along. Her younger brother could be unpredictable and obnoxious at times, but he also had a way of charming people. After Skip's misadventure in the Manzano Mountains, he had returned to his previous job as a collections manager at the Santa Fe Archaeological Institute and had lately been complaining about his life being boring. This interview, Nora reasoned, seemed like a harmless diversion.

She pulled the Jeep into an immaculately graveled area in front of an adobe wall with a massive set of carved mesquite doors bossed in brass. As she parked, the doors flung open to reveal the homeowner himself, framed between them and flashing a big smile.

Edison Nash was a famous collector of Indian artifacts. Most importantly to Nora, he owned the only two prasiolite lightning stones in existence—until the other two Corrie had found with the body.

Nash was fit and chiseled, curly black hair flopping over his brow, wearing skinny jeans, a cowboy shirt, and ostrich boots. Nora was surprised; she'd expected someone older, more staid, and standoffish, given his controversial history with the archaeology profession and the Institute in particular. She hadn't expected someone quite so young and hip—or welcoming.

As they got out, Nash advanced through the gate, hand extended. "You must be Dr. Kelly."

"Nora, please," she said.

"Call me Edison." Nash grasped her hand and gave it a hearty shake, then turned to Skip.

"Skip Kelly," he said, grabbing the hand with enthusiasm of his own. "Heard a lot about you!"

Nash led them through the gate and up a flagstone path into the house, where they walked into a soaring entryway with diamond plaster walls and skylights. A gorgeous, carved Spanish Colonial chest stood on one side, while a Mexican Baroque reredos depicting the immaculate conception graced the other side. The walls above and around them were decorated with a miscellany of rare artifacts, among which Nora recognized beaded Cree firebags, a Chilkat weaving, and a number of Kwakiutl transformation masks—an array of relics so spectacular that she unwittingly halted and stared.

Nash said, "Welcome to my collection."

"It's remarkable."

"There's quite a bit more," he said dryly, ushering them down a hall and into his study. This room was even more stunning, its walls covered with splendid examples of Native American beadwork, painted parfleches, masks, decorated cradleboards, and—she recognized with a start—an extremely rare Lakota ghost shirt. Nora had refreshed her knowledge of Nash and the history of his collection before the interview. He'd inherited the collection from his grandfather, a self-made industrialist who, later in life, had traveled the country buying Indian art and artifacts. But the grandson had outdone the grandfather in his passion for collecting Native American art, and the young Nash had obviously amassed what might be the finest private collection of its kind in the world.

"Please, have a seat." Nash indicated several plush leather armchairs and a couch. Nora sank into the sofa while Skip followed suit in an adjacent chair. In addition to the displays, there was a kiva fireplace in one corner, and a wall of books at the far end of the room. Nash rolled a chair out from behind his antique desk and took a seat. Clasping his hands and leaning forward, he said, "I don't often get visitors from the Archaeological Institute. They don't seem to like me over there."

"Why not?" asked Skip ingenuously.

Nash gave a chuckle. "I know as much about Indian artifacts as any archaeologist out there—but all I have is a BA. That doesn't sit well with folks who've toiled for years in a museum basement getting their PhD. On top of that, they accuse me of being unethical, paying top dollar for important Native American art." He waved his hand. "Those academic bumblebees are always buzzing around me disapprovingly. They think only museums should own this stuff."

"Um, right," said Nora, realizing the conversation was drifting on a treacherous tangent. The bad blood between Nash and the Institute had started when the Institute turned down a gift he'd offered of a rare, prehistoric Pima feathered basket because it lacked provenance—in other words, there was no history of where the basket came from, which raised the possibility it might have been looted or acquired illegally.

She quickly spoke again. "We're hoping you might help us track down the source of two rare artifacts that recently came to light."

"Of course. Happy to help. Tell me about these artifacts."

"They're two prasiolite lightning stones. Just like the two I believe you own."

At this, Nash seemed to freeze a moment in astonishment, but his smile quickly returned. "My, that's quite a discovery. Can you tell me the circumstances?"

Nora had pondered how much to share with him, and she'd decided it would be useful if he knew at least the basic facts. "I'm working with the FBI on a case. I'm supposed to keep the details confidential."

"The FBI?" Nash was surprised afresh. "Now I'm really intrigued. Of course, I'll keep anything you tell me to myself."

"Thank you. The two stones were found with human remains in the Ah-shi-sle-pah badlands. The victim was apparently carrying them when she died, about five years ago. I've been asked to see if we can't trace where they came from, and how she happened to have them."

Nash was leaning forward in his chair, a look of intense interest on his face. "How'd she die?"

"We're not sure, but it appears to have been heat exposure."

"No kidding." He seemed to think for a moment. "And you've come to me because I've got the only other known pair in existence."

"That's right."

"Would you like to see them?"

Before Nora could answer, Skip said with enthusiasm, "Hell, yes!"

Nora cast him a cautionary glance, but he was too thrilled to notice.

"I keep them in my vault." Nash stood up.

Nora rose, and so did Skip. They followed Nash out of the study and down a long hall to a nondescript door. Nash opened it and shoved aside some old coats to reveal a large steel door at the rear. After punching a code into a keypad and turning a wheel, he eased the door open, reached in, and flicked on a light.

"Holy crap," Skip breathed, staring.

It was a walk-in vault, perhaps ten by twelve feet in size, stuffed to bursting with treasure: hammered gold pectorals, Indian peace medals, ceremonial pipes, framed letters, historic photographs of Native American leaders, and many other strange and precious artifacts. At the far end stood a painted wooden sarcophagus leaning against the wall, containing a full-size Egyptian mummy, arms crossed over its chest. A section of one wall was festooned with Peruvian and Colombian gold ornaments, and other shelves contained small caskets of treasure: one full of loose rubies and emeralds, another stacked with Saint-Gaudens twenty-dollar gold pieces, a third filled with five- and ten-dollar gold coins.

"Come on in," said Nash. "There's plenty of room."

"Are those real gold bars?" Skip asked, staring into a corner that had escaped Nora's attention.

"One hundred ingots weighing a kilogram apiece." He chuckled. "That's for when America's house of cards comes down and fiat currency isn't worth a damn. I've got lots of gold. For example—" He took a key down from one wall, unlocked a metal cabinet, and slid open a drawer to reveal dozens of gold nuggets reposing on black velvet like so many gleaming eggs. "Genuine, historic forty-niner nuggets from Grass Valley and the American River. Almost all the placer nuggets were melted down into bullion—these are among the very few surviving."

"And the mummy?" Skip asked. "Where'd that come from?"

"Oh, just a traveling companion I picked up in Egypt," he said.

Nora could see that Nash was having a marvelous time showing off his collection, and that Skip's enthusiasm was only urging him on. But she needed to get the conversation back on track. "Mr. Nash, we'd love to see the stones."

"Of course." He opened another drawer full of prehistoric fetishes, with the central compartment containing two lightning stones almost exactly like the ones found with the dead woman.

Nash picked them up. "Want to see a demonstration?"

"Well—" Nora began, but was interrupted by Skip, who nodded eagerly.

"Hit the lights, Skip, and shut the vault door."

Skip shouldered the heavy metal door shut and flicked off the lights, plunging the vault into darkness.

After a brief silence, a sudden *click-click* sounded, then in rapid succession—*click-click, click-click*—and each time the stones flashed with internal fire of the most lovely, mysterious lime-green hue: just like the pair Nora had demonstrated to Corrie in the FBI lab.

"Awesome!"

"Lights."

Skip turned the lights back on.

Nash held the stones in front of him, a boyish grin on his face.

"Thank you," said Nora, despite herself enthralled all over again. "The FBI asked me to find out the history of your stones, where they were found, by whom—anything that might help identify the woman and learn what she might have been doing."

"Of course," said Nash, putting the stones back in the drawer, then shutting and locking it. "Let's go back to my study."

Once they were seated again, Nash leaned forward. "Those stones are from my grandfather's original collection. He was a self-made man, no academic background—a high school dropout. But he was a brilliant collector with a good eye, and he picked up stuff back in the thirties and forties before it was considered valuable. But—" here Nash opened his hands— "he wasn't good at keeping records. He would scrawl some basic information on a piece of paper and stuff it in a box with an item. Specifically, I still have the piece of paper for those stones, but all it says is *Gallina, Hibben, 1935*."

"Hibben?" Nora echoed. "You mean Frank Hibben, the discredited archaeologist?"

"He explored the Gallina area back in the thirties and wrote several monographs about it. The article I'd recommend is 'Murder in the Gallina Country,' published in the *Southwest Review* in 1951. Still available through JSTOR."

"You're confident your grandfather got these stones from Hibben?"

Nash shrugged. "All I know is what's on the note. According to his own published work, Hibben tramped all over that country during his lifetime. Allegedly, he wasn't above keeping some of the artifacts he found or giving them to friends."

"No indication of where in Gallina they came from?"

"None. The Gallina people lived in a labyrinth of canyons—Gallina Canyon was the epicenter, but they also spread out in Chama River Canyon and up on Mesa Golondrina—that whole area is rugged as hell and most of it is designated wilderness today. Gallina was a strange tribe—you know much about them?"

"Just a little." Among mainstream archaeologists, the Gallina were considered a minor group that all other Pueblo Indians disavowed as their ancestors. Access to their scattered ruins, often in inaccessible cliffs, was difficult; there was no professional glamour in studying them.

"It seems they were wiped out around 1200 CE. The entire population massacred. Hibben excavated some of their ruins and found skeletons of people who'd been brutally killed and dismembered, chopped up, feet cut off, babies' skulls crushed, some full of arrowheads. Their houses were burned, the adobe walls blackened by fire."

"What do you think happened?" Skip asked excitedly.

"Nobody knows. It's one of the mysteries in Southwestern archaeology. I have my own theories—but of course I don't have a PhD, so what I think doesn't count."

"What *do* you think?" Skip asked.

Nora suppressed a smile. Skip was indeed connecting with Nash, who she could see was enjoying the attention.

"I think the Gallina were up to no good. Witchcraft, maybe. Not that I believe in actual black magic, but witchcraft was a much-feared force among the Pueblo and Navajo Indians. I think the Gallina were some bad dudes, and at a certain point the Pueblo Indians decided to wipe them out. Their sacred kivas—those underground circular chambers they used for ceremonies—were burned, and the murals on their walls defaced and profaned."

"Sort of like a prehistoric genocide."

"You might call it that," said Nash. "I've also got a collection of stone knives from Gallina that came from my grandfather. I had them residue tested, and the results showed human blood. So I think there might even have been human sacrifices."

"Like the Aztecs?"

"Exactly. You want to see those knives?"

"Yes," Skip said.

Nora realized the conversation was starting to veer off again, and she felt she had gotten what she needed. "I don't want to take up any more of your time," she said, rising. "We should be heading out. It's after five o'clock."

She could see Skip looked disappointed. "What about the knives?" he asked.

"I've got to run," said Nora.

Nash turned to Skip. "You're welcome to stay and have a look."

Nora got up and exchanged glances with Skip. She hesitated a moment. Skip needed friends—and he could do worse than Edison Nash.

"No problem," she said with a smile. "You two stay here and take a look at the knives—I can see my way out."

"Great!" Skip said. "I'll see you at home later."

"Nice meeting you," Nash said, rising and shaking her hand.

As she left, she heard Nash's voice coming from the study. "Skip, all this talking has made me thirsty. I've got a bottle of Don Julio Añejo..."

She almost stopped and went back to fetch Skip, but he'd never forgive her if she dragged him away and humiliated him like that. He was a grown man, for God's sake.

She closed the door and went to her car, gritting her teeth, suddenly sorry she had brought Skip at all.

# 13

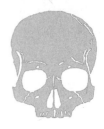

Corrie entered the conference room, trying to look as self-assured as possible. Agents Bellamy and O'Hara were waiting for her, each with their laptop computers and brief-cases open, files spread across the table. The two agents looked almost like twins, both blond, tall, and Nordic, with buzz cuts, blue suits, white shirts, and muted ties. They were a few years more senior than her, and she could imagine what they'd felt when Sharp told them, in terse terms that left no room for questions, that she was lead agent in the case. She had gotten to know the two agents reasonably well during her last, rather notorious investigation—the Dead Mountain case—and despite the physical resemblance, they couldn't be less alike. Bellamy was a whining, sexist, self-important douchebag, while O'Hara seemed more of a quiet, stand-up guy. And, naturally, they were in competition with each other, especially now that they'd been assigned a new case. All FBI cases were code-named, and this one had been labeled Badlands.

"Greetings," said Corrie, laying her briefcase on the table and unhooking it, taking out her own laptop and files. "I hear you have some good stuff for me today. But first—coffee?" This might prove to be a long meeting, and she was dying for a cup herself.

"Sure," said Bellamy. "I'll take mine with cream and sugar."

Corrie realized too late the trap she'd walked into. But before she could think of how to respond, O'Hara rose. "And you, Agent Swanson? How do you take it?"

Now she felt even more awkward at inadvertently triggering this Goofus and Gallant exchange. "Why don't we all just get our own?" she said with what she hoped sounded like a genuine laugh.

They went down the hall to the kitchenette, served themselves coffee, and returned to the conference room.

"Okay," said Corrie in her best supervisory tone, "I'm all ears."

O'Hara was about to talk but Bellamy interrupted him. "We've made really good progress," he said, rapping away at the keyboard of his laptop. "Using the AI baked into the latest NamUs release candidate, we trimmed down that list from one thousand seventy-one names to thirteen."

"Thirteen?" Corrie said, surprised. "That's terrific."

"Got 'em right here." Bellamy whipped a folder out of his briefcase, slapped it on the table, and slid it over to Corrie.

She opened it. Inside were thirteen missing persons reports, each with a photograph clipped to the front. She sorted through them, amazed at how thirteen missing women could all look so much like her forensic reconstruction. Each report had, in addition to the picture, a host of personal details: addresses, employment history, bios, where last seen, investigative summaries, and in some cases much more.

"This is awesome," said Corrie, looking up. "No way to narrow it down further, I suppose?"

O'Hara spoke. "Not without unwarranted guesswork."

"I see." She paused. It was possible, of course, that the actual victim was among the thousand-odd names that had been tossed aside, but she had enough confidence in the ever-stronger NamUs beta AIs that this baker's dozen seemed a good enough place to start. "Agent O'Hara, what are your thoughts?"

O'Hara gave a small smile. "Since you asked, number three is my guess. Number ten a close runner-up."

Corrie pulled out number three and glanced over it. Joyce Pollard Black, thirty-eight, freelance web designer, Albuquerque. Disappeared six years ago; BA in anthropology, University of New Mexico; single.

She looked up. "Why her?"

"She's a dead ringer for your reconstruction. More than the others."

"Maybe so," interrupted Bellamy, "but you've got to take forensic reconstructions with a grain of salt."

Saying nothing, Corrie pulled out the file on number ten. Martha Jane Markey, thirty-nine, high school social studies teacher, Corrales. BA in anthropology, New Mexico State University; single; disappeared five years ago. "And why her?"

"Anthro major, teaches social studies, single...but primarily because her parents were dead, and she had no siblings—which means no one to push for a thorough investigation into her disappearance. If you look at the file, you'll see the investigation was cursory. And she had a drug problem. Arrested for opioid possession."

Corrie looked at the bio and saw that her parents had died in a car crash when she was eighteen. She scanned the rest of the folder, but found nothing further to sink her teeth into. No smoking gun—but she couldn't afford to ignore it. "Looks promising," she said to O'Hara. "Worth following up in the field."

She glanced at Bellamy. He looked eager to say something.

"And you, Agent Bellamy? Thoughts?"

"Number one," he said.

She pulled it out. Molly D. Vine, forty, high school science teacher. MA in anthropology, UNM; lived in Tesuque; disappeared five years ago. "And your reasons?"

"Look at page three."

She flipped to the page and gave the short bio it contained a cursory scan. "What about it?"

"She was headed for a PhD in anthropology, then dropped out suddenly. Why? And compare her picture to your reconstruction."

This, from the guy who'd just expressed dubiousness for such forensic work. Corrie compared the two and was unimpressed. "Number one has brown eyes. And of all the pictures, she looks the *least* like the reconstruction."

"So?" said Bellamy, a challenging tone in his voice. "Your own report said only seventy percent of natural blonds have blue eyes. That leaves thirty percent with a different color."

Corrie, irritated, nevertheless had to concede the point.

"And the chin's the same. Funny-looking, pointed, like in your reconstruction. None of the others have that chin. *That's* the facial detail I'm focusing on."

Corrie gritted her teeth but said nothing.

"Now, take another gander at the bio. It shows instability in her life—and not just the sudden abandonment of her degree. Her father left home when she was two. He gets remarried, drops out of her life totally. That must've hurt. And look— married at twenty, divorced at twenty-one? That's a red flag.

She's a science teacher, but she moved schools three times in nine years and changed her habitation four times. Restless? Unhappy? I mean, if we're looking for somebody likely to just call it quits, walk off into the desert, take off all her clothes, and fry from heatstroke—she's my choice."

Once again, Corrie had to admit that, despite Bellamy's annoying bluster, the agent was making a certain amount of sense. She flipped back to Vine's bio and read it more carefully. Vine may have dropped out of the PhD program, but she did get her MA in anthropology, and later a teaching certificate. Corrie read more carefully this time, curious to see the subject of her MA thesis at UNM. And there it was, staring her in the face: "The Late Chacoan Cultural Phase in Northern New Mexico."

She stiffened: Was this the smoking gun she was looking for? The Gallina culture was late Chacoan.

"So," said Bellamy, in a self-satisfied tone, tapping his finger obnoxiously on the file, "number one here, this Molly D. Vine, is your victim. I'm sure of it."

She looked up at him, amazed to find that Bellamy wasn't such a dolt after all—and realized she'd just learned a valuable lesson about never making assumptions of another agent's work just because they were a douchebag.

"Agent Bellamy," she said, "I believe you're right."

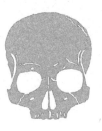

# 14

So, HAVE YOU discovered the lost manuscript of *Götterdämmerung* yet?" asked Mike Finch with his usual good humor, looking up as Nora entered the Institute's soundproofed studio.

"No, but I've got a puzzle for you."

The Institute's small recording studio had recently been updated with a thirty-two-track digital mixer, a high-end mic cabinet, and new pro audio software and hardware. It had been made possible by the $100 million endowment—and the advisory position that came with it—given to the Institute by Nora's boyfriend, Lucas Tappan. The timing of the studio upgrade turned out to be perfect: Nora had been poking around in one of the older storage areas, looking for a conquistador sword that had allegedly been unearthed a century before. Instead of the sword, she came across something far more precious: an old wooden cabinet, its drawers stuffed with cardboard boxes containing orange-colored cylinders wrapped in paper. They were wax cylinder recordings—the original method of recording sound—dating back to the 1890s. An early ethnologist at the Institute named Morrisby had made them, and the collection included songs of Pueblo, Zuni, and Hopi Indians. They were in pristine condition, the cylinders having been played rarely, if ever, before being forgotten in storage.

It was a phenomenal discovery, and no one was happier about it than Mike Finch, the Institute's part-time audio engineer.

Nora, too, was fascinated. She'd grown up playing the oboe and flute, and supervising the curation process would allow her to combine her love of music with anthropology. Most of the cylinders were documented in a logbook found in the cabinet, where Morrisby had written down when and where they were recorded and what the recordings were supposed to mean. There were harvest songs, kachina chants, healing ceremonials, deer songs, marriage songs, and much more—a treasure trove of Native American music. Some involved singing or chanting, others drumming, while a few contained melodies played on Native American flutes. It was an amazing and deeply moving experience to listen to these ancient songs from beyond the grave—music and voices that otherwise would have been lost to time.

The biggest obstacle to curating this unexpected find was the very first step—how to transfer the sound from the brittle 130-year-old wax cylinders to a computer, where it could be processed. Equipment for transferring audio tape, turntables for playing old records—those were easy to find. But the wax cylinder was a technology so old the only solution appeared to be to play them back on an original cylinder phonograph, collecting the sound via condenser microphones and piping it into a digital audio workstation…a far from ideal solution, not only because fidelity would be lost in the process, but because each time a cylinder was played it damaged the wax. A cylinder could be ruined in as few as ten to fifteen playthroughs.

A little research on Nora's part found a different solution: a company that specialized in audio restoration of outdated media, which had built a modern wax-cylinder transfer machine. In short order, one of the exotic and expensive machines had been installed in the studio, and Mike Finch had fallen avidly upon it and had been hard at work for weeks.

But on this particular day, Nora had a special cylinder she wanted Finch to play—and to listen to herself. She had brought into the studio a curious wax cylinder. She handed it to Finch.

"A puzzle! About time," Finch said, rubbing his hands together gleefully, his wild head of black hair bobbing in interest. He peered at it this way and that, holding it carefully by the edges. "I don't think it's been played since it was recorded. What's the documentation say?"

"Not much." She pointed to a scribbled label stuck to the top of the box written in a nineteenth-century hand.

### for repulsing skinwalkers
### do not play

"What's a skinwalker?" Finch asked.

"They're a kind of Pueblo or Navajo witch—male or female— who acquire evil powers by killing people, sacrificing them to malevolent gods. That's my understanding, anyway—they're shrouded in mystery, and nobody who knows anything cares to talk about them." Skinwalkers, Nora knew from previous experience, were nothing to joke about. Even today, many Native Americans of the high desert believed in and feared them.

"Sounds cool. Where'd you find it?"

"I almost didn't. It had been separated from the rest, hidden behind a drawer. There's no documentation of it in the logbook."

"You want to hear it now?"

"Absolutely."

"You sure? It says *do not play.* Might suck out your soul or something." He winked.

"I think we'll survive listening to it just this once," said Nora.

Finch began setting up his equipment. Knowing this would take some time, Nora sat down in one of the mixing console's chairs. She watched as Finch went through his checklist, enthusiastically telling her what he was doing, half of which she didn't understand: assessing the cylinder for efflorescence or eccentric grooves or divots; making measurements before sliding the cylinder onto the proprietary mandrel; determining the proper stylus; and setting the vertical tracking angle. Then, with a flourish, he turned on the preamp and the converters and initialized the computer's audio workstation. He turned in his swivel chair, finger poised above a switch. "Ready to digitize a preservation master?"

Nora nodded.

He adjusted the gain and delicately set the stylus onto the near end of the soft wax cylinder. A melody played on a Pueblo flute came drifting out of the control room speakers, remarkably clear. As Finch hovered over the spinning cylinder, ensuring the stylus didn't skate over any damage grooves, Nora quickly realized this melody was something way out of the ordinary. She could tell it had been built on the pentatonic scale, like most Pueblo music. But the tune had added several musical intervals that were outside of Western norms. It was strange and haunting—more disturbing than it was beautiful. A queer feeling took hold in her gut. As the melody progressed, it got faster and more atonal, until slowly dying out in an otherworldly string of augmented triads.

When it ended, even Finch was quiet. Then a voice came from the direction of the door.

"What the hell was that? Charles Ives on acid?"

It was Skip. He must have snuck into the booth unnoticed while Nora and Finch were preoccupied with setting up the cylinder.

"Nora," he said, flopping down uninvited at the mixing desk, "you should learn that piece on your flute or oboe. It's crazy."

Finch had taken the wax cylinder off the mandrel as carefully as he'd put it on, and now laid it on a bed of acid-free paper. He fussed around a moment, shutting down various machines. "Pro Tools has gotten really good at making sheet music from digital recordings," he said. "I wonder if it could handle those weird quarter tone intervals."

"Give it a try," said Skip. "I'll work out a chord progression on my uke, and Nora can play the melody. We'll be like Billie Eilish and her what's-his-name brother."

"One minute." Finch moved over to his computer. For a minute or two, the control room of the studio fell silent save for the rapping of keys. Then a nearby printer hummed and Nora, looking over, saw a page of sheet music spooling out in standard notation, with special marks for the quarter tones.

"Let me see that." Skip took it. "Nora," he said after scanning it, "this is going to get us a Billboard top ten!"

Sometimes she had difficulty figuring out when her brother was joking or serious. But he loved noodling around on his ukulele in the evening, and she wondered if this could turn into another of his fantastical projects.

"See you at the Grammys," he said, and left, taking the sheet music with him.

Finch turned to Nora. "I've still got a soul—as far as I can tell."

Nora laughed a little weakly, still aware of an unnerving sensation left in her gut by the music.

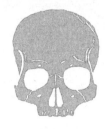

# 15

THE VINE PLACE in Tesuque, New Mexico, was a rambling old ranch set back from the village road, with irrigated fields in front, a horse barn with an alarming lean to it, corrals, and weathered outbuildings. It had, Corrie thought, a picturesque charm: despite its ramshackle nature, the place gave off a whiff of quiet wealth. Before driving to Tesuque, she'd done a little research on the pretty little town. More or less unknown to the public, it had become a stealthy retreat for movie stars like Robert Redford, European royalty, billionaires, and other celebrities seeking privacy.

As she pulled into the graveled area in front, Corrie felt a twist in her gut as she thought about breaking the news of Molly's death to her mother. Looking through the records, Corrie found the woman had not only reported Molly's disappearance, but followed up on it assiduously. She was also all too aware that—while Molly checked all the boxes for being the victim—she was in the uncomfortable position of having to relate the strange circumstances to the mother.

She mounted the creaking steps of the wooden porch lining

the front of the old adobe house and knocked on the door. It opened almost immediately, and a woman who could only be Molly's mother stood in the doorway, a stoic look on her face. Catherine Vine was dressed like the horsewoman she clearly was, in jeans, boots, a cowboy shirt, and a bandanna around her neck held by a silver-and-turquoise slide. Despite her seventy years, she was remarkably handsome.

"Thank you for coming," she said in a soft Texas accent. She turned and led Corrie through the entryway into a living room. "Please, have a seat."

Corrie took a seat and Mrs. Vine did the same, then folded her hands and gave Corrie a disconcertingly direct stare. "You found her, I assume."

"Yes, Mrs. Vine, it's my belief that we did," said Corrie.

The woman waited, hands folded, gray eyes alert and keen. She was obviously a no-nonsense type who would not appreciate a litany of condolences and small talk, so she got directly to the point, explaining how the remains were found, and where. The mother listened with fixed attention, leaning forward, her sharp face betraying little emotion. Corrie concluded with a description of the undressing and, finally, the discovery of the lightning stones and what they were.

When she was done, there was a short silence.

"Do you have any questions, Mrs. Vine?" Corrie asked after what she considered an appropriate interval.

She looked at Corrie steadily. "I have many questions, but none, I believe, that you can answer—at least, not yet. But," she added, "I'm sure *you* have questions. I'm ready to do whatever I can to help you find answers."

"I appreciate that very much," said Corrie. "Do you feel able to continue now? I can always return if this is a difficult moment."

"It's no more difficult than the last five years, dealing with slapdash investigations, second-rate detectives, and uncaring police departments. I sense with you, Agent Swanson, someone who actually cares—at last."

"I'm sorry," said Corrie, careful not to show any reaction to this unexpected compliment. "Thank you for your trust."

The woman nodded crisply.

Corrie took out her notebook on which she had jotted down her questions. "Before leaving, I'll need to take a DNA sample from you, for legal confirmation."

The woman nodded.

"Would you mind giving me an idea of Molly's life situation in the year or so before her disappearance? We're trying to get a picture of what led up to her, um, trek into the desert."

"Molly taught English at Santa Fe High. She commuted there from Tesuque."

"She seems to have changed teaching positions often. Any reason for that?"

The woman let out a sigh. "Even from a young age, Molly was restless. She was a seeker and questioner. She always hoped that a change would somehow make things better."

"Why did she abandon her PhD?" Corrie asked.

The woman shrugged. "I wish I knew. She was so excited about her subject, her professor, her fieldwork. And then...all of a sudden, she dropped it all. After that, she drifted around a bit, tried her hand at modeling and acting. Finally, when I shut off the funds, she went back to school and got a teaching certificate. But not with any great enthusiasm."

"She lived here in Tesuque?"

"Yes. Not with me, though. We somehow drifted apart. At least, she drifted from me—I don't know why. She had a little house in the village and would come by occasionally for dinner. But she became distant, and nothing I did seemed to help." The woman paused. "We never had a falling out, just a drifting away."

"But you did discuss it with her—if anything in particular was going on, or if she had something on her mind?"

"I tried to, but she was evasive."

"Her MA was in archaeology," said Corrie. "The Gallina culture, I believe."

"Yes. She was deeply, deeply interested in the Gallina, spent several summers doing fieldwork out in those remote canyons. I just couldn't understand why she dropped out. Everything I'd heard up to that point implied her work was brilliant. Her PhD advisor was Carlos Oskarbi, you know."

The name did not ring a bell with Corrie. "Oskarbi?"

"The fellow who wrote the book about the Totonteac Indians of Mexico. A seminal work. I met him a few times when Molly was working with him—an interesting man."

"Is he still teaching at UNM?" Corrie asked. He would be an obvious person to talk to.

"No. He left the university years ago. Went back to Mexico."

Corrie glanced at her notes. "The investigation into her disappearance—what can you tell me about that?"

Vine leaned back, a disgusted look on her face. "It was a perfunctory nightmare. The police, detectives, investigators all made it quite clear from the beginning that they had no interest. They assumed she'd run off somewhere, no doubt getting away from her rich, domineering mother."

"And Molly's father? What role did he play?"

The look of disgust deepened. "Last I heard—which was twenty years ago—he was a drunken beach bum in Hawaii. I doubt he even knows she disappeared—assuming he's still alive."

"So you don't have his contact information?"

"No."

Corrie looked through her notes. The remaining questions were increasingly awkward.

"Did your daughter ever show signs of suicidal ideation or ever attempt suicide?"

"No."

"Was she ever treated for depression or any psychological issues?"

"Not that I know of. I believe she saw a therapist for a while after she dropped out of the PhD program—but that was just one of the many subjects she wouldn't talk to me about."

"You wouldn't know the name of the therapist, by any chance?"

"No. But if you're implying Molly committed suicide, I can assure you she did not."

"Forgive the question, but how can you be so certain? In many ways, walking out into the desert as she did seems like a voluntary act."

The woman's eyes widened, their whites showing. "I may not have been as close to my daughter recently as I once was. But whatever problems she may have had, whatever troubles she faced, she had a steady core. Always. I gave her that, if nothing else. She wouldn't just throw her life away. Not uselessly. Not on impulse, the way people who string themselves up in their bathrooms seem to do."

Now seemed a good time to change the subject. "Would you mind please telling me the source of your family's wealth?"

The woman was taken aback. "How is that relevant?"

"It probably isn't, and again I'm sorry for the intrusive questioning. But we need to gather as much information as we can.

There's no way to know in advance what might be significant later on."

"Oil," she said crisply. "Texas."

Corrie wrote this down. "By the time she was twenty-one, Molly was married and divorced. Can you tell me about that?"

"Ugh. She'd just graduated college. Married in haste. Not long into the PhD program, she realized he was a bum and got rid of him."

"Why did she marry him?"

"I wondered that myself. He had nothing obvious to recommend him. Nothing at all. Perhaps he was well hung."

Corrie covered up her surprise by pretending to take notes. "Can you give me his name?"

"Kenneth Curtis."

"Did she have a current boyfriend at the time she disappeared?"

"Not that I know of."

"Any close friends?"

"She had some friends among her colleagues from her time at UNM. I have her old address book and can look them up for you."

"Could I borrow it?"

A hesitation. "I suppose so." She got up and walked over to a large cupboard across the living room and unlocked and opened it. Corrie could see it was filled with memorabilia—graduation diplomas, framed photos, a bundle of letters, some books, a bound thesis, knickknacks, and a beaten-up teddy bear—clearly a sort of shrine to her daughter.

"Excuse me, Mrs. Vine. Would you mind if we borrowed some of this material?"

The woman turned. "It's all I have left of my daughter. I would hate to lose it."

"I understand. We're experts at handling evidence. I'll send over our Evidence Response Team, and they'll inventory every item and pack it up with care. I promise you'll get everything back as soon as we've reviewed it."

Corrie looked into the woman's gray eyes, and for the first time she could see the depth of anguish in them. Grief was finally breaking through the façade of this tough old Texas rancher lady.

"All right," she said as she picked up first an address book, then a hairbrush, from the makeshift shrine. "Molly was no stranger to the desert. She never would have gone out there unprepared without a reason. I...hope and pray that you find that reason."

# 16

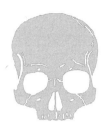

Aʜ, ʏᴇs," sᴀɪᴅ Ralph Lemmon. "Sure, I remember Molly." The professor of archaeology lounged in his office chair behind a cluttered desk, one leg thrown over the other. He wore a rumpled tweed jacket with leather elbow patches and sported dirty eyeglasses, prematurely graying hair in a ponytail, bushy sideburns, and shoulders flecked with dandruff. His socks didn't match.

Nora occupied the lumpy sofa next to Corrie, who had her FBI cell phone out, recording the conversation. The office was claustrophobic: journals and books were piled up in tottering stacks, the desk heaped with loose papers. Even the sofa had to be cleared of books before they could sit down. Corrie had requested that Nora, as a fellow academic, take the lead in questioning Lemmon. The DNA from the brush had been sequenced, and there was no longer any question: the bones in the desert belonged to Molly Vine. The primary reason they were interviewing Lemmon at all was that he occupied the Morris F. Cliffe Chair of American Studies—a position Vine's PhD advisor, Oskarbi, had once held. But Nora wasn't particularly pleased to be here—she'd slept poorly the night before, mostly because of that weird tune on the wax cylinder they'd digitized, which had kept twisting its way into her dreams. Now she felt tired and on edge.

"When was Vine a graduate student here?" she asked.

"Let's see now," Lemmon said. "She'd just arrived as a grad student when I got my doctorate, so that would be about sixteen years ago. She became one of Oskarbi's groupies."

"Groupies?" Nora asked. "How so?"

"Oskarbi liked to surround himself with pretty girls. It was sort of his thing."

"Was he sleeping with them?" she asked.

At this, Lemmon gave a little laugh. "I wouldn't be surprised."

"And what makes you think that?"

"Oskarbi was a real charmer—handsome, funny, char- ismatic, full of interesting stories about his life. He was also kind of famous back then, thanks to that book he wrote. He'd made a lot of money on it, and those students of his just wor- shipped him. He wasn't a bad dude, really, and if he *was* sleep- ing with any of them, I'm sure it was consensual. They were all graduate students in their early twenties, so it wasn't like he was boning undergrads." He shrugged. "He was just one of *those men.*"

Nora thought she picked up a faint note of envy in his voice. "More specifically, was Molly sleeping with him?"

"I've no idea. But I'm sure he would have if he could. She was one gorgeous creature."

*Creature.* Corrie shrugged that one off. "Do you have any idea why she left the program?"

"Not specifically. But it may well have had to do with Oskarbi going back to Mexico and resuming his, ah, discipleship." A snort followed.

"When was that?"

"That would be...about twelve years ago. As I recall, Molly had met all PhD requirements except the dissertation itself. A classic ABD."

"ABD?" Corrie broke in.

"All but dissertation," Lemmon said airily. "It's not uncommon. But in her case, I don't think it was the writing of the dissertation that, ah, blocked her. I think it was Oskarbi taking off like that, with essentially no notice. You could have expected he didn't have the discipline for any extended amount of time in academia. Naturally, it was irresponsible of him, abandoning his students, but then he was always a flake. Too much peyote, taken for 'research purposes.'" He made air quotes with his fingers and laughed.

"Did you keep in touch with her after she left?" Corrie asked.

"No. I think she continued to pal around with the Oskarbi group, though. They were a closed circle, having done fieldwork together every summer. Most are still around. Some are professors now, a couple here at UNM. Others went into the contract archaeology business." He paused. "You should talk to Olivia Bellagamba. She's director of the Archaeology Center now, but back then she was one of Oskarbi's minions."

"Were these groupies all women?" Nora asked.

"No, no. There were a few men, too. He wasn't sleeping with the guys—at least, I don't think so. They all adored him, though."

Nora looked through her notes. "And Molly did fieldwork every summer?"

"Right. Oskarbi directed a field school for UNM, and every summer he'd take a group of his grad students on a dig. They'd hike into the wilderness and camp out for a couple of weeks. I imagine it was a lot of fun, digging up cool stuff during the day,

cocktails around the evening campfire, tent crawling at night."
He chuckled cynically again.

"Where'd they go?"

"Up in the Gallina cultural area, in those canyons along the
upper Chama River. There are literally thousands of ruins up
there, mostly unknown and unsurveyed. That was Oskarbi's
specialty, Gallina. Pretty mysterious culture."

"Mysterious? How so?"

"That's not really my area of research," said Lemmon, with a
sniff that to Nora seemed dismissive. "You should really talk to
Olivia. She's the expert."

Professor Olivia Bellagamba occupied a sunny corner office in
the Archaeology Center, with windows overlooking the campus and the rugged outline of Sandia Peak. Bellagamba herself
was slim and stylish, wearing a professorial suit in gray worsted
wool, a silk blouse, expensive pearls, and Louboutin pumps. She
couldn't have made a greater contrast to the slovenly Lemmon.
To Nora, she looked more like the CEO of a high fashion company than a dirt archaeologist.

Bellagamba received Nora and Corrie right away, inviting
them into a lounge area of her spacious office while a gofer ventured to ask if they wanted coffee, tea, or water. After they were
settled with their proffered refreshments—coffee for Corrie,
Perrier for Nora—Bellagamba took her own seat opposite them,
crossed her legs, folded her hands, and asked in a cool, low voice,
"How may I help you?"

Nora took the lead again, explaining that they were looking
into the mysterious disappearance and death of a former col-
league of Bellagamba's. They briefly outlined the circumstances

of Molly Vine's death. Bellagamba listened with attention. Finally, Nora got to the questions.

"How well did you know Molly?" she asked.

"Quite well," said Bellagamba. "We were all graduate students together."

"Under Professor Carlos Oskarbi, I understand?"

"That's correct."

"Do you have any idea why she might have gone off into the desert like that?"

"None," said Bellagamba. "She was an old hand with the desert. It makes no sense to me."

"We're interested in knowing more about her research with the Gallina culture."

"That was due to Professor Oskarbi. He was fascinated with the Gallina and communicated his interest to all of us."

"Tell us more about them. I understand a certain mystery surrounds their culture."

"That's putting it mildly. First of all, the Gallina were different from the ancient Pueblo cultures that surrounded them—different pottery, different houses, different way of life. Who they were, what language they spoke, and where they came from is all a mystery. They thrived for roughly two hundred years in a rugged canyon complex in northwestern New Mexico, and then, around 1200 CE, they were apparently invaded. And wiped out. It was brutal. Early excavation accounts speak of the almost innumerable skeletons of people who'd been beaten to death, dismembered, burned—men, women, and children. Sacred kivas had been desecrated and set on fire. And no present-day Pueblo Indians claim descent from the Gallina—quite the opposite, in fact. That alone is extremely curious."

"I understand Oskarbi ran a field school up there."

"The professor had his theories about what happened." She pronounced the word *professor* as if it were some sort of holy title. "He did a lot of excavating with his students, looking to shed some light."

"Did he? Shed light, I mean."

"Unfortunately, he left before he could publish his results."

"We heard his departure was rather abrupt. Why did he leave the university, exactly?"

A pause. "As fascinated as he was with the Gallina culture, the Totonteac and their peyote religion was his first and—it seemed to me—greatest interest. He was obsessed with that Indigenous culture, and at the field school he frequently talked of going back there. No doubt he resumed his earlier studies with his spiritual teacher, Don Benicio."

"Molly was part of that field school, wasn't she?"

"We all were as graduate students."

"How did that work?"

"It was a typical field school. Professor Oskarbi would identify a site in the area he wanted to excavate, and we'd pack in, set up a camp, and dig for a couple of weeks."

"When was this?"

"Four summers. Fifteen to twelve years ago. Then the professor left. Most of us disbanded after that, going our separate ways. We finished our dissertations, got jobs in the field, or went on to do other things, like Molly."

Corrie leaned forward, notebook out. "When was the last time you saw Molly?"

A pause. "Twelve years ago."

"Did she show any signs of psychological issues? Depression, suicidal thoughts?"

"Not at all."

"What was she like? Her personality, I mean—interests, social life, that sort of thing."

Bellagamba shrugged. "Normal."

"'Normal' doesn't tell me much. Can you be more specific?"

"Well-adjusted. Nice. Smart. A good field worker."

"Boyfriend?"

"Not that I knew of."

"Was she sleeping with the professor?"

At this, Bellagamba straightened up in her chair. "I find that question offensive."

"My apologies," Corrie replied with an edge to her voice, "but we're conducting an investigation and asking offensive questions is sometimes necessary."

"The answer is no," said Bellagamba, her own voice a few degrees above zero. "The professor was very correct with his students, and nothing like that ever happened."

"That you know of," said Corrie.

Bellagamba said nothing.

After a chilly silence, Nora resumed her own questions. "Are you familiar with lightning stones?"

"Of course."

"Molly's remains were found with two of them. Rare green prasiolites. Any idea what she was doing with those?"

"No."

"The only other two prasiolite stones came from Gallina," said Nora. "Is that where Molly might have gotten them?"

"It's possible. But in our field seasons, we never found anything like that."

"Could she have picked them up and not told anybody?"

"Highly unlikely. It wasn't like summer camp—everything

was done by the book. You don't just pocket artifacts. It would be a gross violation of ethics."

"So where were these excavations, exactly?" Nora asked. "Is there anything published on them?"

"As I said, the professor left for Mexico before publishing."

At this, Corrie broke in again. Nora could hear the suppressed impatience in her voice. "Dr. Bellagamba, we at the FBI would like to get a list of Oskarbi's graduate students during that period, 2010 to 2013. We also would appreciate more specific information on these field excavations—what sites were dug and where. Can you provide us with that information?"

A frosty silence ensued. "I'm afraid not. You'll have to get that from the university records office."

"Why not from you?"

"That was a long time ago. I don't remember who exactly was in the group."

"How many were there?"

"I'm not sure."

"Do you have a map showing the sites excavated?"

"Those would be in the professor's notes, which I don't have."

"Who's got them?"

"I wish I could say."

"And you don't remember where the sites were." This was a statement—a skeptical statement—not a question.

"They were in the Chama Wilderness, not accessible by road. We had a commercial wrangler who packed in our supplies on muleback. I doubt I could find them now." Bellagamba spread her hands.

"Where is Oskarbi now?" Corrie asked.

"I told you. Most likely living with the Totonteac Indians and carrying on the studies he cut short to join academia."

"You haven't been in touch with him since he left?"

"No."

"Do you know anyone else who has?" She tried to keep the irritation out of her voice. This woman was going out of her way to be unhelpful.

"No."

"Where exactly in Mexico are these Indians?"

"I don't recall. It's all in the book he wrote about them. You can look it up yourselves."

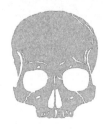

# 17

As they walked back outside, Corrie muttered, "Bitch."

Nora was a little surprised at Corrie's vehemence, but she couldn't deny the sentiment.

"What's she hiding?" Corrie went on. "And there's something about this Oskarbi that stinks, too."

"You mean the sleeping with his students?" Nora asked. "I know the type—the charismatic male professor who gathers female students around himself to bask in their adulation and then, if he can, fuck them. Anyone who's been to graduate school has seen that phenomenon."

"I'm not surprised," said Corrie. "And did you notice her tone of voice when she talked about *Professor* this and *the Professor* that? It was like when she spoke his name it was some sort of talisman."

Nora had noticed. "You think that this somehow connects with Molly's death?"

Corrie shook her head. "All I know is, I'd sure like to talk to the *Professor*."

They got back into Corrie's vehicle, she started the engine, and they began making their way off the university campus. "Let's establish a timeline of sorts, then, between Oskarbi and Molly," Nora said. "You spoke to the girl's mother—what did she have to say?"

"Molly had pretty much distanced herself from her mother. She told me that Molly had been very excited about her graduate work, and her advisor—"

"Oskarbi."

"Yes. She'd spent a few summers with him in the field. According to the mother, her work had been first-class. But then she abruptly dropped her doctorate studies, saw a therapist for a while, drifted around, and finally got a teaching certificate."

"Dr. Lemmon speculated the sudden dropping of her studies coincided with Oskarbi leaving the university."

"'Abandoning them' was the way he put it."

"I'd take that with a grain of salt," Nora said. "I got a pretty strong whiff of professional jealousy from Dr. Lemmon."

Corrie nodded. "It's true, Molly's mother had only good things to say about Oskarbi. But then, she was also adamant her daughter didn't commit suicide...despite living through what I have to believe was a pretty rough decade or more."

"Oskarbi's other 'groupies' seemed to rebound well enough. Look at Bellagamba: she was one of them herself, but I don't see any signs of resentment about how her advisor left. If anything, she was overly defensive of him."

"Exactly."

They had cleared the grounds of the university and were now headed for the interstate. "But Bellagamba also said that she knew Molly quite well," Nora added. "She called her an old hand with the desert. If that's true, she wouldn't be the kind of person likely to end up stranded without water and dying of heatstroke, unless it was deliberate."

After a moment, Corrie shrugged. "I can't deny that obnoxious professor got my goat. But still, I can't help but wonder if the two disappearances are related."

"You mean, Oskarbi and Molly Vine?" To Nora this seemed like a long shot, even for Corrie: not only were the two events separated by almost a decade, but there was no mystery surrounding the professor's return to Mexico.

Just then, Corrie's work phone rang. She picked it up. "Agent Swanson."

As Nora watched, Corrie's knuckles whitened around the cell phone. "Yes. Yes. I'll be there in forty-five minutes. Thanks."

She ended the call and looked over at Nora. "They just found another body."

"*What?*"

Corrie nodded. "One of our search helicopters spotted it. The sector's totally different—the chopper was actually on its way back to the airfield when the body was spotted. Pilot said the surroundings were too gnarly for a landing, but telephoto images show a lot of similarities: absolute middle of nowhere, mostly nude, young…at least, apparently young."

"You mean, there's a body—not just bones?"

"So it seems."

"Did they say where the body was spotted?"

"Near something called Pierre's Ruins—in case that rings a bell."

"Oh, Christ." It certainly did. "The pilot was right—that area's so remote and broken up you couldn't get in there with a Bradley."

"So how do we get to the body?"

"On horseback. Unless you want to walk."

Corrie drove in silence a moment, taking this new development in. "Horseback sounds better to me. And I think I know just who to tap for a guide."

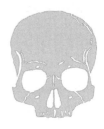

# 18

THE 3500 HEAVY Duty pickup moved northeast along IS Route 7023, Sheriff Homer Watts driving slowly to make sure the bad road jounced the attached horse trailer as little as possible.

He looked over at Corrie. "You've been in New Mexico now—what? Eighteen months? You've seen more of the state than most natives."

"I never knew it was so big—or varied," replied Corrie as she looked out the window at what could only be called another trackless landscape. It couldn't be called beautiful, but it had a sort of Zen-like purity to it that Corrie found evocative, albeit intimidating.

Corrie had worked with Homer Watts on several cases. The elected sheriff of Socorro County, he had successfully kept himself above the kind of politics rife in law enforcement. Despite his silver-belly Resistol hat and six-gun cowboy rig, Watts was not a typical good-old-boy sheriff. Not only was he absurdly young, but he was quick-witted, modest, and far more experienced than his fresh-faced good looks would imply. Corrie had felt attracted to him from the first, and the attraction was mutual—but they had both held feelings in check until the end of the Dead Mountain case, when she'd almost gotten killed. She realized then that life was not something to be put off. Their romance was still new—they'd spent two weekends together camping in the mountains but saw each other infrequently, trying to keep their relationship separate from work. She hadn't yet seen the inside of his cabin.

"Well, you picked a doozy this time," he told her, chuckling.

"Why's that?"

"The first body was found in the Ah-shi-sle-pah Wash badlands—right?"

"Yes." She'd never heard anybody actually pronounce the name before.

"This spot is even more remote."

Corrie already knew the site was difficult to reach. Too remote for a drone, far from a road or trail, and in a wilderness area that precluded motorized transport, even if it were possible. Horses were the way to go; for help, Corrie had turned to Watts, who had good horses and a lifetime of experience in the saddle. The plan was to find the body, process the site, gather evidence, and then call in an FBI chopper to drop a litter and airlift out the body and evidence.

She swallowed. Of course, there was no certainty yet that this corpse was connected in any way with Molly Vine. But simply looking at the blurred images taken from the helicopter convinced her it wasn't going to turn out to be a coincidence.

Watts slowed and swung the big Dodge Ram into a turnoff, sending up roiling clouds of dust as he came to a stop. He glanced in the rear-view mirror. "There's a trailhead, King of Dreams, a little closer at the wilderness boundary. But the road to it is too rough for a trailer." He unfastened his seat belt, looked at his watch. "Let's unload the horses and saddle up."

Within ten minutes he had the horses ready to go. Corrie couldn't help but notice his affection and pride for the animals as he murmured and stroked them while putting on the saddles and cinching them up.

"Ready?" he asked, holding the bridle of Corrie's horse.

"Sure," Corrie said, trying to sound confident, as she contemplated the large, powerful beast, who was eyeing her as well with bright eyes and perked ears. She was intimidated by horses, but she didn't want to show any sign of it. She fitted her boot to the stirrup, gripped the saddle horn and reins, and hoisted herself up, hoping she didn't look too awkward.

Watts checked her cinch for tightness. "His name's Jackaroo," he said, patting the horse's neck and letting go of the bridle. She walked the horse away from the trailer and turned, watching Watts check the panniers on the pack horse and his own saddle rigging. He then swung himself lightly onto his horse, which she gathered from his soft chatter to the animal was named Chaco. He took a final look around, consulted a map tucked into a pouch hung off the saddle horn, then clicked his tongue to set Chaco off at a fast walk, trailing the pack horse on a lead rope held in his right hand. Corrie followed behind. Despite her lack of experience, she could tell Homer had taken care in choosing an animal for her. Jackaroo was a well-built paint with what felt like an amiable character. Some horses she'd ridden were quick to take advantage of an inexperienced rider—but as she followed Homer along a dry wash and into a labyrinth of hoodoos, she could tell Jackaroo was too well trained for that.

The air was hot and dry, but not unbearable, and it smelled of dust and sagebrush. The terrain reminded Corrie of her walk to the first body—scattered with toadstool rock formations, giant nodules, and swellings of sandstone like warped stone trees. The formations were crowded together, and it was hard not to feel claustrophobic. Within a few minutes she'd completely lost her sense of direction and was reliant on Homer, who stopped now and then to glance at his map, adjust his hat, then move on.

"Don't you have a GPS?" she asked, as he checked the map yet again.

"I'm old-fashioned," he said, "and besides, the batteries in my map last forever."

"Have you ever had a case like this before, someone who died in the desert?" she asked, trying to shake off her sense of unease.

"Oh, yeah," he said. "There's even a medical term for it—'desert death.' It's not as studied as it should be. You won't find much literature about it."

"Why is that?"

Watts shrugged. "There are all kinds of deserts in the world, each with its own set of dangers. Here in New Mexico, for example, you've got hypothermia, hyperthermia, envenomation, lightning strikes, dehydration, quicksand, and flash floods. And that's just a starter."

"And your experience?"

"I've personally dealt with two," he said after a moment. "One was a fiftyish hiker who missed the trail, wandered miles in search of water after his canteen ran dry, then finally gave up, sat down with his back against a rock, and died. A lot of inexperienced people just don't realize how quickly you can die of thirst. The other was a dirt bike rider, a crazy kid who went out into the desert just to crank the throttle and raise dust. Got way the hell out there, took a spill, and punctured his gas tank, putting him on foot. Took days to find the body."

"But I mean, any murders or suicides? Like this one?"

Watts gave a chuckle. "No suicides, one murder. Meth killing in Albuquerque, body dumped in my county. We basically followed the tire tracks back to their meth lab in the South Valley. Those meth guys can't do anything right, even murder."

Watts stopped to check the map again, reorient himself in the alien landscape, and then clucked Chaco into motion. "See that mesa over there?" he asked, pointing to a distant rim of sandstone barely visible over the intervening cones and hoodoos. "That's where we're headed."

They rode in silence awhile before he spoke again. "I do remember as a kid, when my pa was sheriff, he had a few head-scratchers. Bones in the desert. Excepting migrant deaths, that stuff was more common then than it is now."

"Accidents, you mean?"

"Anything. Take a person far enough into the desert, strangle them, dump the body...in a year, maybe less, Mother Nature will make sure there's no obvious cause of death."

*No obvious cause of death.* "That's one thing that troubles me," Corrie told him. "Molly Vine knew the desert. But she walked straight out into it, without water, shedding her brand-new clothes as death approached."

"It feels to me like a suicide. But it must be said: heatstroke can make people do crazy things."

They'd just made a tight turn around a precarious-looking hoodoo and were climbing up an embankment. At the top, he motioned for Corrie to stop, then pointed. Not far away, beyond the last of the hoodoo rocks, rose the mesa he'd pointed out earlier. Ruins of prehistoric dwellings could be seen along its rim. It was surrounded by a number of cone-shaped hills, each topped with a ruined structure of its own.

"Welcome to Pierre's Ruins," Watts told her. "Three great

houses, several kivas, and more smaller dwellings than you can count on both hands. That large, central roomblock on the big mesa is known as the Acropolis."

"How do you know this?"

"I looked it up on the maps before we came."

Corrie felt a twinge of embarrassment that she hadn't thought to do that herself.

Beyond the eroded cones of land, Corrie noted a swale leading up to one of the black, stubby fingers of rock that dotted the landscape. It looked similar to the one where Molly Vine's remains had been found; in the aerial photographs, taken during late afternoon from above, its striking height had not been as recognizable.

Her eye was drawn to the base of the finger, where she spied activity.

"Uh-oh," said Watts, staring, and then urging his horse into a lope. As they approached, two coyotes fighting over something broke off and scattered, clearing away from what Corrie now saw was the corpse of the victim.

One was trotting off with something in its mouth.

"Son of a bitch!" she yelled, pulling out her handgun and firing. The horse jumped at the boom and began prancing about as she gripped the reins in a panic, almost dropping her weapon. And of course, she missed.

Watts coolly pulled a revolver and fired, taking the coyote down. A moment later, a second shot dropped the other.

Corrie finally got her horse under control and was able to reholster her sidearm. "Nice shooting," she said, embarrassed. "I'm not much of a shot myself."

"It's super difficult to shoot off the back of a horse," he said, in a kindly tone. "Luckily, these horses go hunting with me and are used to hearing gunshots—otherwise, you might have been in quite a rodeo there."

"I hate to kill a wild animal like that, but couldn't let it run off with human remains," said Corrie, lamely.

"Of course. Let's dismount and take a look."

He got off his horse and untied the lead rope, letting it drop to the ground. He tossed the pack horse's lead on the ground as well. "Just drop the lead rope," he said. "These horses ground tie."

Corrie didn't know what he meant, but did as he suggested, dismounting and letting the halter rope fall to the ground. She walked toward the huddled body, partially torn apart and shriveled from the harsh sun, but still mostly intact. Coming up to the coyotes lying in the dust, she saw one had a human hand clenched between its jaws.

"Jesus," she murmured.

She moved closer to the corpse and stared down at it. For perhaps a minute, she remained where she was, Watts silent behind her. The body lay in a fetal position at the base of the witch's finger, arms outstretched. The one remaining hand was clutched in a half-open position, and nestled inside its shriveled fingers was a lightning stone. A second lay in the dust nearby, darkly green and asleep despite the midday sun.

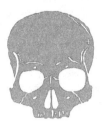

# 19

Skip Kelly arrived early and waited nervously in the parking lot of the Institute for Edison Nash to arrive. He eventually did, twenty minutes late, driving a 1960 Ford F-100 in two-toned white over turquoise. It swung into the lot with a scurry of gravel. If ever there was a vehicle that stuck out, this was it. Skip hoped to hell that no one was working at the Institute on a Sunday.

"Nice ride," Skip said as Edison hopped out.

"I just love these old Ford trucks," said Edison. "I got three more in the garage—I'll show you sometime." He pulled off his sunglasses and looked around at the low-slung adobe buildings tucked among the cottonwood trees. "Nothing ever changes around this pile, does it?"

"It's a stuffy old place."

"I'll say. Hidebound. Did I tell you, around ten years ago, when I first inherited the collection, I offered to donate a few really nice pieces to the Institute? Not that I'm some sort of philanthropist—I was looking for a tax deduction." He gave a quick laugh. "The bastards turned me down, saying the stuff had been collected 'improperly.'"

Skip shook his head. Nash had in fact mentioned this story before, and it was obviously a sore point. "They have all kinds of rules about provenance and so forth."

"Yeah, but the fact is, archaeologists were the nastiest looters and grave robbers of all time. Now they've cleaned up their act and put on a holier-than-thou mug. I'll bet half the stuff in here was collected 'improperly.'" He gave a cynical snort. "Well, let's go check it out. I've always wanted to see their shit. It's supposed to be one of the finest collections in the world."

"It is," said Skip, pride mingling with anxiety. The other evening, Nash had talked him into a behind-the-scenes tour of the Institute's collections, and the man was, if anything, persuasive—especially after a few rounds of reposado. Skip wasn't sure if showing Nash around was strictly kosher. He was permitted to escort credentialed visitors through the collections, but whether Nash was "credentialed" or not was questionable. At least, Skip thought, it was Sunday, and they weren't likely to be challenged. Even if they were, Skip figured he could justify it by saying Nash had been asked by the FBI to provide information on lightning stones, and for that reason he needed to see the collection.

Skip slipped in his card and pressed the code at the main door of the collections building, and Nash followed him in. The reception area was dark, lights turned off. After crossing the lobby and heading down a hall, Skip filled out the logbook. He hesitated, wondering whether to put down Nash's name in the visitors' column, and then decided not to. Why raise questions? There was, of course, security video, but Skip knew that no one ever looked at it and wouldn't—unless there was a robbery or some other problem.

"This way," he said.

They headed down a hall to the open collections. This was storage, but it had been set up in such a way that the finest objects were displayed on shelves and in glass cases, visible and accessible to visitors, so they could be seen and studied without the hassle of opening cabinets and drawers.

Skip flicked on the lights. A slight gasp came from Nash, who stared into the generous space packed with row after row of ancient Pueblo pottery.

"Incredible!" he muttered.

And it was incredible, thought Skip, even though he had gotten used to it over years of working there. The front part of the room was where the finest examples of prehistoric pottery were stored: thousands of Chaco black-on-white ollas; Mimbres bowls painted with stylized fish, birds, and insects; Sikyátki dragonfly vessels; gorgeous Tonto polychrome jars; Jeddito black-on-yellow ware—not to mention a shelf of extremely rare golden micaceous jars and funerary urns. As the collections manager, Skip had learned all the types and kinds of pots.

He glanced over at Nash, who seemed almost thunderstruck. "I had no idea," he finally said. "This is amazing."

"And it's just the tip of the iceberg," said Skip, feeling a flush of pride.

Nash strolled slowly down the main aisle in reverential silence, looking left and right, occasionally stopping to scrutinize a pot.

"May I photograph?"

"It's allowed for private use," Skip said.

After a while, they worked their way into the historic pottery section, equally stunning. At last, Nash turned toward his guide. "Can we see the artifacts—the lightning stones and such?"

"Right through here." Skip led him through another door into a smaller room, this one with numerous cabinets and drawers along the walls. In the center was an open storage system similar to the previous room's, with the best items in glass-covered cases, selected for viewing.

Nash hurried over and stared at row upon row of beautifully flaked spearpoints, arrowheads, and stone knives; at stone fetishes in the shapes of bears, mountain lions, and deer; at ceremonial pipes, carved bones and teeth, crystals, and turquoise pendants. Silence reigned as he bent over the items, stepping from case to case, from time to time taking pictures. Skip could hear him breathing hard. The guy, he thought, was really into this stuff.

"The lightning stones are over here," he said after a while, worrying at the length of time Nash was taking.

Nash walked over to a flat case where Skip was waiting. The case contained a score of paired lightning stones, all in white quartz. There were no green ones, none of prasiolite. But they were nevertheless beautiful and mysterious, softly rounded by tumbling and time, some clear as water, others milky.

"Holy fuck," said Nash. "I'd love to have some of these in my collection."

"Yeah, but you've got the two best," said Skip.

"Too bad we can't take them out and knock them together— test them out." He hesitated. "There isn't a way to, ah, open the cases?"

Skip quickly shook his head. "They're locked and alarmed."

"Too bad." Nash ogled them for a while and then straightened up, his brow furrowing in thought. "I can't stop thinking about how the dead woman they found in the desert was carrying lightning stones. The more I try to picture that, the more it flummoxes me. Do they have any theories about what might have been going through her mind?"

"I don't think so—not yet, at least."

"Do you think she might have been out there at night, using them to light her way?"

"Interesting thought." This idea hadn't occurred to Skip, and he made a mental note to mention it to his sister.

"You really think the FBI is going to be able to solve this case? I mean, what do those dipshits know about archaeology?"

Skip shrugged.

A thoughtful silence lengthened. Then Nash spoke again. "I think—" he started, then paused a moment. "I think the time might come when we should do a little investigating on our own."

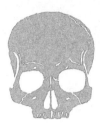

# 20

CORRIE PUSHED AWAY the overhead boom mic, walked over to the sink, stripped off her nitrile gloves, and dropped them in a bio-waste container, then soaped and washed her hands and forearms for thirty seconds. After drying them, she walked over to her workstation and sat down. Beyond the computer monitor, against the far wall of the forensic lab, stood a row of refrigerated lockers where bodies were kept.

She had maintained self-discipline during her exam, confining herself to observations and evidence. Now, sitting at the desk, it was time to give herself some slack and—hopefully—try to process and analyze what she had just seen.

She and Watts had carefully packed up the body and evidence, which they had tied into a litter lowered by a hovering FBI chopper. The evidence had included the lightning stones, as well as the victim's discarded clothing and other bits and pieces that might be relevant—including the carcasses of the two coyotes, in case there were human remains in their stomachs. Everything had been flown back to the Albuquerque FO and transported to the forensics lab.

Those coyotes were also in the fridge, and Corrie would have to dissect them soon, a job she was not relishing.

Opening a new document on her screen, she paused, putting her thoughts in order before typing up a prelim forensic report. Many details would have to await the test results, but Corrie had a clear picture of the basic facts. The body was no more than two to three months old. The girl had almost certainly died, like Molly Vine, of heatstroke and dehydration. Like Molly, she had shed her clothes—cheap and newly bought. She appeared to be in her late thirties, African American, in good health, well-groomed and fit, with no obvious signs of pathology. While she had walked into a different area of badlands than Molly—and this time on Navajo Nation land—she'd nevertheless ended up near a strikingly similar geological formation. The elements in common were remarkable, especially the lightning stones and the badland terrain chosen to die in. Her nude body had been lying on its side, in a quasi–fetal position, but given the angle of her legs, Corrie believed she might have originally arranged herself in a lotus position, maybe holding one lightning stone in each hand, before she toppled over from heatstroke. Coyotes had pulled her apart and chewed off half her face. Unlike Molly, her teeth did show dental work. Corrie had recovered excellent fingerprints from one hand, but there were no hits in the databases.

The two-to-three-month window meant that there might still be recoverable footage of her somewhere, as well as eyewitness memories, gas station receipts, and other avenues of investigation not available in Molly's case. She already had asked Bellamy and O'Hara to check out security footage at big box stores within a fifty-mile radius, showing a woman purchasing clothes.

Now that there were two points of comparison, Corrie hoped to retrace their walking routes back to their starting points. At Corrie's request, Homer Watts was already working on this problem with topo maps.

Taking a deep breath, Corrie began typing, getting her observations down while they were still fresh in her mind. Eventually, her fingers slowed on the keyboard and halted. She pushed back from the terminal, thinking. There was a brand-new instrument in the lab that she'd been dying to try out, a FireLight 3D imaging and CBCT scanner. Even though half the victim's face was gone, she wondered if it might work if she scanned the other side and then flipped it, as if in a mirror, to reconstruct the face. As a forensic tool, this kind of imaging was still in its infancy, but the machine used an array of eight dedicated IR cameras plus a sophisticated AI program to scan, align, and reconstruct both existing and missing features. It was still said to be inferior to an old-fashioned forensic reconstruction using clay, but supposedly, with the addition of facial modeling AI, getting close.

Temporarily closing her report, she rolled the gurney to the FireLight machine and positioned the camera array over the victim's upper body. It scanned it from multiple directions with IR light, which took about thirty seconds. When the imaging was completed, she initiated the analysis and waited in the silence of the lab while the computer, goosed by AI, delved into databases containing countless images, identifying and comparing hundreds of tiny anatomical reference points, to create a preliminary 3D reconstruction of the victim's face.

It took a while, requiring a lot of computational bandwidth.

Once the initial scan was done, it was up to Corrie to refine it, based on her own forensic reconstruction principles. Thanks to her interest in photography, Corrie had developed a familiarity with Photoshop, and the FireLight software was comfortingly similar. She used the program's software to symmetrically apply the intact portions of the face to the missing areas. As the process neared completion, Corrie watched as the software assembled layers of bone, muscle, and tissue—much as she did in clay—to build back the original face. Once this was done, she called up a suite of AI-assisted manipulation tools and requested that the program add the age, fitness level, adipose tissue data, skin color, and racial data.

A window popped up, admonishing her to wait while the machine did the necessary rendering. Fifteen seconds later, a complete face materialized, staring back at her, shocking in its photorealism.

The scalp in particular was badly mauled, but she had recovered enough samples of hair to know the hairstyle had been cornrows on the scalp transitioning into many long, braided strands. She instructed the software to render three variant cornrow hairstyles and then printed them out.

She stared at the face, of a Black woman in her late thirties with regal cheekbones, ebony skin, liquid eyes, and long, naturally colored hair. Of course, this was only a computer reconstruction, and Corrie was still skeptical of how accurate it was. She could always go back, reconstruct it the old-fashioned way, and compare the two. That would be an interesting exercise—especially after they had ID'd her and had a good photo. But for now, this would be enough.

In ten minutes, she was upstairs at her desk, feeding the image, as well as some dates and other data, into the NamUs database. And in another ten minutes, she had a hit: Mandy Driver, thirty-eight, who'd graduated from UNM with a PhD and worked as a geological consultant for a large, diversified energy company.

Corrie stared, astonished. Driver had been Carlos Oskarbi's personal research assistant in the year before he left the university. And she had been reported missing by her father two months ago, to the day.

# 21

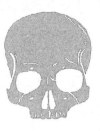

CORRIE DROVE SLOWLY through the town of Bernalillo, New Mexico. Although it was a suburb of Albuquerque, she'd never been there and was curious about what the place looked like. With a population of ten thousand, it was the seat of Sandoval County, remarkable for being home to a dozen Indian reservations within its boundaries. The downtown itself was unremarkable, mostly a continuation of Albuquerque's sprawl, the only charm being its location along the Rio Grande.

Corrie had done what research she could on Mandy Driver. She'd grown up in Bernalillo before going off to college. Her mother had died two years ago, and her father, Horace, still lived in town. In fact, he was employed by the same company—Geo Solutions GmbH—where his daughter worked. Like father, like daughter—except that Mandy Driver's residence was on the opposite side of town.

Corrie had also learned that, since Mandy's disappearance, Horace Driver had been raising hell with the local police department, apparently without much success. He made many visits to the police station and sheriff's department, demanding they find his daughter, and he raised such a ruckus that he'd been threatened with arrest. And from what Corrie could ascertain, Driver was justified in his frustration: the police and the county sheriff's office had done squat in investigating the disappearance.

As a subtle rebuke at the tepid law enforcement response, Corrie had passed off to the local sheriff the task of breaking the news to Driver of the discovery of his daughter's remains—and to let him know that the FBI was now involved in the case and would be contacting him. She had a lot of questions for Driver, but she'd wanted to give him time to process the shock before she interviewed him.

That had taken place the day before yesterday. And now, after driving through a small commercial area boasting an Applebee's and a Motel 6, she pulled into the entrance to Enchanted Hills: a sprawling, fake-adobe apartment complex off Highway 550.

The elder Driver had an apartment with a balcony on the second floor, and his door was marked only by a number. It took him nearly half a minute to answer her knock. When he did, she found herself looking at a man of sixty with grizzled white hair inching up from his ears toward a well-trimmed crown of black. His face was weather-beaten and lean, his eyes intense but guarded. He was wearing jeans and a chambray work shirt. Corrie had made the appointment the evening before and wondered if he'd taken the day off to see her. Then again, it was twelve thirty—maybe he was on his lunch break.

She introduced herself and showed her badge. The man wordlessly stepped aside to let her in, gesturing her into a combined living and dining area. The balcony overlooked the highway—with the windows tightly shut, traffic sped noiselessly past in both directions.

He motioned her to a seat. "Would you like coffee? Tea? Water?"

"A glass of water would be great, thanks." She watched as he moved off into the adjoining kitchen. She wasn't thirsty, but she wanted time to collect herself and examine the room. It was sparely decorated but fastidiously clean, walls hung with water-color landscapes of New Mexico and framed family photographs. In these latter, she recognized Driver, a woman who was clearly his wife—and Mandy.

He returned with a glass filled with ice and a small bottle of spring water, chilled from the refrigerator. She thanked him, cracked it open, filled the glass, and took a sip.

"Beautiful paintings," she said, nodding at the watercolors to break the ice.

"My wife did them."

There was a brief, uncomfortable pause. His face was closed and without expression, but his eyes drilled into hers.

"Mr. Driver," she went on, "I want to express my sincere con-dolences for the loss of your daughter."

He gave a curt nod.

"And I want to assure you we're doing everything we can to find out what happened."

A stony silence. Corrie felt her nervousness rise. "I can't tell you how much we appreciate your willingness to see me at this difficult time." She sensed he did not particularly want to sit through any more expressions of sympathy or chitchat, and so she took out her notebook.

"So you're the one who found her?" he asked with a bass voice, low and resonant.

Corrie nodded. "I did."

"The cops who had me ID her body didn't say much. But then, they never *do* say much. What can you tell me about what happened?"

The gleam in his eyes, combined with the expressionless face, unnerved her. Normally it was not good to begin an interview by answering questions instead of asking them, but with Driver she would make an exception. Taking her cell phone out, she placed it on the table beside her water glass. "May I record this conversation, Mr. Driver?"

He glanced at the phone, then nodded. She tapped the button, stated a few particulars about the impending conversation, then looked back at the man.

"I can't tell you much at this point, as we haven't gotten back any lab work. What I can tell you—" she swallowed— "is this: Mandy wasn't the first woman to die in this manner."

The man took in a deep, long breath, his eyes on her. She knew the police hadn't told him about Molly Vine—and so far, that investigation had been kept under wraps.

"What do you mean?" he asked.

"Sir, what I'm going to tell you is confidential." She went on to sketch out, as briefly as possible, the discovery of Vine's remains, and how that in turn led to a helicopter search and the finding of Mandy. As she spoke, Driver remained as stone-faced as ever.

When she had finished, he sat in silence, and then spoke. "Let me see if I get this: Both women were found naked, in the desert, having taken off all their clothes. No water, no cell phone, no ID—no nothing. Holding green rocks in their hands."

"That is correct. The main difference is the time period. Molly Vine has been dead around five years—your daughter, two months."

"And this other girl—you say she was studying archaeology at UNM as well?"

"Yes, sir. Did your daughter know Molly, by chance?"

"That motherfucker Oskarbi," Driver burst out, not answering the question. "Wrecking students' lives with his mind games."

This was completely unexpected, and Corrie quickly revised her line of questioning. "Mind games, Mr. Driver?"

"I met that bastard twice when Mandy was starting grad school—that was enough. Smooth-talking, drug-taking, jive-ass hippie punk."

Driver's face, which before had been stoic, seemed now to move through a range of emotions: grief, anger, disgust, loss.

"Um, can you elaborate on that?"

"When I was a young man in Detroit, I worked for a while in the dean's office of the local community college. I must have seen half a dozen of his type go through the disciplinary process—*professors*. It's a type. Passing themselves off as hip, dope-smoking mystics, more interested in getting laid than teaching. I had him pegged from the jump." Driver shook his head. "But he was slippery. When I asked him about Mandy's future, what kind of job she'd get, how she was going to make a living, he went all woo-woo on me, telling me that she would 'figure it out in her own time.' And him there, just slavering."

Corrie frowned. "Slavering? Are you implying that Oskarbi, ah, slept with her?"

"I'm not *implying* it. That's what he did. And not just her. I saw those girls he surrounded himself with."

"Was he sleeping with them, too?"

"Sleeping with them or trying to. I was fixing to come after him just before he disappeared."

Corrie took a moment to consult her notes and let Driver cool off. "To get back to an earlier question, did Mandy know Molly?"

He shook his head. "Probably. They were in the same department with that bastard."

"Just so I understand," Corrie went on. "You believe that Oskarbi was—what? Psychologically manipulative with his students?"

"That's putting it mildly. He was a narcissist. He went around implying that book he'd written was a sacred text. Mentioned it both times we spoke. And to hear him talk, that was just the beginning. The next one was supposedly going to be a *real* humdinger."

"The next one? You mean next book?"

"Right. That's what he kept telling Mandy, anyway." He shook his head, scoffed. "Made Mandy his lab assistant. Filled her head with a lot of nonsense."

Corrie glanced up again at the pictures framing the walls. Mandy Driver had been exceptionally pretty—even more than the reconstructive software had shown. "Did Mandy tell you she was having a relationship with him?"

"No, she was closemouthed about it, but I knew."

"Did you share your concerns about Oskarbi with her?"

"*Certainly* I shared my concerns. But what can you do with a starry-eyed daughter? She'd had boyfriends before, but they were chickenshit compared to the Great and Famous Professor."

Privately, Corrie tried to imagine a high school boy passing muster with this formidable father. "Do you think this relationship with Oskarbi had anything to do with your daughter's death? He left twelve years ago, and I understand Mandy went on to finish her degree, went on with her life."

"His leaving almost broke her. Of course, my wife and I were glad to see the backside of that con. My wife and I, we never stopped supporting her. Her dream had been to become a research professor. That's what Oskarbi had promised—but of course it was all bullshit, and then he disappeared. I didn't spend twenty years working oil fields so my Mandy would follow in my footsteps."

His voice was rising again, and Corrie took a moment to pause and consult her notes.

"My understanding was you both worked for the same company?" Corrie had assumed that the father had helped the daughter land a good job at his own firm, but maybe that wasn't the case.

"Geo. We both worked for Geo."

"And what kind of work was that?"

"Fracking," he said, an instant defensiveness creeping into his voice.

"Geo Solutions is an oil company involved in...*fracking?*"

"We're a supplier of fracking equipment in the San Juan Basin oil field." The defensiveness in his voice had risen a notch.

Corrie swallowed. She wasn't a fan of fracking, but as an FBI agent it was not her place to express an opinion on that. Her voice hadn't betrayed her private thoughts...had it? Damn it, she had been taken off guard.

Then she looked up into the face of Driver—and the expression she saw alarmed her. He had picked up her tone. He wasn't outraged anymore. He was now incensed.

"How's that water tasting?" he asked.

Quickly, Corrie took a sip. "Good, thank you."

There was an uneasy silence and the man said, "You have no right to judge what I do—*or* what my daughter did."

"Mr. Driver, I meant no disrespect—"

"I'm not ashamed of working with my hands. These hands got my Mandy through college, got her a scholarship to graduate school, got me promoted to foreman." He looked out the window. "But *she* deserved better. She had a brilliant mind. Straight A student all the way. She wanted to be a professor, to teach and write books. Oskarbi was too selfish to let that happen. First, he built up her dreams. Then he vanished...not a word...just abandoned her and sucked out her ambition in the process. So she ended up at Geo, like me, doing contract archaeology for fracking. What you so disapprove of."

"Sir, I don't disapprove."

"Sure," said Driver. "I saw you drive up—nice-looking ride, that taxpayer Tahoe. I'll bet it glides over these New Mexico roads like silk." He paused. "Any idea how many gallons of gas it guzzles per mile? Or where all that gas came from?"

Corrie was desperate to get the interview back on track. "Can you tell me more about Mandy's work?"

After a glaring pause, he said, "She mapped the proposed fracking leases, showing where the archaeological sites were so they wouldn't be disturbed."

"And this was her employment when she disappeared?"

"Yes. It paid well, sure, but it wasn't the life she dreamed of. She was like you—she disapproved of fracking and hated working for Geo."

Corrie let that go. "This is a difficult question—but was she depressed?"

"Absolutely not. Next question?"

"What was her connection to Gallina archaeology? Those rocks she was found with were Gallina artifacts."

Another freezing silence. "Years ago, she did fieldwork up there with Oskarbi, who seemed to have a hard-on for all things

Gallina. And the San Juan oil field extends into the Gallina area. Geo's going to begin fracking up there. Which was why she got hired, in fact: because of her knowledge of the area. Next question?"

Corrie went to her notes once again, fumbling through them this time. "Do you have any idea why she might have done what she did?"

He stared at her. "So you're assuming *she* did it?"

Corrie realized she'd made another mistake. "Not at all, but it's a possibility we're exploring—"

"How do you know someone *else* wasn't there, forcing her?"

"We're considering every avenue—"

At this, Driver stood up. "You're starting to sound like the cops I've been dealing with these past two months. '*Considering every avenue,*'" he mimicked. "Look, I'm done with this conversation. My daughter's dead—now go do your shit. There's no way she would have done something like that on her own. Or been stupid enough to go into the desert she loved and die of heatstroke. Someone *did* this to her. You find that motherfucker."

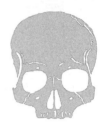

# 22

CORRIE SAT NEXT to Detective Sergeant Benally in his squad car—a white pickup truck emblazoned with Navajo Nation Police logos—watching as they drove deeper into the badlands. The latest victim had, like the first, been found in the Checkerboard part of the Navajo Nation, but this time on land belonging entirely to the Navajo Trust, which meant Benally was nominally in charge. This was fine with Corrie; Benally was a stand-up officer, low-key, sensible, and easygoing. The only problem was he, like Sharp, drove like a maniac over the reservation's prodigiously bad roads, pounding and lurching along to the point that Corrie had to brace herself with the "oh, shit" handle to prevent her head from slamming into the roof. When she'd suggested he might slow down just a bit, he'd said with a laugh, "If I slowed down on these roads, I'd never get anywhere."

Corrie watched the landscape pass by. It was a brutally hot July day, and she was glad for the air-conditioning. They were going to visit a man named Jack Bia, the allotment holder for the section of land on which the woman's body had been found. He didn't live there; his own home was in a settlement called White Horse, south of the badlands.

"Do you know this guy?" Corrie asked as they careened along.

"Never met him. I hear he's a young fellow, studying to be a medicine man."

"And what exactly—if you don't mind my asking—is a medicine man?"

"Don't mind at all. It's someone who conducts ceremonies to restore balance in people's lives, restore harmony, and cure them of mental or physical illnesses. I've heard Jack Bia is learning the Enemy Way ceremony."

"What's that?"

"It's mostly for people returning from military service—especially if they've been involved in battle. It's a long, chanted series of invocations and stories in Navajo that goes on for several nights, along with sand paintings, a battle reenactment, and other things. Afterward there's usually a dance for young people called a Girl's Dance. Used to be called a Squaw Dance, but that term's totally uncool these days." He laughed again.

"And this—as you said—restores their harmony?"

"Coming back from war, you've been around killing. You're tainted by death, especially if you've killed other people yourself. You're troubled by the chindi, or ghosts of those dead. The Enemy Way lays those ghosts to rest." He paused. "Your culture calls those ghosts PTSD."

Corrie was struck by this. "The Enemy Way is meant to cure PTSD?"

"Specifically, cure soldiers dealing with the horrors of war. Just about every Navajo family around here has members in the armed forces, so the Enemy Way is one of our important ceremonies."

"Does it work?"

Benally turned to her with a faux-stern look, and Corrie realized she'd said the wrong thing. Back came the memories of Horace Driver—which were never far away, as it was. Why the hell couldn't she remember to ensure her brain wasn't in reverse...before letting her mouth step on the gas?

"Of *course* it works," he said. "You think psychiatrists and pills do any better?"

"Sorry. That was a stupid question."

"No worries. And here we are."

It didn't seem to Corrie as if they'd arrived anywhere at all, but Benally turned off the rudimentary road onto a track, which wound among some sand hills before approaching a prefabricated HUD house, a large and beautiful hogan made of adzed logs with a mud roof. As was customary, Corrie now understood, Benally stopped the truck well before the house and waited.

The door opened almost immediately and a young, energetic-looking man emerged, waving and calling out. They exited the truck and, as they approached, he invited them in. Corrie found herself in a spacious and comfortable living room, with a carpeted floor, a wood stove, sofas and chairs, a giant flat-screen television—and above the sofa, an arrangement of photographs of young men and women in uniform standing against American flags.

"Jack Bia," said the young man, shaking their hands in a curiously soft manner. "Coffee coming up."

He was full of activity, pouring coffee, dumping in sugar and Cremora without being asked, and serving it around. It was exactly as Corrie liked it, and so, apparently, did Benally.

When the coffee had been served, Bia sat down, put his

elbows on his knees, and leaned forward. "So," he said, "what's going on?"

Benally glanced at Corrie. Given where the body had been found, they'd already decided he would take the lead. "Well," said Benally, "as I mentioned on the phone, we're investigating the death of a young woman on your grazing allotment up by Betonnie Wash. Apparently, she walked out into the desert, took off her clothes, and died of exposure."

Bia said nothing.

"And we were wondering if you could shed any light on it."

Bia remained silent another moment. "I got that allotment from my grandmother, but I haven't ever used it. I don't have time to run sheep. I'm studying to be a medicine man."

"When was the last time you were up there?"

"Oh, at least ten years ago. When I was a teenager, helping my grandmother herd sheep."

"Do you have any idea why someone would go into that area?"

"The only outsiders I've ever heard about are rockhounds wandering in there, looking for fossils or petrified wood. Oh, and supposedly the oil company has people in there now and then."

"Speaking of the oil company, the victim was named Mandy Driver. She was an archaeologist working for Geo, which is fracking up in that area."

"Right. Those fracking leases include my allotment."

Corrie spoke. "You mean they're fracking on your land?"

"Not yet, maybe never. But they have leases covering that land."

"How do those leases work?" Corrie asked. "Do you get money from it?"

At this, Bia made a wry face. "Me? Get money? I wish! That land is Navajo Nation Trust Land. They lease it to the oil companies and collect the royalties. The state and BLM also own land in that checkerboard, and they do the same—lease it and collect royalties. They all cooperate together so the leases aren't broken up. The royalties get divided, some to the Navajo Nation, some to the state, and some to the feds. I don't see a dime of it. It's not *my* land—I just have the grazing rights."

"I see." Corrie glanced at her notes. "Did the victim ever contact you about visiting your land in her capacity as an archaeologist for Geo?"

"No. They come and go without informing me, and I'm never up there anyway."

"There's a rock formation out there, black and rather weird. That's where the victim was found—at its base. Is there any significance to that particular landform?"

At this, Bia's face tightened a little. "Why do you ask?"

"The other victim was found near a similar formation. It just seems like an odd coincidence."

Bia looked down. "In Navajo belief," he began again, much more slowly, "every landmark, every mountain and canyon and mesa, has a story behind it. Our land, the Diné Bikéyah, is sort of like your Old Testament, in that our creation stories are told not by words on paper, but by landforms."

"And that black formation has a part in this story?"

"Yes."

He seemed reluctant to continue, and Corrie felt similarly hesitant to inquire further.

Benally nodded at Bia. "It's okay to share the story. She's on our side."

Bia thought for a moment, then nodded. "All right. In the beginning of time, when the earth was young, the Navajo people emerged and came to live on this land. But they found someone had been there before, leaving their ruins behind. We used to call them the Anasazi, the 'ancient enemies.'"

He paused, drew in a long breath.

"I know the word *Anasazi* is no longer supposed to be used to describe the ancestral Pueblo people. And that's fine. But I have to explain something. The translation of the Navajo word *Anasazi* as 'ancient enemies' is a mistranslation. The word *ana* means 'stranger' or 'outsider,' not necessarily 'enemy.' Anyway, since *Anasazi* is a Navajo word, I'm going to continue to use it."

Corrie waited as Bia took a long sip of coffee, as if preparing himself.

"The story my grandmother told me—and it's an old story, one of the most important in our creation cycle—goes like this: the Anasazi who lived here before us were very powerful. They had medicine men, lots of sacred turquoise, and potent ceremonies. One medicine man was the most powerful of all, called the Noqoìlpi, the Great Gambler. The Great Gambler tricked the people in gambling games and eventually won everything they had. Then he ruled over them, drunk on his own power. He misused the ceremonies in order to control and enslave the people, forcing them to build the great houses at Chaco Canyon and other places. But this displeased the Yei, the gods. Wind, Darkness, the Bat, and the Great Snake came down. They challenged the Great Gambler to games. He eventually lost everything. He began making threats, so to get rid of him, Darkness made a bow and shot him far into the sky, way into the south. Some say he became the god of the Mexicans, others the god of the Americans. After he left, the people were freed and moved away from the great houses. All those places fell into ruin and were abandoned—left as a warning about arrogance and the misuse of power. And that is how we Navajo look on the ruins of Chaco Canyon and elsewhere today—as a warning."

There was a brief silence, then he resumed. "That black spire on my allotment—my grandmother said it, and the others like it, were left by the Great Gambler as a sign of his lingering evil. I've never been up there...and I don't intend to ever go."

Bia drained his coffee, put down the cup. And Corrie could tell from the expression in his eyes—although still friendly—that he wasn't going to answer any more questions about the witch's finger.

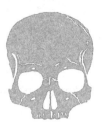

# 23

NORMALLY, WHEN CORRIE descended into the basement of the Albuquerque Field Office, she took a right into the forensic lab. In fact, she couldn't remember ever heading left from the bottom of the stairs, even during her initial tour. But this time, she turned left.

The corridor was long, ending in a wall without windows or glass to soften the door set into it. The signage was equally spare: to one side was a white square with a military-looking acronym stamped in capital letters: ALQ FO / OPR.

She hesitated a moment, uncertain whether to knock. She was uncomfortably aware of her heart thumping in her chest. She knocked, and ten seconds later, a woman in a blue blazer and matching skirt opened the door.

"I'm Corinne Swanson," Corrie told her. "I have an eleven o'clock appointment."

Wordlessly, the woman let her in, then waved toward a tiny alcove with a handful of chairs that reminded Corrie of the place in pharmacies where you wait your turn for a vaccine. The woman returned to a front desk and consulted her computer.

"Yes, you're logged for eleven," the woman told Corrie almost before she'd taken a seat. "Please come with me, Agent Swanson."

Corrie rose again and followed the woman out of the vestibule, past some workstations, then down a short corridor. There were only two doors on each side, with a frosted-glass window set high in each. The décor, such as it was, had the beige neutrality of an interrogation unit. Which, Corrie realized, wasn't necessarily far from the truth.

Horace Driver hadn't wasted any time. She must have still been on her way back to the FO from Bernalillo when he began preparing an official complaint about her conduct. He'd known just how to go about it, too, no doubt from long experience filing earlier complaints with the police and sheriff's department: he'd contacted the FBI's Office of Professional Responsibility. Like Internal Affairs in police stations, the OPR was a feared and often hated unit: those who spied on their own, enforcing laws on those whose duty it was to enforce the law. Corrie had heard the department mentioned numerous times, usually in low tones, but she hadn't paid much attention. Its staff members didn't fraternize with other agents. Corrie hadn't recognized the woman who opened the door, nor any of those sitting at the workstations. By now, she knew most people in the FO by sight, passing them on the way in or out of the building or in one of the cafeterias. But this—this felt like a foreign country.

Yet in another way it was depressingly familiar. She could not help but be reminded of her high school years, when she'd been hauled a number of times into the holding cell of the Medicine Creek police station for some minor infraction or disturbance.

Because Driver had submitted an official complaint, it had to be dealt with in the official FBI way. And that meant a formal debriefing—a gentler-sounding word than *interrogation*—by the OPR.

She'd worked so hard, kept her head down and shoulder to the wheel, getting straight As through John Jay and doing her best afterward to keep her impulsivity and temper in check. Had she *really* screwed up so badly with Driver?

Her flow of thought was interrupted when the woman opened the last door on the right. Agent Sharp stood just inside a small room almost entirely filled by a table: four chairs on one side, two on the other.

"Agent Swanson," Sharp said, nodding at the woman, leading Corrie inside, and directing her toward the two chairs. "Take a seat."

She walked around the table and sat down. The wall was not painted, but covered in some kind of cloth or felt that made her wonder if the room was soundproofed. A large condenser microphone hung from the ceiling, encased by a shock mount. Sharp took a chair on the far side of the table, which she noticed had an array of knobs and buttons set into it, along with a portable microcassette recorder. Her side of the table had nothing. It was all she could do not to examine its wooden surface for grooves left by scraped fingernails.

Another man was sitting across the table. He, too, was a stranger, dressed in the standard FBI uniform, perhaps thirty, with very blond hair cut short but carefully layered. For whatever reason, he and Sharp sat apart, two empty seats between them. The man nodded silently to Corrie.

"Before we start," Sharp said, glancing down at a lone folder in front of him, "would you like a glass of water?"

Corrie shook her head. She was determined to say as little as possible—and to betray a similar neutrality of emotion.

There'd been nobody at the office she knew well enough to ask how to handle this kind of situation. She wasn't that close to the other young agents, and in any case she'd never heard of anybody except the former forensic examiner, Lathrop, getting entangled with OPR.

Sharp snapped a button on the desk. "Checking for sound," he said, glancing at the other man. He nodded in return. Only now did Corrie notice he had an earpiece, its wire running unobtrusively back down the nape of his neck.

There was another brief pause, during which Sharp pressed a few more buttons on the desk. There was a small square of dark glass set high up in the opposite wall: Corrie wondered if a camera was concealed behind it.

She watched as Sharp took a deep breath. He opened the folder, spread out a few pages, then gave the time and date for the benefit of the recorder, as well as the names of those present.

"Agent Swanson," he said, "as you are aware, Horace Driver has filed a formal complaint against you." He glanced down at the papers spread before him. "Specifically, he attests that you treated him in a cavalier manner, were highly disrespectful, showed a lack of empathy in your questioning, and in general handled the interview with an attitude that demeaned not only him, but his daughter." He paused. "The Department of Justice requires us to investigate all allegations of misconduct against law enforcement officials of any type, so long as they were acting in an official capacity at the time. Our conduct is governed by statute 18 U.S.C. § 242, which protects the civil rights of any defendant or potential defendant." He paused to look at her, eyes as sleepy as always. "Do you understand?"

"I understand."

"Based on our preliminary review, nothing about your actions or the recording of your interview would indicate that you violated Mr. Driver's civil rights, engaged in fabrication of any sort, or otherwise conducted yourself unlawfully. We do not believe you committed a federal crime. However, we must nevertheless review the substance of Mr. Driver's complaint for two reasons: so we can show due diligence, and so that, for your protection, we can provide proof we have examined the matter beyond the point of reasonable doubt."

*Jesus God.* Just listening to this recitation had made Corrie's throat go dry. It sounded like the opening statement of a court-martial. She wished she'd accepted the offer of water.

"We are fortunate that you taped the entire exchange. That allows us to evaluate it in light of his allegations. Shall we begin?" Without waiting for a reply, Sharp reached for the recorder, checked the counter, then snapped it on.

The three of them listened in silence as Corrie offered her condolences to Mr. Driver; affirmed that she was the one who'd found the body; then, in response to Driver's pointed questions, gave him details about the manner of his daughter's death and the particular importance of gaining any information he might have—because, among other reasons, Mandy had not been the first woman to die this way. This in turn led to Driver's sudden rant about Oskarbi, accusing the long-gone professor of sleeping with students. Then they reached the part when Corrie had inquired about Mandy's work. Sharp played this, then stopped, rewound, and played it a second time.

*"Geo. We both worked for Geo."*
*"And what kind of work was that?"*
*"Fracking."*

*"Geo Solutions is an oil company involved in…
fracking?"*

Corrie looked down at her hands. There was no denying it—
her voice had clearly betrayed her private feelings—and Driver,
his antennae already tuned to a sensitive degree, had picked up
on it—and immediately transferred his anger to her.

Mercifully, Sharp did not play it a third time. Rather, he let
the tape continue. After another, briefer rant—this one directed
at Corrie—Driver resumed answering her questions, now with
cold suspicion and biting, cynical replies. Then came her second
mistake: phrasing a question about Mandy in a way that implied
she might have taken her own life.

*"How do you know someone else wasn't there, forc-
ing her?"*
*"We're considering every avenue—"*
*"You're starting to sound like the cops I've been
dealing with these past two months…Look, I'm done
with this conversation. My daughter's dead—now go
do your shit."*

Since this was essentially the end of the interview, Sharp did
not replay the final, bitter exchange. He didn't need to. Instead,
he snapped off the recorder and let a brief silence settle over the
room. Then he looked questioningly at the OPR representative,
who gave a faint shake of his head. Sharp turned back to Corrie.

"Agent Swanson, we've now listened to the conversation that
prompted Horace Driver's complaints. At this time, it seems
most germane to ask: Do you feel his complaints are justified?"

*Justified? Hell, no. This bastard is so zealous about filing complaints he had to be threatened with arrest. I'm just a fresh victim he can spew venom on.*

Corrie didn't say this aloud, of course: looking on herself as a victim was the wrong approach. Instead, it was her turn to take a deep breath.

"Sir," she said, "listening to the conversation, I can see why Mr. Driver was offended. He was overwhelmed by grief over his daughter's death. The mindset in which I approached the interview was primarily what he might be able to offer me to help solve this case." She paused to lick her lips. "In retrospect, I can see I pushed ahead too quickly in my eagerness to question Mr. Driver. I carelessly conveyed personal feelings about an issue sensitive to him. I was not as tactful as I should have been, or cognizant of Driver's state of mind...which, by that point, he'd made clear. I ignored my training at the Academy and the mentoring I'd received from Agent Morwood and yourself. There is no excuse I can offer. All I can do is tell you how sorry I am that this happened. I realize Mr. Driver was offended not without reason. I let you and the Bureau down, and I will make every effort to learn from this mistake and ensure it never happens again."

She exhaled with a long shudder. There: she'd said it all. She'd laid it all out on the table, plowing ahead even as Sharp had once or twice opened his mouth to interject. It had been important to her, she realized in hindsight, to do this: she knew she'd screwed up, but deep down she felt this was an overreaction by both Driver and the Bureau—and she wanted to make it clear, without needing to be told, that she understood her mistake... but clear on her own terms.

Now she glanced from Sharp to the OPR rep and back again. Her mentor was looking a little less sleepy than usual. For a moment, their eyes locked silently. And then he nodded.

"I think, Agent Swanson," he said, "that you've done as good a job at getting to the crux of this issue as we could have. But you're going to have to tell all this to Mr. Driver as well, in the form of an apology. In this kind of situation, it's as important you go through the process with him as you have with us. *You* need to own your actions; *he* needs to know you'll use this to do better."

Corrie had wondered if this would be one of the conditions. The good news was that—seeing the OPR rep unexpectedly stand up from his seat and start moving away from the table while adjusting his tie—there might be no further consequences: no keelhauling, no flogging round the fleet. But the thought of seeing Driver face-to-face again, in any capacity, was sufficiently unnerving as to almost mitigate the relief she felt.

The OPR worker nodded to each of them in turn, then left the room, silently closing the door behind him. Sharp closed his binder, snapped off the buttons on the desk, put the recorder away. His slow, deliberate movements seemed gauged to let the pressurized atmosphere in the interview room deflate a little. Finally, he sighed and glanced at the overhead mic—signaling it was off—then turned his eyes to Corrie.

"I'm sorry you had to endure that."

He stopped. When it became clear he was waiting for a response, Corrie nodded.

"I've been in rooms like this before—on both sides of the table. There's always a reason these reviews take place. In this case—" he stopped to pat the folder— "I have two takeaways. The first is that Driver was an exceedingly difficult interview. He was hurting, but he was also eager for confrontation. He'd been badly treated by law enforcement—and you took the brunt of that." He paused. "He'd lost a daughter—and, by the way, he lost his job, as well."

"I didn't know that," Corrie said.

"He missed work searching for his daughter, and Geo, being the giant company it is, simply fired him.

"Sometimes it's the people we're sworn to protect that can be a big pain in the ass. We can't change that. And we can't change the Bureau's red tape, which you've just experienced here in this room."

Now he pushed his chair back from the desk. "Now that I've said that, I wonder if you might hazard a guess as to my second takeaway."

Corrie was still getting over her shock of learning Driver had been fired. It made her feel even worse about her screwup.

"Sir, I believe the other takeaway is that I still have a lot to learn."

Sharp raised an eyebrow. "That, Corrie, is what I'd hoped to hear. Interviewing a victim—as Mr. Driver was—requires great sensitivity. It requires that you keep your personal opinions scrupulously under wraps. Now you've had your baptism by fire. Yes, you have a lot to learn, but you've also come a remarkable distance in a short time." He hesitated, as if pondering whether to say something, and then said it, all in a rush. "You're one of the most promising agents I've ever come across."

He stood up, and Corrie quickly followed suit, stunned by this last statement, her face flushing.

"Back to work, Agent Swanson," he said with a ghost of a smile.

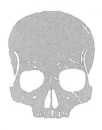

# 24

Sᴋɪᴘ ʜᴇsɪᴛᴀᴛᴇᴅ ᴀᴛ the huge mesquite doors, then took a deep breath and knocked. Almost immediately, Edison Nash threw them open.

"'Sup, man?" he asked. "Come in!"

Skip followed him through the grand entryway and into the study, impressed all over again at the mansion and collections—owned by a guy in his mid-thirties. A couple of years older than himself—and already a billionaire. A fire was burning in the kiva fireplace, the crackle of juniper wood adding its ambience to the dying light outside. On the coffee table sat several items: a bottle of expensive reposado tequila, some limes, a dish of salt, margarita glasses, a bottle of Cointreau, a jar of simple syrup, some lime juice, a bucket of ice, and a shaker.

Nash flopped down in a leather armchair as Skip took the sofa. "It's five o'clock somewhere," he said. "Got all the mixings. What say?"

"I say yes," said Skip.

Edison deftly began mixing ingredients into the shaker: lime juice, Cointreau, syrup, and a massive pour of tequila. He added ice and gave it a brisk shake, then—after running a wedge of lime around the rims of the glasses and dipping them in salt—strained the mixture into them with a flourish. Skip watched, feeling a tickle of anticipation.

Edison raised his glass and Skip followed. "To our investigation!"

Skip took a goodly sip, feeling the warm, tart liquid go down.

"Now," said Edison. "You're not going to believe what I've found out."

"Tell me." Skip began to reach for his glass and a second big gulp, then resisted the temptation. He was determined not to overdo it; after his first drinking session with Edison, he'd ended up with a wicked hangover.

"So I started looking into the Gallina, the ruins, all those canyons up there. I read Hibben's book—you should read it, too—and I did some informed poking around. After your sister's visit, I'd begun wondering if maybe there aren't more green lightning stones in the Gallina country. Maybe there was a source of prasiolite around. And in the process I learned about a really bizarre, unsolved murder."

"Really?"

"About twelve years ago a body was found washed down the Gallina River from upcanyon. It was lodged in a sandbar where the Gallina flows into the Chama River. Found by some river rafters. It was a middle-aged guy, and he'd been beaten up, stabbed, generally trashed. But here's the kicker: when they did the autopsy, they found someone had carved a symbol into his belly. Postmortem."

"What kind of symbol?"

Nash rose, picked up a photograph off his desk, and handed it to Skip.

"Jesus," said Skip. It was an image of a body lying on a gurney, in a disgustingly half-decayed state. "Is that a—spiral?"

"That's right."

"How'd you get this?"

"I have my ways."

"Anybody know what it means?"

Nash shook his head. "That's what makes it even stranger. It looks to me like the spirals you see on prehistoric petroglyphs, but who knows? A spiral could be anything."

Skip handed back the photograph. "Who was the guy?"

"That's a mystery. Nobody knows who he was, what he was doing there, or who killed him."

He drained his margarita and rocked the shaker fetchingly. "Another?"

"Sure." Skip quickly finished off the remainder of his glass. Edison refilled it as well as his own.

"I also dug up my grandfather's notes about the Gallina. And can you believe it—I discovered he'd been up there with Frank Hibben himself! This was back in the thirties. They camped out and Hibben showed him some of his favorite ruins. I'm pretty sure they did a little digging—there weren't many rules back then. Maybe that's where my grandfather got those lightning stones." He paused. "Stands to reason. I'll bet there are more up there."

"Maybe even the mother lode of prasiolite up there." Skip was starting to feel the effect of the strong margaritas.

"Exactly what I was thinking!" Nash leaned forward, giving Skip a wide-eyed stare. "I love a mystery. How about you?"

"Absolutely."

"You do much camping?"

"All the time. Spending time out in the desert, under the

stars, is a Kelly family tradition. My father was kind of a crazy treasure hunter, and he dragged us kids into the great outdoors almost before we could walk." Skip found himself smiling at the memories that arose. "I'm never happier than sitting around a campfire, a steak sizzling over the coals, strumming my uke... dozens of miles from anything."

"You play the ukulele?"

Skip nodded. "My father had this old Martin 1930s soprano uke—Style 1, if you know your ukes. Mahogany and Brazilian rosewood. He won it in a poker game. He taught me every Tin Pan Alley and cowboy song he knew. It's gotten a little dinged up over the years, but I still treasure it. Every time I play it, I'm reminded of my dad."

Edison's eyes shone. "Let me show you something." He stood up and walked out of the room, returning a minute later with what looked like a long, straight object. He handed it to Skip.

"An Anasazi bone flute," Skip said in an almost reverential tone, turning it over in his hands. "I've never seen one in such pristine condition."

Edison laughed. "That's because there isn't one."

"What do you mean?"

"You can't play those old flutes—most of them are so cracked and decayed, they'd come apart in your hands if you tried to play. I had this one re-created by a luthier in Denver."

"So it's playable?"

Edison took it from Skip, played a few bars of a plaintive melody, and handed it back.

"Wow," Skip said. "It sounds fantastic."

"Damn right it does. We took three old flutes apart to get the interior measurements and the finger stops just right."

Skip looked at him. "Three original flutes?"

"Sure. Couldn't get the tonalities or the finger stops right otherwise. It's not like those old things were worth much—I've got half a dozen others stored away someplace. I did keep the mouthpiece of the nicest one, though, and had the luthier attach it. See how it's carved?"

Skip looked at the faded rings and geometric patterns at one end of the flute. Then he handed it back. "That's pretty awesome." He wasn't so sure about the destruction of the old flutes to make this one, but he said nothing.

"Remember what I said last time we met? How's about you and me doing a little investigating on our own? We could get some supplies and backpack into those canyons—camp a few days and do a little exploring. Nothing illegal, of course—just poking around. Bring your ukulele and I'll bring my flute. It'll be a blast. What do you think?"

Skip opened his mouth to say *Hell, yes*—but he stopped himself. He was both flattered and thrilled with the idea. It would be a fantastic outing—and they might just make some interesting discoveries. While going into Gallina Canyon wasn't illegal, he sensed that Nora would take a dim view of him, an Institute employee, "exploring" ancient ruins with a guy like Nash. She had already hinted to Skip more than once that she thought Nash was a bad influence.

"I—" he stammered. "It sounds great. Do you mind if I just, ah, take a day to arrange it with my work schedule?"

"Well...sure. But don't dally too long. I might just get antsy and head out there on my own."

"Don't do that!" Skip said. Maybe, he thought, he could work this out with Nora, persuade her he would be a restraining influence on Nash when it came to picking up artifacts.

Nash smiled. "I'll check in with you tomorrow. Meanwhile, I'll take care of the provisions." And he patted the bottle of tequila with a grin. "Such as a goodly amount of this firewater to nip around the campfire. Eh, Skip?"

Then he raised his glass. They clinked them together and drained them both down.

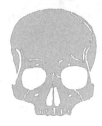

# 25

THE FAT BINDER landed on Corrie's desk with a thump, shaking her abruptly out of some unpleasant reveries.

"What's this?" she asked, looking up to find Nora standing in the entrance to her cubicle at the Albuquerque Field Office, a smile on her face and a visitor's pass around her neck.

"The PhD dissertation of Miranda F. Driver."

"Hefty enough. Did you read it?"

Nora took a seat in the cubicle's only free chair. "I looked through it. It doesn't exactly break new ground, but it's nevertheless a sterling piece of scholarship. Driver would have made a fine professor if she'd taken that route."

"Any insight into the case?"

"From what I can tell, the dissertation brings together pretty much everything known about the Gallina culture, which isn't much. And it has a brief section covering the archaeological field seasons Oskarbi directed—not as much detail as I'd hoped, but then again not surprising, given that he never published any of the team's findings and all his notes, photographs, and journals seem to have disappeared."

Corrie picked up the tome, flipped through it. "How did you get this?"

"From UNM. Dissertations are available online, and you can order hard copies." She paused a moment, fiddling with the visitor's pass that hung from her neck. "But this one was harder to find than it should have been."

"How so?"

"It was indexed incorrectly, effectively rendering it nonexistent to searches. Take a look at the title."

Corrie looked. "The Decline of the Galina Culture in the Badlands of the American Southwest."

"See the misspelling of the word *Gallina*? Now look at the name."

Corrie looked: *Miranda F. Diver.*

"Name misspelled, too. That prevented a hit on searches for either author name or title."

"Deliberate?"

"It could have been a data-entry error...But you gotta wonder."

"What's in there someone would want to hide?"

Nora paused, as if choosing her words carefully. "It's what's *not* in it."

Corrie raised her eyebrows as Nora hefted the dissertation, opened it to the table of contents, and turned it around for Corrie to see. "It looks normal, right?"

"As far as I can tell." Corrie scanned the chapter titles. "What am I supposed to be looking for?"

"And the page numbering is all in order?"

"Seems so."

Nora turned the page. "Now look at the table of figures."

Corrie looked. Each entry gave the relevant chapter number, followed by a dash, then the figure number—a standard format.

Again, this seemed normal. She scanned the table a second time. "Wait. Some of these figures are misnumbered."

"Right."

She looked up to see a broad smile on Nora's face. "The last two chapters have been removed. Everything's been readjusted, pagination and chapters renumbered, table of contents updated—except whoever did it forgot to renumber the figures."

Corrie stared. "Nice detective work. So what do you think was in those chapters?"

"I don't know. But even as I was reading the dissertation over, I felt that Driver was holding something back, as if lining up her evidence for a final, perhaps even unexpected, argument or theory. But then it never materialized. I think that theory was taken out at the last minute—probably in a rush—and a new, more banal conclusion substituted in its place."

"By whom?"

"The most likely person would have been the dissertation advisor. And as you see from the title page, that was Oskarbi." Nora paused. "But even so, we just might be able to find those missing chapters."

"Really? How?"

"I wrote a dissertation myself. You end up going through ten, fifteen drafts before it's done," Nora said. "And you save every draft. If this material still exists—" she paused and smiled at Corrie— "I'll bet her father has it. And, Miz FBI Agent, *you* need to go get it."

Late that afternoon, Corrie, a lump of stone-like dread in her gut, pulled into a parking space in front of Driver's apartment building, got out, went up, and rang the doorbell. She hadn't called ahead to make an appointment: she was worried he wouldn't see her. She had an apology to make—and in addition, if she was going to get his help with the dissertation drafts, she hoped she might have a better chance at persuading him in person.

Another long wait, and then Driver opened the door, looking at her with a cool gaze. "Come in," he said, stepping aside.

Corrie entered, feeling nervous and tentative although doing her best not to reveal it.

"Have a seat," Driver said.

Corrie consciously chose a different chair to sit down in this time. "Mr. Driver," she said, starting with the lines she'd rehearsed on the drive over, "I'm really sorry that I offended you when I first—"

Driver held up his hands. "Say no more. I don't know what I was thinking at the time, and I hope that complaint didn't get you into trouble." He took in a deep breath. "It's just...I've been so frustrated about the do-nothing police. It was obvious they didn't give a damn from the jump—that they assumed she'd run away. I couldn't help but think if she were a white girl, they'd have paid more attention. I let my temper get the better of me."

This was not the response Corrie had expected. "I'm sorry for not being more...discreet in my opinions."

Driver waved this away. "The best thing you can do for me is make progress on this case. Is there any more news?"

"Nothing yet," Corrie said. "I did have a few follow-up questions, along with...well, a request."

"If it can possibly help, go right ahead and ask."

"You mentioned a group of graduate students around Oskarbi. I'm trying to put together a list of who they were."

"The university doesn't have it?"

"Their records aren't good."

He slowly nodded. "Let's see. Mandy talked a lot about them, they were a pretty close group, but I saw them rarely if ever. Molly Vine was one, of course. And then there was another one, Italian name...Bellagamba. I think she's still with the university."

"Olivia Bellagamba?"

"Right. There was Susan Franco...A woman, Elodie Bastien... A big square fellow by the name of Bromley. Morgan Bromley. Another fellow named Grant. That was his first name, can't remember the last." He thought for a long while. "There were some others, but I just can't recall." He shook his head.

Corrie, writing down the names, was surprised by just how good his memory was. No doubt he'd had time, in his bitter reflections, to recall just about everything his daughter had told him before she vanished. "How many in total, would you say?"

"Not that many. Maybe eight, ten?"

Corrie nodded. Now felt like a good time to make the ask. "I think there might be useful information among your daughter's dissertation notes and drafts. Do those still exist?"

"They certainly do—in a filing cabinet right here, as a matter of fact. She didn't have room in her apartment for all her books and papers, so she stored her research stuff with me, in the spare room."

He rose, and Corrie followed him past the living room and into a hallway. The last door opened into a small bedroom almost entirely filled with shabby filing cabinets, books, journals, and papers. A tiny twin bed was crammed into one corner.

"This was her crash pad when she visited. And where she stored all her stuff." He spread his hands. "Feel free to take a look, search everything, take what you want." He hesitated. "I'm just thankful that somebody finally cares."

Corrie looked around the room. This could be a gold mine. "I do care," she said forcefully. "And I promise you, Mr. Driver, we're going to get to the bottom of this case."

# 26

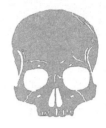

CORRIE DIDN'T SPEAK much on the drive out to Sandoval County Jail, content to let Agent O'Hara take the wheel while she flipped through her notes. Despite Sharp's reassurances and the mutual apology session with Mandy's father, Corrie was finding that the aftermath of her disciplinary interview was lingering. Most of the time she managed not to think about it, but there were other times when she'd ended up second-guessing herself—when she wondered if she'd ever be able to shape her excitable, impulsive nature into the ideal of a cool, confident FBI agent.

She'd asked O'Hara to come along this morning, not only because it was pro forma to have a partner under the circumstances, but because it would give her a chance to hang back a little, let someone else do the questioning. She liked Brendan O'Hara; he was a good guy, friendly, intelligent, hard-working, and—unlike his frenemy Bellamy—seemed to have no issues working under a less-senior like Corrie.

She glanced briefly at her notes once more, then looked up as she felt the vehicle slowing down. The jail was in Bernalillo, of course, which was rapidly becoming her least favorite town, a place destined to be for her like those text-based computer adventure games she played as a kid, where you'd end up in a maze, turn left, then right, and somehow end up back in the room where you'd started.

The Detention Center was a cluster of low buildings, painted sand gray, that could have passed for a distribution facility were it not for the chain-link fence topped with concertina wire that surrounded it. There was precious little greenery in the landscape to begin with, but that was all suffocated by a vast concrete expanse the same color as the building.

Corrie followed O'Hara in, letting him take the lead as they showed their IDs, handed over their sidearms at the entry barrier, and were led through a short series of passages to a standard prison visitation room: two pairs of seats facing each other, between them a thick pane of Plexiglas with a circular speaking grill bored through it, and video cameras in the ceiling corners. Although Corrie didn't tell O'Hara, she'd been in more of these during Quantico simulations than on the job.

She knew they had only a minute or two to themselves. "So, we're good?" she murmured. "You'll take the lead, and depending on how cooperative he is, I might or might not step in."

"It's your party," O'Hara said.

The door opened, and a massive figure appeared. Kenneth Curtis stepped forward, then stopped, overtly examining the two FBI agents through the Plexiglas. He had an insolent gaze, and the way he ran his eyes over them implied he'd arranged this interview, not the other way around. Two guards were barely visible behind his bulk. Curtis had his hands cuffed behind his back. One guard undid the cuffs while the other stood back, mace and ugly stick at the ready. Then the guard with the handcuffs withdrew, the door slammed and locked. Only then did

Kenneth Curtis deign to sit down, massaging his wrists as he did so.

There was a silence while they took the measure of each other. Corrie had seen the man's rap sheet, of course, but the perp photos didn't do justice to the menacing presence that now faced them. She guessed he weighed at least three hundred pounds—one of those hulking frames that seemed as much muscle and sinew as fat. His prison shirt was short sleeved, showing off the myriad tattoos encircling his arms and rising up his neck. He'd shaved his head bald, but hadn't stopped there: the eyebrows were gone, as well.

Corrie had done her homework. Over the last twenty years, Curtis had enjoyed a fraught relationship with law enforcement. Not including the various issues that took place during his divorce from Molly Vine—including a restraining order from Oskarbi—he'd been busted half a dozen times for disorderly conduct and assault. It was the assault charge for busting the ribs of an anti-fracking protestor that had landed him in the pen. He'd pled down to a first-degree misdemeanor and was now in the last week of a ninety-day sentence. Interestingly, he'd been represented with the help of a lawyer provided by his employer: Geo Solutions.

Corrie remained silent while O'Hara ran through the initial questions. She wondered what an educated, sophisticated student like Molly could have seen in Curtis. She reminded herself that people could change, especially over a span as long as twenty years.

Among the knickknacks, letters, and other material Mrs. Vine had lent Corrie was a small photo, unframed and soiled, of Molly in her wedding dress. Curtis was only partially in the frame, but there was enough to indicate he'd looked lean and handsome—hard to believe he'd morphed into the creature sitting across from them.

Formalities over with, O'Hara got down to business. "Mr. Curtis, do you have an idea why we wanted to speak to you today?"

Curtis shrugged.

"Aloud, please, for the microphone."

"No."

"We're here about your ex-wife. Molly Vine."

Curtis showed no sign of interest. He knew Molly had disappeared, of course, but he may not have known her body had been found—jailhouse TVs weren't usually tuned to news channels.

"You knew she was missing?" O'Hara asked.

"Sure. Good riddance."

"Are you aware her body was just found in the desert?" O'Hara said.

"Her...*body*," Curtis replied after a moment.

"Yes."

"And you're here to, what—get a confession out of me, or something?" Curtis scoffed.

"She'd been there about five years," O'Hara added.

The only response Curtis made was to slowly roll his tongue across his teeth: upper set first, then the lower.

Corrie leaned forward to ask a question. "When was the last time you saw Ms. Vine?"

Curtis wheeled his eyes toward her in mock surprise. "She *talks!*" he said. A leer came over his face. "Does she do anything else?"

"Answer the question," O'Hara said.

"Look, I broke up with the bitch, what, twenty years ago? I ran into her once or twice, maybe nine, ten years back."

"Where?" O'Hara asked.

"Gas station in Tesuque."

"Did you converse?"

Curtis laughed. "I wasn't sure it was her, to be honest—until she caught sight of me. Then she got in her car and peeled out of the station like a NASCAR driver."

"How much did you know about her life after the divorce?" O'Hara asked.

Curtis shrugged again. "It's a small world. You hear things. I know she dropped out of grad school, got a job as a teacher somewhere."

"Do you know why she left school?" O'Hara asked.

"Probably couldn't handle the grief. Of losing a prime specimen of masculinity like myself."

"Try again," said Corrie sharply.

Curtis looked at her appraisingly a moment through the scratched and greasy Plexiglas. "I figured she'd probably realized what a fake and a loser that professor was."

"You mean Oskarbi," Corrie said. "The one who filed a restraining order against you."

"Yeah. The punk."

"What was the basis for that restraining order?"

"Because I came home from work one day and found him boning my wife. I did my best to crack his skull, but Molly got in the way and he took off. Fucker."

"So you two had been having marital problems?" Corrie asked.

"That professor was the marital problem. He had this

hippie-dippy charm, answered your questions with riddles of his own, all deep sounding and shit. Smelled like weed. Randy motherfucker, too—I wouldn't be surprised if he was dipping his wick all over the damn place."

Corrie looked down at her file. None of the trouble Curtis had gotten into after the divorce related to Molly—apparently, he'd left her alone. On the other hand, he had not been in prison five years ago when she walked into the desert. He had a motive as well for getting rid of Oskarbi.

"What was the state of your marriage before Dr. Oskarbi entered the picture?" she asked.

"She couldn't get enough of me. I'm the kind of guy that attracts women—just like moths to a candle."

*Where they crackle and burn up*, Corrie thought to herself.

"I figured once she finished her PhD, she'd start bringing in some serious dough. Even if she didn't, her old lady was loaded."

So Curtis was an easy rider on top of everything else. "You say you tried to break his skull," she said. "Can you be more specific about what took place during the assault?"

Curtis thought for a moment—perhaps mentally computing the statute of limitations. "I got a couple of good ones in before Molly broke it up, gave the fucker some cracked ribs and a black eye." He grinned.

Oskarbi had filed a restraining order—but he'd quickly dropped the assault charges. Why? As soon as she asked herself the question, Corrie knew the answer: he didn't want word of his philandering to spread any farther than necessary.

"Did you ever see him again?" O'Hara asked, picking up on her line of thinking.

"No. Heard he went back to Mexico." Curtis paused.

"You were not in jail when Molly died in the desert," Corrie said slowly, looking at Curtis to gauge his reaction.

Curtis was silent for a moment. "Let me put it this way. I didn't kill Molly. But if I *had*—well, you'd never have found her." He eyed them each in turn. "Draw your own conclusions."

And with that, he leaned back from the glass.

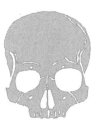

# 27

Corrie and Sharp made their way to the FO's interrogation rooms. She had asked O'Hara to locate all of Oskarbi's graduate students during the period before he went back to Mexico and then persuade the local ones to come in for questioning. It had to be voluntary, since Corrie didn't have enough evidence to get subpoenas, but "voluntary" didn't mean coercion might not be employed.

O'Hara turned out to be good at that. Of five who were local, he'd lined up three for questioning. Sharp had stayed out of that process, but once the witnesses were brought in, he became involved—pointing out to Corrie that she'd had very little experience handling interrogations, and that he was there to observe and only intervene if necessary.

Corrie had to admit she was green when it came to questioning witnesses—and, in these circumstances at least, was glad of having backup.

The interrogation rooms at the FO were on the first floor, bare and intimidating. Each had the usual one-way mirror, through which observers could watch and listen to the proceedings, and it was in one of these observation rooms that O'Hara, Corrie, and Sharp had gathered with their morning coffee to discuss the upcoming interrogations.

"So," said Sharp, looking at Corrie and O'Hara with his sleepy, heavy-lidded eyes. "What is the goal here? What information do you want to solicit?"

Corrie had written down a list of questions. "Maybe it would be easiest if I explained the thought process that led me here. You see, I'd begun to wonder to myself if Oskarbi wasn't at the center of some kind of cult."

At this Sharp's eyebrows shot up. "A cult?"

"Yes, sir. You have this charismatic professor, Oskarbi, celebrated author of a bestselling book about drugs and phony Native American spiritualism. He gathers around him a bunch of starry-eyed students, coerces the female ones into having sex with him, and his male students into a sort of cowed obedience."

She paused.

"Go on," said Sharp.

She glanced at O'Hara, who had a skeptical expression on his face.

"And then, years later, two of the followers go off into the desert, strip naked, and die horribly—probable suicides. And they're carrying these rare, ancient artifacts. One could make an argument for cult-like behavior."

Sharp tilted his head. "And yet they and Oskarbi's other students went on to lead productive careers and lives. Normal. Respected."

"I'm aware of that, sir. I did some research into the FBI databases about cults, and you're right, it's clear that in many aspects this does not resemble a cult. The two women were successful and confident, no drug or alcohol issues that we know of, no mental disorders, they weren't abused as children—they're not the kind of easy pickings a cult leader is on the lookout for. And speaking of cult leaders, Oskarbi vanished twelve years ago—so it seems unlikely he's still running a cult here from wherever he is. There's no indication of recruiting new members."

"So," said Sharp, "seems to me you just made an excellent argument why it isn't a cult."

"And yet," said Corrie, "there's the suicidal behavior, which looks *very* cultish. As I see it, these interrogations now are a chance to make sure these former Oskarbi students really *are* normal—and not hiding something."

Sharp gave a slow nod. "And how do you propose to do that?"

Corrie had thought about this. "I propose to get in their faces."

"And why do you think that will work better than, say, non-confrontational questioning?"

"As you said, sir, they seem to be leading normal, productive lives. If that's just a front, I want to see if we can't break through and see what's behind it."

"And Agent O'Hara's role?"

Corrie swallowed. "Good-guy, bad-guy routine. I know it's hackneyed, but it works."

Sharp turned. "Agent O'Hara—how do you feel about this?"

"We discussed it already and I'm game," said O'Hara. "I don't mind playing the good guy to her bitch—I mean, her bad guy. Sorry."

At this, Corrie laughed. "No, *bitch* is okay. *Bitch* is good. Let's call in the first one."

Corrie watched through the glass as the first, Morgan Bromley, was led in by two officers; seated; and offered a cup of coffee or a soft drink, both of which he refused. Then they left him to sit alone in the room for five minutes—SOP. He was fit, at least six feet, four inches tall, handsome, clean shaven with deep-set brown eyes and an aquiline nose, his prematurely gray hair gathered in a long ponytail.

"Okay," said Corrie, after the five minutes were up. "Let's roll."

Sharp stayed behind to watch, while Corrie and O'Hara left the observation nest and entered the interview room. Bromley sat at the table, an arrogant expression on his face.

"Mr. Bumly," began Corrie, "I am Agent Swanson, and this is Agent O'Hara."

"That's *Bromley*," the man said, "and it's *Doctor*. I have a PhD."

Corrie didn't apologize. She just smirked. O'Hara took a seat on the opposite side of the table while Corrie remained standing.

"Dr. Bromley," Corrie said, "we're recording this interview, and you are under oath. Please state your name, occupation, and confirm this interview is voluntary and that you understand you're free at any time to request an attorney or leave."

"Dr. Morgan C. Bromley, PhD, professor, librarian, and archivist, New Mexico State Library. As for being here voluntarily, I was threatened that if I didn't come in, I might be subpoenaed."

"Please give a yes or no answer: Are you here voluntarily?"

"Yes. I suppose."

"Let the record state," said Corrie in a loud, unpleasant tone, "that the witness is here on a voluntary basis. Now, Mr. Bromley—"

"*Dr.* Bromley."

"My first question: Were you aware that Professor Oskarbi was sleeping with many of his female students—your colleagues?"

"What kind of question is that? What are you, the morality police?"

Corrie privately gave the man points for this comeback, but she kept her face tight and bitchy. "Please answer the question."

"Do I have to answer?"

"No. However, please note you are under oath and lying to a federal agent is a felony."

"Well, *I* was not sleeping with him."

"And the other students? I mean, the female ones."

A hesitation. Then: "Yes."

"Which ones?"

Bromley gave a nasty laugh. "All of them, I think. And why not? It was consensual."

Corrie took a moment to consult her questions. "Did you know Miranda Driver and Molly Vine?"

"Yes."

"How well?"

"As colleagues. Fellow students."

"Are you aware of what they did? Going out into the desert, stripping naked, and essentially committing suicide?"

"I read about it in the papers."

By this point, news of the deaths had been allowed to spread under controlled conditions, but the FBI had withheld the information about the lightning stones.

"It seems a rather *strange* coincidence that two of Oskarbi's former students would do such a crazy thing. Do you know why?"

"No, I don't."

"When was the last time you saw Miranda Driver?"

"I don't recall."

"But you've seen her since the days you were students together?"

"I've run into her. Same with Molly. We don't keep in touch."

"Is that so? I have reports that you did keep in touch with both of them—regularly." She didn't actually have reports to that effect but wanted to see his reaction.

"Sorry, is that a question?" Bromley asked.

"I am questioning the veracity of your statement that you didn't keep in touch. I think you did."

"I still didn't hear a question."

"Did you keep in regular touch with them?"

"I already answered that question."

*He's a regular damned lawyer.* "How about Oskarbi? Are you in touch with him?"

"No."

"When was the last time you had contact with him?"

"Not since he went back to Mexico. That would be...about twelve years ago."

"He was your dissertation advisor. Tell me about him."

"What can I say? He was charismatic. He drew you in. But I realized he was a phony pretty quickly."

"So why did you remain his student?"

"Because it's academic suicide to change your dissertation advisor halfway through."

"Are you familiar with lightning stones?"

"Yes."

"How about prasiolite lightning stones?"

"Yes."

"And what do you know about them?"

"I understand they are associated with the Gallina culture. That's all I know."

"Speaking of the Gallina culture, you used to go on field excavations with Oskarbi and his other students—including Vine and Driver, correct?"

"Correct."

"What took place during those field seasons?"

"Digging. And they were usually extended weekends, not 'seasons.'"

"How about sex?"

"Back to the morality police? Sure, there was tent crawling—but it was mostly Oskarbi, sniffing around like a dog."

"You didn't like Oskarbi?"

"Oh, does it show?"

Corrie was starting to feel frustrated. "How many field expeditions were you on?"

"Three."

"When?"

"2011, 2012, and 2013."

"And besides tent crawling and digging, did anything else happen on these expeditions?"

"There was eating, drinking, and sleeping. And swimming in the river. And s'mores around the campfire."

"Anything unusual?"

"Not that I recall."

"Did you find any prasiolite lightning stones?"

"No. I wish we had. There are only two known examples, belonging to a dodgy collector named Nash."

"What *did* you find?"

"A lot of interesting material: lithics, ceramics, human remains. Unfortunately, Oskarbi never published and the stuff is still sitting in the basement of UNM somewhere. Except the human remains, which of course we left in situ, as required by NAGPRA."

This was getting nowhere. Corrie looked at O'Hara. "Agent O'Hara, I believe you had some questions for this witness?"

O'Hara nodded. "I do have a question," he said, his voice

suddenly taking on a razor-sharp edge. He leaned forward toward Bromley. "We have reason to believe Oskarbi was involved in a drug-fueled secret society, of which you were a member. Is that true?"

At this, Bromley began to laugh. "A secret society? You mean a cult, don't you? Secret societies are for the Founding Fathers and Ivy League students."

"Just answer the question."

"You FBI are still really defensive about Waco, aren't you? I can answer in one word. No."

A silence. O'Hara looked at Corrie. "Back to you, Agent Swanson."

"I have no more questions," said Corrie. She stared at Bromley, who still had an amused, half-incredulous look on his face. "Thank you, Dr. Bromley. You may go now."

He got up, shaking his head, and left.

As the door slammed, Corrie turned to O'Hara. "I thought you were going to be Mr. Nice Guy."

He grinned. "Well, the guy was so slick, I just had to pop him one. And I thought I could do you a favor by dismissing one theory in particular. He may be an asshole, but he's no cult member."

Corrie had to admit, as much as Bromley was a slick and evasive interlocutor, he was convincing. "Noted. Let's bring in the next one."

# 28

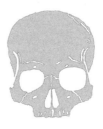

Nora knew it was a bad idea from the start. Corrie hadn't been available—she was spending the weekend at Watts's cabin, off the grid. Skip had to catch up on some work he'd neglected at the Institute and would be occupied both Saturday and Sunday. Tappan had gone off to the East Coast, as planned. Nora didn't want to involve anyone from the Institute.

So she'd decided to go on her own.

Corrie had found and given her the two missing chapters in Driver's dissertation. Nora had read them with interest and astonishment. And now she was impatient beyond all reason to "ground-truth"—as the archaeological term went—the conclusions and theories in those two chapters.

She slowed her Jeep, realizing she was nearing the end of the rutted track. As she came around a hoodoo rock, she could see up ahead the staging area where the film crew had parked, their disturbances in the sand now erased by wind. She had plenty of water in her vehicle, and she would carry more in her pack. It was a relatively cool day—in the mid-nineties, with intermittent clouds—and the hike to the black formation where Vine's body had been found was only a mile. This was something she could do by herself. As far as climbing went...well, it was a steep pitch, class 3 and 4, but not one requiring ropes, belay, and a partner. Or so she hoped.

Nora parked the car, got out, and looked around. It was a great deal more lonely than it had been when the film crew was parked there. But there had been a change for the better. It had recently rained, and although the ground was dry again, the wetting was just enough to encourage wildflowers to pop out of the tawny sand, little dabs of color like stray flecks of paint on a dull canvas. The incessant wind wove skeins of dust over the ground, but Nora was glad of that: it was a cooling presence. In the distance, she could see the tall black butte outlined against the sky, looking as forbidding as ever.

She shrugged on her CamelBak, with a full gallon of water and some snacks. She took a long drink; smeared a fresh layer of sunscreen over her face, neck, and arms; donned a hat and sunglasses—and then, with no further ado, set off.

The way was easy to follow, the footprints of those many who had gone before still visible. She walked fast, the physical activity quelling a sense of unease. In truth, it was never wise to hike in a desert without a partner, nor was it smart to go rock climbing alone. She had left a message on Corrie's voice mail telling her where she was going, in case something should happen; but it was Sunday morning, and Corrie probably wouldn't be back in range until the evening.

As she hiked, the tent-like spire of rock with its flat top loomed ever closer. She took long strides, eating up the ground, and in twenty minutes she had arrived at the base of the pinnacle, in the swale where the body was found.

She gave it a closer inspection. It was about a hundred feet, give or take, to the top. She slowly circled the base, eyeing the best route up. Damn, it looked harder than she had recalled—but still doable. It was a class 4 most of the way, with the crux at the very top, where the volcanic rock became almost vertical: still nothing that required roping up. And because it was rough lava rock, it afforded many excellent and secure hand- and footholds. She brushed away any thought that what she was doing was still reckless—it would be like climbing a ladder, she told herself. It was unlike her to take a risk like this, she had to admit, but she was burning with impatience to see what lay at the top. Driver had advanced a remarkable, even revolutionary theory about the purpose of the witch's fingers, but it seemed that, inexplicably, she had never actually ground-truthed her theory by climbing to the top.

Completing her circuit of the pinnacle, she decided on the best route and began to climb, lodging her boot on a foothold, grabbing two handholds, and hoisting herself up from there. It was indeed not much different from climbing a ladder. The lava was a little crumbly and friable, though, and about halfway up a foothold gave way. She still had three points secure, but it gave her a scare.

She continued on, the space below her becoming a yawning void. As she gained altitude, the angle grew steeper. Finally, after about fifteen minutes, she reached the "crux" of the climb—the hardest part: a sheer girdle of rimrock surrounding the flat top of the mesa.

She paused to catch her breath and look up. Son of a bitch, this section of the climb was definitely a class 5 pitch. There was a single visible fissure among the basalt pillars that she could "crack climb," jamming her fingers and toes in and hauling herself up. *Stupid, stupid. Don't do it. Go down. Come back another day with a partner, ropes, nuts, and cams.*

But she couldn't. She was almost there.

It was impossible not to look down, to make sure of her foot placement. A fall now would likely be fatal, and if not, she'd wish the rest of her life, sitting in a wheelchair, that it had been.

She told herself to focus. Another rise, another finger jam and foot jam, another rise. She placed a hand on the rim itself, felt around for a hold, found one. As she was shifting one foot, the other slipped, and she was briefly hanging by a single hand, dangling, before she found another hold on top and managed to wedge her toe into the crack again.

A moment later she had hauled herself over the edge and onto the top, breathing heavily, her heart beating wildly as the terror subsided.

"Idiot," she muttered, angry at herself. What was wrong with her?

But at least she was at the top.

She looked around. At one end of the pinnacle stood a small stone structure, stout, flat roof mostly intact, covered with dirt and latillas, and with a tiny keyhole entry. Next to the hut, the small mesa-top had been paved with flat stones. She walked over and stared; the stones still bore the scorch marks and fissures of countless gigantic fires.

Nora approached the mysterious hut with a certain sense of trepidation. It had thick walls—a dark, hunched structure. She could see something piled inside the hut, a jumble of shapes. Removing the headlamp from her pack, she strapped it on. The door was so low she had to get down on her hands and knees to crawl forward to look inside, imagining as she did the presence of rattlesnakes and black widow spiders.

The light flashed toward the heap and she gave a yelp of horror, scrambling back and banging her head on the door lintel. She fell back and lay on the ground, her head pounding, breathing hard and trying to wrap her mind around what she had just seen.

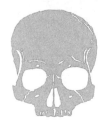

# 29

L<small>EAVE IT TO</small> Watts to have a place in one of the prettiest spots of the New Mexico mountains. Nora could see it on a nearby ridge: a perfect little log cabin with a green corrugated roof, tucked in among ponderosa pines, looking out over a meadow of wildflowers. The late afternoon light was turning everything from green to gold. Nora crept along the road in her Jeep. She wasn't happy about interrupting their romantic weekend getaway—but, damn it, Corrie had dragged her into this, and she needed to learn of Nora's discovery right away.

As she approached the cabin, a figure came out on the porch, followed by another—Corrie and Homer Watts had evidently seen the car approach. Nora was relieved—at least she wasn't intruding on them at, perhaps, a most inconvenient time.

Neither looked pleased as she drew closer, until Corrie recognized her car and waved.

"This is a surprise," said Watts, standing on the porch. "What brings you out here?"

"I'm sorry to interrupt," said Nora, "but there's something Corrie needs to know. It can't wait."

"Come on in," said Watts, "and have a cup of coffee, glass of wine, or something."

"Thank you." Nora hauled her briefcase out of the passenger seat of the Jeep and followed them inside.

It was a genuine old-time hunting cabin, built of hand-adzed logs notched, fitted, and caulked with oakum. A Franklin stove sat at one end, with a fire going—at nine thousand feet, the cool afternoon was turning into a chilly evening. An elk trophy with antlers was mounted on one wall, and a crossed pair of old snowshoes made with bentwood and gut were nailed to another. An old flintlock rifle hung over the door. A cribbage board hung on a hook, and an untidy shelf contained stacks of games and cards and old, half-full bottles of whisky and bourbon. A couple of battered leather chairs and a leather sofa stood in front of the stove, with a crude wooden table that looked like it had been made with a hatchet.

"Very authentic," said Nora, laying her briefcase on the table and opening it.

"Thanks," said Watts. "The place belonged to my granddad and I've left it as is."

"I wish this could have waited until tomorrow," Nora said. "But it couldn't. Not after what I read in the missing final chapters of Driver's dissertation you gave me."

Corrie's eyes widened as Nora pulled the chapters out of the briefcase, along with some maps, and spread them out on the table, laying her cell phone next to them.

"Before you begin, sun's below the yardarm—I'm having a bourbon," said Watts. "Will anyone join me?"

Nora said, "If that's coffee on the stove, I'll have a hit of that."

"Coffee for me, too," said Corrie.

He poured her and Nora mugs of coffee and, for himself, two

good fingers of bourbon. "Okay," he said, smiling as he put down the glass, "now that I'm properly fortified, let's have it."

"Before I get into the details, I need to give you a little background on what's known as the Chaco Phenomenon."

"Chaco Phenomenon?" Corrie echoed.

"That's what archaeologists call the civilization that thrived, and then mysteriously collapsed, in the Four Corners region a thousand years ago. From 900 to 1200 CE. It was a remarkably sophisticated and complex culture. The many tribes—they used to call them the Anasazi, but no longer—came together and built a city of immense buildings in Chaco Canyon. These dozen or so gigantic stone structures were four to five stories high and totaled many thousands of rooms. The largest of these was Pueblo Bonito, the largest prehistoric structure in America."

"I've been to Chaco," said Watts. "Amazing place." He took another slug of bourbon.

"But there was something they built that was as impressive as Pueblo Bonito," Nora went on. "An elaborate system of so-called roads. These roads radiated out from Chaco like the spokes of a wheel, spreading across parts of New Mexico, Arizona, Colorado, and Utah. But these weren't 'roads' in our sense of the word—the Chacoans hadn't discovered the wheel and didn't have any beasts of burden. They had no need for straight, wide, surfaced roads. But they built them nevertheless—running in absolutely straight lines of precisely the same width: thirty feet. Instead of going around hills and zigzagging into canyons as normal roads do, they sliced through hills to stay straight. The longest of these roads, called the Great North Road, goes for over a hundred miles in a perfectly north-south direction, better aligned than even the surveying lines laid down by American engineers in the early twentieth century. And they did all this without compasses, using only the sun and stars to fix direction." She paused for a sip of coffee. "For these reasons, and more, scholars and historians believe these roads had some sort of ceremonial purpose beyond mere travel."

"So the chapters were about these Chaco roads?" Corrie asked.

"Indirectly, yes. But not just the roads—the lighthouses that ran alongside them, as well."

"Lighthouses?" Corrie asked in a slightly skeptical tone. "In the desert?"

"On the tops of pinnacles and buttes, the Chacoans laid down massive stone hearths, where they lit gigantic fires that could be seen from afar. These lighthouses were aligned in such a way that, in a single night, messages could be sent, by fire, across the entirety of the vast Chaco domain: over a hundred thousand square miles. And the roads seemed to follow the longest paths of the light."

"So what were they for?" Watts asked. "Navigation?"

"Definitely not, since the landscape already had many highly visible landmarks. Exactly what they were for is still a mystery. Was it to call the faithful to assemble, marching down the roads into Chaco for religious ceremonies? Or to communicate with the gods? Or to pass along vital information about weather systems, rain, and crops? Or did the system of roads and lighthouses have a military purpose? And if so, what? Who were they afraid of?"

"Aliens?"

"Very funny," Corrie said, nudging him as he grinned and took another sip.

"The lighthouses are, in some ways, more mysterious than the roads themselves. Nobody knows their full extent, how many existed—there are so many spires of rock in the Four Corners area, it would take ages to inspect them all."

"Sounds like an obvious task for archaeologists," Watts said.

"You're welcome to try. Anyway, here's where we get to Driver's last chapters. Once I read them, it became clear what the rest of her dissertation was leading up to. Take a look at this map of hers." Nora pointed to one of the unfolded sheets. "You see this line of dots, heading northwest? Those are known Chacoan lighthouses. Now, look here—farther along." She pointed out several more spots, marked on the map in a rough arc. "You see this arc? It represents seven lighthouse towers, extending the arc of known lighthouses. And each of those seven towers is a black volcanic plug. This one, and this one, are the badland pinnacles where the women's bodies were found. There are five others."

"No shit!" murmured Corrie, staring.

"Driver's missing chapters speculated that the invaders the ancient Chacoans were so afraid of were none other than the Gallina tribe. And this arc of lighthouses—beyond any known before—was directly in line with the Chama River area, where the Gallina lived. Driver believed those seven lighthouses served as an early warning system, a kind of ancient DEW line, against a possible invasion from the Gallina."

"How could she know that?" Watts asked.

"I'm not sure. It seems Driver never visited, or at least summited, the pinnacles she marked here across the badlands. It looks like her chapters were withdrawn before she could verify that the arc of volcanic plugs was, in fact, lighthouses."

Corrie and Watts peered at the map.

"How weird," said Corrie.

"It gets weirder," Nora said. "Driver's dissertation advances a theory that she ascribes to Oskarbi. The origin of the Gallina has always been a mystery. Driver, quoting Oskarbi, says that the Gallina were a branch of the Totonteac Indians of Mexico. They somehow had a falling out, or split, and the Gallina people came north, up here, bringing with them their culture and religious practices. They ultimately came in conflict with the people of Chaco, who thought they were witches, or evil, or dangerous in some way—and wiped them out." She paused. "That last part, at least, is consistent with what is known: there was a devastating genocidal attack on the Gallina people around 1200 CE, which wiped them out in one hammer-like blow."

"Jesus," said Corrie, shaking her head.

"I'm a little confused," said Watts. "Who were the bad guys and who were the good guys here?"

"We archaeologists don't make moral judgments like that. What seems evident is that the Chacoans lived peacefully until the Gallina arrived, who threatened them with violence and witchcraft. The Chacoans first built the lighthouses to protect themselves, but when the Gallina continued to menace and even kill them, the Chacoans finally retaliated—invading and success-fully wiping them out."

"Okay," said Watts. "I get it now. Being law enforcement, I like to know who's right and who's wrong."

"In this case, as I'm about to show you, the Gallina were the aggressors. You see—" She hesitated. "I drove up here to tell you what I found when I climbed the badland pinnacle above Molly's corpse."

"You did?" said Corrie. "When?"

"Today."

"By yourself? Alone?"

"Well, yes."

Corrie laughed. "That's crazy. That's like something *I* would do."

"Maybe—if you knew how to free climb. But anyway, what I found at the top was a great hearth of flat stones scorched and cracked by fire, along with a sort of hut or storage chamber. Here's what I found inside." Nora picked up her phone and handed it to Corrie. "Swipe through those photos."

Corrie began swiping through them, her face turning pale.

"They weren't just lighthouses," Nora said. "See all those bones? They're a thousand years old, but you can still see the evidence of burning, the cut marks, bashed-in skulls—all signs of violent death." She paused. "Driver never explored the top of one of those seven black lighthouses. But I did get to the top of one. And I believe those bodies I found—the photos you're looking at—are the remains of the lighthouse guardians."

"You mean, Chacoans?" Watts asked.

"It makes perfect sense. The Chacoans hated and feared the Gallina—and the Gallina couldn't have been pleased having these watchtowers on their border, keeping track of their movements. I'll bet the Gallina did something about it. The fact those bodies were burned indicates they might have been sacrificed... by the Gallina. And, if you take that assumption to its logical conclusion, the killing of the keepers—seizing the DEW line, to follow my analogy—might in turn have been what precipitated the Chaco invasion of Gallina...and the subsequent genocide."

She fell silent. For a long time, there was no sound but the crackling of the fire.

"Human sacrifice," breathed Corrie at last. "So these women who killed themselves, who went out to the pinnacles and died—they might have been part of some sort of resurrected sacrificial rite?"

"This thing runs very deep," Nora said. "And I don't have a lot of the answers. But yes—the signs point to our dealing with human sacrifice. Today."

"A cult," said Corrie, a note of satisfaction in her voice.

"Yes," said Nora after a moment. "Yes."

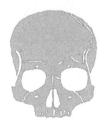

# 30

AFTER ANOTHER PROTRACTED silence, Corrie said, "I think I'm going to need a little fortification myself."

Watts poured her a drink and then waggled the snout of the bottle at Nora.

"No thanks. I have to drive."

"It's getting late—you shouldn't be driving back through the mountains in the dark. You need to stay here, if you don't mind the sofa. I've got a sleeping bag you can use."

Nora was grateful for the offer. "In that case," she said, "pour me one of those, too. We still have a lot to talk about."

He handed her a drink. She took it and sipped, the fiery liquid going down nicely. "To sum it up: Driver believed there were a total of seven lighthouses, built by the Chacoans as an early warning of any dark doings by the Gallina."

Corrie nodded. "And you're wondering—do they *all* have bodies at their bases?"

"Exactly," said Nora.

Watts lit a couple of kerosene lanterns as the evening dusk settled in.

"Okay," said Corrie slowly. "I think the FBI should investigate these five unexplored sites for human remains." She gestured at the documents and maps on the table. "Can I take this stuff?"

"It's all for you—and I'll AirDrop the photos to your phone."

Corrie shook her head. "I'm still trying to wrap my head around this. Human sacrifice—here and now? Willing sacrifices, at that. What could possibly have precipitated it?"

Watts spoke up. "Oskarbi."

Nora looked at him. "Exactly. Somehow, Oskarbi must be at the center of this. He gathered all these acolytes around him. He was sleeping with the women. He wrote a book that made his name—and that just happened to be about taking hallucinogenic drugs. He led field excavations into the Gallina Canyon every summer. And for some reason, he suppressed this crucial conclusion to Driver's dissertation. He didn't want anyone to know this stuff."

"Hold on," said Watts. "As I understand it, Oskarbi disappeared like a dozen years ago—long before these women died."

"They say he went back to Mexico to continue his studies," said Nora. "But I'll bet he's stayed in touch." She turned to Corrie. "The FBI need to go down to Sierra Madre, find him, and bring him back for questioning."

Corrie didn't respond for a moment. Then she said, "That's a problem."

"How so?"

"You know how hard it is for the FBI to get authorization to send agents into a foreign country? Especially Mexico? It's a bureaucratic nightmare, it would take months, and in the end it probably won't work. And the truth is, we don't have any solid evidence against Oskarbi, let alone a smoking gun. It's just supposition."

"Then I'll go."

"Into Mexico? Are you nuts?"

"I'll go as a tourist. A lot of people travel to the Sierra Madre to see Copper Canyon and the Tarahumara Indians. I'll go as a tourist, arrange to run into Oskarbi, and then we'll have a nice chat."

"And just how do you plan to find him?"

"I've traveled all over Mexico—and I speak enough Spanish to get along. From his book, we know at least approximately where he was with the Totonteac Indians."

"That sounds dangerous as hell," Watts said. "In those backwaters of Mexico, with all the drug smuggling and cartels. And on top of that, if Oskarbi is somehow involved in these deaths—voluntary or not—he isn't a safe person to confront."

"I'll be fine," Nora said.

"If something happens, I won't forgive myself for dragging you into this."

"For better or worse, I'm already dragged in. I can take care of myself. Someone needs to talk to Oskarbi—he's the missing piece."

"Don't—" Corrie began.

"I can't believe you're asking me to back off this late in the game. You don't have a choice in the matter. I'm going."

"Nothing of what you find out will be admissible in court or officially actionable by the FBI."

"Maybe. But interviewing him will at least shed some light on what's going on, help us fill in the gaps. I'll talk to Don Benicio while I'm there." She laid a hand on the map. "And meanwhile, you can search for the rest of those lighthouses—and possibly more victims."

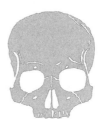

# 31

SKIP THOUGHT THE idea of Nora going down into Mexico all by herself, deep into the mountains no less, was totally crazy. He'd told her so repeatedly, standing in the tiny living room of their shared house, hands on his hips, a frown on his face, watching as she packed her bag. "Is that all you're taking?" he asked. "You need to bring a gun. You can borrow one of mine."

"Skip, you know you can't bring guns into Mexico."

"Hide it in the door panel of your Jeep."

Nora shook her head. "And end up in a Mexican prison cell?"

Skip shook his head. "Got your knife, at least?"

Nora dug into the bag, withdrew her blacked-out Zero Tolerance 0888, and waved it at him.

"Just how long do you plan to be gone?"

"According to Google Maps it's a twelve-hour drive. So I figure, a long day down, two days to find Oskarbi and talk to him, then a day's drive back. Three or four days. Done."

"You don't know his exact location—all you have is the name of a village. Finding him could take a lot longer than that—in difficult country, too."

"Okay. Maybe four or five days, then."

"The Federales will stop you and extort bribes."

"I know how to handle the Federales. I'm bringing down plenty of twenties and a carton of cigarettes."

"The narcotraffickers will shoot you."

"The last thing they want is to kill an American tourist. As long as I stay out of their way, they won't bother me."

"You'll be a good-looking single woman traveling alone in a macho-man country."

"I'll be in my own car, driving straight through. Skip—please don't worry."

"But where are you going to stay when you get to—what's the crazy name of that village where Oskarbi's supposedly living?"

"San Luis de Majimachi. In places like that you can always find someone to put you up. I don't mind sleeping on the floor." She pulled out a piece of paper. "Meanwhile, here's a honey-do list to keep you busy while I'm away."

"I hate that term." He was annoyed but had long ago accepted that his bossy older sister was in charge of their household—and in her own way, sort of in charge of his life. But not totally. And it had occurred to him that the three or four days she would be gone was an ideal time for him and Edison to make their trip into the Gallina country without her finding out. He sensed—or rather, he knew—that his sister would not be happy with him going into the wilderness with Nash. In fact, that might be the incentive behind this punch list she'd drawn up.

Nora spoke again, as if reading his mind. "Look, Skip," she said. "While I'm gone, I just want you to...well, be a little careful with your new friend."

"Edison? What's wrong with him?" he asked, flaring up.

"I'm not sure he's on the up-and-up. As a collector, I mean.

You work for the Institute. You don't want to be seen as too palsy-walsy with that guy."

"The Institute has no say on who my friends are," Skip said, feeling self-righteousness suddenly kindling within him.

"I agree in principle, but let's live in the real world. Nash's a sketchy collector, and you manage the collections of an archaeological institute. The two don't mix." She hesitated. "He's also... kind of weird."

"I will choose my friends as I wish," said Skip stiffly.

"And," Nora plowed on determinedly, "he drinks too much. Just take it easy with all that expensive tequila. Okay, younger brother?"

Skip felt heat creep into his face. Nora was right, of course. But a few drinks now and then were definitely not a problem—he could manage that and stay in control. "Caveat noted," he said, careful to moderate his tone.

"I'm going to text you every day, at least when I'm in range," Nora said. "And I'll call you when I get to San Luis."

"Great. And don't worry about me—just be sure to take care of yourself."

They hugged. She gave Mitty, their golden retriever, a hug as well, and then she zipped up the duffel she'd just packed. Skip watched her head out to the Jeep and heave her duffel into the trunk, feeling more than a twinge of anxiety. Mitty stood next to him, looking worried, as he always did when anyone went away. Skip did not have a good feeling about this last-minute trip to Mexico. But...at least it freed him up.

As her vehicle disappeared down the street, he shook off the feeling of doom and pulled out his cell phone. "Hey, Edison. It's Skip. Listen, the trip is on, and it's on *now*. Get your shit together—we're heading to Gallina!"

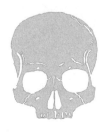

# 32

Skip's car was a piece of crap, so he was glad Edison had offered his F-150 as their expedition vehicle. Gallina Canyon—where the heart of the Gallina ruins were hidden—was located within the Chama River Wilderness, which meant they could not simply drive to the spot and camp. A pack mule would be too much of a pain, so in the end they decided to backpack in. After poring over maps, they worked out the best route. But there was a hitch: to get as close as possible to the wilderness boundary before abandoning the pickup, they'd have to drive through the western portion of the San Juan Basin oil field, negotiating a warren of dirt roads built by the fracking companies leading to their wellheads and pump jacks. Those roads were out of bounds to all but oil field workers.

"The hell with those fracking bastards," Edison had said, staring at the maps over glasses of tequila, neat. "It's public land that belongs to the American people. We'll sneak through."

At the time, Skip had thought it a reasonable idea—but now, as they turned into the dirt road leading into the fracking badlands and were greeted with a huge, threatening NO TRESPASSING sign, he wasn't so sure. He'd recently had a disagreeable brush with the law, which had included an arrest, jailing, and a trial. He'd been resoundingly acquitted—but it had been a terrifying experience, and he really, really did not want to get into any kind of trouble again.

"Someone should unload a twelve-gauge into that sign," said Edison, giving it the finger as he accelerated past.

They entered a maze of dirt tracks, Edison driving and Skip navigating, using his iPad and Google Earth. They were, he saw, already three-quarters of the way to their destination, if not more. A few miles on, as they wound among the dry washes, buttes, and arroyos of the terrain, a battery of giant fracking tanks, painted green, came into view in the middle of a large area bulldozed flat and surrounded by a dirt berm—a horrible excrescence on the landscape. Nobody seemed to be there.

"Look at that," said Edison.

"Unbelievable."

They drove past the tanks, where the dirt road divided yet again. Skip checked his iPad—there were no mapped roads here, but he could still guide them using GPS. "Take the right-hand road up that mesa."

They climbed up a zig-zag cut into the mesa rim, and came out on a sagebrush-covered flat. There were views all around, and now the full extent of the fracking field could be seen: a plethora of dirt roads leading hither and yon in no discernable pattern, each terminating in a bulldozed flat with a well and a row of tanks containing fracking fluid. Piping coiled like snakes around each of the wellheads. The field extended westward as far as the eye could see.

"Disgusting," said Edison. Skip viewed the expanse with anxiety: this was what they'd have to drive through. And he could see three white pickups parked at a wellhead not far below the mesa—oil service vehicles. A bunch of roughnecks were there, working on something.

Skip looked at the GPS. "Um, it looks like our route goes past that."

"Is there a way around?"

"No."

"Then we'll just speed past them."

"They'll see us coming."

"Screw them. We *own* this land."

Edison might be right, but the fact it was public land hadn't stopped the oil companies from putting up a bunch of NO TRESPASSING signs. Skip reminded himself that, Edison being a billionaire, he could buy his way out of all sorts of trouble. Wasn't that what rich people did? Of course it was.

Edison drove to the far side of the mesa, where the road dipped down into the next valley. At the lip, Skip wondered if the workers would see their vehicle, now prominently outlined against the sky. And see them they did: several began pointing up, then running toward their trucks.

Edison accelerated, slewing around a couple of hairpin turns before they reached the bottom. The day was relatively cool, but the road was still parched and they were sending up a corkscrew of dust that could be seen for miles.

Once on the flat, Edison really opened it up. "Easy, now," said Skip, gripping the door handle.

"We've gotta get past them before they can block the road."

The fracking well was temporarily invisible, blocked by some badland formations, but as they came around a hoodoo at high speed, Skip could see the workers in their vehicles, pulling out of the flat and heading for the main road.

Edison floored the accelerator as they fishtailed on gravel and dirt. Two of the pickups had now reached their road ahead.

"They're going to block the way," said Skip.

Edison didn't answer, his hands gripping the wheel, face tense.

The third pickup also halted on the road, which was now fully obstructed.

"We'll go around them," Edison said. "To the left."

Skip could see what he was talking about: the left side of the road, while rough desert with scattered rocks and gullies, might still be passable.

The roughnecks had gotten out of the pickups. Several were holding metal bars. Skip could see their dirty faces sadistically grinning with anticipation.

But Edison did not slow down. A hundred feet before reaching the blockade, he veered off the road, their truck leaping a dirt ridge. He headed for a gap between two rocks, made it by mere inches, swerved and braked as they lurched over a small gully, then swerved again, the dust billowing up in huge clouds. Edison reached out of the window and gave the roughnecks the finger.

Skip heard some shouted obscenities. He turned back and got a glimpse of the men, piling back into their pickups.

"They're coming after us," he said.

"Of course they are."

Edison veered back onto the road, once again going flat out. For a while there was too much dust for Skip to see behind them, but then they rounded a curve, and then he could see that, indeed, at least two of the trucks were giving chase.

Their vehicle was briefly airborne as they cleared a small hump. Edison gave a whoop as they slammed back to earth.

Skip consulted his GPS. They were now about halfway across the fracking area. Beyond, in the blue distance, the land rose as the badlands gave way to a piñon-juniper forest. Even farther beyond that was the wilderness boundary, where even these dirt paths would end.

"See if you can figure out a way to lose those bastards," Edison said.

There were so many roads up ahead, so many rock formations, that it would have been easy to shake their pursuers—were it not for the plume of dust they were sending up. It was like a running advertisement of their location.

"Take a right at the next fork," Skip said.

He continued to give Edison directions, threading them through a maze of roads, dry washes, abandoned pumpjacks, fracking tanks, and hoodoo rocks, all the while headed toward the national forest. Skip wondered if the workers could continue to pursue past the oil field. He wished to hell Edison had not given those guys the finger.

Still, the two white pickups followed. And now, finally, they reached the end of the fracking area and dove into the piñon-juniper woodland.

"They're still following," said Skip. "Gaining."

"Shit," said Edison. "This damned truck is just too heavy to outrun them. Time for plan B."

"Plan B?"

Edison popped open the glove compartment and removed a massive handgun.

"Whoa. No way," said Skip. "That's insane."

"Don't worry, I won't shoot anyone," Edison said, waving the gun around. "This is strictly for self-defense."

"Maybe they've got weapons, too."

"I doubt it. It would be against company policy. Anyway, I'm not going to show this unless we're directly threatened."

Skip was seized with apprehension. "Look—I didn't sign up for this."

"They have no right to chase us," said Edison. "They aren't cops. And did you see those iron pipes they're carrying? We've got a right to self-defense."

They drove around a low butte. He braked, then drove off the road, parking the pickup in the shadow of the butte.

"Okay, let's roll." He tucked the gun into the rear of his waistband and started to get out.

"Roll what?" Skip cried in a panic.

"Just follow my lead. Get your phone out and start recording— but surreptitiously. Skip, don't worry—I've got everything under control."

Edison walked back to the dirt road. Skip followed, heart pounding, as he fumbled with his cell phone. This was insane.

In minutes, the two pickups hauled into view. Edison waved at them from the roadside and they braked hard, slewing to a stop. The doors flew open and four guys got out, at least two holding long metal pipes. They came swaggering over, stopping about twenty feet away. They looked fierce: big-bellied, massively strong men with dirty faces. Two wore wifebeaters, one a greasy shirt, and the fourth was, surprisingly, in some sort of uniform, pressed and clean. Skip started to video, holding the phone casually at his side and trying to keep his fingers from trembling.

"You boys are trespassing," said Mr. Clean—evidently the supervisor—stepping forward.

"This is public land," said Edison, suddenly and surprisingly calm.

"Didn't you see the signs?"

"I did. But as I said, this is public land. Now, *I* have a question:

What do you intend to do with those pipes? Are you threatening us?"

Edison's voice was so assured, it was like he'd become a different person.

"You boys are coming with us," said the man. "We're taking you to the sheriff."

"You have no right to detain us."

"Fuck you," said the supervisor, beginning to grow angry. "You're coming with us, whether you like it or not."

"Nope," said Edison. "And you're off your fracking lease. This is national forest land."

The supervisor was now red in the face. He glanced toward his crew. "Guys, show these motherfuckers we mean business."

"We have the right to self-defense."

"Fuck you, Jack," said one of the men, advancing with pipe raised. The others followed.

Reaching around to the small of his back, Edison removed the gun from his waistband and held it lazily at his side.

The men halted. "Cocksucker's got a gun."

"Just so we're clear," Edison said. "I will exercise my legal right of self-defense if any of you takes even one more step forward. If you don't believe me, go ahead and try calling my bluff." He looked at each of them in turn, his gaze falling on Mr. Clean. "I can see you're the supervisor. So you're going to collect everyone's IDs for me to examine. I'm reporting you to the oil company. My associate here has it all on video—and your bosses aren't going to like what they see."

The men looked at Skip in surprise. He nervously raised the phone. As he did so, the irate look on the supervisor's face began to morph into an expression of apprehension and uncertainty. It was astonishing how quickly Edison had turned things around.

"Mr. Supervisor? Let's have those IDs. Toss them on the ground, and my associate will record them with his phone."

"Go fuck yourself. You've no right to collect our names or anything else." The man's tone was not as bellicose as his words implied.

"Just as you have no right to detain us."

There was a silence that stretched into minutes.

"Tell you what," said Edison with a sudden smile, tucking the gun back into his waistband. "I'm willing to let it go. We'll go on our way, and you go on yours. No harm, no foul. What do you say?" His voice was laden with sarcasm.

The roughnecks looked at each other, shuffling their feet. Finally, the supervisor hawked up a gobbet and spat it on the ground, then without another word turned, making a brusque gesture for his crew to go back to their trucks. In a few minutes they had climbed in and were gone.

Abruptly, Edison started to laugh, shaking his head as they walked back to their own vehicle. "Guys like that are the proverbial dog that caught the car. You know, Skip, most people in this world are dumbasses: they take a leap, only to find themselves waist deep in shit."

Skip tried to laugh along with this bit of philosophy.

Edison pulled out the revolver again, this time showing it to Skip. "You ever seen one of these?"

"Never." It was massive, a handgun on steroids.

"It's called the Judge. This particular model, in fact, is known as the Raging Judge." Edison laughed. "Stainless, six shot, six-point-five-inch barrel. Fiber optic sight. Impressive, don't you think?"

"Hell, yes." And it *was* impressive—a huge, terrifying gun.

"Takes either Colt .45 rounds or .410 plated disc buckshot. Or a quarter-ounce slug, for that matter—if you think your wrist can handle it. She's gotten me out of a pickle more than once."

Skip wondered what sort of "pickle" he might be talking about, but felt disinclined to ask. They got back in the pickup and Edison put the Judge back in his glove compartment.

"Carry on, Navigator," he said, face flushed and triumphant from the encounter.

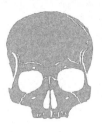

# 33

It felt like the end of the world: mountains beyond mountains, dissolving into blues and purples in the vast distance, the landscape prostrate below a hot afternoon sky. The Jeep was straining to keep its interior cool in the beating sun. Nora had left Santa Fe at five AM, crossed into Mexico through the Columbus port of entry around ten, and continued on into Chihuahua.

She had finally arrived in San Luis de Majimachi. She pulled off the road at the top of a ridge and looked down into the town that lay below. It was five o'clock and the village was bathed in a yellow light, the whitewashed cinderblock and log houses with their red corrugated roofs scattered among dusty fields, pine trees, and bleached rock formations. She could see, near the center of town, two crude towers of a small mission church, built in stone, standing in a field of yellow grass.

It had been far more challenging getting to San Luis than she had thought. She had lost cell reception and navigation hours before, but she'd been ready for that and was prepared to work from paper maps. But as she penetrated deeper into the back country of Mexico, and the towns turned to villages—La Junta, San

Juanito—the roads on the maps corresponded less and less to the roads on the ground. The journey involved driving across several rivers, some of which were so deep she was worried the water would run into the car. And San Luis de Majimachi itself seemed almost like a mirage. Twice she'd gotten directions from local peasants, and twice she'd ended up in minuscule hamlets that, apparently, had no names. It occurred to her that mentioning Don Benicio might have had something to do with their misdirection, and the third time she asked directions, she mentioned nobody's name—and, it appeared, she had finally arrived at the right town.

Shifting the Jeep back into drive, she descended the road and in five minutes had pulled up in front of the church. She got out, the smell of dust and heat hitting her like an anvil. She was relieved to see the church door was cracked open, which she hoped meant someone was inside. She eased the door open with a creak and entered the silent space, blessedly cool and scented with wax and myrrh. After the dazzling afternoon light, it took her eyes a moment to adjust to the gloom. As they did, she noticed a form hunched over in one of the pews, praying. She walked down the central aisle, looking for the priest, but the altar area was empty. The only person in the church was the praying figure, face bowed and wrapped in a brightly colored shawl and scarf.

Nora took a seat in a pew behind her and waited, unwilling to interrupt her prayers. After a few minutes the woman rose, and Nora watched as she went over to a small bank of candles below an image of the Virgin of Guadalupe, took one out of a box and lit it, and then knelt and prayed at the shrine.

Nora had begun to fidget when the figure at last rose again and walked across the pews to the central aisle, heading out of the church. She raised her head and Nora saw her face for the first time. It wasn't the old lady she'd expected, but instead a young, attractive woman.

Nora rose and approached her. "Buenas tardes, señorita."

The woman smiled. "Buenas tardes, señora."

Nora introduced herself in her workmanlike Spanish, explaining that she was in San Luis to visit a certain Don Benicio Bawi, and wondered if she knew where he was. Nora was hoping to find him before dark, and further hoping he might offer her a place for the night.

The woman introduced herself as Maria. At the mention of Don Benicio, a troubled look passed across her face.

"Don Benicio lives up in the mountains," she said. "A long way from here."

Nora tried to hide her dismay. A long way? She had hoped that San Luis de Majimachi, mentioned several times in the book, was where she'd find Don Benicio. "How far?"

"Twenty, maybe twenty-five miles."

Nora winced inwardly. "That's...not too far, I guess."

"The road is bad. The maps are bad. You won't be able to get there before dark—and the chances of your getting lost on the way are very great."

When she saw the look on Nora's face, she quickly added that she lived with her father and family, and that Nora would be welcome to spend the night at their place, at the edge of town—and of course share their evening meal.

Nora gratefully accepted and gave the woman a ride back to her house. They drove through the small, dusty town and out the far end, where the woman indicated a shotgun house, built of whitewashed logs, with a deep and shady portal.

At the approach of the car, it seemed that all the inhabitants of the house came out to meet them: an old man in a straw cowboy

hat and two shy boys about eight and ten. Maria got out of the
Jeep and spoke in an Indigenous language to the man, who was
leaning on a cane. He was clearly the *padre de familia*, and she
introduced him to Nora as Don Alvaro. He took off his hat,
smiled toothlessly, and gave her a little bow, his hat on his chest,
without extending his hand.

"He doesn't speak Spanish," Maria explained.

Inside, the house was mercifully cool. "Let me show you
where you can sleep," Maria said. She led Nora to a *banco* in her
own room, covered with a thin straw-filled mattress and pillow
and a brightly colored weaving, and then gave her a quick tour of
the house before bringing her back to the living area.

"I'll make dinner now," she said.

Maria prepared a meal of tortillas, chicharrones, nopalitos,
and beans over coals in a kiva fireplace in one corner. Nora
helped, grateful to be able to refresh her Spanish, while Don
Alvaro sat in a large chair near the fire, hands propped on his
cane, smiling broadly and smoking a corncob pipe, watching
the two women work. The two shy boys sat on a *banco* nearby,
also watching Nora with apparent fascination. Cooking finished,
they sat down to dinner as the light vanished over the mountains, filling the house with a purple twilight. A single kerosene
lantern was lit and hung from a hook above the table.

Don Alvaro, who had said nothing up to this point, spoke to
Maria in their Indigenous language. Maria turned to Nora. "My
father wants to know if the dinner is satisfactory."

Nora assured him that it was very good and thanked them
again for their hospitality.

A few more superficial questions followed, and then the old
man asked—with Maria translating—why she was going to

see Benicio. Apparently the old man knew a fair amount about him—or, at least, appeared to.

Nora had already worked out the answer to this question in her mind. Although she hated to lie, she couldn't tell the truth about the investigation: the strange deaths and other details would likely put people off. She told them she was an anthropologist, that she had read about Don Benicio in the famous book by Professor Oskarbi, and that for this reason she wanted to meet him herself.

When Don Alvaro heard this, he frowned, his face becoming impossibly wrinkled with displeasure and disapproval. He responded at such length that Maria grew uncomfortable.

When he had finished, Nora said to Maria, "Please translate directly—don't worry about offending me. I want to know what your father said."

Maria shifted in her chair. "My father says that Benicio is not a good man. He practices the old ways, the devil ways. He thinks you should not go to him for spiritual advice."

"Why does your father think so?"

Maria translated. "He chews the devil's root, and his ways are not that of a Christian. And, he says, he lives so far up in the mountains you will never find him, but fall off a cliff in your car. Besides, he has not been seen or heard of in several years. My father thinks he is probably dead."

Nora frowned, then leaned forward. "Did Oskarbi tell you that?"

Maria translated, and the two of them looked back at Nora with blank expressions. "Who?"

"Carlos Oskarbi. One of Benicio's followers was a man named Carlos Oskarbi. Do you know of him?"

Maria translated and the old man looked blank. "We have never heard of him."

"What?" There had to be some mistake. "But he came down here over a decade ago. To join Don Benicio and to continue his...his discipleship. Perhaps you know of him, under a different name?" Oskarbi cut a charismatic figure that, she knew, would not be forgotten by the closest villagers.

The old man shook his head. "I do not know of any white man living up there—with him, or anyone else."

This was beyond strange. "But this is the closest village to Don Benicio's residence—right? He would need to come here for supplies."

"Don Benicio left his house very rarely. In the old days, followers would bring him what he needed."

"Followers?"

"Long ago there were many. More recently, only a few. But nobody goes to him now."

"Did you know there was a book published about him, written by Professor Oskarbi?"

"I know of no book." The old man hesitated, then spoke again, Maria translating. "You are clearly a good lady, so I want to tell you something. Please be careful. If he is alive, and you find your way to him: do not believe what he tells you. Be doubtful, do not give him money—and afterward, go to the church here and confess to the priest."

She assured the old man she would be careful, and with that the dinner drew to an end. The family, clearly all early risers, began to prepare for bed—but not before the old man extracted a promise from Nora that she would let the older boy guide her part of the way to Don Benicio.

As she lay on the narrow, hard *banco* in the dark, Nora felt sleep eluding her. Nothing Maria or the old man had told her aligned with her expectations—or what she'd understood to be the case. Oskarbi, as a disciple, must have taken up the reclusive, hermit-like ways of his teacher. She wondered about that teacher: if, assuming Benicio was still alive, he was the wise, Yoda-like figure depicted in Oskarbi's book...or if he practiced the "devil ways" as the old man had said. Tomorrow, if all went as planned, she would finally meet him, along with the elusive Professor Oskarbi—and then she would know the truth.

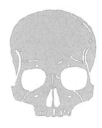

# 34

THE DIRT TRACK they were driving on ended abruptly. No sign indicated this was where the wilderness area began, but Skip could nevertheless see it on his GPS. Ahead, the land kept rising through shelves of yellow sandstone toward the rim of Gallina Canyon, a few miles distant.

Skip was not looking forward to the hike. Edison had insisted on bringing all kinds of unnecessary stuff in their backpacks, including the cannon-sized revolver, a machete, a trowel, and far more alcohol than they could ever hope to drink. But Skip had kept his mouth shut and, as a reward for his circumspection, was now stuck with a sixty-pound pack, which included his uke strapped on the back. Edison, for his part, had a swollen pack that probably weighed twenty pounds more. Skip was an experienced backpacker and he knew this was no way to proceed, but he felt intimidated and didn't want to get into an argument with Edison over everything he'd insisted on bringing.

"Ahoy, Navigator! Which way?"

Skip consulted his phone. There was no cell reception, but he'd downloaded the USGS maps ahead of time. And the satellite

GPS connection was working well, showing where they were on the topo map. He consoled himself with the fact that it was not a long hike—six miles at most—and after the first gentle uphill part, it would be all downhill. There were no trails, but the ponderosa-and-fir forest along the rim had broadly spaced trees, and a ridge ahead of them, descending to the canyon floor, looked like a possible way down.

"This way," he said.

Edison was in an expansive mood and took the lead, hiking fast along the ridgeline. Soon, views opened up into the canyon— a stunningly picturesque and dramatic rupture in the earth formed by the Gallina River. Skip could see it far below, a shining ribbon winding in sinuous curves and lined by gigantic cottonwoods. Beyond the grass-covered canyon bottom stood sandstone walls that glowed in red and orange bands, carved by time and water into otherworldly spires, slots, and alcoves.

They started down and—winding their way along the descending ridge—at last reached the bottom. By then, Skip's back was killing him, and he gratefully dumped his pack on a grassy flat above the river—a beautiful, shaded campsite. It remained cool at eight thousand feet of altitude, and the summer rains had generated an explosion of wildflowers.

"Four hours of daylight left," Edison said. "Plenty of time to explore!"

Dumping his pack next to Skip's, he set off practically at a jog, binoculars in hand, stopping from time to time to scan the canyon walls, benches, and hills above the river, full of excited chatter about the Gallina and their mysteries. It was, Skip thought, like a fairyland for him.

They forded the river and began scrambling up the steep prominence on the far side, Skip struggling to keep up.

"The roomblocks where the Gallina lived," Edison panted as they reached the height of land, "will be concealed and hard to find. Most of them are probably up various side canyons." He scanned the landscape with his binoculars for a moment, then pointed. "See that slot canyon over there? I guarantee there's a ruin in that."

He charged down the far side of the slope. Skip, barely recovered from the climb after the river, followed. Crossing a grassy floodplain, they reached the rock wall in which the slot canyon lay, little more than a crack in the sandstone façade—carved by flash floods, the walls sculpted and smoothed. It narrowed still further as they moved up it, enclosing them in shade and cool stone. A thread of water wound down over a bed of light sand.

"Whoa!" said Edison, stopping and bending down. Lying on the pale sand was a perfect arrowhead, knapped from black obsidian.

"Wow," said Skip, "that's a beaut."

Edison slipped it into his pocket.

"Um," said Skip, "you know, we shouldn't be taking anything."

"An arrowhead?" Edison gave a snort. "Everyone takes arrowheads. I mean, if I didn't, the next person up here would. Or it'd be washed into the river and disappear forever."

"Right," said Skip dubiously, reminding himself of the many arrowheads he'd found—and kept.

They continued up the twisty canyon, jammed with fallen fir trunks and boulders. The stream of water created a cool, fragrant ambiance.

Suddenly, Edison pointed. "There!"

Skip looked up and was amazed to see a perfect little cliff dwelling in an alcove about thirty feet over their heads, built on a wide, flat ledge. The sandstone face that rose above it was covered with petroglyphs pecked into the rock—spirals, images of deer, and a spectacular stylized bear with four-pointed stars on its body. A steep crack led up to the ruin, evidently used by the former inhabitants. It was incredible—beautiful.

Without another word Edison started up, making his way along the narrow ledge that slanted upward. Skip followed. At one point the ledge had fallen away, forcing them to step over a yawning gap, but within a few minutes they had arrived. The structure was recessed into the alcove, leaving a flat sandstone patio in front as a kind of work area. Edison crossed it, removed the headlamp from his day pack, and walked over to a dark door leading inside. Putting on the headlamp and ducking, he entered, Skip following.

"Holy crap," Skip said as he looked around.

It was as if the inhabitants had just walked out, leaving their stuff behind. In the rear was a row of corrugated clay pots with stone lids. A small black-on-white bowl stood in a niche, filled with carbonized corncobs. Broken potsherds were scattered on the stone floor, and the roof was dark with ancient soot.

"Let's go into the inner rooms," said Edison. His face was shining with excitement.

Bending lower, he went through a still smaller door in the back that led into rooms wedged beneath the lowering ceiling of stone. As Edison shined the light around, Skip froze.

"Holy mother of God," breathed Edison, his headlamp illuminating a sprawl of human bones, including a human skull split in two. Lying next to the pieces of skull was a hafted axe, wooden handle still present, the blade made with the same shiny black obsidian as the arrowhead they'd come across earlier.

Edison knelt and reached out for the axe.

"Better not touch that," said Skip.

But Edison ignored him. He grasped the handle and lifted it, turning it around in the beam of his headlamp as it glittered and threw flecks of light around the small room. He looked at Skip. "This is an incredible artifact. Just look at the knapping—and with an intact handle!" He took off his day pack as if to put the object inside.

Skip swallowed. "Taking that is a felony."

At this, Edison began to chuckle. "You don't think I'm just going to leave it here?"

"I do, actually."

Edison gave a sigh. "All right." He laid it back down among the bones. "I'll just leave it here like this, okay?"

"Thanks," said Skip, feeling awkward. He didn't like being put in the position of artifact cop, but taking something like that was illegal as hell, and wrong—and Edison knew it.

"Hey, will you look at this?" Edison cried, his light landing on another object—a stone mountain lion fetish, broken in half. He reached out and picked up the pieces, examining them with reverence, while Skip looked on in dismay. "Don't worry, I won't take them." He put them back. "Let's keep going. After you."

Skip worked his way out of the small room and Edison soon followed, joining him in the cool air of the plaza. "This place is incredible," Edison said. "And what we've found is just the beginning."

*Incredible* wasn't quite the word Skip would have chosen for this scene of violent death. Spooky was more like it. He felt a shiver of creepiness.

They explored side canyons until darkness forced them to return to their packs, where they set up camp. It was, Skip mused, a place of wonders, chock full of untouched ruins, but also unsettling. Edison seemed to have an uncanny knack for knowing exactly where to find them; it was almost as if he were channeling the ancient Gallina Indians. Several times he'd vanished among the labyrinthine roomblocks—once for nearly a quarter of an hour. They had found several other skeletons, many with arrowheads or axe heads mingling with the bones, some with their skulls bashed in. Edison had kept a few things—arrowheads and several axes—arguing with Skip each time but leaving the truly important stuff behind. Skip remained uneasy, but said no more about it once they'd left the ruins. Edison was so thrilled by everything that there was little Skip could have said that would have stopped him anyway. And there was, he told himself, some truth to the idea that it was only a matter of time before looters discovered the canyon. In fact, he wondered why they hadn't already. That was strange—very strange. When they got back out, he decided, he would definitely tell Nora about their discoveries. He'd been noting them on his GPS, dropping pins at every location, many of which had probably never been recorded before.

Even in July, when the sun went down a chill came into the air. They set up the tent and lit a cheerful fire for dinner. After a meal of steaks—Edison had brought down a couple of New York strips in a soft cooler pack—and a bottle of wine, out came the bottles of tequila. Edison cracked the seal of one, pulled the cork out with a pop, took a swig, then passed it to Skip, who took his own good swallow of the fiery liquor.

"Twenty-year reposado," said Edison. "Five hundred bucks a bottle."

"It's amazingly smooth," said Skip, taking another sip.

"Only the best," said Edison. "Isn't this place just incredible?"

Skip nodded.

"You could spend a month in here and not explore it all. Just imagine this canyon during its heyday! Those meadows along the river planted with irrigated fields, kids playing in the river, women cooking, men coming back from the hunt with deer slung over their shoulders...And then—" he paused dramatically— "the invasion comes." He took a long pull of tequila, eyes shining in the firelight. "They come in from both ends of the canyon, I'll bet, in a pincer movement. Warriors are already secretly deployed along the canyon rims. The Gallina are trapped. They run screaming for their dwellings in the side canyons, mothers scooping up their kids. They pull up the ladders, man the arrow ports, and fight like hell. But it's too late. The invaders are too many, the surprise too great." Edison swept a dramatic hand over the dark cliff faces. "It wasn't just a war. It was genocide. One by one, the Gallina's cliff dwellings fall to the invaders and they're massacred: men, women, children, skulls split, brains beaten in. The invaders are not there to steal, but exterminate. They don't loot the dwellings. Oh no: they leave everything as is, the bodies left where they fell, to show the world what they did."

At this, Edison rose and bowed extravagantly. "And that, ladies and gentlemen, is what happened."

Skip applauded. He was feeling good, his earlier apprehension dispelled by liquor and a full belly.

"Bring out your uke," Edison said, "and let's make some music."

"Sure thing." Skip opened the lightweight traveling case, pulled it out.

"I thought you had a vintage Martin," Edison said as Skip pulled out a small blue ukulele with a fretboard of dark wood.

"I do, but no way in hell am I gonna bring that out here. But this—" he patted the instrument proudly— "is a pretty sweet substitute. An Enya 25D, less than a hundred bucks, if you can believe it."

"Really?"

"Yup. That way, I don't mind the dings and dirt."

Edison reached for his own pack and drew out his expensive replica bone flute. Then he paused, eyes drawn once again to the canyon walls. "You can tell," he said, "by how carefully those cliff houses were hidden, and by their arrow ports and thick stone walls, that the Gallina must have been really, really afraid." Edison's words were beginning to slur together. "And with good reason! But here's the question: Were the Gallina afraid because there were bad dudes out there...or because they, *themselves*, were the bad dudes?" He laughed and swigged, then handed the bottle to Skip.

Skip had had plenty, but he thought, *What the hell?* and took another good pull himself. He could feel his head starting to reel.

And now Edison leaned toward Skip, his face glowing with liquor. "My friend, I've got a confession to make," he said in a confidential whisper.

"What is it?"

Without another word, Edison put the flute aside, reached for his daypack, and drew it toward him. He unzipped the top and felt inside, pulling out a large Ziploc bag with something inside wrapped in a paper towel. He drew it out. It was the obsidian axe.

Skip stared, a creeping feeling of alarm coming over him, dulled by alcohol but not extinguished.

"I was naughty," Edison said, now taking another bag, and then another, out of his backpack. He opened them, then unwrapped and displayed the items within: the obsidian axe; a small but exquisitely painted effigy pot of a bird; a polished stone pipe; a child's finely woven yucca sandal—and something Skip had not seen in the ruins that Edison must have picked up in secret: a pair of prasiolite lightning stones.

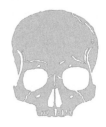

# 35

THE FIRE HAD died down to coals. The instruments had been played, with decreasing virtuosity as additional liquor was consumed, then put away. The empty bottle of tequila lay to one side, glinting in the reddish light from the coals. Skip looked at it—had they really consumed the whole thing? Jesus.

He looked over at Edison, stretched out beneath his rumpled sleeping bag, mouth open and drooling. Skip, drunk as he was, could not get to sleep. He felt nauseous and hoped he wouldn't throw up as Edison had, stumbling out into the bushes to heave. He had staggered back into the firelight, slurred something incomprehensible, tried to crawl into his sleeping bag, gotten all tangled up, then passed out. Now he lay on his back, hands behind his head, listening to the night sounds.

It was getting cold. Skip was desperate for sleep, but every time he closed his eyes things began to whirl, his gorge began to rise, and he had to open his eyes again to hold back the nausea. Christ, he should've restrained himself—that tequila was wicked stuff.

What time was it? They had talked and talked—or rather,

Edison had talked—for what seemed like hours. Skip had listened, his own thoughts lingering on the artifacts Edison had taken—taken in spite of all his warnings. And those lightning stones: Where the hell did those come from? Skip knew that such ceremonial objects were supposedly found only in kivas. Had Edison managed to find a kiva during one of those intervals when he'd vanished?

Skip closed his eyes again, but then the whirling started, right on schedule. He might just as well puke and get it over with: some desert creature could enjoy what had once been a delicious strip steak.

He fumbled to his knees and felt around unsuccessfully for his headlamp. *What the hell.* He exited the tent. The coals in the fire were collapsing, opening red gashes. There was no moon, and the ground was so dark, it was like standing in a pool of night. He couldn't see his feet but he shuffled forward anyway, holding his arms out in front of him. The dark shape of a ponderosa was just visible, maybe fifty feet ahead. That would be far enough.

Groping and shuffling in the dark, he reached it just in time to retch once, then a second time. He stayed there, hunched over, for another minute or so. Then at last he straightened up, spat a few times, and wiped his mouth with his bandanna. God, he felt better. Amazing what a good puke could do.

A cool, piney air was drifting with the breeze and he took a long, deep breath. His head was clearing a little. He stood still, taking in the night air, feeling its salubrious effect on his drunken state. He didn't want to go lie down again and start whirling. No—he'd stay here for a moment, just standing, just breathing. He could see the faint glow of the dying coals, a smudge of red in the sea of black. It looked inviting and he shivered a little, feeling the edge of cold. Sliding into the sleeping bag would be nice—but before he lay down again, he had to get his head clear.

As he gazed around, he saw something: the reddish smudge of the fire winked out, then reappeared a second later. Skip blinked. It was almost as if a dark shape had moved in front of it. He squinted at the faint, distant glow. Nothing. As he stared, a small collapse of ash opened a slash in the heap of coals, and the fireglow brightened a little.

But then, silently, the glow was blotted again, and then again, by shapes—dark shapes, moving more slowly this time. Skip stared, his heart pounding. It wasn't some drunken figment of his imagination; he was certain of it. Several shapes had moved past the fire, blotting it out as they went. Were animals circling the fire?

He hardly dared breathe, listening intently. The only sound was the distant murmur of the Gallina River, invisible behind him. He wanted to yell, call out, do something—and yet a most dreadful fear seemed to paralyze him. All he could do was stare.

But the glow remained steady. Again, he listened, motionless. Nothing.

Okay—so it *was* just his imagination, or more likely a hallucination, brought on by the expensive tequila. Skip didn't know what, exactly, was in that reposado to make it so costly, but he made a silent promise to himself and Nora not to drink any more of it.

But he couldn't seem to move his feet back toward camp. He was still afraid.

And then he heard a sound: a stealthy footfall. Then another. And above the susurrus of the river, he heard a whisper that might have been wind, or might not.

Another whisper.

And now he knew there were people there. People sneaking closer, gathering around quietly in the dark. Instantly, he recalled the story Edison had told him: of the mutilated body that came floating down the Gallina River many years ago—the murder that was never solved.

The intense fear began clearing his head. What he needed was to find the headlamp. Maybe he had left it on the edge of the tarp next to the tent. It would be to his right.

But no—that would be a huge mistake. What he needed to do was circle around somehow, get close to Edison's pack, and slide out that mother of a gun.

He took a step forward, then another, the soft grass muffling any sound. Suddenly, he sensed beyond any doubt the presence of humans—it could only be humans—gathering and circling around the tent.

Plan thwarted, Skip froze for a second. Then, very slowly, he eased down onto his hands and knees. His headlamp was close now. But it wasn't that he was after: it was the EDC knife he kept for quick access in the front Velcro pocket of his pack.

Suddenly, he heard the loud tearing of tent fabric and a *thump!* sound, followed by a hideous groan. Another *thump!*

*What the hell?*

*Thud!* And then a muffled voice, a garbled, groaned-out "Fuuuuck"—a voice that was unmistakably Edison's.

Instantly, Skip broke out of his paralysis. *Oh God: they're beating Edison.* His fingers found the edge of the tarp, and he frantically swept his hands over it, quickly making contact with his pack. He snatched at it, fumbling it in his panic, trying to grab his knife. There was a muffled scream. He could hear what sounded like Edison fighting drunkenly, in the tent thrashing, grunting, followed by more horrible blows.

"Hey! Hey, you!" he screamed, rising to his feet and stumbling forward, orienting the knife with nerveless fingers and then flicking its blade open—only to feel it slip out of his hand again. "What the hell—"

Skip crouched blindly, frantically searching the grass. He heard a rush toward him and, instinctively, began rising to meet it. A second later he felt a soggy blow to his ribs that sent him to his knees with a grunt, then a second blow to the side of his head, sending him to the ground and into oblivion.

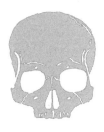

# 36

At dawn, the Bell 407 FBI chopper had risen from its pad at Kirtland AFB, where the Bureau kept its air assets. Corrie was in it, along with Sharp and four Evidence Response Team spotters. Corrie was nervous: her request for a search of the other five prehistoric lighthouses marked on Driver's map had not been met with enthusiasm and had been approved only after many questions. Helicopter time was expensive, it required a lot of personnel, and it generated a ton of paperwork. They had already used a lot of chopper time wandering over the badlands before finding the second victim. Nora's speculation—seconded by Corrie—that there might be other recent victims at the bases of the five lighthouses on Driver's map was met with skepticism from the special agent in charge and a lack of enthusiasm from Sharp.

But now they were up in the air, the sun just breaking the horizon. Sharp was quiet—it was hard to carry on a conversation with the thud of the rotors, even wearing headphones. Corrie looked out the big window as the Bell headed north, over the Pueblo reservations along the Rio Grande, past Jemez Springs, over the Valles Caldera, before angling westward toward the great badland region surrounding Chaco Canyon. As she stared at the passing terrain, she was once again struck by just how big and empty New Mexico was—how most of it was basically uninhabited deserts and mountains.

*Please, please, God, give me a dead body,* she found herself thinking. She tried, at least half-heartedly, to shake this grim prayer out of her consciousness.

As they approached the vast badlands, the landscape below transitioned from the green slopes of the mountains to grays, whites, oranges, and purples. Looking down, she could see how the land had been stripped down to rock and sand by erosion, with countless wandering dry washes, arroyos, hoodoo rocks, lifeless escarpments, and mesas. Beyond the tiny Navajo settlement of Nageezi, she could see the western section of the San Juan Basin oil field, recently rejuvenated by fracking. Sprinkled amidst the rock formations were rows of fracking tanks and piping all coiled together, pumpjacks, and fresh dirt roads going every which way. This was the area leased to Geo Solutions GmbH, the company at which Horace Driver and his daughter worked—or had worked.

"That's some hellacious country down there," said Sharp, speaking at last.

Corrie nodded and checked the paper map she had unfolded in her lap, so she could follow the landmarks. "We're getting close to the first lighthouse."

Before leaving Watts's cabin, Nora had marked—as best she could—the locations of the other five lighthouses, based on Driver's own rough map. It was not easy, given how many black fingers of lava stuck up like cruel spires all across the wasted landscape. The chopper pilots had been given the coordinates of the five badland formations she wanted to search around. They were widely separated, but the Bell 407 was a fast machine and they would be able to complete the search in three to four hours.

The drone of the engine changed as the chopper slowed and began to descend toward the first target. Corrie raised her set of 10×50 binoculars and squinted through them, looking down at the landscape, doing her best to match the various landmarks beyond the window to the map in her lap. She could see the first of the possible lighthouses coming into view: a steeply eroded cone, rising higher than the others around it.

The captain brought the Bell into a hover to one side of the cone and about seventy above it, allowing the spotters time to scan the ground. Corrie drew in a breath: she could see the vague outlines of ruins atop the formation, a large flat hearth of stones and a ruined hut. So Driver was right: it, too, was an ancient lighthouse. She wondered if the stone hut contained more human bones. She scanned it with her binoculars, but the ruins were almost buried in windblown sand and it was impossible to tell what, if anything, was inside.

Slowly, the chopper circled the cone, sometimes angling one way, then another, giving the spotters on either side the angles they needed to locate anything unusual on the ground. After ten minutes, the spotters shook their heads. Nothing. It was time to fly to the next target.

They followed the same procedure at each pinnacle, moving northward along the course of the Great North Road toward Bloomfield. There was nothing at the second and third formations—nothing on the ground, nor visible ruins on top. Perhaps Driver had been wrong about these, or the remains of the lighthouses and huts on the summits had eroded away.

At the fourth spire, they found the remains of a lighthouse... but nothing else. Corrie began to feel a little sick at heart. This was not turning out well.

The fifth and last formation lay in a place called Kutz Canyon, south of Bloomfield. According to Driver's theory, it marked the northern terminus of the Great North Road. As they approached, the canyon came abruptly into view: a broad gash in the earth, eroded into a crazy labyrinth of humps, spires, and buttes, riddled with bone-dry arroyos whitened with salt. It was a forbidding place, grim and unrelievedly frightening.

The chopper did its usual routine, coming into a hover to one side of the pinnacle. Corrie could see that it was in fact a real lighthouse, with an area of flat stones forming the fire hearth and another hut, roof still intact. She felt a momentary relief. But as the pilot moved the bird around in a slow circle, and the spotters scoured the ground with their powerful binocs, it became clear they could see nothing.

Time stretched on.

Corrie glanced at Sharp. He was not looking at her; instead his eyes were fixed on the metal floor, elbows on his knees, hands clasped. He looked neutral, calm, but Corrie could imagine what he was thinking.

After twenty minutes, she saw the spotters shake their heads, heard the chopper's rotors power up. They began to rise.

Sharp finally raised his head. "Agent Swanson? Next steps?"

She flushed. There was really nothing else. "I guess head back to base. Looks like this was a bust."

When he didn't respond, she looked back out the window, a sick feeling in her stomach. The chopper began to move away from the pinnacle, banking in the direction of Albuquerque.

And then, through her headphones, she heard one of the

spotters speak to the pilot. "Can you slow down and descend? I see something on the ground at two o'clock."

Two o'clock was on the other side of the chopper. Corrie leapt up and scrambled over.

The spotter pointed, and Corrie raised her binoculars.

It took her a minute to bring the dual images into single focus. Then she made out a person, walking—staggering, really—across the sandy wastes.

The pilot brought the chopper into a hover, then descended. The figure below looked up, pale white face indistinct in the blowing dust.

When they had sunk below a hundred feet, Corrie could make out the figure: a woman with long black hair. She abruptly broke into a run, heading up a wash toward the formation they had just searched.

"Put the chopper down!" Corrie cried.

The pilot hovered over the fleeing figure until a landing zone came into view. Then he expertly put the bird down with a small tornado of dust. Meanwhile, the woman, still running, had gone ahead out of sight.

Corrie waited impatiently for the rotors to power down. Then she watched as the ERT, having already slipped on their packs, took off in the direction of the figure, following her footprints in the sand. Corrie threw on her own pack and ran after them. The woman had put distance between them in the time it had taken the chopper to land and power down, but Corrie had seen that she was weak, moving erratically. She soon came into view, tumbling and lurching. The four ERT members quickly surrounded her, and she fell to her knees with a sob.

"Water!" Corrie shouted, coming up running. "Get her some water!"

The woman was a wreck: hair tangled, her skin burned and peeling, her lips cracked and bleeding, green eyes filmy and bloodshot. And yet, underneath this ravaged exterior, Corrie could see—like a palimpsest—signs of what had been a healthy woman about forty years of age.

Corrie grabbed the canteen offered by one of the ERT members, went over to the woman, and knelt, trying to take her hand. It was enclosed around something, and the woman snatched her hand away, concealing what was in it.

Corrie held out the canteen. "We're here to help you. You need water."

The woman eyed the canteen with wild eyes, hesitated, shook her head. But Corrie could see she was severely dehydrated, and so she unscrewed the cap, took a sip herself, let a few glistening droplets fall into the dust...and then held it out again.

After a moment, the woman grabbed the canteen with both hands and started gulping down the water.

As she did so, two green lightning stones fell into the sand. The woman, following her stare, snatched up the stones and stuffed them in her pocket before gulping down more water.

"Easy with that," Corrie said gently.

The woman drank some more, then spat out some water and tossed the canteen aside. The expression in her green eyes was dark.

"I'm Corrie. What's your name?"

The woman didn't respond.

"We're from the FBI. What were those objects in your hand—lightning stones?"

No answer.

"Was that pinnacle over there your destination? You were walking toward it when we first saw you."

Still no answer—just a sullen look.

"This is a dangerous place to be. You've got no water, and you clearly need medical attention. We'd like you to come with us."

To Corrie's surprise, the woman did not resist. Without a word, she rose, staggering once again. Corrie tried to support her, but she brushed off any effort to help and made her way unsteadily toward the helicopter.

Corrie buckled her in. As they dusted off, she asked: "What are you doing out here?"

The woman said nothing.

Corrie asked another gentle question, then one more—but the woman merely stared straight ahead, her face slack and apathetic as a zombie's, uttering not a single word.

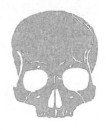

# 37

Maria's family had risen in the dark, and as a result Nora, along with the older of the two young boys, set off at first light. To her surprise, now that it was necessary for him to provide directions, the youth proved to speak decent English. He would guide her for the first ten miles or so himself, then explain the rest of the route—or, at least, to a point where she could find others who knew more. Nora protested at his having to walk back such a distance, but he said it was nothing; the road was good and he'd be home again before dark.

The road was not good. It was a one-lane track with no guard-rails chiseled out of the sides of mountains and cliffs, winding up and down in a terrifying manner. It also crossed and recrossed other, identical-looking roads until she was not sure she'd ever find her way out again.

It took two hours to travel the ten miles. Then the boy got out; pointed out the road that, supposedly, would take her where she wanted with no further forkings; then turned and began scampering back to San Luis.

Nora watched him for a minute as he grew smaller and smaller in her rear-view mirror. Then, with a deep breath, she continued along the dreadful road. She wound her way around several more heart-stopping cliffs, but as she'd been told, there was only one road, and after another two hours and ten additional miles she finally emerged into a hanging valley high in the mountains. The climate here was much cooler, the slopes clad in pine trees, and a few farmhouses were scattered among the emerald patchwork fields that clung to the steep slopes.

She stopped at the first house she came to and asked directions. To her consternation, here too nobody professed any knowledge of Oskarbi or any other white man in residence nearby—but they knew Benicio, and she was directed to a little white hut clinging to a promontory above the valley so far up a distant hillside as to be barely visible.

The road—such as it was—ended on the far side of the farmhouses, and she was forced to get out of the Jeep, shoulder her pack, and climb the last few miles to the little white hut. After a few false turns, the steep, rutted trail came out onto a clearing. The simple house had a portal overlooking the yawning chasm of Copper Canyon and the mountains beyond.

An old man was on the porch, sitting in a rocking chair, wearing a straw cowboy hat, a clean white shirt, and dungarees. A large mongrel dog lay at his feet, and upon Nora's appearance leapt up and began barking frantically.

She hesitated. But when the dog made no aggressive moves beyond the terrible racket, she approached slowly. The man's eyes were closed, the chair still. Was he sleeping? It hardly seemed possible.

A few feet from the porch, she stopped, assumed the least threatening pose she could imagine, then said over the barking and baying: "Disculpe, es Usted el señor Don Benicio?"

The lids slowly opened to reveal two brilliantly black, large eyes. "Sí, soy yo. *Yes, it is I.*" He spoke sharply to the dog, who instantly went silent.

Nora stepped guardedly up onto the porch and extended her hand. "My name is Nora Kelly. Enchanted to meet you."

"And I also." He took her hand.

Given her recent discoveries, this was becoming more promising than Nora had hoped. If nothing else, the old man was still alive. She paused a moment. "Don Benicio, I am here to seek your counsel."

"You are the first in many years to do so."

Once again, she felt a vast surprise. She did her best to conceal it. "*Maestro*, I've come looking for Carlos Oskarbi."

Now it was Benicio's turn to pause. He gazed at her for a long time.

"And?" he finally asked.

"I understand he may be here."

There was no reply. At last—when Nora felt certain this was not simply a pause, but that the old man had no intention of responding—she continued. "He was a professor of anthropology in New Mexico. He left the position twelve years ago, to return here once again, as a *discípulo*."

There was another pause, but after a time Benicio responded. "Coffee?"

"Yes, please," Nora said.

The man stood up and went inside with the dog. Nora, who had intended to follow him, found the door shut in her face. She told herself this was not rudeness; it must simply be the old man's way. After about ten minutes he came out again, carrying two mugs. He sat down, handed one mug to Nora, and nodded for her to sit on the only other seat available—a woodpile on the far edge of the porch.

She sat down and an unhurried silence ensued. He did not ask any questions or even evince any curiosity. Finally, Nora cleared her throat. "It is good to meet you in person, Don Benicio."

At this, he said nothing.

"I read all about you in Professor Oskarbi's book. I'm looking for him. I expected he would be here, but if not, I hope you can tell me where I can find him."

Benicio remained silent, taking the time to sip from his mug, then sip again. And then finally he spoke. "Is the coffee to your liking?"

"Yes," she said. "Thank you. Now, about Oskarbi—may I speak to him?"

"No," he said. "You may not." And with that, he rose, nodded gravely, then disappeared again into the hut with his dog.

After the door had closed behind him, Nora remained in her seat on the woodpile, recovering from this sudden surprise and trying to understand what had just happened. Was Oskarbi inside—perhaps as an immured disciple, currently undergoing a spirit journey? Had he taken a vow of silence? Had he moved on, or up, somehow? The people in the farmhouses below professed not to have seen him—but then again, Oskarbi would have come here twelve years ago. A lot could have happened to him in that time. He might well have changed under the tutelage of Don Benicio—the tutelage that Maria's father had warned her against.

It was now late in the afternoon and the sun was about to fall behind the mountains. She considered knocking on the door, or calling out...but something told her this would not help. He clearly knew she was still there and was ignoring her. If Benicio would not speak to her willingly, there was no way she could induce him.

She rummaged in her pack and pulled out a couple of protein bars and her canteen. It was cool, but not chill, and she took out her jacket not so much for warmth as for something to sit on. She rose, draped the jacket over the lone chair, then sat down, rocking back and forth as she ate the protein bars, watching rather idly as the landscape darkened around her. She felt a strange, and most unexpected, sense of peace settle over her: now that she was here, she found herself in no hurry. Que será, será.

In time, as near total darkness enveloped the clearing, she placed the jacket on the hard wooden floor of the porch and lay down upon it, making herself as comfortable as possible. She'd expected to find sleep even more difficult to come by than it had been the night before, at Maria's house. But all the recent surprises, and the questions arising from them, seemed—mercifully—to be somnolent as well, and she soon found herself nodding off to the chirruping of crickets.

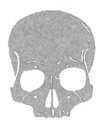

# 38

Nora was awakened by the smell of fresh coffee. Opening her eyes, she saw Don Benicio bending over her, offering her a cup.

She sat up, wincing a little from the night spent on the floorboards of the porch. Despite the discomfort, she'd slept well, disturbed only occasionally—when the dog had woken up and remembered to bark at the intruder before curling up and going back to sleep.

Now Don Benicio gestured her toward the door, which was standing open. She stepped inside what appeared to be a two-room hut, spare, cool, and whitewashed. One room served as a kitchen, dining, and living area, with a single window looking out over the distant mountains. The other, windowless room was the sleeping area.

As she sat at the crude table, drinking coffee, Don Benicio prepared a simple breakfast of esquites. He joined her at the table and they ate together in silence, glancing now and then out at the landscape beyond the window. Finally, the old man said: "He is not here."

It took Nora a moment to realize he was picking up the

conversation where they'd left off the evening before. Why, exactly, he'd left her outside, so abruptly and for so long, she couldn't be sure. Maybe it was an old man's eccentricity.

"Where is he?" she asked.

Don Benicio shrugged.

"Do you mean to say," said Nora, "that he has gone somewhere and will return, or that he isn't here at all?"

"I have not seen Carlos in many years," said Benicio.

Although the others she had met hinted at this possibility, Nora was taken aback nevertheless. "How many?"

Another shrug. "He left long ago. He never came back."

"Wait. You mean he hasn't been in contact with you since he wrote his book?"

"That is what I mean."

Nora was shocked afresh. "So…" She paused to organize her thoughts. "You haven't heard from him at all? He didn't present you with a copy of the book?"

"He gave me nothing. I know nothing of any book."

At this, Nora took a long, deep breath and drained her mug. This surprising revelation overturned all her assumptions. How could Oskarbi have written a book about Benicio and never told him? And if Oskarbi wasn't here—where was he?

"Years ago, Oskarbi was a disciple of yours, a student. Isn't that correct?"

Benicio didn't seem to hear. His eyes were on the distant horizon.

Nora realized she was getting ahead of herself. Peppering Benicio with questions, so soon after he'd allowed her into his home, was no way to get answers. She stopped herself for a moment and let the silence gather, let the peace of the morning return.

"Thank you," she said. "For the *desayuno*."

Benicio nodded. "Another cup?"

"If you wouldn't mind."

He rose, went over to the stove, and brought back the pot, refilling both cups.

"Don Benicio," she began again when her second cup was half-empty, "may I ask you some questions about Oskarbi's apprenticeship with you?"

He shook his head in a silent no.

Nora took some time to rearrange her thoughts. Finally, she said, "May I tell you why I have an interest? Why I have come all this way?"

No reaction.

"When Oskarbi returned to the States after the time spent under your tutelage, he wrote a book. It was about you and your teachings. Even though it was somewhat scholarly in nature, it was a bestseller and millions of people read it—read about the teachings of Don Benicio and how they transformed his life. He became a professor and gathered around him a group of students. And then, twelve years ago, he abruptly disappeared. Everyone said—believed—he'd grown disenchanted with the academic life and returned here, to continue his discipleship. But, obviously, everybody was wrong." She paused. "But here's the reason I've come: in the last five years, there have been at least two ritual suicides among his former students. I'm looking into what might lie behind those suicides."

At this, a subtle change took place in Benicio's face. Its lines deepened, the eyes growing cold and even more distant.

"I need your help," Nora said. "*We* need your help. We're trying to find out why these former students killed themselves in a most horrible way. It seems possible that it connects, somehow, to what Oskarbi learned down here."

Finally, Don Benicio replied. "I cannot share with you this knowledge," he said.

"Why?"

"It is dangerous. Even to mention it is dangerous."

Nora let a beat pass. "If that's true, then Oskarbi is dangerous. It can't be just coincidence—one way or another, he must have had a role in those suicides." She paused and waited.

After a moment, Benicio asked the question she had hoped. "How did they die?"

"They took off all their clothes in the desert, in the full sun, and died of dehydration and heatstroke."

Benicio went very still, deliberately turning his head toward the window and the distant canyons and mesas beyond. He remained this way for a long time—long, no doubt, even by his own standards. Minutes passed. Then a quarter of an hour.

Nora picked up her empty coffee cup, toyed with it, put it down. "Don Benicio—"

He held up his hand in a gesture of restraint.

Yet again the silence gathered. It seemed to Nora that Benicio was pondering something, his brow creased, eyes inward-looking despite the vista, expression quiet. And then—at last—he began to speak, hesitantly, in a low voice.

"Carlos came to me," he said. "It was, perhaps, twenty-five years ago. I don't know how he found me. He said he was an anthropologist seeking traditional knowledge. Before, all my teachings were with my own people—to bring them back to the ancient truths. But students were scarce and growing scarcer. My people were losing interest in the old knowledge. Yet here was this person who not only learned about my existence but sought me out. And so I agreed to teach him—*provisionalmente*. For a long time, perhaps a year, he was a very good student. Maybe the most attentive and eager of all. He was greedy for information, always..."

His voice trailed off. Nora waited patiently.

"The traditional way to knowledge is to open a door to the powers that live invisibly in the world around us. The key to that door is *hikuri*—peyote. There are many spirits that come through doors opened by *hikuri*. Some of these are spirits of light. Some are of the dark. And then, there are the spirits we call *duende*, which can go either way. These last are spirits of trickery and gratification."

He finished his own cup. "Carlos chose as his spirit a *duende*. That spirit found a receptive soul, took him by the hand, and led him down the paths to the dark powers."

"You couldn't stop it?" Nora asked. "Keep him from that path, or perhaps guide him back?"

Benicio shook his head. "The attraction of power, especially the power of darkness, is very great. When Carlos first came here, he followed my lessons, wanting to learn. He wasn't sure if the teachings were real or perhaps just old Indian superstitions. But in time he took *hikuri*—and, eventually, met his *duende*. Only *then* he realized the power was real, and that he, Carlos, could harness it. But a *duende* spirit is not only full of deceit, but patient. The process was slow, subtle. By the time I realized what had happened, he was already lost."

"What then?"

"I told him to leave. He took the power and knowledge with him and disappeared. I never heard from him again."

"But..." Nora had become increasingly shocked. "He wrote a book. You really never knew that?"

Don Benicio shook his head again. "I never knew it. Perhaps he did not want me to know it. I fear—"

He stopped. But Nora guessed what he might be thinking. Despite being scoffed at by certain scholars as fantastical, or even fiction, Oskarbi's book might well have been academically sound—revealing truths that were never meant to be revealed.

"Do you think," she pressed, "the deaths of these women might have something to do with all that you've just told me—of Oskarbi trying to harness these dark powers?"

Benicio bowed his head. "It is possible. In fact, it is likely. Dark spirits are attracted by sacrifice—especially human sacrifice."

Another silence fell. The temperature of the room, already cool, seemed to fall several degrees.

"And yet Oskarbi disappeared twelve years ago," Nora said, almost to herself. "Nobody has seen him—he seems to have left no trace."

Don Benicio turned his dark eyes on her. "He was already far along the dark path when he left—and he would only have increased his power since. Wherever he is now, you can be sure that his *duende* is there, too."

# 39

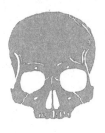

Sᴋɪᴘ, ᴇɴᴄʟᴏsᴇᴅ ɪɴ cool darkness, swam back into consciousness. For a moment he had no idea who he was or what had happened, and he was abruptly seized by panic. But as he struggled to sit up—gasping for breath, head pounding, and black spots blossoming in his vision—the attack came back to him, first in fragments, then in force. Once again he realized he was bound in the dark with leather straps, his hands behind his back and his ankles tied together. How long had he been there? It felt like days he had been drifting in and out of consciousness.

Panic blanketed him once again. He made another effort to sit up, every bone in his body aching. They had beaten the crap out of him. At least his head seemed finally to be clearing—a little.

"Hey!" he cried out. "What's going on? *Hey!*"

Nothing. The air smelled of earth and dirt, and the darkness was absolute. He was still underground. He practically choked, hyperventilating in terror. Who had attacked them—and why? Where was Edison? He dimly remembered, through a haze of pain, Edison getting a terrible beating.

He struggled and screamed, then screamed again. The sound was muffled, dead. But there was no sound, no light, nothing.

At last, he managed to struggle upright, then began pushing himself backward with his feet—the only way the leather strips allowed him to move. The ground was hard dirt, and his heels dug in as he forced his way backward. And then, suddenly, he encountered something—a wall. He felt with his hands. It was smooth and felt as if it had been plastered. He could tell it was slightly curved.

"Hey! Someone! *Anyone!*"

It was like shouting into a hole.

The panic surged again, and Skip fought to tamp it down. He had to think, figure out what to do. If only he knew what was going on, where he was, who these people were, what they wanted, then maybe...

He heard a faint groan in the darkness.

It came from the other side of the cave, or well, or whatever hole he was in. With an effort, he turned around and began digging his feet in, pushing himself in the direction of the sound. His head pounded, and one of his eyes felt swollen, almost shut. There was blood crusted around his nose. He was thirsty and hungry.

He gave a cry of surprise as his tied hands encountered something soft and yielding—a body. He slowly let his hands crawl over the clothing, the skin. He opened his mouth to cry out *Who is it?*—and then, for the first time, realized it might in fact be better if he made no sound at all.

The body moved, and he heard another groan. Christ, it sounded like Edison.

"Edison!" He shook the body as best he could. "Edison, is that you?"

No answer. Skip prodded again, eliciting another moan. It sure as hell sounded like Edison. It had to be Edison. He must be badly injured.

"Edison," he whispered. "It's Skip."

A groan, followed only by heavy, stertorous breathing.

*Oh my God.* Skip felt panic seize him again. What had they done to trigger this? Had they come across a group of killers dwelling in a remote canyon? Had they stumbled onto a crazed militia, or a group of paranoid back-to-the-land survivalists?

And then he heard another sound in the darkness. This one came from above.

He listened intently, holding his breath. There was a muffled scraping, and then a narrow rectangle of light appeared overhead, growing wider as some sort of covering was slid back. It sent down a shaft of light that, quite suddenly, made clear to Skip where he was: at the bottom of an ancient kiva, a circular underground chamber that was the center of religious ceremonies for Pueblo Indians. A square hole in the roof had opened up, and now a crude wooden ladder was descending. A face appeared in the square of light, backlit and featureless.

Turning, Skip saw that the body next to him was indeed Edison. He felt horrified: the man was savagely beaten, face purple and swollen, blood caked around his nose and mouth. His feet were bound together by the end of a thick cord, and another dozen feet of what looked like steel cable was loosely coiled nearby. His shirt was torn and his eyes were but half-open, unseeing slits. Good God, he looked as if he was dying.

"*What's going on?*" Skip cried, unable to keep himself from shouting. "Why are you *doing* this?"

The dark silhouette in the square of light did not move, simply looking down on him.

"My friend needs medical attention!"

No reaction. And then there was another scraping sound, the square of light became a quickly diminishing rectangle—and then silence once again reigned in the cool dark. His head began to whirl, and he laid it down and sank back into unconsciousness.

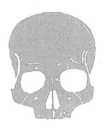

# 40

AFTER SOFTLY KNOCKING and receiving no answer, Corrie entered the hospital room. The black-haired woman was sitting up in her bed, staring at the blank screen of a TV set attached to the wall. She did not look over as Corrie took a seat next to the bed. Without the IVs, Corrie thought, one would hardly know the woman had been gravely ill with dehydration only sixteen hours before. Her hair had been washed and combed, and aside from a horrible sunburn and swollen lips, she looked remarkably improved.

The doctors had made Corrie wait before they would allow the patient to be questioned, which was fine with her. She'd spent the time identifying the woman. It had not been difficult. Starting with the assumption that the woman was another of Oskarbi's original students, Corrie got the list and photos Agent O'Hara had assembled and immediately recognized her. Her name, in fact, had already come up in the investigation—Elodie Bastien. What amazed Corrie, as she paged through the file O'Hara had prepared, was that Bastien was a successful and respected archaeologist with her own private firm, doing contract archaeology for the New Mexico Department of Transportation, surveying and identifying archaeological sites prior to road building or construction. Her parents lived in Santa Fe, and her life—at least from what Corrie could see in the file—was normal. Single, forty-one years of age, place of residence Santa Fe, registered to vote, taxes paid, no criminal record or even unpaid speeding tickets—mundane in the extreme. And yet here she was, having just attempted to commit ritual suicide in the most utterly bizarre and insane fashion imaginable. She didn't seem to be close to her family. And she had no boyfriend or romantic involvements—at least, none that O'Hara had identified.

Bastien had not been reported missing—perhaps because she'd not yet been gone long enough. In hoping to encourage the woman to talk, Corrie had faced a difficult decision: Should she notify her family now, or wait? She was desperate to get the woman's explanation of what she was doing and why, and wondered whether bringing her family into the picture would help... or hinder. The woman had declined the use of a phone and would speak to nobody. After discussing the matter with Sharp, Corrie had decided to hold off telling the family while she tried to get the woman talking on her own. If that didn't work, then they could bring in the family.

"Elodie?" Corrie said gently.

At the sound of her own name, the woman finally reacted: she turned her head around and looked at Corrie for the first time. And then, just as quickly, she looked away, her face once again a mask of nothing.

"My name is Corinne Swanson, and I'm an agent with the FBI here in Albuquerque. I want to assure you that you're not in trouble, you haven't broken any laws that we know of, and your cooperation with me is voluntary. Do you understand?"

Bastien said nothing.

"I'd like to ask you a few questions."

When the woman still didn't respond, Corrie went on. "We're working on a case involving the deaths of two women: Miranda Driver and Molly Vine. I believe you knew both of them. They were colleagues of yours when you were a graduate student in the Anthropology Department at UNM. Professor Carlos Oskarbi was your thesis advisor."

No reaction.

"Both women died by walking out in the desert, in the blazing heat, with no water, dressed improperly. Just as you seemed intent on doing."

It was as if Bastien were frozen, rigid, like a statue.

"I'd simply like to know why you—and they—acted in this way."

A pause. It was as if the woman didn't hear her at all.

"Elodie, please. It's important for us to know why those women died."

She waited.

"I'd like you to consider their families, desperate for closure. Desperate to know what happened to their daughters and why. I was speaking with Horace Driver, Miranda's father, the other day. He's almost at the point of a breakdown over his daughter's death. You can help by telling us what you know."

Nothing.

"If not for the families of Molly and Miranda, think of your own family."

She just wasn't getting through. Corrie suppressed the impulse to stand up and shake the woman in an effort to snap her out of this silence. There had to be some way to get through to her.

"You were in Kutz Canyon, walking toward a badland formation—a prehistoric lighthouse. Do you know what I'm talking about?"

Nothing.

"That's where you were going—right, Elodie?"

Corrie waited, keeping her breathing even. All right: step two. "I'm going to contact your parents and let them know what happened. I expect they'll come here and see you. I hope you'll share with them what you're not willing to share with me."

Nada.

It was hard to look at, even harder to comprehend. This woman just sat in her bed, as rigid as a stone, saying nothing, reacting to nothing. She was like a catatonic, or someone who'd been brainwashed. *Like a member of a cult.* And it was a cult, Corrie was sure of it now, with Oskarbi as its leader, controlling his disciples with sexual coercion, drugs, and bogus religious twaddle. She wondered how Nora was doing in the Sierra Madre of Mexico, whether she'd tracked down Oskarbi. It might be worth the FBI issuing an extradition request to get him back here and make him explain what was going on. But Nora would be back in a day or two, and then she would know a lot more.

But Oskarbi had gone back to Mexico a dozen years ago. Was he running the cult from afar? And why were these suicides happening only now? Or had there been others, as yet undiscovered? It made no sense.

In a final attempt to get a reaction, Corrie reached into her briefcase and brought out the green lightning stones. She held them toward Bastien. "You were carrying these. What do they signify?"

Elodie Bastien turned and looked at them for a brief moment, with a flicker—finally—of something like emotion passing across her face. But then her face set into a mask once again, and she turned her gaze back to the dead television set.

# 41

SKIP EMERGED FROM a groggy stupor in the pitch dark. He must have dozed off, helped along by what was probably a concussion. But how much time had passed? A day? Two? It seemed like he'd been there forever. The fear—and the cloud of pain in his head—was distorting his perception of time. He had a vague recollection of someone giving him water. But no food—and he was ravenously hungry. He'd stopped calling out: it was a stupid exercise in futility. Attention, right now, might be the last thing he wanted. He took a mental inventory of his aching, battered body: nothing seemed to be broken, just a lot of painful bruises and cuts, and his lip was as swollen as a kumquat.

"Edison?" he ventured into the dark. "Are you there?"

Silence.

"Edison, God damn it!"

Was he dead? Skip tried to banish the out-of-control fantasies of torture, rape, and death that were crowding into his head. Who were these people? Crazy survivalists? Satanists?

His rampant speculations were interrupted by a noise from above, and the rectangle of light reappeared as the covering was slid back. A beam of sunlight came in, illuminating drifting motes of dust. It was daylight, of another day, he assumed. Skip glanced over to where Edison had been tied up before, but he was now gone.

A ladder was lowered, then a figure began to climb down. As the person became illuminated by sunlight, Skip could see him more clearly. But what the hell was this? He was naked, smeared head to toe with a thick layer of red clay, wearing a mask of smoothly carved wood, also painted red. A hairpiece of woven grass stuck up from the mask like some outlandish hairdo. He carried a wooden baton in his left hand, the fist-sized sphere at one end carved with a grotesque face.

The man reached the bottom of the ladder and straightened up. Skip could see the gleam of the man's eyes through holes in the mask. The figure moved toward him. There was something odd about the way he walked, a sort of shuffle, as if his feet were too heavy to lift much above the ground. Was he blind? Drunk? High?

Skip stared, fear surging again. "Who are you?" he demanded.

The figure bent down and fumbled with the leather straps holding Skip's ankles together. He loosened the straps, then lengthened and retied them—creating a pair of hobbles that allowed limited movement of the feet.

"Stand up."

The voice was flat and neutral. Skip staggered up, hands still tied behind his back, fighting a momentary dizziness. The man took out a long cord made of leather with a slip knot at one end and wrapped it around his neck, tightening it until it functioned as a collar. The man stepped back, looping the leash around his left wrist.

The man gave the rope a savage jerk, which tightened the cord around Skip's neck until he coughed and choked.

After a second or two, the figure loosened it. "Message received, thief?"

Skip was surprised by the normal, even educated, sound of the voice.

The man jerked the leash. "Respond."

Skip nodded.

The man now untied his wrists. "Climb."

Skip shuffled over to the ladder. The hobbles made climbing difficult, but the ceiling of the kiva was low and it was only moments before he emerged into the sunlight. He blinked in the dazzling light as his handler once again tied his arms behind his back.

"I'm no thief."

"Desecrator."

"Hold on, that wasn't me—"

The handler struck him a sharp blow on the back of his head with the club. "Shut up."

Skip's headache burst back into his consciousness, temporarily forcing everything else away. He closed his eyes, fighting another spell of dizziness, which gradually passed. When he reopened them, he made an effort to focus on his surroundings. He was atop a steep, long mesa about a hundred feet above the river, but still enclosed within the walls of the broad canyon.

Three other men were gathered at the end of the mesa. They were naked as well, two of them smeared with red clay and wearing the same polished masks and grass headdresses. They were shuffling in a crude circle around one of two tall tripods of lashed poles. Something was hanging from the tripod they circled. Skip could not make it out clearly from between the passing forms, but as the three stopped again and began a low chant, he saw, with a spasm of terror, that it was a body, beaten and covered in blood, hanging head down from the tripod by a cable. Son of a bitch—it was Edison: hair matted and stiff with curds of blood, tongue lolling.

These motherfuckers had killed him.

"Jesus Christ!" Skip cried out in dismay.

He felt another blow to the back of his head. "I said, *shut up,*" his handler murmured.

Skip felt himself go weak, sagging down to his knees. His handler jerked him back up with the leash, grabbed his jaw in one meaty paw, turned it upward, then blew some powder he'd cupped in his other paw into Skip's face.

Skip coughed, choked, and sneezed as he felt the unknown substance enter his nostrils, mouth—even his open eyes. It felt like a million tiny pieces of grit, each of them on fire. He struggled and gagged, even as the fiery pain receded to be replaced by a fog of delirium. What had been men lost focus and became shapes. Skip collapsed onto the ground, but his handler no longer tried to keep him standing. Through blurred and watering eyes Skip could hear—as if from far away—a low chanting arise as the three figures began circling Edison's corpse. Then, vaguely, Skip saw the leader raise one arm, and something gleamed darkly. It was a dagger, made of flaked stone—long and black and cruel. More chanting…then the three men stopped circling, moved in tighter around the tripod—and, abruptly, screams broke out.

Skip tried struggling to his knees, fell again. The screams were growing louder and louder, throat-shredding, more animal than human…but nevertheless Skip recognized the voice as that of Edison.

So he wasn't dead after all.

He blinked and blinked, trying desperately to clear the swirling mist from his eyes. But the leader blocked his view and he could not see what was happening. But the screams continued, growing louder and more agonized. Since his hands were bound behind him and he could not cover his ears, he shouted, "Stop it! Please stop it! *Stop it! Stop it!*"—until the shadow of his handler fell over him, the wooden club came down on him again, and a merciful darkness claimed him.

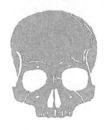

# 42

On long drives, Nora often listened to audiobooks, and for her roughly thirty-hour roundtrip drive to Mexico she'd come prepared with a couple of good thrillers by Preston and Child. But the more time she spent on the road driving home, the harder she found it to concentrate. What kept intruding was a melody, an earworm of sorts: the one from the wax cylinder recording that Skip had taken home a transcription of. He'd harmonized it and played it incessantly on his uke, and then gotten her to accompany him on flute, talking excitedly about all that he was going to do with it. And then, in usual Skip style, he'd moved on to some other interest. It was dissonant, unsettling, with quarter tones that were not known in Western music. It sounded a little like that weird, final string quartet of Shostakovich's maybe. Idly, she wondered what Shostakovich would make of it. But the relief at identifying, and thus ridding herself, of this unsettling earworm gave way to other intrusive thoughts—in particular, what she'd learned from Benicio, and the mystery of Oskarbi supposedly turning to the "dark side."

Now it was clear Oskarbi was running a cult. And yet, it was like none she'd heard of before. Oskarbi wasn't a David Koresh or a Jim Jones. Its members were not a collection of lost souls, brainwashed and shut away in a remote compound. Instead, they appeared to be educated, intelligent, high-functioning professionals who—at least on the surface—lived successful and productive lives. Was it possible—really possible—that people like Molly Vine and Miranda Driver were in a cult? Where and when did they meet? What did they do—and why?

As she drove through the darkness, these questions wove themselves within her brain. And as they did, Nora found herself led inevitably to the question of whether Benicio's claims of dark powers, *duende* spirits and an unseen world, were real. Could there be a hidden world behind the real one, accessible through secret rituals or hallucinogenic drugs like peyote? This wasn't a new concept to her: as an anthropologist, she was well aware that many ancient cultures around the world believed hallucinogens could put you in touch with a hidden and often dangerous world lurking behind the visible. Whatever the cultish dogmas were, Vine and Driver had apparently believed in them passionately enough to commit horrific, ritual suicide.

It was midnight when Nora finally turned into the driveway of the little house she shared with Skip. The place was dark as she pulled her car up next to Skip's crappy old beater. She was intensely relieved to be home; it had been a grueling trip in more ways than one, and on top of everything else the fifteen-hour drive back had just about fried her brain. She couldn't wait to get into bed.

She got out of the car and went to the door, inserting her key; she would unpack in the morning. She heard the reassuring barking of Mitty, their golden retriever, and when she opened the door he rushed to her, wagging the entire back half of his body in a fervor of welcome, whining and licking her hand. The excitement of the greeting gave her pause; it suggested he had been left alone in the house. She stepped into the kitchen, Mitty following eagerly.

The house felt empty.

Passing through the kitchen and dining area, she went into the hall. Skip's bedroom door was open. She stepped inside and flicked on the light. The bed was unmade—but then, it was always unmade. She returned to the kitchen. Mitty had been fed and there was water in his bowl—so Skip either was out for the evening, or, if he'd gone away, had arranged for their dog-sitting friend to feed and walk Mitty. But if he was out for the evening, why was his car in the driveway? Had a friend picked him up? Maybe. He did, on occasion, spend the night away from the house, especially if he'd gone to a party and had too much to drink. Or met some woman.

She felt a rising irritation at her irresponsible brother and his doings. But she was tired and it was too late to do anything about it. She'd call their dog sitter in the morning and find out if Skip had engaged her, but for now all she wanted to do was collapse in bed.

The sound of her phone booming out the *1812 Overture* woke Nora in a panic. She fumbled at her nightstand and lifted the phone; it was Corrie, calling at seven o'clock sharp.

Jesus. There were times when Corrie was relentless. She swiped the answer bar and put the phone to her ear. "Yes?"

"Nora? It's Corrie."

"I know."

"Sorry to disturb you." The words tumbled out in a rush. "You must've just gotten back. But I'm really anxious to hear what you found out."

Nora sat up, her head clearing, and tried to focus on the torrent of words. "I didn't find him. But I learned some things... interesting things."

"Can we meet in half an hour? I've got news for you as well. I'm on the interstate just coming into Santa Fe—I've got an interview there at nine. We can grab coffee before."

Nora groaned inwardly. "Okay, fine," she said.

They met at a coffee shop around the corner from Nora's house. She'd just had time to shower and dress, managing to arrive right as Corrie pulled into the little parking lot. They walked in together. Nora ordered a triple espresso and a chocolate croissant, while Corrie had a gigantic, sweet coffee drink, and they sat down outside.

After a few gulps of espresso, Nora felt herself returning to normal. First, Corrie told her the astonishing news about finding a third woman out in the desert—this one still alive and currently recovering, but refusing to speak. Next, she peppered Nora with questions about her trip. Nora related the whole story: tracking down the elusive Benicio, spending the night on his porch, and ultimately learning the truth about Oskarbi. Corrie hung on to every word, leaning forward, elbows on her knees.

When she was done, Corrie eased back in her chair and, after a silence, said, "Let me get this straight: Oskarbi left Benicio's place twenty-five years ago, never went back, never even communicated with the guy ever again, published a book, got rich and famous—but through it all he'd gone over 'to the dark side'—" she formed air quotes with her fingers— "then gathered a bunch of cultish followers around him, mostly women, and disappeared without a trace. Years later, some of these women started committing ritual suicide."

"That's about it," said Nora.

"Sounds like he signed a pact with the devil," Corrie said.

"Or at least believed that he had." She paused. "But where the hell is he?"

"According to the FBI databases I checked," Corrie said, "all traces of him vanished twelve years ago—no credit card or bank activity, no social media posts, no contact with friends or relatives, no driver's license renewal—nothing."

"So maybe he *did* go to ground and is running the cult from some secret location."

"Seems unlikely."

"Why?"

"When all electronic traces of a person vanish, it usually means one thing: that they're dead. That's an FBI rule of thumb, anyway."

"Dead? Really?"

Corrie held up her hands. "It's awfully hard to disappear or establish a new identity in this day and age. Maybe the cult is hiding him. But what kind of cult is it where the members have PhDs and lead professional lives?"

Nora smiled ironically. "The question occurred to me, too—although I know quite a few PhDs who are totally nuts. Tell me more about this woman you found. Bastien. Has she really refused to say anything?"

"Yes, but she's back with her family, which might help—I'm seeing her at nine."

Nora thought for a minute, then glanced at her watch. Eight o'clock. "Would it be okay if I came along? It would require a brief stop at the Institute—but I just might know a way to get a reaction."

She described her idea to Corrie, who nodded. "Anything that might help."

It was now late enough for Nora to call the dog sitter. "Listen, Corrie, mind if I make a quick call? I'm worried about Skip."

"Skip? Go ahead."

Nora called the dog sitter and learned her brother had, indeed, engaged her to feed and walk Mitty twice a day. The sitter said Skip was going camping with a friend. He didn't say where, and he'd been vague about when he'd be back, but he'd mentioned the friend's name—Edison. Nora hung up the phone, more anxious than ever.

"Everything all right?" Corrie asked.

Nora shook her head. "Seems he took off the day after I left for Mexico. Camping with that guy Edison."

"That rich young collector you told me about? Where?"

"I don't know."

"Do you have a reason to be concerned?"

Nora gave a small, ironic laugh. "With my brother Skip? Yeah. Always."

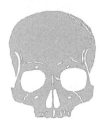

# 43

Slowly—very slowly this time—Skip rose back toward consciousness. Each time he felt himself rise, he tried to dive down again into the safe and enfolding dark. But it grew more and more difficult until—at last—he opened his eyes.

The scene had changed. The tripods were still in place, and Edison still hung from one of them. But his body looked different—a ghastly marbling of red and white—and then, as the final strands of fog fell away, Skip realized that the bastards had flayed him alive.

The group that circled Edison's skinned body was much larger now—perhaps a dozen. Most appeared to be women, naked and smeared with red clay as well and wearing the same masks. As they circled the tripod, their movements were herky-jerky, as if under the influence of drugs—which, he thought, was probably true.

Skip managed to sit up, fear churning his stomach. *My God.* Despite the roughness with which he and Nash had already been handled, the brutality and sadism of this act shocked him to the core. *Why is this happening? Am I going to be next? What did Edison do to deserve being flayed alive?* Earlier, his handler had called him a thief, a desecrator—but of what? Were they being punished for violating some sacred place, or picking up artifacts?

It was Edison's idea to keep this little excursion a secret. They'd told no one where they were going. No one knew where they were. No one would come looking for them here. Besides, Nora was away in Mexico—she'd promised him she would be back in just a few days, but there was no way of knowing how long she would be gone.

Another thought occurred to him: they were not going to let him live after this. He was a dead man, for sure. *God, poor Edison...*With an effort, Skip tried to force away the memory of those prolonged, soul-wrenching screams.

The group stopped dancing, stirring with excitement. Two women appeared at the edge of the mesa, carrying a litter made of two poles on their shoulders, a platform of wooden planks in between. Coming up behind was a tall, muscular figure painted in white clay, with handprints of black paint imprinted all over his body. Instead of a bundle of tied grass, a pair of deer antlers rose above his head—clearly a person of authority.

Skip stayed silent, looking at them with curiosity and terror. A person sat on the platform, cross-legged, swathed despite the heat in a woven Pueblo-style poncho blanket with a drooping hood.

The crowd fell into a hushed silence and parted to let the litter pass through and approach the pole. This, Skip thought, must be the big boss, the man—the one that even the figure in white drawing up the rear would answer to.

The bearers circled the pole, obviously to give the hooded

person on the litter a good view of Edison's mutilated corpse. Then the litter was borne back out of the circle and set upon a large, flat boulder nearby. The bearers flanked the litter in ritual fashion as the figure in white stepped forward, reverently took up the corners of the blanket and, after a brief chant, whisked it off.

# 44

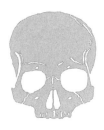

THE BASTIEN HOME was in Las Campanas, a fancy golf development outside Santa Fe. As they pulled into the driveway, Nora took it all in: the sleek adobe-and-stone house in contemporary Santa Fe style, the four-car garage, the infinity pool, the tennis court, the sweeping views.

"Not bad," said Corrie as she parked the car.

They got out. As they came up the flagstone walkway, the door opened, revealing a young blonde woman dressed for riding in breaches, leather boots, a silk shirt, and a vest. In one hand she was carrying a crop and helmet. Before they could introduce themselves, she turned and called back into the house: "Randolph, the FBI are here."

She stepped aside to let them in without introducing herself. A moment later, the man named Randolph arrived, much older, heavyset, with a neatly curated salt-and-pepper beard.

"I'm going riding," the woman said from the door. "I'll leave you to entertain these people."

"Yes, darling," he said, turning and gesturing Nora and Corrie inside.

The woman turned and skipped down the walkway, leaving behind a cloud of expensive perfume.

Nora had initially assumed the woman must be Bastien's sister, but the exchange made it clear she was the wife—of the trophy kind, apparently.

Corrie wasted no time showing her badge. "Special Agent Corinne Swanson," she said, "and FBI consultant Dr. Nora Kelly, here to interview Elodie Bastien."

"Right, right. Have a seat," said the man, leading them into a vast white living room. "She's still not talking."

"And you are Mr. Bastien?" asked Corrie.

"Randolph Bastien, Elodie's father," he said, not offering his hand.

"Could we ask you a few questions, Mr. Bastien, before we see her?"

"Go ahead."

They settled into several ultra-contemporary, ultra-uncomfortable chairs. Corrie took out a phone. "Mind if I record?"

"Go ahead," said Bastien.

As Corrie set the phone down, microphone pointed at him, Nora took the opportunity to examine the elder Bastien more closely. He wore a blue blazer with gold buttons, white slacks, black loafers with horse-bit buckles, and a burgundy ascot plumped up around his neck. His hair was brushed back and his face was fleshy, the cheeks ruddy and varicose.

"And that," asked Corrie, "was Mrs. Bastien, I assume?"

"Yes," he said.

"Elodie's mother is...where?"

"Denver. Divorced. Why is this your business?"

Corrie gave him a cool smile. "Just getting a picture of the family, that's all."

"Elodie's not talking," he said brusquely.

"You mentioned that," said Corrie. "I have a few questions about her life, education, employment, and state of mind. If I may?"

"Fine." He glanced at his watch.

"Elodie had a PhD from UNM in archaeology, is that correct? I understand she studied with Professor Oskarbi."

A curt nod.

"Do you know if she had a relationship with Dr. Oskarbi?"

"What do you mean?"

"A romantic relationship."

"I don't know. I don't vet her boyfriends. How is this relevant?"

"Mr. Bastien," Corrie said, her voice sharpening, "the FBI will decide what's relevant or not. Of course, you're not under any obligation to answer questions."

"I'll answer them," he said with irritation. "Elodie was a grown woman. She lived her own life. I didn't interfere."

"Did she have a history of depression? Was she ever treated for any mental health issues?"

"Not that I know of."

"But as her father, you would know—wouldn't you? At least, during the time she was a minor?"

"You'll have to ask her mother. I was very busy during Elodie's childhood, and my wife was in charge of family matters." He fidgeted in his chair.

"And what did you do that kept you so busy?" Corrie asked.

"I managed a hedge fund."

"I see. Now: after she got her PhD, did she continue to associate with Professor Oskarbi or his former students?"

"I've no idea. I didn't track her life."

"She owns a small contract archaeology company, correct?"

"That's right."

"And how does it operate?"

"It's just her—a one-woman firm. As I understand it, she does contract work for the New Mexico Department of Transportation. Identifying archaeological sites during road construction projects, that sort of thing. That's all I know."

"Did or does she have any boyfriends or romantic partners?"

"I don't know. I never met any."

"How often do you see your daughter?"

This question was met with a short silence. "Since my remarriage, not often."

"Can you be more specific? When was the last time you saw her? Before now, of course."

"A year, eighteen months."

"But you live in the same town."

"Like I said—she lives her life; I live mine."

"Do you help support her, give her money?"

"Of course I give her money. You think she makes anything as an archaeologist? I advised her not to go into that profession, but she didn't listen."

Nora opened her mouth, thought better of it. Corrie was peppering the man with questions as it was.

"And Elodie's relationship with your new wife? How is that?"

"Laurie is ten years younger than Elodie. That didn't go down well." He laughed harshly.

*This is going nowhere,* Nora thought as she listened to the back and forth. But if nothing else, it illuminated why Elodie might have fallen in with a cult. What a childhood she must have had, growing up with a distant and uncaring father like this—just the type to be susceptible to the brainwashing of a charismatic, faux-paternal figure.

"Is there *anything* you can tell me, Mr. Bastien, that might shed light on why Elodie did what she did?"

"Nothing," Bastien said.

"In that case, may we go in and speak to her?"

"Be my guest. The doctors say nothing's wrong with her brain—she just refuses to talk."

He stood up and led them through a succession of more spare, white rooms and corridors, arriving at last in a beautiful room with windows overlooking the Sangre de Cristo Mountains. Elodie was sitting up in bed—as Corrie had described her in the hospital—staring at a dark flat-screen TV.

"Here she is," Bastien said, and withdrew.

Corrie sat down in a chair next to the bed, while Nora took a seat on the opposite side.

"Elodie," Corrie began, in a gentle voice. "I'm Agent Swanson from the FBI—you remember me, I hope—and I've brought Nora Kelly, an archaeologist working as a consultant to us. We'd like to ask you some questions."

No response.

Corrie then proceeded to make a series of inquiries, but Elodie remained stone-faced throughout, always staring forward, never reacting. It was almost as if she was catatonic. After a while, hoping to make a connection, Nora reached out and took Elodie's hand lying on top of the bedcover. The hand was ice cold. The woman didn't flinch at the touch, but she did slowly withdraw her hand from Nora's and slide it under the bedsheets.

Corrie glanced at Nora and gave her a subtle nod. Since nothing had worked, it was now time to try the idea she'd suggested. Nora reached into her briefcase and removed a small metal box, which contained protective padding around a heavy Ziploc storage bag. The bag itself held a large, flat piece of stone, its edges roughened and coarse, as if it had been knocked or chipped from its original position. On its flat side, a design had been inscribed. Very carefully, she lifted the bag from the box, holding the face of the stone away from the girl in the bed. "Elodie, I'd like to show you something," she said. Cradling the stone within its protective casing, she brought it closer.

No response.

Nora turned the stone around, bringing the design into Elodie's field of vision. At first, the girl's gaze remained straight ahead, staring at the television—but then Nora saw a flicker of movement and the eyes turned toward the stone. They widened abruptly, and she issued an involuntary gasp. Her face drained of color, and her lips trembled. But this reaction lasted barely a moment before her gaze once again swiveled back toward the television set and her near-catatonic composure returned.

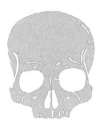

# 45

Back in the car, Corrie turned to Nora. "So what *does* that strange design mean?"

Nora took the metal box out of her bag again, opened it, and showed the chunk of stone to Corrie. On it had been drawn, quite carefully, a spiral design ending in a snake's head.

"It's from the Institute's collection of items of Gallina origin."

"How did you know it would get a reaction?"

"I didn't," said Nora. "But a reverse spiral like this is known to the Pueblo Indians as a sign of evil. It is believed witches use the reversed spiral to project their evil power. The Gallina ones always have the Feathered Serpent as a head." She paused. "I took the trouble of getting an authentic specimen from the Institute collection—we could never put it on display, given its associations—because I thought that might get more of a reaction out of her than simply a sketch I made myself. She recognized it—but she didn't talk."

"I don't think she's ever going to talk," Corrie said. "I think she's withdrawn from the world—and no wonder, with that monster of a father."

Nora paused, wondering if this was the right time to mention something she'd been mulling over. She decided that, with this unsuccessful interview concluded, there was no point in waiting.

"I've been thinking about what you said over coffee this morning," she told Corrie. "About the FBI's tenet that if a person disappears from the public record, it means they're probably dead."

Corrie nodded. "What about it?"

"Remember my telling you that a mutilated body came washing out from the Gallina River about a dozen years ago?"

"Sure."

"The body was in pretty bad shape, but the mutilation kind of resembled the petroglyph I showed to Bastien just now."

"No shit." Corrie thought a moment. "How common is this symbol?"

"To actually see a representation of this symbol is very, very rare. Most Indians around here won't even *discuss* witchcraft, for fear of somehow bringing it upon themselves. But that's not what I've been thinking about. I've been wondering if maybe that body that washed down from the upstream canyons might have been Oskarbi's."

She watched as, with admirable speed, Corrie followed her line of reasoning and put the pieces together. "Wow. When was the body found?"

"Twelve years ago. Around the time Oskarbi supposedly went back to Mexico. And I looked up old newspaper stories about it—the body was never identified."

"Wow," said Corrie. "This is amazing work, Nora." She paused, her brow creased. "The local sheriff's department would have investigated the death. The autopsy must still be filed away somewhere. You know who could look into the possibility that the body was Oskarbi's? Sheriff Homer Watts."

Taking out her phone, Corrie dialed the sheriff, brought him up to speed, told him of Nora's theory, listened for a moment, then thanked him and hung up. "He's on it," she said. "Gonna look at the evidence file and autopsy ASAP."

"Thanks," Nora said. Then: "Do you have anything else to do this afternoon?"

"Just some paperwork on the case."

"Would you mind if we swung by Edison Nash's house? I'd like to see if the housekeeper knows where they might have gone camping."

"You're still worried?" asked Corrie.

"I'm more worried than ever."

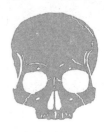

# 46

As THEY DROVE up to Nash's house, Corrie gazed up at it with a laugh. "They just get bigger and bigger."

"There's a ton of money in this town," Nora replied. "I grew up here, and I watched it pour in. It's still pouring in."

They parked and walked up to the heavy antique mesquite gates in the wall surrounding the house. Corrie pressed the bell. After a wait, she pressed again.

A voice crackled over an intercom. "Who is it?"

"Special Agent Corinne Swanson, FBI."

A silence. "Is this joke?" came the voice.

"No, it's not a joke."

A few moments later, the gate was unlatched and opened, and a battle-axe of a housekeeper stood before them, arms crossed, like some medieval guard. "You really FBI agent?" she demanded, staring at Corrie with an openly disbelieving look.

Corrie held up her badge.

The woman stared at it. "Oh."

"May we come in?"

"All right."

They followed her across the inner courtyard and into the house. Nora remembered it from her earlier visit, the walls and surfaces crowded with Native American artifacts.

"We'd like to speak to Mr. Edison Nash," Corrie told the housekeeper.

"He not here. What this about? He in trouble?"

"No one's in trouble," Corrie said, speaking calmly. "We're just hoping he can help us with a few questions. Where is he?"

"I don't know."

"When's he due to return?"

"He was supposed to be back yesterday."

"You have no idea where he went?"

"Camping. He got the gear and they pack it in the truck."

"'They'? Who was he with?"

"The tall skinny friend. I not remember his name."

"Skip?"

"That's it."

Nora broke in. "He didn't say where they were going?"

"No. They look at maps and then they leave."

"Which maps?"

"They in the study."

The housekeeper led them into Edison's grand study. There, on a large marble coffee table, were scattered several USGS topographical maps. Nora went over and had a look. They were of Gallina Canyon and the badlands to the east. Squinting more closely, she made out pencil marks tracing a set of roads that led through the fracking badlands to a dead end at the eastern rim of Gallina Canyon.

"Oh boy," said Nora. She turned to the housekeeper. "Did they take Edison's car?"

"Truck."

"What kind?" Nora asked.

"A brown F-150."

Nora paused. "Why did they go camping?"

"Mr. Nash often go camping. He like to see old ruins."

Corrie glanced at Nora, who looked more worried than ever. "What now?" she asked.

Nora checked her watch. "It's just one. If we leave now, we can be at the trailhead by four thirty and down into the canyon by seven."

"You mean go get them?"

"Yes."

Corrie said nothing, thinking this was an overreaction. Skip wasn't the most reliable individual—but he was an adult, and she had long felt Nora was too protective of her brother. "Maybe we should wait until tomorrow and see if they show up. Doesn't it seem likely they just decided to stay a little longer than planned?"

"Maybe. But I just don't have a good feeling about this."

"What do you think they might be doing? They're just camping, right?"

"I don't know. But Gallina Canyon..." She drew in a breath. "I'm going now. If you'd like to come, I'd sure appreciate it, but I'm not going to wait."

"Well, how can I say no? I can't let you go alone." Corrie made a little effort to squelch her irritation. Nora had, after all, made the crazy trip to Mexico that broke wide open her investigation, and she owed her a big one for that.

"Thank you, Corrie, really, thank you. I appreciate it."

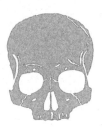

# 47

Behind the wheel of the black SUV, Corrie did her best to thread her way safely through the fantastical landscape of spires and hoodoos. They had passed several large NO TRESPASSING signs put up by the oil companies, and now far ahead she could see a large drilling rig, a row of green fracking tanks, and several white pickup trucks. A group of men in hardhats and orange vests were working on a cluster of pipes nearby. As Corrie and Nora approached, the men saw them, turned, and jogged for their pickup trucks.

"What are they doing?" Nora asked.

"Looks like they're blocking the road," said Corrie.

And they were, in fact, pulling their trucks into a line across the road. Once they successfully obstructed the road and both sides of it, the men got out of the pickups and waited.

"This is strange," said Nora. "I wonder why they're so touchy."

"I guess they think we're trespassers."

The SUV reached the flat and Corrie slowed to a halt as they approached the roadblock. The half a dozen or so men were

leaning against their open truck doors or lounging around, dirty
and grinning. Several had taken the opportunity to light up cigarettes. One had a cigar.

"Kind of ugly to be Harvey Girls," said Nora. "Besides, I don't
see any restaurant around."

Two of the men sauntered over. The one with the cigar tapped
on the driver's window. Corrie rolled it down. The man looked
inside, turned to his friend, and said, "Looky what we have
here." He turned toward Corrie. "Wanna party?"

Corrie stared at the man. He was so disgusting—unshaven,
dirty and sweaty, stinking of cigar smoke—that she almost
laughed. The days when she'd feel cowed by a miserable bunch
like this were long gone.

"We'd like to pass," she said.

The man turned to his friend. "The buckle bunnies want to
go through."

"Gotta pay the toll."

"What toll?" Corrie asked.

"What's the toll?" the man called back to his friend.

"Show us a titty."

"He wants you to show us a titty," the man at the window
said, blowing a stream of smoke into the cab.

Corrie gazed at the man steadily. "A *titty*? Half a dozen good
old boys like you—and all you want as a toll is to see one titty?"

The man was momentarily taken aback. Then, aware of the
others staring at him, leered. "What you offering, girlie?"

"How about something spicier?" Corrie asked.

"Hell, yeah!"

"You sure you're man enough, now—to see it, I mean?"

"Oh, yeah," he said, cackling. "Let's see it."

Corrie reached into her jacket and removed her FBI wallet,

held it inches from the man's face, and let it fall open, displaying her badge and ID. "Spicy enough for you?"

There was a freezing silence as the man stared.

Corrie let a beat pass and said: "Special Agent Corinne Swanson, Federal Bureau of Investigation, Albuquerque Field Office—in case your reading skills are as bad as your breath."

Beads of perspiration popped out on the man's forehead and his whiskers quivered as he stared at the ID. "Um, sorry. Sorry, ma'am. No disrespect meant. We were just having a little fun."

Corrie put away the badge. "Fun. Right. Get that goddamned cigar out of my face."

He sheepishly dropped the cigar to the ground and stepped on it.

"I have some questions for you."

"Sure, of course." The man had become so obsequious, so quickly, that Corrie was amused and disgusted at the same time.

"Did a couple of guys come through here a few days ago, driving a late-model brown Ford F-150 pickup? One tall and skinny, the other one shorter and stockier?"

"They did." He was suddenly willing to talk. "They tore through here like a bat out of hell, and when we ran them to earth the short guy pulled a gun on us and gave us a bunch of bullshit. The tall guy videotaped the whole thing." He looked positively eager. "They in trouble? You looking for them?"

"When was this?" Corrie asked.

"Three days ago."

"Time?"

"Afternoon. Around three thirty. What'd they do? I hope you catch those motherfuckers."

"Tell your people to move their vehicles out of our way."

"Yes, ma'am." He shouted and gestured at the men, who were

standing around looking confused. They climbed into the pick-ups and moved them off the road.

"Listen up," said Corrie. "I'm going to let this slide. But if you and your boys harass anyone coming through here again, I'm going to come back for you with some friends—the badge-carrying kind. And we'll toss you so far up shit creek you'll find yourself in the rectum of the devil himself. You understand?"

"Yes, ma'am. Sorry, ma'am."

She rolled up her window and the man stepped back, nodding obediently, then turned and began yelling for the men to get back to work.

As Corrie eased the SUV forward, Nora laughed—a laugh with a naughty edge. "That was fun."

"Yup. Can't usually take advantage of that kind of thing—but those shitheels deserved it."

They continued on, the land rising, piñon-juniper scrub giving way to ponderosa forest. The road, already tentative, got rougher and was washed out in places. Finally, as they emerged from the forest, Nora saw a glint: Edison's truck.

They pulled up alongside it, parked where the road ended. They got out. Corrie went to the truck, peered in the window, and then tried the door.

"Locked."

Nora circled the truck. "Footprints," she said.

They shrugged into daypacks containing water, snacks, and a few supplies. Nora waited while Corrie buckled her service weapon into place, then began following the prints over the sandy ground. In less than a mile, they came to the edge of the canyon.

"Looks like they went down along that ridge," said Nora.

Corrie took out a pair of binoculars and scanned the canyon

floor. "Is that a campsite there, by the river?" She handed them to Nora.

"Sure looks like it."

Nora started down the slope, watching for loose rocks; Corrie followed close behind.

# 48

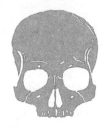

As they hiked down the ridgeline, Nora was able to follow Skip's and Edison's footprints. Judging from the deep impressions and frequent gouge marks left in the soft ground, it looked like they had been carrying heavy packs. She wondered if this was evidence that they'd decided to spend a few extra days in the canyon. She hoped so—she'd much prefer learning she and Corrie were on a wild-goose chase and they'd find Skip and his friend camped peacefully in the canyon.

About halfway down the far side, the trees along the ridgeline opened up, giving them a view northward upcanyon. They paused a moment to take it in. It was magnificent: sheer walls of sandstone striped in red and yellow, a lush bottomland of green grass, and groves of old cottonwoods. Many narrow side canyons branched off at various points. The last of the late-July sun flooded the canyon floor and gleamed off the scimitar curves of the river. The wind was picking up, carrying the scent of flowers. As they watched, the sun fell below the rim and a purple gloaming began to form in the valley.

"It's like a little Eden down there," said Corrie.

"Hard to believe this was a place of genocidal killing—by Native Americans, no less."

"Human nature is the same everywhere," said Corrie. "Violent and tribal."

"That's a rather cynical take."

"Think so? You wouldn't believe some of the stuff I've seen in my short time with the FBI. It's not limited to modern society, either. Studying anthropology, you must've learned about a lot of the bad things humans do—right?"

"Maybe, but anthropologists aren't supposed to judge. We're trained to accept cultures as they are."

Corrie gave a short laugh. "We agents are just the opposite. We're trained *to* judge. It's our job to know right from wrong— or rather, know the difference between what's legal and what's criminal."

Nora stopped to look at her companion. This was—not for the first time—a more philosophical Corrie Swanson than she was used to. "How'd you end up an FBI agent, anyway?" she asked.

"I guess I have a strong sense of justice—or rather, injustice." Corrie hesitated. "It started at home, really, with my mother. She was a mean drunk, and she treated me like shit. The local sheriff seemed more concerned with getting in his daily donut quotient than enforcing the law. It pissed me off, and growing up there was nothing I could do, really, but act the rebel...but, I realize now, the older I got, the more I wanted to do something about it. So I became an FBI agent, with the help of our mutual friend. Crime is simply a kind of injustice, imposed on innocent people."

Nora listened, surprised. "That's an interesting way of looking at crime."

"That's the way our friend in New York sees it."

They lapsed into silence as they descended into the beautiful valley. The ridge ended in a lush, grassy benchland—and not a hundred yards distant was Skip and Edison's camp.

Immediately, Nora saw something was wrong. The tent was partially collapsed, its fabric torn. Stuff lay strewn about.

The campsite had been trashed. She was seized with a feeling of panic.

As they hurried closer, the full dimensions of the wreckage became clear. The fire was dead. A broken tequila bottle lay on the ground. The packs had been opened, their contents pulled out and strewn about, freeze-dried food packets lying around, clothing mingled willy-nilly with camping gear, a trowel, brushes, a compass, and even a pair of night-vision goggles. But what horrified Nora most was the smashed musical instrument tangled up on the ground—Skip's much-beloved ukulele in turquoise blue.

"Oh my God," she said, horrified.

Corrie eased her sidearm from its holster and looked around. Dusk had gathered in the canyon, twilight collecting around them.

Feeling sick with dread at what else she might find, Nora got on her hands and knees and stuck her head inside the slashed tent. The sleeping bags were rucked up, but the tent was empty. Then she saw a stain along the edge of the fly. Quickly, she rubbed her fingers on it.

"Corrie, look at this. Blood." Her insides seized up in dread.

Corrie joined her at the door. "Oh shit," she said. "Okay, what we have here is a crime scene. Let's not mess it up anymore—and talk about what we're going to do."

Nora tried to get her emotions under control.

"Okay, first thing," Corrie said, "we call for backup."

"Backup?" Nora said. "How long will that take? It's eight thirty. By the time we hike out of here, get in the car, and drive to where there's reception, it'll be after midnight. Corrie, we've got to do something *now*. Skip is out there somewhere, very possibly hurt!"

"I understand," said Corrie. "But, Nora, just think this through. We've no idea how many attackers there were, where they are, or why any of this happened. There are only two of us."

"We can't just abandon my brother!"

Corrie put both hands on her shoulders. "Nora, we're not going to abandon anybody. But if we just rush in impulsively—and fail, which is likely—nobody's going to rescue them...or us."

Nora was silent for a moment. "We need to at least scope out the situation."

"Okay. What do you propose?"

"I'm going to climb that hill over there and see what I can see."

"All right. Maybe it's not a bad idea to gather some intel. But *carefully*—and stay out of sight."

Nora started at a jog toward the base of a small, rocky covered hill rising above a grove of cottonwoods, Corrie following. They kept to the darker twilight under the cottonwood trees. They soon reached the bottom of the hill and began to climb, keeping low among the scattered boulders. In a few minutes Nora reached the top, crawling to the summit on her belly. Corrie came up next to her.

The view from the top was unobstructed, and the sky was still light enough to see clearly. Nora slipped off her daypack and removed the binoculars, then scanned the canyon to the south— slowly, methodically—then turned and glassed to the north. Corrie now had her own binoculars out and was searching.

"There are people over there," said Nora.

Corrie trained her binocs in the same direction. "Oh Jesus."

Perhaps a thousand yards distant, Nora could make out a group of about a dozen people on a peculiar-looking mesa top. It had a gradual, south-facing slope that rose to a flat top, ending in a towering cliff on the north end. Two tall tripods were sticking into the sky, one with something hanging from it. It was hard to make out much detail, but it seemed the people were dressed in red, or maybe painted red, and wearing headdresses. Several of them were parading around while bearing something on a litter.

And off to one side, Nora could see a figure dressed in normal clothes—a green shirt, jeans—sitting on the ground with his hands tied behind his back and watched over by a guard. While his face was not visible, she knew right away it was Skip.

Her hands trembled and the image got shaky, then steadied as she forced her breath to stay under control.

"You see what's hanging from that pole?" Corrie muttered.

Nora moved her field of vision from Skip to the poles. The base of one pole was piled with wood—apparently, the makings of a bonfire. But what was that hanging from the pole, ready to be burned? Nora squinted, trying to make it out.

A carcass of some kind, skinned and hanging upside down. But, she realized, not just a carcass—a body. A human body.

As she stared, hands trembling again, she felt a lick of wind, and another, and then a gust. The body began to sway a little in the approaching storm. And the wind brought to her, faintly, the whisper of chanting.

She turned to Corrie. "You still think we go for backup? Nash's dead already—and my brother's next."

Corrie said nothing for a moment, then spoke. "Point made. We've got a gun. We've got a knife. Now we need a plan."

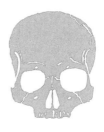

# 49

SKIP, FROZEN WITH horror, stared at the litter. When the blanket was whisked off, he saw, with shock, that it wasn't the leader of the cult after all. In fact, it wasn't even a person—at least, not one still alive. It was a desiccated body, sitting cross-legged in a lotus position, hands pressed together as if in prayer—and grotesquely mummified, the skin pale as dust and as wrinkled as a dried apple, the wizened lips drawn back from a gleaming row of perfect white teeth. Most bizarrely of all, the figure wore a pair of thick glasses, the shriveled-raisin eyes behind them disgustingly magnified.

At the unveiling, a murmur of veneration rose from the group. The sound grew in volume until it became a thrumming chant. One by one, each in turn bowed down to the figure—in a pantomime of worship. Skip's handler dragged him to his feet and, when the bowing reached their position in the line, forced him to genuflect like the others.

The handler then pulled Skip back to his feet and half-dragged, half-jerked him along. For a terrible moment he thought he was headed toward the second tripod and the agony that would follow, but then it became clear he was being pushed in the direction of the kiva entrance. He could see the rough ladder poking out of the hole.

Without warning, the guards shoved him into the hole and he tumbled down the ladder, landing hard on the dirt floor.

As he lay in the dirt, half-dazed from the impact, needles of agony shot through the shoulder he'd landed on, the pain driving away his anger and replacing it with fear. He couldn't get the grotesque vision of Edison out of his head: skinned, hanging upside down like a butchered cow. He'd seen the second tripod—they were going to do the same to him.

One of the guards descended the ladder and busied himself in a corner of the kiva, picking up torches, lighting them, and placing them in holders around the interior. For the first time, Skip got a clear look at the kiva. It was stunning. The walls were covered with an ancient mural, cracked and faded, of a giant snake, its body seemingly made of feathers and smoke. It coiled around the circular space, mouth open, fangs spouting fiery venom. In a series of niches carved into the walls of the kiva, Skip could see a number of prehistoric treasures displayed: golden micaceous pots; glittering obsidian spearpoints and knife blades; bones flutes; carved fetishes of mountain lions and bears; painted kachina masks with grimacing visages; a bow and arrow set and some clubs. And finally, in one niche, stood a large bowl filled with emerald-green lightning stones.

Beside it, in a throne made out of sandstone slabs, sat a figure in white.

In his haze of fear, Skip had forgotten about the leader. He hadn't seen him since the procession that brought up the wizened corpse. How, or when, this figure had gone into the kiva, Skip wasn't sure. But now—as the guard dragged Skip over and threw him down at the man's feet—it was clear he was about to be given an audience.

He opened his mouth, then shut it again. Blustering and cursing at the man who'd presided over the skinning of his friend was not, he thought, a good idea. He stared at the white figure; at the black handprints that covered him like leopard spots. Through the eyeholes carved into the mask, he could see a pair of eyes staring back at him—glittering in the firelight, bloodshot, pupils contracted into points.

"Why...," Skip began, tasting blood in his mouth. "Why are you doing this to us?"

No response.

"You killed my friend. Why? You skinned him alive! Are you crazy?" Skip realized he was starting to babble—but he also realized he was fighting to save his own life. "We didn't mean any harm. Let me go. Let me go, and I'll never come back...I swear."

The figure in white stirred, and then—at last—spoke. "You don't understand."

Through his haze of dread, Skip was shocked to hear a smooth, educated voice.

"What don't I understand?" If this masked person was cultured, maybe he could reason with him. Skip had to keep the conversation going, look for an opening—*any* opening.

"You think coming here was a mistake," the figure said. "It was not. You were *summoned.*"

*Summoned? What the hell?*

"Summoned by who?"

"By our *diablero.*"

Jesus, this really was some batshit crazy cult. Out of the corner of his eye, Skip saw the guard begin to approach. What did they want? Power? People groveling and writhing at their feet? He had to think of a way to get out of this.

"I was summoned," he said, seizing on the figure's words. "Well then. I...I wish to join."

"Join," the figure repeated slowly.

"Yes. Join. I...You said I was summoned. It must have been for a reason." Skip was thinking furiously. Even fanatics could be reasoned with. After all, the man painted white was surrounded by other followers. *Find an opening.* "I can offer a lot. I work for the Archaeological Institute. They have collections, wonderful collections. Things you need."

The figure remained silent. He appeared to be listening. Skip, encouraged, went on.

"And I have a knowledge of ancient things, a deep knowledge that could help you. I want to be part of all this. Become one of you."

"Is that truly your wish? To become—like him?" And the man gestured toward the guard standing behind Skip.

"Yes. *Yes.*" God, if he could just prolong this, maybe they'd have a council or something to determine if he could join. The more time he could buy, the better his chances of getting the hell away...

These thoughts were cut short by the leader, barking what sounded like an order to the guard in a strange tongue.

As Skip watched, the guard bowed deeply, walked to the far side of the kiva, and then returned with something wrapped in animal hide. He held it out to the leader with both hands and stepped back.

"Those who join us," the leader said as he held the raw leather bundle, "must abandon their future and choose our path instead. We will give you something that wasn't offered to your friend. Are you willing?"

"Yes. *Yes.*"

"We can trust that you are sincere in making this gesture? If so, it will spare you the agony your friend went through. Can we trust you?"

"You can trust me, I swear I'm sincere. I swear it."

"Very well." And the man on the throne unwrapped the hide to reveal an obsidian dagger, long and wickedly sharp, similar to the one used to flay Edison. In fact, it was the one: it was still streaked with blood.

"In that case," the man said, "you must sacrifice yourself."

Skip wasn't sure he'd heard correctly. "What?"

"You now have the choice to sacrifice your own life. It is my gift of mercy to you—compared to what happened to your friend."

Skip, staring at the glittering blade, felt sick. "You want me to...kill myself?"

The figure paused. "Of course."

"No. Hell no. That's not what I meant."

"Ah. Not so eager, after all?"

"I want to join, but not that way!"

For a moment, the figure did nothing. Very slowly, he wrapped up the dagger again and handed it to the guard. Then, to Skip's vast surprise, he raised his hands and removed his mask.

# 50

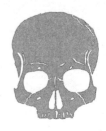

The EVIDENCE ROOM at the Rio Arriba County Sheriff's Department was hardly, Watts thought to himself, a high-tech affair. It was more like a dusty and abandoned library, with shelf after metal shelf covered with identical cardboard boxes, most of which hadn't been opened in a decade. For a small county, he had to admit, it seemed like a lot of stored evidence. At least nobody could claim it was disorganized; on the contrary, every box was labeled and recorded and in its proper place, with its own three-by-five card stored in a big oaken antique card catalog. The sheriff's department had received a grant to computerize the evidence room files, but the project was not yet completed. In a way, this was a good thing: Watts knew the old filing system like the back of his hand, and he felt more than a little apprehension about the new system working—or, as he fully expected, not working.

He went to the catalog and looked up the John Doe homicide of the body found by some hikers at the confluence of the Gallina and Chama Rivers in July twelve years ago. He already knew the victim was not Oskarbi—the body couldn't be Oskarbi's, because one glance at the autopsy indicated it was a good five inches shorter than the tall professor. And nothing else about the victim matched Oskarbi: age, hair color, eye color, body type, and so forth. It had been a savage murder. The autopsy Watts reviewed indicated the victim had been tortured, a spiral carved into his torso in vivo, and the man garroted so violently that his neck had been partially severed.

For all these reasons, Watts was pretty sure this was a wild-goose chase, with absolutely no connection to the women found in the desert. But since he'd promised Corrie he would review the evidence, he decided to give it a brief look.

The evidence card revealed the case file was, thankfully, limited to one evidence box. The mutilated John Doe had been wearing nothing but shorts and carried no ID, and the card indicated the total sum of evidence consisted of a few items of jewelry and some "unidentified items" recovered from the pockets.

Watts looked at his watch. Christ, it was after eight o'clock—and a Friday night, no less. About this time, he could normally be found shooting pool with friends. The things he did for Corrie.

He walked down the main aisle of the evidence room checking number tags; took a turn, another, then another; and finally found the location he was searching for. The place was like a tomb, dark and silent and smelling of musty paper and cleaning fluids. The box was on a high shelf, out of reach—naturally—so he was forced to find a ladder, roll it over, and fetch down the files. The box was light: at least there wouldn't be much evidence to paw through.

He carried it over to an examination area, set it down, then hit a nearby switch, flooding the nearest tables in bright light. After filling out the chain-of-custody paperwork, he undid the twine holding the box lid in place, took it off, and peered inside. The box was practically empty.

First to come out were the man's shorts, sealed in a plastic bag. Then the underwear. Then came a silver-and-turquoise ring, a man's woven parachute-cord bracelet, a silver neck cable, and two small plastic bags. The labels said only *two unidentified quartz minerals, found in victim's pockets.*

He picked up one of the two bags. It held a smooth, water-worn pebble about the size of a golf ball. Raising the bag up to hold the stone against the light, he was suddenly stunned: the pebble inside glowed a rich grass-green color. He picked up the other bag: the same.

Prasiolite lightning stones.

*Jesus.* Just like that, the twelve-year-old unsolved John Doe murder was suddenly connected to Corrie's active case.

He pushed his chair back from the table, the facts and near facts aligning themselves in his mind almost faster than he could recall them. Oskarbi bringing back some drug-fueled wannabe-Indian ritual from Mexico. Oskarbi collecting his groupies. Oskarbi's "archaeological" field trips into Gallina Canyon. Oskarbi's disappearance. The John Doe murder in Gallina Canyon…and then, more recently, the string of suicides. There was no longer any question in his mind they were dealing with a cult—a highly unusual and dangerous one—and the locus of its activities was Gallina Canyon.

He suddenly felt uneasy. When Corrie had asked him to look into the John Doe, she'd mentioned Nora was worried about Skip, fearing he and Edison had gone camping in Gallina Canyon. They were, she said, more than a day late in returning.

He sat frowning for a moment, staring at the two prasiolites glowing under the lights. This was something Corrie needed to know about immediately. He took out his phone and called her cell. It immediately went to voice mail. He tried her FBI number: same thing.

Now he was genuinely alarmed. He called Nora's number, and that too went straight to voice mail.

"Son of a bitch," he muttered. He tried Skip Kelly: also voice mail. What the hell? He didn't have Edison Nash's cell, but he quickly located the man's home number and called it.

"Hallo?" a female voice answered. "Nash house, who calling?"

Watts identified himself as the sheriff and asked for Edison.

"He not here," she said, in an irritated voice. "Why more questions?"

"More questions?" Watts echoed. "What do you mean?"

"Two were here earlier. A woman FBI agent and another. And now you."

This gave Watts further pause. "Do you know where Edison is?"

"The FBI lady talk about camping in Gallina Canyon," the woman's voice said.

"Muchas gracias, señora."

Watts hung up, his feeling of alarm now increased exponentially. Skip and Edison had gone camping in Gallina Canyon, and he had little doubt Nora and Corrie had gone in earlier that day looking for them. All four were deep in the wilderness, cut off from the world. He looked at his watch. Half past eight...and they were evidently still in Gallina Canyon, out of range.

After a moment's hesitation, he placed a call to Special Agent Sharp.

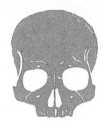

# 51

As the figure put the mask aside, Skip saw revealed, to his enormous surprise, not the crazed cult leader he expected, but an ordinary-looking Caucasian man of about forty: good-looking, with a salt-and-pepper beard, brown eyes, and an obviously expensive haircut.

"It would have been infinitely preferable for you to have accepted my gift, especially on this day of days."

"Day of days?" Skip echoed numbly.

The man nodded. "One prays for it, prepares for it—yet though one knows it will eventually come, when it finally arrives, one is awed nonetheless." He paused. "You said you wanted to become one of us. Your wish will be granted."

"But...in what way?"

The man pursed his lips. "A rubber tree might wish to flap its leaves and, birdlike, take to the skies...but not, I imagine, in the form of a floor mat in the restroom of an airplane." He shook his head. "You are the vessel through which we will realize what we've so long prepared for—which our visionary founder promised."

"Your founder?"

"You met him. Just now, on the mesa top. Dr. Carlos Oskarbi."

Skip, struggling with confusion and fear, realized he was referring to only one thing—that shriveled mummy figure in the litter.

"Oskarbi?" he said, whispering because his mouth had suddenly gone dry.

The man on the throne nodded. Then he gestured to the guard, spoke once again in what sounded to Skip like a nonsense tongue.

The guard responded and busied himself on the far side of the kiva.

The white-painted figure looked back at Skip. "We have a moment while he makes up a preparation for us. I'm ready to help you understand why your impending sacrifice is of such consequence. Ask what you will."

*Impending sacrifice.* Skip tried to speak but found himself unable to utter a sound.

The man shook his head sympathetically. "Then I will explain. In your world, I am Dr. Morgan Bromley, professor. Here, in Gallina Canyon, I am the leader of the *Convocatoria de Brujos.*"

"The convocation of sorcerers," Skip said, finding his voice.

"We are seekers of a particular kind of knowledge that confers great power. Those who fear this knowledge for centuries have tried to erase it—destroy it through massacre and genocide. Look what they did to the Gallina people: our spiritual forebears, whose kiva we now occupy. It has taken decades to reconstruct what was lost. Many times, in that other world where I run a library and teach anthropology, I've wished I could tell of the effort and scholarship that went into that reconstruction, first by our spiritual father, Carlos Oskarbi, and then by myself as his heir. Carlos first traveled the path to power in Mexico, where the Totonteac Indians had preserved the knowledge. He persisted even in the face of efforts by his teacher to hinder him. And then he brought the teachings out of the mountains and gave them to us, his students. He wrote a book, but withheld the central teachings—those that could be shared with only the select few. When he passed on to a higher plane here in the canyon, due to an unfortunate accident, I undertook to complete his work. I refined and perfected the ceremonies. I began the sacrifices. Your arrival was the sign we were waiting for. The sacrifices were not in vain. And as you see, his sacred remains are still presiding over our ceremonies."

"What's this sign you're talking about?" Skip managed to ask.

"You think you came here of your own free will. But in reality, you were summoned here by our *diablero*. You're confirmation that our annual rituals of devotion, combined with the sacrifices of our three members, have pleased our *diablero*."

*Three members?* "You mean the women who died in the desert?"

"Not 'died.' Voluntarily and joyfully elevated. They have now joined Dr. Oskarbi on the higher and far more beautiful plane of consciousness."

This was so fucked up—this guy was nuts. "But no one brought us here," Skip protested feebly.

"You two were summoned to us for a vital reason. Your sacrifices will power the ceremony in which we finally summon Xuçtúhla."

"Xuçtúhla?"

"Our founder was taught, from his years immersed in the ancient Totonteac religious tradition of Mexico, that there's a way to tap into this power of the unseen world that lies behind this one. There's a way to open the door and raise the *diablero*, the master of smoke, the feathered creature of darkness, who offers us knowledge and power...Ah." Abruptly, Bromley stood up, nodded at a sign from the guard, and then placed the mask back on his head. "I see the preparations are complete."

Skip swallowed. "But...Wait. I want to know more."

"And you will." Bromley gestured to the guard, who brought a small, lidded pot over which he'd been toiling with a pestle. Bromley took it and removed the lid. In a paralysis of dread, Skip watched Bromley approach him, holding the outstretched bowl. In it was a paste of some greenish, sticky, gum-like substance. Bromley scraped it from the pot, rolled it into a small bolus with his hands, and held it out toward Skip's face.

Instinctually, Skip turned away.

The guard grasped Skip by the hair and jerked his head back around. In his other hand he had the obsidian knife, which he now pressed against Skip's throat.

"Please accept the gift of transformation," said Bromley in a mild voice.

Skip opened his mouth and the thing was thrust in, like a foul communion wafer.

"Chew," said Bromley.

He bit into it, his mouth flooding with the bitter astringency.

"Swallow."

Skip obeyed, the acrid taste drying up his mouth and throat once again. He shuddered, trying to get down the substance sticking to his throat.

Now the guard handed Bromley an ancient clay beaker, which he in turn offered to Skip. In it was a vile-looking brown brew, with bits of beetle wings and insect bodies floating on the surface.

"Drink," urged Bromley, holding the cup to his lips.

When Skip hesitated, the knife dug again into his throat; he felt its sting, sensed the trickle of blood. He drank the brew, swallowing it as fast as he could, made all the more difficult by the stone blade pressed into his throat.

Forcing down nausea, Skip watched as the guard lowered the knife and then put away the cup and the bowl. He returned a moment later, still holding the knife.

"Compared to all our years of study and preparation," Bromley said to Skip, "doesn't your own sacrifice seem small?"

He nodded and the guard approached, once more with the blade raised.

"Wait! No! Don't do this—!"

"Tonight," Bromley said, "we will *see* him. We will *experience* him." Raising his voice like a camp-revival preacher, he cried, *"Tonight, you will be the conduit through which we summon Xuçtúhla!"*

The guard seized Skip and muscled him over to the ladder. Looping his arm under his shoulder, he hauled Skip up and outside, dragged him over to the base of the second tripod, and threw him to the ground. The white figure retreated.

Lying on his side, frozen with terror, Skip could hear around him the swelling of a breathy chant from the congregants. A formal ceremony of some sort seemed about to begin. He looked on with a dull sense of unreality. The humming chant continued, the white figure leading it with swaying motions and a dramatic swinging of his arms. Moans arose, and weird gestures filled the air. Occasionally, one or another of the cultists would fall to the ground and writhe. A pile of wood had been arranged beneath Edison, and now—at a shouted order from Bromley—the group began collecting kindling from a nearby heap and stacking it beneath the second, empty tripod.

It was all too obvious what they were planning to do.

Now Skip saw someone attach a thin steel cable to the straps tying his ankles. He stared at the tented pile of wood at the base of the empty tripod. He saw the other tripod, with Edison's carcass still hanging from it. A strange lassitude came over him as two naked women, smeared in red ocher and holding burning torches, circled the pile of wood beneath Edison's corpse and set fire to it.

Now the drugs, or poison, or whatever Skip had been given truly started taking hold. Colors became brighter, the hum of chanting drilled into his brain. The ground seemed to shift. And the dreamy sensation that suffused his brain began to quell his anxiety and fear, replacing them with a dull sensation of uncaring acceptance.

He heard a low, hissing chant slowly fill the air like steam. The flames leapt up and he saw the sparks, distorted and hallucinatory, begin to whirl into the night sky.

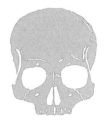

# 52

NORA CROUCHED BEHIND a fallen cottonwood, watching with rising panic the activity on the top of the mesa. She and Corrie had decided on a plan, split up, and gotten in position—but just as they were about to execute, Skip had unexpectedly been thrown down into the dark hole of what appeared to be an underground kiva.

Nora felt an excruciating anxiety: they might be killing him in the kiva as she and Corrie helplessly waited. Corrie, as per the plan, was in position on the other side of the mesa, and there was no way to contact her or alter their plan. All Nora could do—with bitter irony—was to hope the second tripod had been erected for Skip. Because that meant they'd have to bring him back up—alive. And when they did, she'd be ready.

She clutched Corrie's Glock in her hand, the rubber grips slick with sweat. Like most people who had grown up on a ranch in the West, she'd fired many a gun, but she'd never fired a Glock. She reminded herself that the goal wasn't to kill anyone, but to create a distraction and uproar that would allow Corrie to carry out her part of the plan.

She waited, heart thudding painfully. Full night had fallen.

It was moonless, and an infinitude of stars covered the sky. She could hear the gurgle of the Gallina River, the summer frogs croaking, the crickets trilling. A rising wind was stirring the cottonwoods. All her senses were on full alert.

And then, to her enormous relief, she saw—through the flickering firelight—a figure haul Skip out of the kiva and throw him to the ground beside the second tripod. Her relief quickly turned to horror as she saw the fire being lit under the first tripod, tongues of flame leaping up almost immediately.

Now was the time to act. When Corrie heard her gunshots, she'd know what to do.

Nora ran at a crouch toward the base of the mesa, then started up the slope, scrambling with one hand through the rocks and brush while gripping the Glock in the other, moving as fast as she could. The chanting, and the gusting wind, covered any noise she made, but she had no light and the ground was pitch black. She fell once, slamming her knee into the dirt; got up; kept on at a limp; fell again. Her lungs were burning. But she ignored this, just as she ignored the pain in her knee: all her thoughts were on Skip and what they were about to do to him.

She slowed as she approached the lip of the mesa, taking cover behind a sandstone block and making a recon of the ritual or whatever the hell was taking place. She could hear more chanting and humming. The fire under Nash's body was quickly mounting, being whipped back and forth in the rising wind and throwing off a yellow glow that flickered and danced over the ground. The figure in white had also reappeared, and she could see Skip lying on the ground, dazed, as a red-painted man strapped his ankles to a cable that had been flung over the second tripod. The bastards were about to hoist him up as well.

She couldn't get any closer without revealing herself—but she was close enough now. And if she managed to hit one, so much the better. She raised the gun, aimed it at the figure in red, decided he was too close to Skip, and turned instead to the figure in white. But he was a moving shadow on the far side of the firelight. Other figures were even farther away, but much closer to her was the litter that had been paraded around earlier. At this distance, it was a bizarre sight indeed: the withered corpse of a man, sitting cross-legged in a lotus position atop a plinth or platform.

Apparently, it was an object of veneration. Whatever the hell it was, it made a perfect target.

She aimed at the center of the figure, applied steady pressure to the trigger. The noise of the gunshot was incredibly loud, drowning out the low chanting and humming. There was an explosion of dust and the figure was knocked forward, the head snapping off the body like a dry stick and rolling off the plinth, leaving a trail of papery bits behind.

The effect on the cultists was instantaneous. They froze in place, alert, as the echoes of the shot reverberated about the canyon.

She aimed at the figure again and fired, this time striking its shoulder and sending up another cloud of dust and confetti-like streamers.

This second shot had the effect she and Corrie had hoped for: emerging from their shock, the cultists realized they were being fired upon, and they freaked out, running every which way, some falling to the ground in their eagerness to find cover.

Corrie had warned her she only had fifteen rounds in the magazine and to not shoot off the whole wad at once, but nevertheless she fired a third time, aiming at a figure that was fleeing in her direction. He spun around as the round hit him, then fell with a scream. This had a further galvanizing effect. And now she saw Corrie come up over the far side of the mesa, wearing the night-vision goggles. Like a ghost in the flickering firelight, she raced over to where Skip was lying dazed and—using Nora's knife—sliced the bindings from his ankles and hands, loosened the cable, and pulled him to his feet.

But now the leader in white paint appeared, also armed, aim- ing at Corrie as she was bent over Skip. Nora fired, missing but forcing him to drop to the ground. He fired back, but Nora could tell that the monstrous revolver he was holding was unfamiliar to him, and he missed badly.

Skip was now free and, with Corrie half dragging him, ran toward the spot where Nora was crouched. A second cannon blast from the huge revolver went off, kicking up a gout of dirt at least a dozen feet away, as Corrie and Skip dove over the edge of the mesa, landing hard and rolling down the rocky slope. Nora leapt up and, tucking the Glock into her waistband, helped Skip to his feet as Corrie scrambled up herself.

"What?" said Skip, his eyes wild, disoriented. "How—"

Nora shook him. "Shut up and run."

They ran down the slope. Another blast from the gun sounded behind them, but by now they had reached the bottom and were out of range.

"We'll make a feint to the east, and then head north," said Nora. This was what she and Corrie had decided: instead of heading back to their vehicle and civilization, they would ini- tially head that way but then veer north, deeper into nowhere: with any luck, the last direction their pursuers would suspect. Because to the north lay the wildest section of canyon—so rug- ged that not even the Gallina had ever ventured to live there.

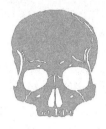

# 53

A̲T̲ ̲T̲E̲N̲ ̲O̲'̲C̲L̲O̲C̲K̲, Watts was waiting at the government heliport in Santa Fe for Sharp and the FBI chopper to arrive. The wind was gusting across the tarmac, stirring his hair.

When Watts had called Sharp, he had expected pushback—it was a big deal to deploy an FBI Hostage Rescue Team and scramble a helicopter, especially when he didn't have proof that Corrie and the others were in trouble. But when Watts explained his concerns, the agent had immediately understood. Then he'd gone to work. It was remarkable how quickly the FBI could move when necessary.

And now he heard the thudding of the helicopter and made out the running lights approaching from the south. He braced himself as it landed, raising a cloud of dust and dry weeds. Watts, one hand clamped down on his hat, ran to the door at a crouch and hopped in. He took a seat as the door closed, put on the headphones. The chopper lifted off at a stomach-dropping ascent.

He turned to Agent Sharp in the adjoining seat. "Many thanks."

Sharp nodded, a serious expression on his face.

"Any developments?"

"As a matter of fact, yes. After your call, we tracked Agent Swanson into Gallina Canyon—FBI cell phones are equipped with a special GPS chip. So at least that much has been confirmed."

The chopper sped northwestward, leaving the lights of Santa Fe behind, then passing over Española before heading into a dark ocean of uninhabited mountains and deserts. Watts could see the onboard Hostage Rescue Team illuminated in the red navigational lights—two men and two women—kitted up and armed to the teeth, faces impassive. As shocked as he was to learn that Corrie was definitely in the canyon, this impressive group gave him a measure of reassurance. If only they could get there in time.

Despite being a law enforcement officer, Watts had not spent a lot of time in helicopters, and he did not much care for them. He could feel the wind buffeting the airframe and the occasional jolts and sinkings caused by turbulence. The weather report had warned of thirty-to-forty-mile-an-hour gusts, but he was too ignorant of helicopter operations to know if that was bad news or not—and he wasn't about to reveal his nervousness by asking.

"So," he asked Sharp after a moment, "does the FBI have a theory of what the hell is going on here?"

"We do, at least in general outline. We're dealing with a religious cult."

"Strange kind of cult," said Watts. "Bunch of PhDs."

"Actually, not strange at all," Sharp said. "We've got a special psychological unit that focuses exclusively on cults and cult behavior. Unlike what people tend to believe, most cult members aren't brainwashed zombies. They're often successful people. For example, we investigated a cult called NXIVM that recruited Hollywood stars such as Allison Mack. Or take Scientology, which we at the FBI also consider to be a cult."

"I see your point."

"I've had one briefing from this unit already, examining the possibilities," Sharp went on. "Based on what we know now, a highly charismatic graduate student, with narcissistic tendencies, goes off to Mexico while still at an impressionable age and learns about an ancient Indigenous religious tradition. He expropriates it for his own purposes and publishes a bestselling book about it. He becomes a respected professor, and it doesn't take long for a group of worshipful students to form something of a discipleship around him—especially since, as their thesis advisor, he already has authority over their intellectual lives. This, over time, leads to ever greater control over the group—not to mention his growing certainty about his own true destiny. He sleeps with the women, dominates the men...and gradually, in this way, they're transformed into a cult."

"Interesting," said Watts. "I've encountered 'wannabe Indians' before—the Anglos who adopt Native American religious traditions for themselves and hang around Native people. The Indians can't stand them."

"That's an operative factor in this case, too," said Sharp. "Cults have a way of turning to doomsday thinking. Many of them end up believing the end of the world is coming, or that they're being threatened by nefarious government forces. They become paranoid and fearful—and that's when they start arming themselves."

"And turn violent."

"It's a side of human nature not all that uncommon. As I said, the FBI has been studying the psychology of cults for decades. It frequently boils down to the desire to belong—the need to simplify life's ambiguities and reduce everything to black and white. The desire to not have to think for yourself. And in the case of the leader—who's almost invariably a man—it's the desire to exercise sexual control and power."

"What a species we are," said Watts, shaking his head.

Abruptly, the chopper was buffeted by a strong blast of turbulence, which tilted it sideways for an alarming moment before it recovered stability.

"Um," said Watts into the headset, trying to keep his voice calm, "is that turbulence something to be concerned about?"

There was a silence. After what seemed forever, the pilot answered back.

"Well, it's not good."

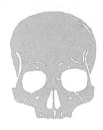

# 54

CORRIE LED THE group northward, up the canyon. It was a moonless night, and they didn't dare use a flashlight, but she had night-vision goggles and could lead them with whispered directions.

For the first half mile it was fairly easy going, and they moved quickly through groves of cottonwood trees alongside the Gallina River. The wind had been steadily rising, and the sound of it thrashing the treetops, combined with the rush of the river, masked any noise they made as they jogged along.

Remarkably, Corrie thought, their hastily assembled plan had worked: they'd gotten away clean from the cult. The firing of the Glock had not only interrupted their ritual—it had been so unexpected, coming when it did, that it had scared the crap out of them...especially when Nora shredded the grotesquely desiccated figure of who, she figured in retrospect, could only be Oskarbi. The cultists had scattered, their sudden panic no doubt exacerbated by their drugged state. During the attack, the only one who'd kept his shit together was the presumptive leader—but he'd been forced to deal with the chaotic aftermath of the shooting, giving the three of them precious minutes to add some extra distance. Their stratagem of going eastward in a feint, as if heading back to their vehicles, and then cutting northward had also worked; the pursuing mob that the white figure had finally assembled seemed to have gone eastward, even as they turned north.

The wind gusted harder, and Corrie could smell dust in the air. As they fled, she tried to put out of her mind the sight of Nash's hanging, burning, grease-dripping corpse surrounded by a painted and chanting mob. Nothing in her training had prepared her for such crazy, unbridled savagery. Was it the drugs, or a love of power, or inner, angry emptiness—or something deeper and even more disturbing—that could make intelligent people behave that way?

She felt the reassuring weight of her Glock tucked into her pocket. Nora had returned it, minus the four rounds she'd fired during the rescue: that left eleven. Still, she wished to hell she'd brought the extra magazine from her car. The cultists had a weapon, too—a big, loud, monstrous thing that reminded her of certain handguns she'd helped seize in an arms-smuggling raid.

"I think they've got a Taurus Judge," she panted. "Fires both .45 cartridges and shotgun shells. But that guy in white didn't seem familiar with it."

"Judge," the zonked-out Skip repeated, as if by word association. "Raging Judge."

So perhaps it had belonged to Edison Nash, Corrie thought, the gun he waved around at those roughnecks. That made sense.

The canyon became narrower and steeper and—constrained by rock walls—the river flowed faster here as it tumbled over boulders. It didn't take an expert to figure out that the easy part of their flight was over. Not even Nora knew what lay ahead. This part of the Chama Wilderness was little, if ever, visited.

"Ow, shit," Skip muttered, tripping and falling. Corrie paused while Nora helped her brother up, warning him to keep quiet.

They continued on at a more gingerly pace, relying on Corrie's whispered directions for the location of rocks and fallen logs. In a few minutes they reached a landslide—fairly recent, at least to Corrie's untrained eyes—which had strewn boulders the size of cars into the rushing river. They were forced to wade through the icy current, holding hands and bracing themselves as best they could.

Beyond the landslide the cottonwood trees vanished, replaced by Douglas firs that crowded the embankment and hung over the river. They had to climb over dead timber and cross the river several times, negotiating slippery, algae-covered boulders in the process. While Nora was keeping up despite an injured knee, it was Skip who was having an increasingly hard time—falling, grunting, and muttering curses under his breath.

Suddenly he halted. "What's that!" he cried.

Corrie stared into the darkness through the goggles. "There's nothing there," she whispered.

"Keep your voice down," Nora told her brother.

"No, no! I can see it! A man with an owl's head!" Skip scrambled backward in terror, and Nora grabbed him before he fell.

"Shut up! You're seeing things!"

"No, I'm *not!*"

Nora held him as he struggled. "Hey," she said in a more calming voice, "it's just the drugs. Okay? If we want to get away, you'll have to cool it."

Skip struggled a bit more, then went limp. "I don't feel good," he moaned.

"I know," Nora said. "But we need to all keep going."

Skip rose unsteadily to his feet, Nora supporting him. He

began muttering again, shaking his head as if trying to rid himself of hallucinations.

Corrie took a few steps. "Log here."

Skip managed with Nora's help.

They went on, Corrie doing her best to describe the hazards of the terrain ahead. It seemed Skip was getting better at keeping the demons at bay, even though he still fell on occasion, sometimes taking down Nora with him. The walls closed in even tighter, the canyon growing as dark as a cave.

"Maybe we can chance a light," said Nora. "They can't see us in this hole."

Corrie considered this. It would make traveling a lot safer, given that one of Skip's falls might result in a serious injury. "Okay," she said.

The night-vision goggles had a mounted light that could be turned on when the goggles weren't in active use. She aimed them downward and switched it on.

"Fiat lux," Skip muttered.

Now Corrie could see him more clearly. He looked terrible, his face bruised, nose bloody, hair matted and askew. His jeans were torn, and he was cut and bleeding in several places.

"Oh, Skip!" said Nora, involuntarily.

"Don't say it," Skip gasped. "It's all I can do to move. You may not see them but there are owls just ahead, and this horrible face, too—hovering just beyond."

"Ignore it," Nora said.

"I'm *trying!*"

They struggled on. Half an hour passed, then an hour, as the canyon continued narrowing into a slot. They worked their way up the steep embankments, bracing themselves against the rock walls. Corrie felt her muscles beginning to spasm, her limbs aching with the effort. Then, suddenly, they came upon a giant boulder jammed between the canyon walls, along with a tree trunk and its giant root ball.

"What the hell!" said Skip loudly.

"We've got to climb over this," muttered Corrie.

They scrambled up the debris, clinging to roots and branches. At the top, Corrie shone the light toward the route ahead. She felt stunned: the slot canyon ended, broadening into a flat meadow. Shining the light left and right, she could see fat cottonwoods lining the embankments of the winding river, with a curving bar of sand—an enclave as beautiful as it was small.

Nora joined her at the top. "Wow. Look at that."

"Too bad we can't stay here," said Corrie. "We've got to keep going."

"Agreed."

Skip pushed up beside Corrie, all three now atop the debris. There was a drop-off on the far side, and it looked to Corrie like a bitch to descend.

"That face!" said Skip loudly. "Don't go down there."

"There's nothing down there," said Nora.

"No," said Skip, grabbing his sister. "Don't. You mustn't. *There's a face!*"

Nora shook him off. "It's the drugs, Skip."

"Corrie?" said Skip, his voice rising, tight with fear. "Take out your gun. Get ready."

"It's nothing," she replied, trying to keep the annoyance out of her voice. "I need my hands to climb."

"Let me go first," said Nora. "I've got the experience." She began working her way down through the debris choking the canyon ahead, soon disappearing from view.

After a minute, Corrie turned to Skip. "You're next."

"I'm not going down there."

Corrie took a deep breath. "You want to go back? And face that fucker in white again?"

There was a silence. Then Skip gave a loud sigh and started down, grasping at roots and branches, his feet scrabbling on the sloping face of the boulder. Corrie leaned over to shine her light down as an aid, but the slope's angle was too steep and he, too, disappeared from view.

"Clear?" she called quietly after a moment.

No answer.

She leaned over the edge of the rock and shone the light down. Skip wasn't visible, and neither was Nora. She looked out across the open canyon, but she couldn't see them there, either. On the other hand, the auxiliary light of the goggles didn't reach very far into the blackness.

"Hey," she said, raising her voice a little. "Where are you?"

No answer.

Clearly, they couldn't hear her over the sound of the wind and water. She started down slowly, one hand and one foot at a time. It wasn't far—about fifteen feet. It wasn't even as hard as it had looked from above. A moment later, she felt her feet land on a solid bed of sand. She sighed with relief, then started to look for Nora and Skip.

She froze as something cold pressed into her ear.

"Don't move," came a hoarse voice. "Now: hands up slowly."

She raised her arms. A hand went into her pocket and pulled out the Glock. Then her night-vision goggles were yanked from her head and she was searched more thoroughly, her cell phone and badge also being confiscated.

"Okay," the voice said. "Turn around. Slowly."

Corrie turned, arms still raised. There he was, the crazy

bastard, covered in white with black handprints, pointing the monster .45 directly at her. And behind him stood a half dozen red-painted men. Skip and Nora were in their midst, hands already bound behind their backs and stone knives at their throats.

"You're all coming back with us," said the figure in white. "And we're going to finish what we started."

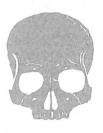

# 55

WHAT DOES THAT *mean*, thought Watts: *It's not good?*

As if in answer, the helicopter dropped like a stone, so quickly Watts felt himself rise out of his seat and his harness pin him in the air; and then the chopper lurched back up, slamming him down again. The engine made a strained, grinding noise as the chopper recovered its equilibrium. Watts stomped down hard on a sudden, rising panic. He'd been in turbulence on an airplane before, of course—but this was different, way different. He found himself being not simply jolted up and down, but rather thrown around in every direction.

A moment of calm passed and then the turbulence lashed the chopper once again. He gripped the seat rests, looking out the window. Solid black—no lights at all. Since their course took them northwestward, Watts figured they must be over the Ah-shi-sle-pah and Bisti badlands now, where nobody lived except a few resilient Navajos.

"Folks," came the captain's calm voice, "what we've got here is some clear-air turbulence." He paused. "I'm going to try to go around it."

The chopper banked and jounced again, hard. Although Watts was scared, he was even more frightened of showing it. He swallowed, hoping they would get through it as quickly as possible. He would say nothing, ask no questions, keep his face set with an unconcerned expression. He glanced around at the HRT: their faces were still impassive, but he could guess that similar thoughts were probably going through their heads. He looked over at Sharp, who was shrugging around in his seat, eyes closed, as if finding the most comfortable position for a nap.

There really wasn't anything to worry about, Watts told himself as he watched Sharp settling down: the FBI had top helicopter pilots, and they wouldn't be flying if it wasn't safe.

Would they?

Nobody spoke as the chopper continued thudding through the night. Watts looked up and saw the stars through a faint haze of dust. He was familiar with this kind of weather in New Mexico: one of those weird windstorms that arrived on a clear night in the desert, a night without clouds or rain—just brutal gusts and scarifying dust.

Lowering his gaze, he could now make out the faint glow of a town on the far northern horizon—actually, two faint glows, side by side, which could only be Farmington and Bloomfield. That meant they must be planning to circle around the turbulence from the north.

"How long is this detour going to take?" he asked the pilot.

"Hard to say. Thirty minutes, maybe more. The problem is, you can't see clear-air turbulence on radar, so I can't determine precisely how extensive it is. That's what makes it dangerous—that, along with updrafts and dust."

Watts sat back, frustration mixing with his nervousness. A lot could happen to Corrie and the others in thirty minutes.

# 56

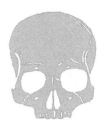

Hands bound behind their backs, Nora and the rest were marched up and out of the canyon on what was evidently a hidden trail the cultists had used to get ahead of them, circle around, and set up their ambush. Nora realized that as they'd been struggling up the slot canyon, thinking they were escaping, the cult members had evidently divined their plan and been lying in wait, ready to spring their trap.

The head cultist—the figure in white—was carrying a big Mag flashlight in addition to the revolver. Several others had headlamps strapped around their red-painted hair. Nobody spoke except Skip, who—his tongue apparently loosened by a cocktail of dismay, resentment, and drugs—started up a refrain of insult. "You people are a bunch of poseurs," he was saying loudly. And "Wannabe jerkoffs playing Indian with stone knives and fake rituals, supposedly divining the wisdom of the ancients—but modern conveniences like flashlights and guns are okay, is that it?" And "Too bad we shot up your founding dickster, Oskarbi, into confetti." He was ignored until he said, "Nora, can you believe this clown in white, with all the scary handprints all over him, is by day just a slope-shouldered academic named Bromley—"

This was when the figure in white turned abruptly and whacked Skip upside the head with the butt of his gun, sending him sprawling on the ground. Two handlers seized Skip and hauled him back to his feet, dazed, blood streaming down his face.

For an instant, Nora was overwhelmed by shock and disbelief. The vicious, bloodthirsty leader was Bromley, the jerk Corrie had interviewed? But almost immediately the pieces fit together and it began to make sense. He hadn't looked like a mentally disturbed cult leader, a Charles Manson type—but wasn't that what people always said about serial killers, when it was too late? But here, in this get-up—a full-blown psycho.

Skip, drugged or not, seemed to have learned quite a bit since he was initially captured. But in retrospect it made sense. Oskarbi hadn't gone to Mexico. He'd died in the canyon. Bromley must have taken over the cult. Briefly, she wondered how Oskarbi had died. In any event, his acolytes had lovingly preserved his body, while no doubt feeding the rumors that he'd gone back to Mexico.

Skip, bleeding and now silent, was pushed forward along the trail, followed by Nora and Corrie and the rest of the cultists. The trail ran along the canyon rim for several miles before plunging down through a hidden cleft in the rimrock.

It occurred to Nora that, from this vantage point along the rim, someone could possibly make out flames at the spot where Skip and Edison had made camp. And somebody with powerful enough binoculars could keep a watch over that side of the river—to see if, indeed, she and the rest had tried escaping in that direction.

The cleft descended to the canyon through a series of steep

stone staircases, cleverly constructed within cracks and fissures in the rock—clearly an ancient trail. When they emerged onto the canyon floor, Nora could see the glow of the fire on the mesa—the place where the rituals were being conducted. They were marched along the canyon bottom, then up to the mesa top. After being manhandled to the opening of the kiva, their hands were untied.

The white-painted figure—Bromley—pointed with the gun. "Down."

They descended the ladder, with Bromley and several cult members following after them. Four torches, burning low, illuminated the space, and Nora was momentarily astonished: the curving wall of the kiva featured a fresco of the Feathered Serpent of Aztec mythology. Carved niches called nichos under the eaves protected various ancient treasures—pottery jars, fetishes, clubs, bone flutes, a bow with arrows, and other artifacts, well preserved and of inestimable archaeological value. In another nicho, all by itself, stood a large, painted pottery bowl brimming with prasiolite lightning stones.

She was abruptly brought back to reality by Bromley, who had seated himself in a ridiculous sandstone throne. "Bring out the *hikuri*."

Two cultists fetched a mortar, from which Bromley removed a waxy substance that he rolled into a large greenish-brown lump. A cult member grabbed Nora from behind, and she felt the cold edge of a stone knife against her throat.

"Take," Bromley said, rising and approaching her, the greasy ball held out in one hand. She felt a concomitant tightening of the knife against her skin. She opened her mouth and he put the disgusting ball in.

"Chew and swallow."

Nora chewed up the horrible stuff, then swallowed, trying not to vomit, knowing that would only mean a second helping.

Next came a bowl of some foul soup, with bits of dead insects floating in it. "Here comes the happy juice," Skip said loudly.

"Drink."

This procedure was repeated with Corrie. They left Skip alone.

Following this nasty ceremony, Bromley stood back, staring at them through his mask while his followers kept the knives at their throats.

"Well, Professor," said Nora. "What now?"

"What now," spoke Bromley, "will be a demonstration of power so incredible that—though you witness it with your own eyes—you will not believe it." His voice fairly quavered in triumph. "Nevertheless, you will be given the privilege of seeing it...before your passing to the higher plane."

Nora began to reply, then stopped herself. It was all too obvious, from his tone and the bloodshot, maniacal eyes behind the mask, that the man was beyond all powers of persuasion—or mercy.

"Yeah?" said Skip, still high. "And meanwhile, you can go fuck yourself."

Rather than doling out another blow, Bromley turned to him. "Even *you* will be rendered speechless. But there is one final step. Tie their hands again."

Their hands were rebound behind their backs. Bromley made a gesture, and one cultist removed the torches from their wall niches and doused them, plunging the kiva into darkness. After a moment, Nora heard a faint clicking noise, then saw flashes of green light as a whispery chant began to rise before them. Bromley was rubbing the lightning stones together, causing them to sparkle and flash in eerie green light, as he chanted. He was mad, Nora knew—mad with the lust and power that drove all cult leaders, made all the more dangerous here by the actual scholarship of Oskarbi, and the treasures of the Gallina that surrounded them, from which Bromley had gleaned God knew what. But that very madness made what, in a very different context, might be risible into something terribly lethal.

Now the others took up lightning stones in turn, and a chorus of chanting began as they moved around the three prisoners, the soft clicking of the stones and the flickering of lightning like green fireflies drifting through the darkness.

*There has to be a way out of this,* Nora thought. These people were not only crazy, but—Bromley excepted—potentially malleable, gullible. That was one weakness of cults...and it just might give them an opening.

But what?

# 57

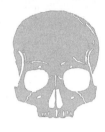

Aɴᴏᴛʜᴇʀ ʙᴜꜰꜰᴇᴛɪɴɢ ᴏꜰ the chopper that threw them all sideways—harder even than before—was followed by a sickening drop and then gravel blowing against the helicopter's Plexiglas canopy that sounded as violent as birdshot.

Abruptly, the pilot spoke through their earphones. "We're close to Gallina, but the terrain is such that we're in for a lot more turbulence. These freak dust storms, coming out of nowhere, can wreak havoc with everything from navigation to rotor lift. Our comms have been dropping out, too—I've been in and out of touch with base. I'm going to try an approach from another angle. But we may have to abort."

"That's not acceptable," said Sharp, opening his eyes.

"As captain, it would be my decision," came the chilly response.

"We've got an agent out there in trouble."

"I'm acutely aware of that, Agent Sharp."

"You said it yourself: we're almost there."

This clipped exchange ended when the pilot didn't reply. Nervous as he was, Watts hoped to God they didn't abort. He had a bad presentiment about what might be happening in Gallina Canyon right now, his imagination made all the darker by his feelings for Corrie.

The helicopter continued over the dark terrain, pitching and yawing—sometimes to a terrifying degree—but always managing to recover. Watts didn't know how much longer he could take this endless battering. He tried forcing himself to think of other things besides pancaking in a ball of fire. Cleaning his revolvers. Riding his horse. Eating a hot chili. When none of those worked, he escalated: a toga party at Hugh Hefner's mansion, with champagne fountains of vintage brut. That didn't distract him, either.

The headphones crackled, then the pilot's voice came on again. "I just received a report from our ground team. A haboob is now being tracked in the badlands."

"A what?" Watts asked.

"It's an intense dust storm that pushes on ahead of a weather front. Very dangerous and unpredictable."

*Wasn't this weather unpredictable already?* "No abort, I hope."

"Not yet. They're monitoring it and updating us constantly. When they can get through, that is—our comms are cutting out more and more frequently."

Ten minutes of tense silence passed, then the pilot's urgent voice broke across the intercom once more. "Base just reported that Agent Swanson's cell phone was destroyed."

"When?" Watts cried.

"Just two minutes ago," said the pilot.

"How do you know?"

"FBI cell phones are equipped with a sat connection and emergency reporting software," Sharp told him.

Every minute counted, Watts thought—maybe every second.

"Circling back around toward the LZ," said the pilot.

At that moment, the chopper was buffeted so hard it was turned ninety degrees on its side. The rotors squealed in protest against the violent change in air pressure, and the engine seemed to cough as dust and sand were sucked into its turbine intakes. Watts clung to his restraints in a panic as the bird began to spin, slowly at first, engine grinding, and then faster, whirling them around.

"Brace, *brace*," came the captain's voice. "Autorotation! We're going down!"

Watts could hear fresh waves of gravel breaking loudly against the fuselage. He took a grip on the restraints as the tail boom whipped around and around, beginning to spin uncontrollably. There was a horrifying jerk, followed by the sound of tearing metal, as a shower of sparks whipped by outside the canopy. Then the cockpit tilted upward, and tilted still further, until with a groan like that of a dying beast, it flipped onto one side and went into a sudden, sickening free fall that—even before Watts could prepare for impact—abruptly ended in a tremendous, jarring crash.

# 58

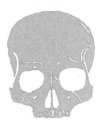

THE LIGHTNING STONES had at last been put away and the kiva torches lit again. They were herded to the ladder and, because their hands were tied, hauled up one by one and dragged toward the rudely built tripod that held the body of Nash. Beside it now was not one empty tripod—but three.

Nora stared at Nash's remains, now unrecognizable as a body, with a combination of horror, pity, and fear. The cultists fed more wood into the fire below them, building it up once again into a raging blaze.

She was beginning to feel the effects of the drugs they'd been forced to take. A sense of detachment—of not quite being there—was creeping over her. The chanting became a hollow echo in her ears. The colors of the fire grew in brightness, the whirling flames like tatters of orange light snapped around by the wind. A lassitude was taking hold of her mind and body... and, knowing this would lead to a sense of resignation, Nora tried hard to fight it off.

She met her brother's eyes. Skip had long ceased his sarcastic comments. His face was deathly pale in the firelight, covered with a sheen of sweat. He was back on the ground, his face blood-ied and his hair all awry. She was appalled at the almost unthink-able scene, torn up by her brother's fear as well as her own terror. How could a group of people, no matter how brainwashed, do this to fellow human beings? She felt another surge of alienness cloud her thoughts and a buzzing sound start up in her ears; the drugs were really taking hold. She glanced over at Corrie, saw the terror in her face, the drugged weirdness in her eyes. Like Nora, she was trussed up and unable to move.

This was the end.

Now several cultists surrounded Skip as he lay on the ground, and took up the slender cable attached to the hobbles around his ankles. This was threaded over a reinforcing pulley at the crux of the tripod. Good God—they were going to be hoisted up by their feet, to dangle upside down over the piles of kindling, flayed to death and burned...just like Nash.

And Skip was going to be first.

"No!" Skip screamed as the cable was attached. "Get away from me!"

But the painted figures ignored him and continued their work. He twisted and fought as best he could, but despite his strug-gling, the figures began pulling on the cable now, in a rhythmic, chanted cadence, preparing to hoist Skip up.

"Don't do this!" Skip screamed.

Slowly, Skip's legs were raised from their prone position. The cable snagged in the pulley, and they stopped momentarily to fix it. Meanwhile, the fire beneath Nash's corpse, fed fresh wood, was growing in size. What remained of the body—a lump of burnt flesh with charred ends of bones protruding—was on fire itself, swinging back and forth like a macabre pendulum, gusts of wind tearing off burning bits that swirled into the dark night.

"No," said Nora. "No. *No.*"

The buzzing in her head increased, and the sounds around her grew distorted, as if her skull had expanded into a huge echo chamber. She desperately tried to keep a grip on reality—but that same reality was a mad froth of panic and disbelief.

"God!" Skip screamed as he was pulled into position and began to sway, upside down, stiff hair just brushing the tips of the logs and branches assembled below.

In her drugged nightmare, Nora became aware that Corrie was struggling wildly, trying to wrench herself free. Nora began to do the same, flailing at the nearby guards with her tied hands, trying to headbutt them and lash out with her hobbled feet. She screamed maniacally, cursing Bromley, his twisted gods, and his false religion.

"Shut her up!" cried Bromley.

They smacked her and kicked her as she lay on the ground, but she continued to fight and shriek, drowning out the chanting.

"Put her in the kiva!" Bromley yelled.

Now two of the figures dragged her once again to the rough, round opening and dumped her in, hands and feet still tied. She hit the dirt floor below with a violent impact, briefly stunning her. Then, almost against her will, she swam back into consciousness—as Skip's cries and pleadings drifted down from above.

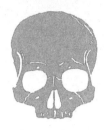

# 59

CORRIE WATCHED AS Nora, screaming and fighting, was thrown into the kiva. Skip was now hanging above the pile of wood, trussed up like a deer about to be butchered. He'd stopped pleading and screaming, and she wondered if he'd passed out—mercifully—or if he was just too paralyzed with fear to make any further protest.

That was going to be her fate as well. They'd had a good plan, and they'd executed it well...but it had failed, and now there would be no getting out of this.

The wind had picked up tremendously, roaring and gusting down the canyon, tearing at the fire and sending embers streaming off into the darkness. If only she'd waited to make voice contact with Watts before heading out of cell range. If only she'd told Sharp about her plan. *If only, if only.* Even if she had—even if by some chance law enforcement had deduced where she was, deduced what dire straits they were all in—she felt certain no rescue chopper could fly in this weather.

Now two of the brutes approached Skip, wielding obsidian knives. Jesus Christ, she thought in horror, recalling the appearance of Edison Nash's body before it was burnt. *They're going to flay him alive.* One gripped his torso while the other sliced off his baggy shirt, tossing aside the pieces and exposing his pasty white chest. This roused Skip again, and he began shouting and twisting, pleading incoherently as he writhed.

Was this really happening? It felt like a dream—a ghastly, unreal nightmare. It had to be a nightmare—something this awful didn't happen in real life. It was found in only the darkest recesses of subconsciousness...

With Skip's shirt off, one of the cultists steadied the flailing body, gripping it hard in order to make the job easier, while the other ran a thumb along the edge of his knife, testing it for sharpness. Then he approached the upside-down figure, raising his knife hand and readying it for a cut down Skip's back.

Corrie turned away, unable to watch such cruelty, such pure evil.

# 60

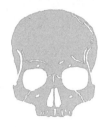

From time to time during his life, Watts had been plagued by a recurring nightmare: of being trapped in a fire, paralyzed and unable to move, unable to breathe, unable to cry out for help, as the flames crept closer...but this time, as he swam back into consciousness, he realized this was no nightmare: he was in a real fire and couldn't move.

It came back to him in a rush: the turbulence, the sandstorm, the crash. And now, behind him, fed like a blast furnace by the wind, was the fire—and he was trapped. It was uncannily like the dream: no matter how he thrashed, he seemed to be bound up, paralyzed, unable to gain traction.

And then, as both consciousness and reason fully returned, he realized he was suspended in the air, hanging from straps and webbing. He stopped thrashing uselessly about and fumbled around for a buckle, found one, and unlatched it. But that wasn't enough; he was still tangled up in webbing as the unbearable heat of the fire drew closer.

In desperation he felt around for the handle of his fixed-blade knife, pulled it out, and slashed at the webbing. He freed himself, falling to the padded metal beneath. He sat up and looked around through the smoke, gaining situational awareness. There was another person—Sharp—also caught up in the webbing. Watts crawled over and, with another swipe of his knife, released him from the nylon web. The man fell to the ground, conscious but dazed.

Choking on the acrid smoke, Watts seized Sharp under the shoulders and dragged him out of the wreckage, upwind, to a safe distance from the brutal heat of the fire. One of Sharp's legs was twisted at an odd angle.

He left Sharp and went back into the wrecked chopper, which was lying on its side. He saw that the fire had started in the engine housing and was propagating fast in the blowtorch wind. At any moment it would reach the fuel tanks and the damn thing would explode. The pilot, still in the cockpit, was horribly mangled and clearly dead. What about the others? As he cast around, he saw a hulking figure stagger out of the smoke, walk several feet, then fall to his knees, coughing.

Watts turned his attention back to the wreckage. There were three others in there.

He rushed toward the billowing smoke and climbed in again, holding his breath. Glimpsing another figure through the swirls of ash, Watts freed her and dragged her outside, only to find that, like the pilot, she was mangled and clearly dead. He eased her body down, and as he turned to go back for another, there was a massive *whump*, and a blast of heat and pressure threw him to the ground.

In a second, maybe two, the chopper changed from wreckage into a ball of fire. He could feel his own hair crisping as he shielded his face from the wave of heat, so hot that for a minute he thought he might catch fire himself. But the explosion

328    DOUGLAS PRESTON & LINCOLN CHILD

subsided as the wind shredded and whipped the fire downwind
and away from him.

Watts rose, then fell back onto his knees, gasping for breath
through a seared throat. He managed to get back to his feet and
saw Sharp and the other survivor huddled in the lee of a rock,
shielding themselves from the explosion. He managed to stagger
over. Sharp was on the ground, wincing in pain.

"Think he's got a broken leg," said the man who'd managed to
stagger out—before passing out.

"It's fine," said Sharp through gritted teeth. It clearly wasn't
fine. "You okay, Watts?"

"Yes."

The two of them stared for a long, awful moment at the flaming wreckage.

"Son of a bitch," said Sharp in a choked voice. "We just lost
four good people."

Watts had no words. He simply stared at the flaming wreckage. What a catastrophe. And Corrie...she and Nora were
trapped in the canyon, probably with Skip and the other guy.
Given the fact her cell phone had been deliberately destroyed, he
had no illusions about her situation. Watts's mind began, unbid-
den, to count off the doomsday cults he knew of—Jim Jones,
Heaven's Gate, the Branch Davidians. When they killed themselves, they inevitably took innocents with them.

He collapsed on his back, groaning, energy gone. The wind
was screaming along the ground, gravel pelting and lacerating
him like buckshot. He was forced to close his eyes and shield his
face with his arm. He cursed out loud the crash, his helplessness,
the loss of life, his fear for Corrie.

What the hell would they do now?

"Where are we?" he shouted over the wind.

He heard Sharp reply. "Help me reach my cell phone."

Keeping his face from the wind, Watts twisted to one side, reached into Sharp's singed jacket, found the cell phone, and plucked it out.

"Give it to me." Wincing afresh with pain, Sharp swiped and fiddled with it.

"Working?" asked Watts.

"Yes," said Sharp. "I've got a sat connection. It shows..." He paused. "It shows we're on the western rim of the canyon, about two miles southwest of our planned LZ."

Watts sat up, momentarily forgetting the wind. "You're sure?"

"Think so. Looks like..." He stopped to take a few breaths. "Looks like the pilot completed his turn and was headed toward the canyon from the west. The ground team will know the chopper crashed and send out a rescue."

"I can't wait," said Watts. "I'm going to find them." He lumbered to his feet after briefly checking on the unconscious man.

Sharp looked at him. "Take my gun. And good luck."

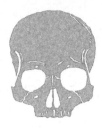

# 61

Nᴏʀᴀ ᴡʀɪᴛʜᴇᴅ ᴏɴ the floor, struggling to break free of her bonds. The leather around her wrists had been tied so tightly that, struggle as she might, she couldn't work it loose. She kept pulling and jerking until she realized she was only abrading her own flesh.

She lay for a moment, breathing hard. Skip's distant crying echoed weirdly down into the kiva, and she shook her head, trying to clear the drug-induced fogginess but only partially succeeding.

*Damn it, think.*

She glanced around in the dim torchlight. The nichos along the kiva walls were filled with ancient artifacts: masks, flutes, pottery, lightning stones—and obsidian blades.

She managed to wriggle herself over to the nearest wall. She braced herself against it and, with a mighty effort, forced herself into a kneeling position. There were the obsidian spearpoints, stacked in a bowl in one nicho. She leaned her head toward the niche and, grabbing the edge of the bowl in her teeth, pulled it free. It fell and shattered, scattering spearpoints over the hard-packed surface of the floor. Falling back onto the ground, she rolled atop one of them, fumbling around with her fingers. It took only a moment for her to grasp it and press it edgeways into the dirt floor. Then she positioned her wrists over it and used the exposed edge to saw through the leather binding. Despite its age, the obsidian was still incredibly sharp, and within moments she'd cut her hands free.

She grabbed the blade and quickly sliced the hobbles from around her ankles. She staggered to her feet only to feel an overwhelming sensation of dizziness.

Skip was still sobbing and pleading—at least he was still alive, thank God. But now she heard a new sound: a guttural snarling that she knew instinctively could not be human. What the hell kind of an animal was it? There weren't many apex predators in New Mexico other than cougars and black bears—and this didn't sound like either.

She looked around, trying to focus. She was free...but what now? How was she going to prevent her brother from being killed?

Even as she tried to think, she caught movement out of the corner of one eye. It seemed to be coming from the far wall of the kiva, and she turned toward it quickly. It was the Feathered Serpent on the wall. It was starting to move, slithering itself free of the adobe, taking form, and sliding toward her...

She slapped her own face, hard, to rid herself of the hallucination. Shaking her head into a semblance of clarity, her cheek stinging, she headed for the ladder.

Then she halted once again. Climbing up to fight them, willy-nilly, would be stupid. There were a dozen of them, or more, and they had a gun. No, two guns—Bromley had taken Corrie's Glock. Christ, she needed a plan, *right now*—but what?

She cast frantically about the kiva.

*Weapons*...there were weapons in some of those niches: a bow and arrow, a club, some obsidian knives with bone handles.

She grabbed the bow and arrow. With a rush of relief, she noticed it was still strung. She hadn't shot an arrow since Girl Scouts, but maybe if she could take down Bromley, the rest would fold. Wasn't that how cults worked?

She drew the bow back and the wood immediately snapped. Dry rot.

*Son of a bitch.*

She seized the biggest knife. It was razor-sharp—but what did that matter against a dozen people out of their minds with blood-thirst and armed with guns? A futile slash or two, then they'd cut her down. Nevertheless, she tucked the knife into her belt and continued to look, but there was nothing.

She felt overwhelmed by panic. If she couldn't fight them, could she do something else? Knock over the tripods with the club? If only she could find a way to interrupt the ritual, something to disrupt the ceremony...

As she tried to focus, she heard, from above, Skip's cries intensify into a scream. She could also hear Corrie's slurred voice yelling at them to stop, her shouting abruptly drowned out by the hideous shriek of the bear or whatever animal was up there, being tortured or something.

*Something to disrupt the ceremony.*

Her eyes lit upon the bone flutes. She grabbed one, put it to her lips, and blew. Nothing.

She tried again, blowing harder—then plucked it from her lips and inspected it. The bone was old and flaking from the embouchure and finger holes, and the body of the flute was riddled with cracks. Useless.

Throwing it to the ground, she plucked up another one. A weak, tremulous sound emerged. She licked the dirt from her lips, blew again—harder, this time—and the thousand-year-old relic broke apart in her fingers.

God *damn* it! She tossed away the pieces in frustration. The desperate plan that had come to her mind was a long shot anyway—the mother of all Hail Marys, in fact—but she couldn't execute it with a fossilized, crumbling instrument.

Now her eyes stopped at something else: a blanket, laid out in a dark corner of a kiva. She'd noticed it before and deduced from the stuff spread on it—artifacts, lightning stones, some camping equipment—that the cultists had taken these things from the campsite. She saw the stem of a stone pipe peeping out from the folds of the blanket, an obsidian axe, some spearpoints, a crumbling sandal, a pair of lightning stones...and a flute. She darted across the kiva and seized it. It was a beautiful modern replica of an ancient Pueblo flute, rebuilt with original turquoise inlays. Taking a deep breath, she closed her eyes, then raised it to her lips and blew—gently.

A remarkably pure sound issued forth.

Now she blew harder, her fingers stopping various holes. The tone holes were spaced in a pentatonic scale, its tone clear and fine—in perfect working order. Against all expectations, she'd found a working instrument...one clear and loud enough to interrupt the ritual. Now it was time to undertake the Hail Mary.

She rushed to the ladder and scaled it, emerging into the heart of a seething ritual. Skip, strung up by his ankles, was missing his shirt and blood was running down his back. He seemed unconscious, a strip of skin about to be peeled off from between his shoulder blades. But the torture of him had stopped. The attention of the group had shifted from Skip to the charred corpse of Edison Nash, hanging from the nearby tripod, above a raging fire. The cultists were transfixed by the corpse, staring, frozen with awe—including Bromley.

She followed their gaze. What had fixated their attention wasn't the corpse, exactly, but rather what was *inside* it—a nebulous apparition, appearing and disappearing amidst flames and smoke. *Something* was animating the charred bones and flesh, and it was also where those muffled animal sounds were coming from.

She stared, uncomprehending. She was still hallucinating, of course.

Or was she?

*No. No, no.*

A hallucination, drug-induced or otherwise, could not possibly seem this real...

...And this overwhelming realization left her paralyzed.

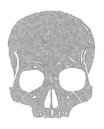

# 62

Nora watched, transfixed. *Something* had begun to emerge from what was left of Nash's body, in a series of spastic, organic contractions, almost as if the burnt corpse were giving birth. Wreathed in smoke, it slowly squeezed out of its womb of charred bone and meat. The shapeless thing that emerged cried out again: not the muffled, guttural sound Nora had heard before, but a soul-chilling shriek so loud and full of triumph that she felt the pinpricks of faintness come over her. In the roiling smoke, she saw two dark spots form, resolving into slitted lizard eyes. Soon the manifestation of a face formed—with a black mouth, which began to move, opening and closing like a fish's, and then a body, appearing and disappearing in the whirling smoke and fire.

Then, abruptly, clouds of smoke billowed out on either side of the thing and began to form into a pair of wrinkled wings. Nora watched as the creature flexed them—slowly at first, as if testing—before starting to unfold them. Instead of feathers, tongues of dark fire flickered over the skeletal body, never fully visible, obscured by whorls of smoke that revealed glimpses of grotesque body parts quickly cloaked again.

Now the smoke-creature moved its wings, fully unfurling them so that they seemed to cover half the night sky. Its head formed: the mouth morphed into an eagle's beak, and it gazed down with snake's eyes upon the beings below it, the head moving jerkily this way and that, like a bird of prey's.

Nora stared at this summoned thing, wreathed in appalling black flame, slowly fanning its skeletal wings. It seemed to be waiting, looking down at the puny creatures that had summoned it—waiting for purpose.

Her paralysis at the sight vanished when the smoke-creature opened its monstrous beak and let out another unholy shriek— and then she remembered her plan.

Bromley and the rest remained transfixed, staring upward, their faces slack. They had the look of children who, having tossed a lit match into a lake of gasoline, were witnessing a terrifying conflagration of their own making.

Tearing her gaze away from the creature, Nora put Nash's flute to her lips and blew a note, and another. She closed her eyes to shut out the horrific sight, but especially to recall the ancient melody from the wax cylinder that she had played with Skip. It was in a pentatonic scale, but with added quarter and half tones, which she had earlier learned how to make by half covering the holes with her fingers. Eyes still squeezed shut, but confident now, she raised the flute skyward and unleashed the thousand-year-old melody, the song to repel skinwalkers.

The melody swelled as she gained confidence: louder, faster, the notes rising cleanly above the snarl of wind and fire.

It had an instantaneous effect. With an unearthly screech, the apparition began beating its skeletal wings, stirring the pyre below. It flared up with a crackling hiss, spewing vast showers of sparks into the wind. The blackened corpse swung and twirled madly on the tripod, as if assaulted by some demonic wind, before coming apart, bones and burnt flesh scattering.

"No!" screamed Bromley, shaken out of his own paralysis.

She continued to play, faster and louder, even as the skeletal thing thrashed amidst the fire, its shrieks and bellows mingling with the melody.

Bromley dashed at her in a frenzy. Nora yanked the obsidian knife from her belt and lunged toward him, arm extended, bracing herself. In his mad rush, Bromley ran himself directly onto the knife. He grunted, his mask jarred off by the impact. He stepped back as she pulled the knife out, and he stared down at the blood gushing from his solar plexus. Staggering backward, he fell to his knees among the other cultists, who could only, zombie-like, gape at the events as they played out. She felt the unholy wings beating up a swirl of sparks around her, spreading smoke that surged over the mesa top. As if from far away, she could hear Corrie shouting something, but then the smoke-creature gave another screech that sounded...almost triumphant.

With a terrific effort, Bromley rose back to his feet and now, at last, pulled the Raging Judge from the strap around his waist. Legs spread, bracing and swaying, he tried to raise it toward her with shaking hands.

Nora resumed playing, using all the breath she could muster.

Once again the creature reacted violently, drawing up into itself fire, sparks, and embers until its form disappeared in a maelstrom of fire and smoke. A great tongue of fiery smoke engulfed Bromley even as he leveled and aimed the shot.

He vanished in the smoke. The gun never went off.

Moments later, the smoke drew back, revealing Bromley once more, staggering backward. He flung down the gun, making a keening sound and grasping his head in both hands, spinning around as if in terrible pain.

"Xuçtúhla!" he gasped. "Xuçtúhla!"

The living smoke coiled around him again, caressing him with its tendrils. He opened his mouth in a soundless scream, and the tongue of smoke seemed now to enter into him, take possession of his body. His head snapped backward, his eyes rolled, and he took a spasmodic step, and another, with movements like a marionette's, twitching and jerking his way toward the edge of the cliff. At the same time, he started crying out something above the roar of the wind and flames. It was incomprehensible at first, but then Nora began to make out individual words: *"Day of days...gift of transformation...Xuçtúhla...through the portal of smoke...the black path to the higher plane."*

Now the smoke spread outward, forked with livid lightning, and flowed around the nearby cultists like a gray fluid. To Nora's astonishment they took up the refrain, hesitatingly at first, and then louder. They fell into place behind Bromley, chanting: *"Our gift of transformation...through the portal of smoke to the higher plane..."* Their chaotic movement gradually became coordinated as they surged toward the edge of the cliff, led by Bromley.

*"Through the portal of smoke...follow, follow...,"* Bromley chanted.

Beneath his tone of command, and the chanting of the cultists, Nora was certain she heard another voice, deeper and older, felt rather than heard, repeating the same refrain.

Bromley took a final step forward, teetered at the edge of the cliff, then keeled off and disappeared. The others hesitated, but only for a moment; one went, then another, and in a few moments the rest followed, surging over the cliff's edge and vanishing, followed by the sounds of crashing and tumbling, grunts, and thuddings, as the cultists plummeted to their deaths, impacting the rocks below. The last thing she heard was the deep voice, still intoning...until, with a dry, malevolent laugh like the skittering of leaves, it faded away. All that remained was a slow eddy of smoke that was soon whisked away by the wind.

Leaving nothing behind but a heap of glowing coals.

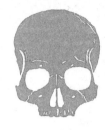

# 63

Nora tossed aside the flute and ran over to Skip. He had passed out. The cable holding him suspended was hooked to a ring in the ground. She knelt beside it, grasped the cable in both hands, lifted it with a grunt of effort, and freed it from the hook. She lowered it gently, easing Skip's hanging body down sideways and away from the pile of wood. Once he was on the ground, she cut away the hobbles from his ankles, freed his hands, then quickly inspected the cuts on his back. She felt overwhelming relief when she saw they were superficial—long strokes that had bled freely, but nothing deep. The cultists had been interrupted by the creature before they could begin work in earnest.

Her brother lay on the ground and gave a loud groan, gasping for air.

"Skip?"

His eyes fluttered open.

"Thank God." She hugged him. "You're safe now."

His mouth worked silently for a moment before whispered words emerged. "They were going to…skin me alive."

"They're gone."

Skip's eyes opened wider, as if in disbelief. "What—"

"Mass suicide. They all went off the cliff."

He tried to lift his head and look around. "Oh my God." He laid his head down again. "They were chanting. I could feel the knife..."

Gently, Nora put a hand on his shoulder. "They're gone. All of them."

Skip's breathing eased, his body relaxed, and he closed his eyes and lapsed back into unconsciousness. Assured he'd be all right, Nora rose and rushed over to Corrie, trussed and lying on the ground in a drug-induced haze of her own.

As Nora cut off her bonds, rousing her in the process, Corrie gasped, her eyes pinpoints. With a shriek, she flailed out at Nora, her face a mask of fear.

"No!" she cried. *"No...!"*

"Easy." Nora grasped her wrists, holding them and gently calming Corrie's struggles. "Easy now. It's me, Nora. We're okay. We're okay now."

Corrie stopped fighting, trying to focus. "Nora...Oh my God... What—what was that *thing?* Jesus, I saw it rise from the smoke and flame...I was sure it was going to kill us all..."

So she'd seen it, too. The rational part of Nora had hoped she hadn't.

"It was the drugs," Nora said, disbelieving her own words even as she spoke them. "Just the drugs."

Corrie lay back, eyes wild and confused. "Drugs? But...it was so *real.*"

"Just the drugs," Nora murmured again.

The mesa top was quiet now; the wind was at long last dying

away; and the fire under the first tripod had burned down into a heap of smoldering coals. Nothing was left of Nash's body—just a meat hook dangling from the cable.

Nora's blood froze as she heard a sound from the edge of the mesa—a rough scrabbling in the loose rocks. Someone was laboring clumsily up the slope.

*Shit.* Could one of the cultists have survived the fall and was now making their way back up the mesa?

The gun—she needed the gun. Where was it? The only light now came from the glowing heap of coals. She rose to her feet and scrambled to the spot where Bromley had dropped it.

There it was.

She seized it. It was heavy as hell, a big stupid revolver. She held it up to the reddish light and could see two rounds left in its five chambers. Grasping it in both hands, she took a deep breath, braced herself, and raised it, aiming toward the sound of grunting and scrabble of footsteps just below the mesa rim. A head appeared, obscured in shadow.

"I've got a gun!" Nora cried out. "Don't fucking move!"

Sudden silence.

"Put your hands in the air!" she shouted, her own voice strange in her ears. "Step forward into the light—slowly—so I can see you!"

*Jesus, the head.* Black against black, it was strangely oblong, with wings, inhuman. Nora's heart accelerated again.

"Easy now," came a familiar voice. "It's just me, Homer. Sheriff Watts."

Nora, astonished, squinted into the darkness. As he rose to his full height and came forward into the faint glow of the coals, she realized that what she'd taken for a head was really just

Watts's cowboy hat—dented and badly dinged. The man himself appeared dinged up, sooty and ragged, as if he'd been in a fire.

"Homer?" Nora lowered the gun. "What in the world—"

He turned slowly, his eyes wide, taking in Corrie and Skip stretched out on the ground, the tripods and the remains of bonfires, the masks and other detritus littering the top of the mesa. He holstered his gun. "Well, I was expecting to be the cavalry, come to rescue you all. But I can see you've done all right on your own."

Now Nora heard another sound—the distant thudding of rotor blades.

Watts gestured toward it. "Here come the rest of them." Even in the faint light, Nora could see Watts was struggling to contain his shock. Nevertheless, he spoke to them calmly. "Those choppers will have you out of here before you know it. We'll get you back to Santa Fe and medical attention. You must have been through hell up here. But they'll get you patched up, and it'll all be good." He went over and knelt by Corrie, who lay on the ground wide-eyed and silent, still in profound shock. He took her hand and murmured, "Corrie, you're safe now. Everything will soon be normal again."

They might be safe, Nora thought. But nothing would ever be quite normal. Never again.

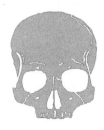

# 64

*Four months later*

Nora had never heard of Piscator, a restaurant recently opened in the Sandia Heights neighborhood north of Albuquerque. But when out of the blue she received Corrie's invitation for dinner at the place, she'd accepted without hesitation. It looked upscale, and she figured Corrie probably wanted to thank her for all she'd done…or perhaps apologize for once again dragging her into unexpected, unwanted craziness.

In any case, Nora was eager to catch up. The usual law enforcement proceedings had followed their ordeal—debriefings, questioning, depositions—until the red tape finally died away of its own accord. The media did not make a huge fuss about the story—for the simple reason, she assumed, that its pieces were too widely scattered and bizarre to connect. In the end, all there had been were a few notices about suicides in the desert; some obituaries and stories about the sudden, tragic death of Edison Nash, wealthy young collector and archaeology enthusiast; and some passing mentions of the arrests of a few professors at the University of New Mexico. Nothing more had trickled out—and thank God for that.

She bundled Skip into the car and headed south on I-25. While Skip hadn't technically been invited, Nora felt she could hardly leave him behind. His trauma had been greater than theirs, and he'd taken a lot longer to recover from it.

During his recovery, Nora had realized more than ever what her brother meant to her. He was the only family she had left. Lucas Tappan, due back from the East Coast next week, might in time end up as family—that remained to be seen—but these days she felt more protective of Skip than ever. In the two months he'd taken off from the Institute to convalesce, lying around their house, catching up on his reading or playing the ancient and irreplaceable Martin ukulele, she'd become aware of just how much he reminded her of their father—and also, in certain ways, of her deceased husband, Bill Smithback. But after a rocky few months, Skip had returned to his old wise-cracking, quasi-irresponsible self, leading life on his own idiosyncratic terms.

Piscator was even nicer than she'd expected: a sleek, minimalist restaurant serving continental fare perched in the shadow of Sandia Peak on a small height of land above a golf course. Almost immediately upon entering she saw Homer Watts sitting at a large round table set before a picture window with a gorgeous vista.

Seeing them approach, Watts rose. The three embraced and spent a few minutes in small talk, laughing and smiling in the manner of old friends temporarily out of touch.

"I wonder where Corrie is?" Nora said, glancing at her watch.

"Not like her to be late, is it?" Watts replied. "Her idea of late is ten minutes early."

Although they were inside, Watts was still wearing his cowboy hat—a new one, Nora noticed, creamy silver—along with a silk high-style cowboy shirt, tight jeans, and ostrich boots. He made quite a contrast to Skip, dressed in an NRBQ T-shirt and baggy shorts.

Twenty minutes later, Corrie came hurrying toward their table. "Sorry," she said as she took a seat. "Sharp called me into a last-minute meeting."

She smoothed down the front of her jacket and accepted a glass of wine. It seemed to Nora that Corrie's face was aglow, and she wondered idly if some field assignment had left her sunburned. They ordered and soon were digging into impeccably prepared dishes. The conversation had wandered all over the place, casual banter that nevertheless pointedly avoided the nightmarish situation they'd all recently experienced.

It was Skip who ultimately brought it up. "I've been doing some research, these last few months," he said abruptly, out of nowhere. "Anyone care to guess the subject?"

The table went silent. Nobody needed to guess.

"And no matter how many other examples of cults I came across, I just couldn't see any way this one matched the standard pattern."

"How, exactly?" Corrie asked.

"*How?* Is that a rhetorical question?" Skip asked. Then he raised his hands apologetically. "Sorry. Okay, in certain ways it was a standard cult—the charismatic leader, the shared beliefs, the sexual domination." He leaned forward, flourishing a fork laden with swordfish and caper berries. "But *they didn't do any recruiting*—job number one for any cult what wants to maintain its membership. Not only that, but the members were almost universally successful, high-functioning members of society... and they flew under the radar *for years*. Even after the death of Oskarbi. Can you imagine the discipline necessary to maintain that kind of façade—when you meet up with your fellow acolytes only once or twice a year?"

"Yes," Corrie replied, "it's the lack of cognitive dissonance—the cult members presenting as normal, productive people—that's what has the FBI behaviorists baffled the most."

"Have the FBI found out any more about Oskarbi or the cult since?" Nora asked.

Corrie hesitated. "Not so much about the cult members. They seem to have been fanatically careful to maintain their façades and left little useful evidence. But...well, we were able to do a deep dive on Oskarbi."

"And?"

Corrie hesitated again. Then she lowered her voice. "I won't bore you with oaths of secrecy and all that bullshit—only because you deserve to know. But what I'm telling you is totally confidential."

There was a nodding of heads, and Corrie continued. "In that kiva, we found a trove of Oskarbi's notes, journals, and papers—along with some of Bromley's. They were stored in a secret compartment, as if they were holy writ." She paused, looking around, her gaze finally settling on Skip. "You sure you want to hear this? It's rough stuff—and maybe you'd just as soon not know more."

"After spending weeks on research, looking for crumbs?" asked Skip. "You're damned right I want to hear more."

Both Nora and Watts nodded.

"Okay. Some of this you already know." Corrie took a deep breath. "It starts a quarter of a century ago. A young graduate student named Oskarbi is looking for a topic. He somehow hears about a Totonteac Indian named Don Benicio who still observes the traditional religious practices of his ancestors in the Sierra

Madre of Mexico. Oskarbi goes to Mexico to become his acolyte. But when Oskarbi grows morbidly interested in the more dangerous aspects of those beliefs—specifically, the path to wielding the powers of darkness—Benicio sends him away.

"So he returns to the States. He writes a book that taps into the new-century zeitgeist and becomes a bestseller. In reality, it's more fiction than fact: including fascinating but ultimately unimportant bits and pieces of his year with Benicio, tossing in some pseudo-academic jargon to give it a glossy veneer—but he keeps the really important stuff to himself. On the strength of the book, he gets a plum appointment at UNM as an associate professor of anthropology. He's hip, popular, charming, and good-looking, and he gathers around him a coterie of worshipful graduate students—particularly women. In the few years it takes him to become a full professor, he becomes increasingly interested in the ancient Gallina culture—and its violent demise. He develops a theory: the Gallina were a branch of the Totonteac Indians who, like him, were expelled for dabbling in dark practices. These renegade Totonteacs migrated northward into New Mexico and settled in Gallina Canyon. It was there that they practiced their dark arts...and this was precisely what brought them into conflict with the Chaco Canyon people. They were feared and hated as witches, skinwalkers, worshippers of evil. And ultimately, they were exterminated in what was apparently a proactive effort of self-defense.

"Anyway, to prove his theory, Oskarbi organizes an archaeological field expedition into Gallina Canyon, bringing along graduate students. And on the very first expedition, fifteen years ago, they discover the Great Kiva of the Gallina people—the one we all saw—filled with priceless treasures. This discovery was not considered a mere stroke of luck. Rather, it seems to have triggered the development of the cult—whose goal was to revive the malevolent powers of the Gallina Indians.

"Oskarbi now shares the darkest and most powerful of the secrets he'd learned in Mexico with his students. They begin coming into the canyon every summer, under the guise of field excavations, to take drugs and perform ceremonies to renew their bond and deepen their connection to the dark powers. This is how the cult sustains itself." Corrie took a sip of wine. "All goes well for four years. Then, tragedy strikes: Oskarbi dies in a fall off the cliff near the kiva."

She set down her glass. The table remained utterly silent, waiting for her to continue.

"It might have been an accident. Or maybe Morgan Bromley gave him a well-timed shove. Bromley had become a sort of deputy to him, his right-hand man. Bromley steps into Oskarbi's shoes...and into the beds of those women. Although Oskarbi's death was clearly a traumatizing event for the cult—Molly Vine, for example, dropped out of her PhD program—they were still totally invested in their beliefs about the Gallina and their dark rituals. They mummify his body and bring it out every year to parade around during their ceremonies, as a kind of god. Bromley was instrumental in this. What happened later—the women sacrificing themselves in the desert, for example—was mostly his doing. He seems to have been leading the cult into a much darker place than Oskarbi—an outgrowth of his own warped personality."

"And the body found in the Chama River?" Nora asked.

"That, apparently, was some fellow who stumbled upon the ruins in Gallina Canyon and decided to loot them...but was unlucky enough to choose the moment when the cult was performing their annual ceremonies. They caught him, killed him, mutilated him, and sent his body downriver. This was in keeping with Bromley's beliefs: no longer constrained by Oskarbi, he had grown eager to perform human sacrifices, which he believed would allow them to raise some sort of spirit or demon. This demon would be under their command, with the power to transform their lives...and perhaps them as well. Sort of like a Faustian pact."

Corrie spread her hands. "And that was the horrifying ceremony we all walked into."

After a moment of silence, Watts cleared his throat. "And what does Sharp think of all this? You mentioned you were just in a meeting with him. What's his take?"

"His take is...that he's no longer my mentor."

"What?" Nora asked.

"He's been kicked upstairs. He's taking over as SAC of the Albuquerque Field Office, and the current SAC, Garcia, is heading to DC."

Murmurs of surprise from around the table. "But what about you?" Watts asked her. "Does this mean you're going to have to break in a *third* mentor?"

Corrie looked down. "Well...I was going to tell you..."

"Out with it," Watts said.

Corrie settled back against her chair. Without looking up, she dug into a jacket pocket, pulled out an official-looking envelope, and handed it to Watts.

He unfolded it, read it—then looked up, with a huge smile. "Looks like Sharp wasn't the only one to get promoted. Corrie's mentoring period is officially over and she's now a GS-11, step 2—a full-fledged special agent."

There was a moment of surprise, followed by a round of cheers, whistles, and applause that turned every head in the restaurant their way. The flush Nora had seen on Corrie's face, she realized, was not sunburn at all.

As the noise subsided, Watts leaned over and gave her a congratulatory and rather passionate kiss.

"That's wonderful news, Corrie," said Skip. "And thank you for sharing that information with us. It...well, it helps to know. But there's something you've left out."

"What's that?" Corrie asked, detaching herself from Watts.

"You've explained what Oskarbi, Bromley, and the cult members believed...but what do *you* believe?"

"Well...," said Corrie, her voice trailing off.

"That's kind of a weird question," Watts said.

Skip turned to Watts. "I know what *I* saw. I want to hear from the others."

"What you saw," Watts replied, "were drug-induced hallucinations. Right?"

This was greeted with a disagreeing silence.

"Whoa. Am I missing something?" Watts finally said, looking around, his eyes coming to rest on Corrie.

"What I saw," Corrie said, "was...quite enough to last me a lifetime."

"Wait a minute," Watts said in a low voice. "You don't actually believe you saw the raising of some fiend from the underworld? Is that in your report?"

There was another long, awkward silence. "What I saw," said Corrie finally, "sure as hell did *not* go into my report." She gave the envelope a flourish. "If it had, instead of this, I'd be in the FBI psychiatric unit."

"As far as that goes," Skip added, "you all know what I think. But am I going to wander around the Institute telling anyone who will listen that I was almost sacrificed in some demon-summoning ceremony? I'm not stupid."

Watts turned to Nora. "And you? You think what you saw was real?"

Nora gave him a long, level gaze before answering. "You heard what Corrie and my brother just said. I'm keeping my mouth shut, too. But we—we three—were *there.*"

"It's like Hamlet told his friend," Skip said. "'There are more things in heaven and earth, Horatio, than are dreamt of in your philosophy.'"

"That's right," Corrie said, looking at Watts. Her voice, which had gone tight for a moment, was once again back to normal. "And just what do you have to say to that—*Horatio?*"

This was so unexpected they all laughed—even Watts.

"Well, shoot." Watts took off his hat, turned it one revolution, smoothed down the brim, then replaced it on his head. "Maybe I shouldn't have skipped that Shakespeare assignment in high school." And he grasped Corrie's hand with a smile as laughter went around the table, dispelling the dark mood.

*That conversation's over and done with.* Nora felt more than a touch of relief, looking around the table. She caught Corrie's eye, then Skip's: whatever ended up in the official reports, they had a shared understanding that required no further words.

*We—we three—were there.*

# Authors' Note

THE GALLINA PEOPLE mentioned in this novel are real. They were a mysterious culture who lived in Gallina Canyon and surrounding areas in northern New Mexico during the pre-European period, from around 1100 to 1275, when they suddenly vanished. The few archaeologists who have worked in this remote canyon discovered evidence of extreme violence directed against the Gallina. Most of the one hundred or so remains of Gallina people found in the canyon show evidence of violent murder—and this is true for all age groups, men, women, and children. These discoveries have led some archaeologists to hypothesize that the Gallina were the victims of a campaign of genocide. Who the perpetrators were and why the Gallina people were targeted remains a mystery.

In our novel, we speculate the enemy of the Gallina might have been the people of Chaco Canyon. This is not improbable. Around 1275, the Chacoans were undergoing a social and economic collapse due to widespread drought. They were abandoning their great houses and settlements, as the entire Four Corners region descended into violence and widespread cannibalism. It appears that the destruction of the Gallina culture happened during this period of turmoil.

While most present-day Pueblo tribes trace their ancestry back to various ancient settlements and specific ruins, no Pueblo tribe has claimed the Gallina as their ancestors—still more evidence they were wiped out and not simply displaced. Adding to the mystery, Gallina ceramics are different from ancient Pueblo pottery, and some Gallina skulls have an unusual flattened shape, unlike anything seen elsewhere in the Southwest. This suggests that the Gallina may have migrated into the region from somewhere else, which could also explain why they came into conflict with their neighbors. The idea that the Gallina engaged in witchcraft and dark practices is our own invention, but it can be argued that indirect evidence supports this theory: the people who exterminated the Gallina made efforts to burn or bury their sacred kivas, possibly as a way of canceling their spiritual power.

The Chaco lighthouses and roads do exist. The seven lighthouses the novel describes along the Gallina frontier are, however, fictional. While the landscapes mentioned in the novel exist and are described accurately—Ah-shi-sle-pah Wash, the fracking badlands, and Gallina Canyon, among others—we took some liberties in moving elements of the topography around to suit the needs of the story. There is indeed controversial fracking taking place in these badlands, which is strongly opposed by the Pueblo people who are the descendants of the Chacoans.

In any case, in addition to our own fictive representation of the long-vanished Gallina culture, and its equally fictive relationship (or lack thereof) to any known culture, extant or extinct, all characters related to that history and the equally fictitious cult—Oskarbi, Don Benicio, Bromley—and its practices that we describe in the novel are entirely creatures of our imaginations.

Throughout, and at all times, we have approached this subject with the greatest respect, while at the same time doing our best to create a novel both exciting and, in many ways, informative. This leads us, finally, to the topic of names. All people, of course, have the right to name their cultural affiliation as they wish. One of us, Doug, has spent half a lifetime in New Mexico and lived on both the Zuni and Navajo Indian reservations. He has asked numerous Native Americans what they would like to be called—and the answers vary a great deal. Many are fine with the term *Indian*. Others prefer *American Indian*, to distinguish themselves from the people of South Asia. Others prefer *Native American* or *Indigenous*. But above all, their strong preference is to be called by their tribal names—Navajo, Zuni, Pueblo, and so forth. Finally, the term *Anasazi*, which means "ancient enemy" or "ancient stranger" in Navajo, for the ancient people of the Southwest has been retired in favor of the more accurate and respectful term *Ancestral Puebloans*.

# ABOUT THE AUTHORS

The thrillers of **Douglas Preston** and **Lincoln Child** "stand head and shoulders above their rivals" (*Publishers Weekly*). Preston and Child's *Relic* and *The Cabinet of Curiosities* were chosen by readers in a National Public Radio poll as being among the one hundred greatest thrillers ever written, and *Relic* was made into a number-one box office hit movie. They are coauthors of the famed Pendergast series, and their recent novels include *The Cabinet of Dr. Leng, Diablo Mesa, Bloodless, The Scorpion's Tail*, and *Crooked River*. In addition to his novels, Preston is the author of the award-winning nonfiction book *The Lost City of the Monkey God*. Child is a Florida resident and former book editor who has published eight novels of his own, including such bestsellers as *Chrysalis* and *Deep Storm*.

For more information you can visit:

PrestonChild.com